W9-AFA-645

Jackie
and
Maria

ALSO BY GILL PAUL

The Lost Daughter

The Secret Wife

Another Woman's Husband

Women and Children First

The Affair

No Place for a Lady

Jackie and Maria

A Novel of Jackie Kennedy & Maria Callas

Gill Paul

HARPER LARGE PRINT

An Imprint of HarperCollinsPublishers

This book is a work of fiction. References to real people, events, establishments, organizations, or locales are intended only to provide a sense of authenticity, and are used fictitiously. All other characters, and all incidents and dialogue, are drawn from the author's imagination and are not to be construed as real.

JACKIE AND MARIA. Copyright © 2020 by Gill Paul. All rights reserved. Printed in the United States of America. No part of this book may be used or reproduced in any manner whatsoever without written permission except in the case of brief quotations embodied in critical articles and reviews. For information, address HarperCollins Publishers, 195 Broadway, New York, NY 10007.

HarperCollins books may be purchased for educational, business, or sales promotional use. For information, please e-mail the Special Markets Department at SPsales@harpercollins.com.

FIRST HARPER LARGE PRINT EDITION

ISBN: 978-0-06-300009-4

Library of Congress Cataloging-in-Publication Data is available upon request.

20 21 22 23 24 LSC 10 9 8 7 6 5 4 3 2 1

For Barbara Douka,
who gave me the idea for this novel

Of all creatures that can feel and think,
we women are the worst treated things alive.
—EURIPIDES, *MEDEA*, 431 B.C.

ACT I

Chapter 1

Hotel Danieli; Venice, Italy
September 3, 1957

"Come with me." Maria felt her elbow being tugged by the party's hostess, so insistently that she almost toppled sideways. "I want to introduce you to your fellow Greeks: Aristotle and Tina Onassis. *Here* they are." Arm outswept, the hostess announced, "*This* is Maria Callas."

Years later, Maria would look back on the seeming ordinariness of the moment. When you meet someone who is going to turn your world upside down and shake it up so violently that nothing will ever be the same again, there should be a warning sign, she thought. In Greek mythology there would be a thunderclap, an earthquake, an eclipse of the sun. Here there was no such thing. Just the murmur of polite conversation, a string quartet playing Schubert, and the clink of champagne glasses under crystal chandeliers.

Of course Maria had heard of Onassis before. Depending upon which paper you read, he was either the world's richest man and a charming host on his yacht, the *Christina*, or a crook and a pirate of the high seas. She was surprised to find that he was shorter than her, because in photographs he had the aura of a tall man, but straightaway she liked the amusement she detected in his eyes, the way he held her hand firmly and bent to touch it with his lips.

"I'm honored to meet the world's greatest soprano," he said, his first-ever words to her.

"*One* of the greatest perhaps . . ." Hyperbole always embarrassed her.

"You must be the only person in this room who plays *down* her achievements," he said, with a tip of his head toward the assembled company. There were actors and socialites, some royals, and a sprinkling of politicians, but few from the world of opera, Maria's usual milieu. The Duke and Duchess of Windsor were holding court, wearing crowns as if to mock the one he gave up when he abdicated the British throne; Princess Grace of Monaco wandered around with a sweet smile pinned to her face despite the conspicuous absence of Prince Rainier less than a year into their marriage; and

Elizabeth Taylor was flirting at the bar with a swarthy man who was definitely *not* her husband.

Maria laughed. "I was assured these were 'Europe's finest,'" she said, mimicking the Midwest accent of their hostess, a gossip columnist who relished bringing celebrities together.

"Of course, one should always believe the word of journalists," Aristotle retorted with a grin, and Maria warmed to him.

"Are you Maria's father?" she heard Tina Onassis asking her husband, Battista, who had been hovering behind her. People often thought that because of the thirty-year age difference between them.

"*Suo marito,*" he replied with a hint of exasperation. He didn't speak much English, only Italian, so Tina switched to that language to chat with him, while Aristotle continued addressing Maria in Greek.

"I'm ashamed to say I've never heard you sing. I'm not a fan of opera. It always sounds to me like a pair of Italian chefs screaming risotto recipes at each other."

Maria laughed. "I don't think I've heard that one. Can you remember what it's called?"

"No idea," he admitted with a grin. "But when Tina took me to an opera in Athens I dozed off in the box. At least they had comfortable seats."

"I think you'll find that operas are as varied as . . ."

She searched for an appropriate simile. "You are in shipping, are you not? As varied as shipping routes."

He pulled a face. "But more artistic, I hope. Despite my tin ear, I would love to hear the voice that all the critics rave about."

She gave a modest shrug. "They don't all rave, I'm afraid. They ran out of superlatives long ago and now they come to my performances searching for things to criticize. I don't want to make their job easy, so the pressure each time I perform is immense."

"That old story: they build you up only to knock you down again."

"Perhaps you have experienced something similar?" She knew that three years earlier he had been arrested in America on some technicality involving his shipping empire, and grainy photographs of him being finger-printed had appeared in the press. It must have been humiliating.

He leaned closer, and she could smell a sweet hay scent that was probably explained by the cigar protruding from his top pocket. "There's a world of difference between us. To get where I am took nothing more than pigheadedness. But you—you clearly have a gift from the gods."

"I work quite hard too, Mr. Onassis." That was an understatement. Maria memorized libretti, practiced all afternoon, and, if she didn't have a performance in the evening, she read opera scores in bed till the early hours. Music was her life. Attending parties like these was a rarity.

"Call me Aristotle. Please." He touched her arm, just above the elbow, where her glove stopped and bare flesh was exposed. "So, when will I come to hear you sing? You be my guide."

She smiled. "I'll let you know when I am singing in a concert hall with particularly comfortable seats. Maybe you should bring your own pillow."

"It's a deal," he said, his hand still resting on her arm.

He was flirting, with her husband just inches away. Maria usually had no time for the directors and fellow performers who made advances, but this was innocent fun and she was enjoying herself. "How can I believe you?" she teased. "Don't they say you should never trust a sailor?"

"My friends can trust me with their lives, my enemies can trust that I have a Greek appetite for revenge—so I suppose that makes me trustworthy." His eyes were flecked with gold, she noticed. Shrewd eyes.

"And I? Do you think I should trust you?" she asked.

"If I make you a promise, I will always keep it," he told her, serious now. "You can trust in that."

Those words stuck in her head long afterward.

Chapter 2

Venice
September 4, 1957

The morning after Elsa's party, Maria awoke to find a note slipped under the door of their suite asking if she and Battista would join Aristotle and Tina Onassis for lunch in Harry's Bar at one o'clock. She stretched and looked at the ormolu clock on the mantel: it was almost twelve. She generally preferred to ease herself into the day with a scented bath followed by a leisurely breakfast, but something about Aristotle had piqued her curiosity. She'd expected the world's richest man to be serious and money obsessed, but instead he seemed fun.

"Battista!" she called. Her husband was reading a newspaper on a sunny balcony that overlooked the Grand Canal. "We're going for lunch in an hour."

Harry's Bar was a short walk away along the water-

front and they arrived only slightly late. A maître d'
in white jacket and black bow tie led them through
the restaurant, past the long, polished-wood bar to a
table at the back, where the Onassises were poring over
menus. Aristotle leapt to his feet.

"I'm delighted you could come," he declared in Italian, kissing Maria's hand, shaking Battista's, then clapping him on the back. "Please, sit. Bellinis all round?
It seems fitting, when they are named after the great
opera composer."

Tall glasses of the bar's trademark cocktail appeared:
white peach juice mixed with Prosecco, so light and
aromatic, it seemed impossible it was alcoholic.

Maria sat on a banquette next to Tina Onassis, a
pretty woman with bleached blond hair and dark eyebrows who on closer scrutiny seemed scarcely out of her
teens; there was clearly a substantial age gap in their
marriage, as in hers.

"I'm honored you could join us," she said to Maria.
"I'm one of your biggest fans. Did Aristo tell you? I first
heard you singing *Aida* at La Scala back in 1950, and
since then I've flown to Milan for all your premières."

"Really?" Maria was touched. "That's very flattering. Do you live in Athens?"

"We have homes all over the place: Athens, Paris,
Nice, Monte Carlo, Montevideo . . ." She gave a quick

eye roll, mocking the length of the list. "But Aristo is usually to be found on the *Christina*. He gets crotchety if he has to spend too long on dry land."

Battista was telling Aristotle about the funds he was trying to raise to make a film of Maria singing *Medea*. She hoped their host didn't feel he was being pressured to contribute.

"How long have you two been married?" she asked Tina, looking from one to the other.

"Forever!" Tina cried. "Eleven years. I was just seventeen at our wedding and Ari was forty, so I'm sure I seemed terribly childish. But then we had children and they make you grow up fast."

She pulled one of those faces that Maria had often noticed mothers make: it was meant to be long-suffering but was really a look of pride. She would rather have joined Aristotle and Battista's conversation about the film business but knew Tina was waiting for her to ask about the children, so she did.

"What ages are they now?"

Tina began to describe them, and Maria's attention wandered. Everyone assumed that she hadn't wanted children because of her devotion to her career, but it wasn't true. She yearned for a baby, ached for one, and it simply hadn't happened. A specialist had told her she had a malformation of the womb that would make it difficult, but not impossible, for her to get pregnant. She was thirty-three years old and all too aware that time was running out.

She blinked, realizing Tina had asked her a question.

"How did you and Battista meet?" she repeated.

Maria smiled. "He saved me from a life typing businessmen's letters and got me where I am today." As she told her story, Aristotle and Battista paused to listen.

It had been hard for Maria to get her break in opera, because her voice was too strong, too mature, for the chorus, and it had an unusual timbre. She needed directors who were prepared to risk giving her lead roles, but most were risk averse—unsurprisingly, given the astronomic cost of staging opera. She had trained in Athens, where she spent the war years living with her mother and sister, then moved to New York, where her father's pharmacy business was based. After more than a year of disheartening auditions, she at last won a lead role, singing *La Gioconda* in Verona, and sailed to Italy alone at the age of twenty-three.

"It was a difficult time," she told the Onassises. "There was resentment toward this young interloper who didn't even speak fluent Italian yet had somehow landed the lead. The cast pushed past me backstage without saying *buon giorno,* and I went home alone most nights."

She didn't add that she was a whale of a girl in those days, over two hundred pounds of blotchy, dimpled flesh, with a nose that was too big for her face, and thick, black-rimmed glasses, without which she was near blind. Her appearance made her shy and awkward, another reason it was hard to make friends.

"I had a guardian angel, though." She turned to Battista with a smile. "I met this man at a dinner party on my first evening in Verona and he took me under his wing. He was an opera aficionado and we bonded over our shared love of music."

Battista took up the story: "When Maria's contract at Verona ended, her father wanted her to return to New York and work as a secretary. To me, that would have been a criminal waste of talent. I offered to subsidize her for another six months while I introduced her to the directors I knew and tried to get her career off the ground."

"What a clever investment!" Aristotle exclaimed. "You gained a beautiful wife and the world gained a magnificent talent."

Battista grinned. "We had luck on our side. One evening, when we were strolling after dinner, we bumped into my friend Nino Catozzo, the director at La Fenice.

A soprano had let him down at the eleventh hour. His production of Wagner's *Tristan und Isolde* had been advertised, tickets sold, and suddenly he had no Isolde—so I suggested Maria for the role."

She interrupted. "You have no idea how terrifying it was. Battista pretended I already knew the part, which is one of the most difficult in opera. I had to audition a week later, sight-reading for Tullio Serafin, the great guru who had conducted me in *La Gioconda*. Fortunately he thought I was capable of the role and arranged two months of intensive coaching to get me ready."

She would never forget the blind panic of that time: the technical difficulties of the part of Isolde, the wild, passionate Irish princess; the immense pressure of stepping out onto the glittering stage where Rossini's and Bellini's works had premièred; the grandeur of La Fenice, with its rows of golden boxes, the ceiling mural of flying Graces, the ornate putti, the plush red-velvet seats. All of it combined to make her feel unworthy.

On opening night Tullio had given her a gift of a Madonna icon—a pretty one in jewel tones with a gilt frame. She remembered trembling as she prayed to the compassionate face of the Holy Mother that she would not let everyone down.

The prayer must have worked, because the production was an astounding success. She couldn't see beyond the proscenium arch without her glasses but could hear that many were getting to their feet, cheering and whistling as well as clapping, and she was called back to the stage a dozen times before she could finally retreat to her dressing room. It felt like a dream.

"You should have seen the reviews." Battista beamed. "I've never read anything like it. The critics were unanimous that a new star had appeared in the firmament. After that, every director in Italy wanted to work with her, and Tullio became her cheerleader."

They had told this story before, and she smiled at him as she delivered the punch line. "Battista waited till the third night after the opening, when he was sure his investment had paid off, before asking me to marry him."

They all laughed. In fact, Maria had been stunned by his proposal. She had so little confidence in those years that she couldn't believe anyone would want her for anything other than her voice. How could he think of making love to a woman so large that no chairs were big enough for her? A woman with thighs the circumference of the average woman's waist? She had been reluctant to remove her tent of a nightgown on their wedding night, but Battista seduced her slowly, awakening sensations she adored. Right from the start, she loved sex, couldn't get enough of it. She loved him too; he was the first person ever to make her feel cherished.

Waiters interrupted them with plates of pink carpaccio, the house specialty that Aristotle insisted they try. Maria was glad he had ordered for them. She couldn't have read the menu without her glasses, and she was too vain to wear them in public. The thinly sliced raw beef was succulent, tender, sublime. When that was gone, he ordered prawns, freshly caught in the Lagoon that morning and grilled with garlic butter. All afternoon, they drank frothy Bellinis and nibbled delicacies, while getting acquainted. Maria felt uncharacteristically light-headed, and more relaxed than she had in many a month.

The windows at the far end of the bar were frosted glass, and cozy lamps glowed on the walls, so it was hard to judge the time. She was astonished when she read Aristotle's watch upside down and saw that it was almost seven. Diners were beginning to arrive for the evening meal, and she spotted their host slipping some folded lire to the maître d' with a sleight of hand as smooth as any magician's. She guessed he was bribing him to let them keep their table.

Weariness engulfed her in a sudden wave. "I'm afraid I must go soon," she said, feeling guilty that she hadn't sung a note all day. It was important that she practice daily.

"I have a final question for you," Aristotle said, waving away Battista's clumsy offer to contribute to the bill. "You are at the very top of the tree. I wonder what ambitions you have for the future. Are there any dreams you have yet to fulfill?"

I want a baby, Maria thought to herself. The desire was overwhelming. But that was too personal to mention in present company.

"My dream was always to become a company member at La Scala. For me, it is the greatest opera house in the world. Now I'm there, I suppose I want to sing with the best musicians and best directors for as long as I possibly can." She paused. "And then I will retire quietly to a lovely part of the world and be a housewife." She laughed as if she didn't quite take her words seriously. In truth, it was hard to picture the future.

"Even your laugh is beautiful," Aristotle replied, his tone heartfelt. He caught her eye and looked hard, as if trying to peer into her soul.

Chapter 3

Newport, Rhode Island
Summer 1956

Jackie Kennedy rocked on the porch, one hand on her swollen belly, the other clutching a glass of icy lemonade, which dripped condensation onto her cotton frock. A cigarette burned in an ashtray, its smoke spiraling upward, and a book lay open beside it. The heat was flint dry and oppressive, with only the faintest whisper of a breeze, but she preferred to be outside, where the air was marginally fresher.

She thought of Jack on a yacht on the Mediterranean. He would be brown as an urchin, hopping around the deck in his shorts with a beer in hand, or splashing about in the turquoise water. There was a hard knot of anger inside her. How could he fly across an ocean to vacation with friends when she was heavily pregnant—especially when she'd suffered a miscarriage the previous year? She'd been distraught, and it made her anxious about this pregnancy.

The man she had married was selfish. Entitled. But so charming, so exciting, that she could forgive him his worst transgressions: forgetting birthdays and anniversaries, sending her home early from their honeymoon because he had meetings to attend, even the occasional hint of perfume in his hair and lipstick on his collar from the women who were always fawning over him. Even that.

They were both independent souls who had spent a lot of time apart during their three-year marriage. Washington gossips kept predicting imminent divorce, but in many ways their lifestyle suited them. Jackie liked to go riding and fox hunting at her stepfather's Virginia estate, to fly to London for some shopping with her clothes-mad younger sister, Lee, or to hop on a train to New York for an early lunch with her hard-living daddy, Black Jack Bouvier, before he got too pickled.

Jack Kennedy's life revolved around politics; it was the oxygen he inhaled, the sustenance he craved. Currently a Democratic senator from Massachusetts, he was one of the party's most glittering young talents, with a reputation for his strong stance on civil rights, as well as international peacekeeping and halting the

Communist threat. Within the Kennedy family, they were talking about a presidential run in 1960—an idea that Jackie privately found far-fetched, but she admired his ambition all the same.

If only she felt as if he needed her more, she would be content. Of course, she knew he admired her intelligence, her style and class, but his life continued much as it had in his bachelor days. As a politician, he had needed a presentable Roman Catholic wife, and it seemed she had ticked the right boxes. Now she hoped to provide another political essential: a couple of healthy kids.

She frowned. When had she last felt the baby move? Perhaps the poor creature was as drained by the heat as she was. She shifted her position on the rocking chair, nudging her belly with the palm of her hand, but there was no movement, not even the flutter of a tiny foot kicking under her skin. Slowly, clutching her lower back with one hand and pressing on the armrest with the other, she eased herself to her feet and waddled around the porch. Nothing. She jumped up and down, then ran her hands over her belly again. Still nothing. Alarm took hold.

"Nelly!" she called. "Can you come out here?"

Nelly, the housekeeper, was a mother three times over and the soul of calm. She felt Jackie's belly and asked her to jump a few more times.

"Little 'un's having a good old nap," she said, her tone even and careful. "But why don't I call Dr. Brady all the same?"

Jackie lay in a hospital bed, surrounded by doctors and nurses, paralyzed with fear. Her mother, Janet Auchincloss, sat ramrod straight by her bedside as the physician ran a stethoscope over her belly. What was wrong? She couldn't lose this child; not after eight and a half months. A miscarriage in the first trimester had been tough enough, but the doctors had assured her it wasn't uncommon. This was different; she already felt she knew this child, after sensing it move and react inside her.

She watched the medical staff's expressions, the way they glanced at one another, sending signals with their eyes that she wasn't meant to intercept. Her mother had taught her it was unladylike to show her feelings, but it was hard not to. One nurse took her hand and Jackie gripped hard, grateful for the human contact. Sympathy was not her mother's forte. Arranging a ball, yes. Managing the staff at her husband's estates, yes. Sympathy, never.

"Can I call your husband?" someone asked. "He should be here."

Yes, he should. Jackie narrowed her eyes.

"He's away on business," Janet told them. "Whatever it is, you can tell us."

It was then they confirmed in words what Jackie had already guessed. Her baby was no longer alive. Sometime between her checkup a week ago and this morning, its little heart had stopped beating and no one knew why. Jackie focused on a cheap clock on the opposite wall, watching the second hand tick. It seemed impossibly loud. She began counting the beats, finding it helped her choke back the emotion that threatened to overwhelm her.

"What happens next?" Janet asked in a practical tone. You'd never have guessed her grandchild had just been pronounced dead.

The doctor checked some papers on a clipboard. "Mrs. Kennedy was booked to have a Caesarean, so we'll bring it forward. We could operate this afternoon."

Jackie turned her gaze to the window, where blinding sun was glinting through the leaves of a red-oak tree. What would Jack say? He'd flown off on vacation expecting to return in time for the birth of his first child; instead he would return to a funeral. She had let him down. He would be crushed. Kennedys didn't do failure.

"That sounds like the best plan," Janet said, without consulting Jackie.

"Can you call Bobby?" she asked, turning to her mother. "He'll know how to get in touch with Jack."

There was a radiotelephone on the yacht, but you couldn't dial direct. The operator had to request a time slot to transmit through the nearest shore station, so it depended on their location. She recited Bobby's number from memory, and Janet rose to make the call, as if glad to have something to do. She still hadn't uttered a word of comfort, but Jackie knew her better than to expect it.

When Jackie came to after the operation in late afternoon, Janet was gone and Bobby was by her bedside. Straightaway he took her hand and said, "I'm so sorry. What a sad loss for you, and for the whole family."

Jackie closed her eyes to stop the tears from leaking out. She didn't want Bobby to see her cry. He was being kind, but he must think she was a failure. He already had four children, and Ethel was pregnant with their fifth. She seemed to give birth like a vending machine: pop in the sperm, and out popped a fully formed, squalling baby.

"I've left a message for Jack asking him to call the nurses' station when there's a connection," he told her. "A nurse will come to fetch me."

"Thank you," Jackie whispered. She was glad he was there, taking charge.

Although more reserved than Jack, Bobby had enough of the family charm that people fell over themselves to help him. She knew the nurses would be fluttery and coy around him.

Jackie wondered what Bobby thought of her deep down. He had always been friendly, although Ethel thought her "hoity-toity." She'd overheard her complaining about the way Jackie set a table, of all things. Seemingly Ethel didn't think it mattered whether the knife blades were facing inward or outward and scoffed at Jackie for adjusting them. She would crow now: she was the successful wife who could produce heirs by the handful.

Jackie was still woozy from the anesthetic and drifted into a doze, but she awoke when she heard Bobby's voice in the corridor outside. A nurse was bustling about in the room, checking her temperature, clattering instruments on a metal tray, so she missed some of the conversation, but what she heard was unmistakable.

"Jack, you *have* to come back. . . . Your wife's just had surgery. She needs you. . . . Don't be an idiot. . . . Of *course* she's upset, but you know Jackie—she doesn't show it. . . . It will be in the papers tomorrow for sure. There's nothing I can do about that. . . . Just think how it will look politically: 'Wife loses baby while senator suns himself in the Med.' Is that the headline you want to see? Well, get your ass back here . . ."

Jackie was stunned. She clutched her throat, finding it hard to breathe. Jack didn't want to interrupt his vacation. That's how much he cared about her. She shivered. Everyone had warned her before they got married that he needed his own space, and she had been willing to allow that, but she hadn't realized till now that his heart was quite so cold.

Chapter 4

Washington, D.C.
August 28, 1956

Five days after their baby died, Jack arrived in D.C.
Jackie was recovering at home in Georgetown,
where she lay on top of her bed with a fan blowing
cool air on her legs. Her sister, Lee, had flown in from
London and was bustling around, fetching drinks and
tidying the bedside clutter of books and lotions, wearing an immaculate silk polka-dot dress from Jean Pa-
tou's spring/summer collection.

Jackie regarded her critically. It had been kind of her
to drop everything and rush over to play nursemaid,
but who wore a brand-new designer outfit to look
after an invalid, for heaven's sake? Lee always strove
to be the better dressed of the two of them, no matter
what the occasion, and her competitiveness could get
tedious.

"How are you, kid?" Jack asked, leaning over to kiss her, a concerned expression on his face. "Are you okay? We had a stopover in Paris and I bought you some perfume." He put a gift-wrapped package in her lap but she didn't touch it. How could he think of perfume at a time like this? "Hi, Lee," he continued. "Good of you to help out."

Lee beamed at him. "Hi, Jack. Great tan!"

"The funeral was last Saturday," Jackie interrupted, poker-faced, trying to snap them both into some respect for the solemnity of the occasion. "She was a girl. Your daughter. I called her Arabella."

Jack nodded, at last serious. "I like the name."

"Bobby made the arrangements," she continued, her voice like a knife.

"Good man," he remarked. "I'll call and thank him, but first I need a sandwich. I haven't eaten since breakfast."

"Let me get your sandwich," Lee insisted, heading for the door. "Ham and mustard okay?" She was dippy about Jack; nothing was too much trouble for her darling brother-in-law.

Once they were alone, Jackie waited for him to apologize for not returning sooner, to tell her how sad he was about the loss of the baby, to share the grief that was lodged inside her, hard and implacable as a bullet—

but instead he began talking about some journalist he'd met on the plane. She watched him, his hair bleached from the sun, his skin as dark as walnuts, and marveled at the electricity he exuded. He had no idea what was going through her mind. None whatsoever. Maybe he never had.

He finished his story before sitting on the edge of the bed and pulling her into his arms. "It's so sad about Arabella," he said. "I can't take it in yet. After all those months of waiting . . ."

His face pressed against her shoulder and she heard him stifle a sigh—or could it have been a sob? He did seem upset now, but he didn't feel the loss; not like she did. Her grief was dark and solitary, and it was mixed with bitter anger at him for being overseas when their baby died and then not coming home immediately.

He broke away before long, the moment over, and she watched as his mind flipped to the next matter to be dealt with. "I'm glad Lee is here for you. It was good of her to come." He glanced at his watch. "Do you mind if I drop by the office this afternoon? Just to pick up messages."

Jackie was so shocked he could consider it that she was lost for words. She kept her feelings buried, but surely Jack must know how devastated she was, and how much she needed him to comfort her? Down the hall there was a beautifully decorated nursery with no baby to put in it.

"I won't be long," he promised, standing up. "We can have dinner together."

The problem was that she had married a man who was an iceberg. A glacier. Deep down, did he care about anything apart from politics and power? It was hard to tell.

Once Jack had gone, Jackie eased herself out of bed, waving away the maid's protests. He had left his suit-case on the floor and she lowered herself to sit beside it, gasping at the tug in her stitches. She didn't know what she expected to find as she rummaged through his sandy swim shorts, casual shirts, and musty towels, but she knew there was something Jack wasn't telling her.

And there it was: when she picked up a copy of a Saul Bellow novel, a Polaroid fluttered out. A girl with white-blond hair sitting on his lap, wearing a skimpy hot-pink bikini. She looked Scandinavian, with a high forehead, laughing eyes, and a slim figure.

Jackie's stomach heaved. *This* was what he was doing when their baby died. Holding the photograph between thumb and forefinger, as if it might contaminate her, she rose, hobbled back to bed, and dropped it into her handbag.

What should she do? Who could she confide in? Definitely not Lee, who would make excuses for her brother-in-law; definitely not her mother. There was only one person she could turn to. He hadn't been able to visit her in the hospital, but she would meet him for lunch in New York just as soon as the doctors told her she was well enough to travel.

Black Jack Bouvier examined the photo for several minutes. They were sitting at a quiet corner table in an Italian restaurant in east Midtown, a bottle of plum-colored Chianti encased in a raffia basket between them.

"He's clearly having an affair with her, isn't he?" Jackie demanded.

Black Jack tilted his head to one side. "A vacation fling rather than an affair. She looks that sort of girl."

"How could he do that to me? To our baby?" Tears began to well, and once she let go there was no stopping them. Her daddy passed her a crumpled white handkerchief with the ease of a man who often dealt with crying women.

"You need to separate this out, honey. Jack didn't know you were going to lose the baby when he slept with this woman. They're different issues. It's sad your baby died but it's not his fault. You married him knowing he was a ladies' man." The tears were rolling silently down her cheeks, and he reached across to stroke her forearm.

She dabbed her eyes. "I knew he was dating other girls before we got married, but I thought he would stop once we were engaged. Was that naive?"

She watched his reaction, aware that Black Jack used to have lady friends back when he was still married to her mother. She remembered him bringing a pretty brunette to watch her ride in a gymkhana one Saturday. She was only about nine, but she saw a knowing look between them, watched her daddy's hand brush the lady's knee, and in a flash gained insight into a whole new grown-up world of understanding. She should have known her father would defend Jack. They were cut from the same cloth.

The difference was that she'd never felt jealous of Black Jack's girlfriends. They made a fuss over her and Lee, letting them eat ice cream and popcorn, and never chastising them the way their mother did. As for her father, she knew beyond a shadow of a doubt that she was his favorite, so she had no reason to feel insecure. He loved Lee too; just not as much.

"Some men have particularly strong sexual needs," he answered. "One woman will never be enough."

"Daddy!" She blushed and covered her wet cheeks with her hands.

"It's not a betrayal of you. It's just something Jack has to do, a physical act like cleaning his teeth or shaving. He doesn't love you one bit less because of it. And I bet they're all brief encounters; he's not going to risk keeping a mistress."

The thought hadn't even occurred to Jackie. Good God, she hoped he wouldn't do that.

"Do you really want a divorce, though?" Black Jack continued. "Think of the heartache caused by your mom and me divorcing."

Her parents' divorce had been a long time coming: First her daddy had moved to a different apartment and she and Lee were told it had something to do with his work. The girls preferred it that way, because they didn't have to huddle in bed at night listening to their parents screaming at each other anymore. Her mother, who had always been quick to lash out with a slap, became even stricter without Black Jack there to restrain her. Good manners were paramount. You had to be on your best behavior when Janet was around.

Jackie was a teenager when her mother announced that she was getting remarried, to the Standard Oil heir Hugh Auchincloss. Hughdie, as he was known to those closest to him, was much wealthier than Black Jack, with estates in Virginia and Rhode Island as well as a Park Avenue apartment. Their standard of living leapt to a whole new level of affluence, with dozens of staff members in each house, their own stables, attendance at top schools, and generous clothing allowances. Jackie and Lee both adored clothes, and now when they pored over *Vogue* and *Harper's Bazaar* or traipsed around stores together they could afford to buy their favorite outfits. They had endless discussions about the new collections, the season's hemlines and colors, and their passion for all things French. The marriage meant they saw less of their daddy, though, because he still lived in New York. By then, Jackie was old enough to know that he drank too much, and she worried about him. She never stopped worrying about him.

"Divorce would kill Jack's career," Black Jack said over their chicken cacciatore, then took a slurp of wine. "It's difficult enough getting elected as a Catholic because Protestants will be biased against him—but if he's a divorced Catholic he won't even get the Catholic vote."

"He should have thought of that sooner," Jackie replied, peering into her compact mirror and wiping away mascara smudges. She didn't want a divorce. She wanted Jack. But she wanted *more* of him. She wanted them to be able to talk about the baby they had lost. She would have liked for him to be with her when she was told Arabella had died. And she wished he wouldn't cheat on her. Was that too much to ask?

"Rise above it and keep your dignity," Black Jack counseled, tilting his head toward the photograph. "Make sure he treats you with the respect due to a wife. No fornicating in your home, or parading other women under your nose. Draw the line at that. But stay married, honey. That's my best advice."

On the train back to Washington, Jackie wondered if other wives put up with this. In novels or plays, cheating husbands always got their comeuppance, but perhaps it wasn't the same in real life. Why had she picked a man like Jack? Was it partly because he reminded her of her flawed but adorable daddy?

Looking back, the only period in their marriage during which she could say for sure he'd been faithful was after he'd had back surgery in 1954 and was laid up for a few months. She'd been a good wife then as now: arranging visitors to entertain him, reading magazine articles to him, feeding him his favorite foods, devising ways to make love without straining his stitches.

But after he recovered he became preoccupied again. He popped home from the office to shower and change his clothes before dashing off to more meetings. Were they really "meetings," or was that a euphemism? Did he have a mistress right on their doorstep in Washington?

She had a choice to make: she could do as her daddy suggested and rise above it; she could turn detective and confront him whenever she caught him; or she could ask for a divorce. Even if she didn't go through with it, she knew the suggestion would shake him up. His political future relied on a stable marriage.

She knew what her mother would say: "Don't wash your dirty linen in public." But Jack owed her for this. He'd have to buck up his ideas big time if he wanted to hang on to her.

Chapter 5

Milan, Italy
December 1957

The week before Christmas, the telephone rang at Maria's Milan townhouse, and when she answered she heard Aristotle's voice on the line. Battista must have given him the private number.

"The forecast is for calm seas so we're planning a New Year's Eve party on the *Christina*. I wondered if you and Battista might come. I could send a plane to pick you up."

She laughed at the ostentation; not many party invitations included such an extravagant offer! "I'm afraid I can't. I'm singing in Rome on the second, to an audience that includes the Italian president. I mustn't let them down."

"I could fly you to Rome on the first," he persisted.

"Thank you," she said, "but it doesn't work like

that. I need to prepare for big concerts. For several days before, I'll either be rehearsing or I'll be resting my voice."

"What a bore!" he exclaimed. "I would be vexed if my work stopped me having fun."

"I've never thought of singing as work," she said, then paused to try and find the words to express herself without sounding too pretentious. "It's the greatest source of joy in my life. When I'm immersed in a production, it's so all-consuming and fulfilling, I can't think about anything else."

"Like sex, then?" he retorted, and she blushed, glad he couldn't see over the telephone wire.

"I suppose there are similarities." Maria giggled, nervously. She wasn't used to discussing sex with anyone—not even her husband. "It's as if something else takes over when I sing—a divine energy, a creative force, call it what you will—and it fills me from top to toe . . ." She stopped, feeling self-conscious. "Now you're going to laugh at me!"

"I wouldn't dream of it," he said quietly. "It's clear this is what you were born to do, and I'm glad it brings you such pleasure. You're lucky."

"I am," she agreed. She didn't tell him that she was insecure, superstitious about her luck deserting her if she changed any of her rituals. She always used the same warm-ups, prayed to her Madonna icon, crossed herself three times, then stepped onto the stage right foot first. Always the right. "But clearly you were born with a great talent for business. I'm sure you get pleasure from striking a new deal and watching the money roll in."

"It's not about money for me," he said. "I love the game. The simple explanation is that I can't stand to lose, so I make sure that when I set my heart on something, I always get it."

His words hung in the air between them, seeming loaded with meaning.

Maria was the first to speak. "I'm sorry not to make your party. Perhaps another time."

"You were going to tell me when I should come and hear you sing, remember?"

"I will." She laughed again. There was an awkward pause; then she said, "Do give my best to Tina," before she hung up.

Maria decided not to mention the call to Battista. He was keen to become best buddies with Onassis. He liked befriending the superrich, whereas she always felt slightly uncomfortable around them, as if they could sense she wasn't their social equal. The rented apartment in Manhattan's Washington Heights neighborhood where she had grown up with her Greek immigrant parents and older sister had been comfortable enough, but her mother was never satisfied with it: "I'm used to better than this," Evangelia moaned incessantly. "I should never have married down. What was I thinking?" As a product of that "marrying down," Maria was still conscious of her place in the class system long after her success had helped her to transcend it.

Rome was overcast, with a damp, penetrating wind blowing up the Tiber when they arrived on December 27. Maria and Battista were staying at the Hotel Quirinale, which was connected by a passageway to the Teatro dell'Opera. This meant she could protect her vocal cords from the chill of the streets, but the auditorium was as cold as the grave when she arrived for the first rehearsal.

"Can we have some heating, please?" she demanded. "*Presto!*"

An assistant stage manager scurried over and promised she would look into it, then sneezed violently. Maria yanked her scarf over her face. She couldn't risk catching cold just days before a concert.

It was *Norma*, Bellini's great tragedy, a difficult part but one she loved to sing. It suited her voice, with all the technical challenges and coloratura. She usually sang in full voice at rehearsals, just for the sheer joy of feeling the muscles working in harmony to create such glorious music. The acoustics were superb, of course, and the orchestra top-notch. She lost herself in such moments. This was the reason she put up with all the pressure and criticism—because the rewards were phenomenal.

On New Year's Eve, four days after their arrival, they joined some friends for a party in a club called Circolo degli Scacchi. Maria permitted herself one small glass of champagne for a toast at midnight, but only sipped it. They stayed for an hour before heading back to the Quirinale.

"What would you like 1958 to bring?" she asked Battista in the taxi.

"I want to get more money out of La Scala when we renegotiate your contract," he said. "They bought you too cheaply."

He didn't ask what she wanted, but he knew. She'd never made a secret of it. She yearned for a baby.

As a singer, Maria had to be very attuned to the state of her health. She imagined it was the same for athletes, or anyone else whose body was highly trained for performance. So when she woke on the morning of January 1, she knew her throat didn't feel right: slightly tight, a little bit scratchy. She nudged Battista and mimed that he should fetch the steam inhaler, then wrote on the notepad she kept by the bed that he should call a throat specialist.

While she breathed steam through the mask, she listened to him make phone call after phone call and became increasingly alarmed. No one was working on New Year's Day. She thought back to that girl who had sneezed on the first day of rehearsal, three days earlier—exactly the incubation period for a cold or influenza virus.

She could tell that one call he made was to the opera's director: "I hope you have an understudy," he said, "because Maria may not be able to sing tomorrow."

There was a long pause, then Battista retorted, "Be that as it may, if a doctor tells her not to sing, she will not sing. She can't risk damaging her vocal cords."

Maria clutched her throat. She couldn't bear to let them down. *Please, God, no.*

The specialist who came that afternoon swabbed her throat and gave her an anti-inflammatory spray. All day she avoided speaking, using her notepad to communicate, sipping water at room temperature, and having clear soup for meals. No meat, no dairy, no solids.

The following morning, as soon as she awoke, she swallowed tentatively, and felt the tightness had eased a little. Still, she rested her voice all day, and an hour before curtain the doctor pronounced her fit to perform.

She did the warm-ups cautiously, scared to push herself. "Please give me good voice tonight," she prayed to her Madonna. The Virgin smiled back, her expression benign.

In the first scenes, the notes were true but she couldn't get much power behind them. The muscles were not responding. During "Casta Diva," with its leap from middle F to high C and those long sustained notes, she could feel the sound weakening and her top notes becoming unsteady. Her voice was hanging by a thread. It was agonizing, but what could she do? There was nothing for it but to press on. After one particularly wobbly phrase, someone in the audience booed, and she winced. There was a shuffling of feet. They were restless.

Then she felt the instability hitting her lower register too, and the grumbling from the audience increased. "Go back to Milan!" someone shouted. She couldn't blame them. They'd paid a fortune for their tickets and they weren't getting value for money.

When she staggered backstage at the intermission, she knew she couldn't go out again. Her forehead was burning and her throat was so swollen that it had almost closed.

"You need to get her to bed," the doctor told Battista, after taking her temperature.

The director came to argue: the show would have to be canceled and he would sue.

Battista told him that he was an idiot for not getting an understudy and led Maria through the passage to their hotel. She wanted to apologize and try to explain, but she was so ill she felt close to collapse.

The next morning she heard Battista huffing and grunting as he looked through the newspapers that had been left at the door of their suite. The headlines were damning: "A Million Lire for a Single Disastrous Act," one said. Another had a photograph of her drinking champagne in that damned nightclub. She hadn't noticed a photographer; it must have been taken in the commotion just after midnight. They claimed that it was her "partying" that had damaged her voice. "*Scandalo!*," "*Disgrazia!*," "*Insulta!*," they all agreed.

The public attack was infuriating and deeply unfair. In the whole of 1957, she had given sixty-seven performances and had postponed only one—in San Francisco, also on medical advice. She had been accused of canceling a Vienna concert, but in fact contract negotiations had stalled, so it didn't happen. Hers was a better record than any other opera singer's, yet the press insisted on portraying her as a spoiled diva who stormed

out of productions on a whim. The media had invented
a scowling persona for her and were sticking to their
story, so there was no sympathy when she caught a cold
in Rome. No, this was Maria Callas being difficult—
again. They accused her of drinking champagne and
staying out until dawn, when it wasn't true. She was
selfish, ungrateful, a disgrace. It reminded her of the
litany of complaints her mother used to hurl at her in
childhood—"Stupid, ugly, good-for-nothing girl"—
and brought back a similar feeling of worthlessness.

As she lay in bed in the Hotel Quirinale, a compress
wrapped around her throat, a telegram arrived. She tore
it open.

"I'm sorry to hear of your malady," it read. "Please
let me know how I can help. May I send my personal
physician? A private plane to whisk you to sunnier
climes? Or a hitman to assassinate disrespectful journalists? Your wish is my command. Aristo."

Maria smiled. All three would have been welcome.
But instead she would keep her head down, recuperate, then work harder than ever to get ready for the
full schedule of concerts already booked for the coming
year—including a run at the Met in New York City in
just a month's time.

Chapter 6

Hyannis Port, Massachusetts
October 1956

"I heard Maria Callas sing at the Met last night," Jackie said during a lull in conversation around the Kennedys' huge oak dinner table. "She was spectacular. It gave me gooseflesh that a human being can produce such a sound."

Jack looked up from sawing his brisket. It was tough as boot leather; Jackie had left most of her portion. If she were in charge of the menu, the meals would be much better, but the Kennedys didn't care about fine food. "Just think of all the votes I could have bought for the price of your ticket," he quipped.

She felt a prick of annoyance. Running their household was her domain, but Jack was forever complaining about money these days, wanting to know how much she spent on drapes, and rugs—even on towels, for heaven's sake. She was about to answer when Rose, Jack's mother, chimed in.

"She sounds like a piece of work. Did you read that *Time* article about her?"

Jackie shook her head. "Not yet."

"It says she is a diva who always has to get her own way." Rose spoke as if this were a criminal act, although the same could be said of any of her children.

"I imagine you have to be very exacting to perform at her level," Jackie replied. "And I also imagine the *Time* journalist went in wielding a hatchet because otherwise there's no meat to the story."

"Henry Luce and Briton Hadden were the cofounders of *Time*, back in the twenties," Jack's father, Joe, added. "Decent men, both of them, but Briton used to drive Henry crazy when he put actors and singers on the cover. He wanted it to be a heavyweight political paper, leaning towards the Republicans. But of course journalists tend to be young men of principle so it acquired its Democratic bias."

"Who do we know there?" Jack asked. And, just like that, the subject switched back to politics.

"Ed Thompson will be with us." Joe began to list *Time* journalists who might support Jack's career.

Jackie would have liked to argue that Maria Callas was every bit as deserving of a *Time* cover as a transient politician, and that her ticket had been worth every last cent she'd paid for it, but she knew from experience that discussions around that table quickly became adversarial. All the Kennedy children were competitive; no one backed down, whether they were playing tennis, swimming, or debating. And none of them shared her belief that culture was equally as important as politics in a civilized society. This evening, she didn't have the energy to fight them.

Jack stood abruptly, scraping his chair against the floor. "I've got a meeting in Hyannis at seven. I'll grab dessert when I'm back, if you hounds leave me any."

"Who are you meeting?" Jackie asked, then bit her lip. She wished she could be the independent, sassy girl Jack had fallen for rather than a nagging wife, but sometimes the questions slipped out.

"You know—the team," he answered vaguely. "I won't be late."

He gave Jackie a quick kiss on the forehead, exactly the same kiss he gave his mother a second later. Not long afterward she heard his car's engine turning over in the drive.

When they finished dinner, Jackie was about to head up to their room, but Joe grabbed her arm. "Let's you and me go for a stroll. It's a fine evening."

She donned a wool wrap against the autumn chill and tied a headscarf over her hair. The Kennedy house was right on the Cape Cod seafront and winds whipped in off Nantucket Sound. The sun had sunk below the horizon but there was still a pinkish glow on the west-facing upper windows.

"You seem unhappy," Joe said as they walked across the lawn toward the beach. "Is my son neglecting you?"

"No more than usual." Jackie forced a chuckle. She and Joe had had this conversation before. Prior to the wedding, he'd warned her that Jack needed plenty of freedom, and she'd been able to tell him she already knew.

"You could have had any man you wanted," Joe said. "I know that; he knows that. You're brilliant, beautiful, charming, and you've got spirit."

"What's with the soft soap?" she asked. "Have you got a favor to ask?"

He spoke seriously. "Just that you don't leave him."

Jackie didn't answer for a long time, but walked along the shoreline, listening to the noise of breakers crashing, then ebbing, sending pebbles scuttling. "Why not?" she asked. "Because it would ruin his political career?"

"No. Because I couldn't bear to lose you as a daughter-in-law. Now, let's talk frankly."

"We always do, Joe," she said softly. It wasn't quite true, but she knew he liked to think they were close, and it suited her to let him think that.

"You've moved around too much since you got married. You need a proper home in D.C., somewhere to raise your family. What if I help you get somewhere real nice?"

"Are you trying to bribe me?" She gazed at the darkening ocean. Fishing boats were heading out, their lights blinking as they rose and dipped on the waves.

"I wouldn't call it that. I want you to be happy and I'm asking you to tell me what that would take."

Her eyes blurred with tears, and she was glad of the dark and the wind blowing into her face, so that he wouldn't realize it. Did any of them know what it felt like to have lost two babies when the other Kennedy wives and daughters were producing grandchildren like clockwork? To have to attend their baby showers and christenings was agony.

"He does love you," Joe continued. "As much as he is capable of loving anyone. But he's thoughtless. You have to be very self-sufficient to be with my son."

"You can say that again." She wiped her eyes quickly with the edge of her wrap.

"You should get pregnant again soon, Jackie," he said. "I can't help you with that, but you know I'm right."

"You're an interfering old goat, Joe." She laughed to mask her embarrassment. Sexual relations with Jack had been almost nonexistent since Arabella had died. She was too angry with him. She should revive their sex life; she knew she should. It wasn't good for a marriage to let these things slide.

They stopped when they reached the end of the beach, where a fence separated them from the rocks beyond.

"Start house hunting," he said. "Let me know when you find one you like. Decorate it however you want. Build a nest."

Jackie nodded. She would enjoy that. As it happened, she already had a picture of her ideal house in mind. And perhaps, if there was any cash left over, they could buy their own place in Hyannis Port and not have to stay at the family home anymore. She'd like that.

A few months later, a Washington paper printed a story claiming that Jackie had been thinking of leaving her senator husband but that Joe Kennedy had bribed her to stay by giving her a check for a million dollars. Where did they get these stories with their tiny kernels of truth? she wondered. It was alarming to think there could be a leak so close to home.

She called her father-in-law, assuming he would have

seen the story too. "Only a million, Joe?" she teased. "Why not ten million?"

He laughed, but she could sense caution. "Worth it at any price," he said at last.

"I've got some news for you." She crossed her fingers before continuing, so she didn't jinx it. "I don't want everyone to know yet because it's early days but I followed your advice. I'm pregnant."

"That's wonderful!" he cried, and she could hear that he was grinning. "Third time lucky, eh?"

"Third time lucky," she agreed, but she kept her fingers crossed after they got off the phone. At long last she hoped to give Jack a child, but she couldn't help feeling scared. She didn't know how she would bear it if anything went wrong this time.

Chapter 7

Milan
April 1958

It was as if the Rome fiasco had unleashed whole new levels of abuse on Maria's head. Her voice was as strong as ever and all her performances were sellouts, but the papers insisted she was a diva, a tigress, a monster, and wouldn't have it any other way. They twisted the facts. One piece reported that she had insisted on rehearsing for six hours straight when she wasn't happy with a production; it was true, but the director had agreed with her, and the press weren't attacking him. She admitted to being a perfectionist about her work, but she always behaved with professionalism and never lost her temper, seldom even raising her voice. Yet when photographers snapped pictures of her in airports and emerging from stage doors, editors always chose the ones that made her look as if she were snarling or scowling.

"Does the public truly believe I am this vile creature?" she asked Battista, wincing at a particularly unflattering shot.

"Ignore it," he said, without answering the question. "Who cares? Your friends know the real you."

He didn't understand her need to be liked. She couldn't stand to have anyone think badly of her. She'd had a difficult childhood, with a mother who blatantly favored her elder, prettier, daintier daughter, Jacinthy. Maria grew up feeling ugly and unlovable, with her voice the only saving grace, so the news stories were rubbing salt in decades-old wounds.

What had she done to deserve this media treatment except be successful? Was she being punished for that, as she had been in the early days of her career when other singers resented her getting solo roles?

Some of the blame lay with La Scala's press office, who fueled the flames by inventing a rivalry between Maria and another first soprano in the company, Renata Tebaldi: "Clash of the Prima Donnas!" It made good copy, but there was little truth in it. Renata was trained in the *verismo* school, which focused on a strongly produced tone and dropped the coloratura, while Maria trained in bel canto and had a full armory of trills and vocal flexibility. That meant they gravitated toward different repertoires. Maria didn't know Renata well, but they were perfectly friendly whenever they met.

All the same, the rumor that they were rivals spread like the plague among Milanese opera lovers. They were a passionate bunch, never slow to express their opinions. If a singer missed a note, they would sing it back to him or her. If a performance was disappointing, the booing and hissing began. Their actions were in complete contrast to the hushed respect of other concert halls, especially London's, where the audience was so polite that they would never dream of interrupting a performance. Maria admired the Milanese's love of opera but not their bad manners.

It got to the point that one section of the La Scala auditorium was occupied by Renata Tebaldi's supporters and another by Maria's. Whenever she stepped onstage, Renata's followers would shout abuse, and hers would try to drown them out with cheers. The moments before she opened her mouth to sing were like an ancient Roman gladiatorial contest: "Kill her!" "No, let her live another day."

"Why can't I just sing, without all the politics?" she pleaded with the press office, but they shrugged in that maddening Italian fashion, as if to say, "What can we do? It's just the way things are."

———

In the spring of 1958, Maria was rehearsing two productions back-to-back: *Anna Bolena* and *Il Pirata*. That was manageable, but for some reason Ghiringhelli, the artistic director of La Scala, was being childish and petulant. One morning, when he saw her entering through the stage door, he ducked behind a piece of scenery and disappeared, knocking over some wooden castle battlements that hit the floor with a resounding clatter.

"What's eating him?" she asked the doorman, and he shook his head in bewilderment.

Ghiringhelli sat near the back of the auditorium during rehearsal that day and rushed out at the end before Maria could ask him for feedback.

"Have I done something to upset him?" she asked a nearby tenor.

"I think it's to do with your contract," the tenor whispered behind his hand. "I hear he's in a rage about your husband's demands."

"Oh, for goodness' sake!" Maria exclaimed. "That's just business. I'll go and speak to him."

"He's not here," Ghiringhelli's secretary insisted, panic etched across her face.

Maria glanced through the frosted glass and saw a figure crouched behind a filing cabinet. He was hiding from her. Unbelievable! She considered bursting in and confronting him but thought better of it.

"Please tell Mr. Ghiringhelli that I merely wanted to ask about my opening nights," she said, making sure her voice carried. "No one has yet told me when they will be." It was a reasonable enough request.

"Of course," the secretary agreed, scribbling on a notepad. "I'll ask him to let you know."

No word came. Two days later, Maria found out by chance, when she saw the dates printed on a poster in the vestibule.

She knew Battista could be aggressive in his negotiations with opera houses, but she never interfered. Their deal was that she focused on the singing while he handled the business side, but it was hard not to feel alarmed. For all its faults, she loved La Scala with a passion. It was the crème de la crème of opera houses, the home of Verdi and Toscanini, the place where every opera singer dreamed of triumphing yet few succeeded. When she had been invited to join the company back in 1952, it had been the proudest moment of her life. They had given her the chance to sing all the choice soprano roles, and she loved working with their top-notch musicians and highly skilled stage crew. It felt as if she had a real home at last, and a musical family to make up for the love she lacked from her birth family.

"Please don't alienate Ghiringhelli," she begged Battista that evening. "You know I would sing at La Scala for no fee whatsoever, simply for the honor."

"Leave the contract to me," he insisted. "I think I'm getting through to them at last."

Anna Bolena premièred and the reviews were glowing, although the audience was rowdier than ever. Booing and cheering at curtain was par for the course, but one night a section of the crowd was so noisy that she could scarcely hear herself sing. In the third act, at the point where the guards came to arrest her character, she snapped. She pushed the guards aside, charged to the footlights, and sang directly at the offenders, shaking her fist, eyes blazing: *"Judges? . . . My fate is decided if my accuser is also my judge. . . . But I will be exculpated after death . . ."*

Her supporters went mad, their clapping and cheering filling the auditorium all the way to the gods. The orchestra had to pause for several minutes till the furor died down, and Maria stood her ground, fists clenched, glaring at the troublemakers.

It was gratifying at the time, and backstage her fellow performers congratulated her, but that's when the trouble began to spill out into Maria and Battista's private lives. Their address was well known—Via Buonarroti

40, in the Teatro district. One day, not long after she had confronted the audience, their driver found a dead dog on the backseat of their car; a few days later excrement was smeared on their railings, and obscene graffiti scrawled on their walls.

Maria began to fear that the hysteria was building to a crescendo and they weren't safe in their beds. The police came and recommended that doors and windows on the ground floor be kept locked. She couldn't walk her pet poodles anymore, couldn't browse in local boutiques or relax outside a café with an espresso—those days were gone.

The price of fame kept getting higher. It was crazy. All she'd ever wanted to do was sing.

Aristotle rang in the midst of that tumultuous time. He caught Maria at a vulnerable moment and she let off steam.

"It's absurd that such beautiful music can provoke such ugly behavior," she told him. "We have policemen patrolling the theater and I have a police escort to take me from the stage door to my car. Can you believe it?"

"I've been following reports in the press," he said. "Can't your publicist release some stories to calm the atmosphere? Perhaps a photo showing you and Renata Tebaldi having dinner together, the best of friends?"

"I don't have a publicist," she said. "Battista handles press inquiries."

"You're kidding! He does that and manages your contracts and bookings as well? It's a lot for one person. A decent publicist could place positive stories and help to kill the negative ones. I've had a PR for years."

Maria wrinkled her nose. She preferred to avoid the press. "I keep hoping it will die down. I'll be in London in June; then we're having a long summer break. Maybe by fall the atmosphere will be calmer. If not, the way things are going I may have to hire a bodyguard."

"Perhaps you should do that anyway," he said. "I don't like to think of you at risk from some lunatic."

She shivered. "I'm safe at Lake Garda at least. We've got a house in Sirmione that is my sanctuary. The locals don't bother me. That's where we'll spend the summer, and I can't wait."

She loved the serenity of the little town on the shores of the lake, where the water was as deep as the Alps were high, the ice-cream shops had fifty different flavors, and there was an old-fashioned civility. Her dogs loved it too.

"I was hoping to persuade you to come for a cruise on the *Christina*," he said. "Would I be wasting my breath?"

She hesitated. It was flattering that he was being so

attentive, and it seemed harmless enough since they were both married to other people. She might have been tempted to visit his famous floating palace, where they would surely be cosseted in the utmost luxury, but she was too exhausted. "This year I need rest and solitude," she said. "But thank you."

There was another reason for turning down the offer. Celebrities were often photographed on his yacht, the women chic in Chanel beachwear and cat's-eye sunglasses. It had been only four years since Maria had lost eighty pounds and slimmed down to her present shape, and she still felt like a fat girl inside. Posing alongside the world's most glamorous women, with press photographers snapping away like sharks, was her idea of hell on earth.

Chapter 8

Milan
May 1958

Maria was in the music room one evening, accompanying herself on the elegant Bechstein grand piano she'd bought with her first paycheck from La Scala, when Battista came in. "They aren't renewing your contract," he announced.

She was horrified. "La Scala? But why not? They have to renew!"

"It's a mixture of money and the trouble that's been breaking out. Plus Ghiringhelli is being a bastard." He shrugged. It seemed he was just going to accept it, as if this were purely a business decision and her feelings didn't come into it.

"No!" She panicked. "Go back to them. Reduce the fee. I can't leave La Scala!" She felt as if she'd been stabbed. It would break her heart to go.

"We've got no choice," he said. "There are plenty of other opera houses, decent places where you won't be intimidated by maniacs."

"Are you sure about that? We've got lawsuits with Rome, Vienna, and San Francisco." When performances were canceled for any reason, it always ended up in the courts. She hated it, couldn't bear conflict. "If I can't work with the best orchestras and top conductors, I would rather retire. I'll give up singing entirely!"

She spoke out of passion, not meaning it. She would miss singing too badly. It had been her whole life. But she also knew that when she did retire, sometime in the far-off future, she would relish the peace. Being able to go out for dinner without dodging photographers would be heaven.

Battista was in a brusque mood, still riled from his conversation with La Scala's manager. "Don't be ridiculous! There are dozens of top places where you can sing: London, Paris, and New York, to name but three. Besides, we can't afford for you to retire. Don't exaggerate and turn this into more than it is."

It was quite a speech for him, delivered with brio. Maria rose and paced to the window, picking up a porcelain vase from the side table. He looked wary, as if worried that she might throw it at him, but instead she stroked the delicate, hand-painted flowers on the sides. It was one of her favorites.

"I've always told you I want to retire at the top. I don't want to be one of those sad old has-beens trailing round dingy clubs trying to remind audiences of their glory days. I'm not there yet, but we have to plan for it."

"For the love of God, pull yourself together," he snapped. "I never had you down as someone who quits at the first sign of trouble, and I'm not going to let you. Do you hear me?"

He turned and left the room, pulling the door sharply behind him. She stared after him, suppressing the urge to scream.

The following day the papers would report she had been "sacked" by the greatest company on earth, and they would blame her for being a "diva." It was humiliating and deeply hurtful. La Scala had made her the star she was and now they were whipping the red carpet from beneath her, after all she had done for them. It was a rejection that resonated on many levels, taking her all the way back, yet again, to the little girl whose mother never loved her.

Maria lay in bed fretting about what the future might hold. Should they leave Italy altogether and try to join the company at another opera house? It would feel like a comedown, because nowhere else was as prestigious as La Scala. The alternative was constant touring, living out of suitcases for more of the year than she did already, and that was a daunting prospect.

Battista was snoring, making a rumbling noise like a lawn mower, and she felt irritated with him. When they'd first been married, she'd relied on his support and his ability to handle her business affairs. She had felt protected. Now he kept alienating opera house managers, and it was a bone of contention that he refused to hire a publicist, as Aristotle had suggested. He claimed they couldn't afford it. Why was *he* always the one who decided how *her* money was spent?

Months had passed since they had last had marital relations. They had become like brother and sister, bickering over trifles such as who hadn't closed the door of their new American refrigerator. Tensions were exacerbated without the glue of passion. She often felt cross with him for no good reason.

Actually, there was a good reason. He knew she was approaching her thirty-fifth birthday at the end of that year and she was desperate for a baby, yet he never wanted to make love. She had tried everything: wearing sexy negligees and sitting on his lap, rubbing against him; sponging him in the bath in her most seductive manner; rolling over in bed to kiss him, then letting her kisses stray lower. Always he would return the embrace at first, then find a reason to push her away. "It's too hot to make love," he had claimed the previous night.

"But I like getting hot with you," she whispered.

"I'm tired, darling," he said. "Sleep well."

She thought back to the early days of their marriage: even then, she had been the one who wanted more. She would have made love several times a day, given half a chance. Battista laughingly called her his "sexy puppy." But back then he was still interested. Now, nothing.

Was it his age that made him less *appassionato*? Did he have trouble getting aroused? She rarely felt any hint of an erection. Was it because they lived and worked together around the clock, so there was no mystique? He saw her shaving her legs; did that dampen his desire? Even if he wasn't attracted to her, could he not make the effort when he knew how much she wanted a child?

A realization hit her, with the undeniable force of truth: *He doesn't notice me anymore. I might as well not be here.* She felt like crying once the words had formed in her head. She would never admit this to anyone, not even her closest friends, such as Biki, the Milanese designer, and Mary Carter, a dynamic socialite who lived in Dallas.

Stop it, Maria, she rebuked herself a moment later.

He is your husband, your beloved. You are not in an opera now. This is what a real marriage is like. Pull yourself together and get on with it.

She leaned over and kissed his brow, trying to feel tenderness toward him. He didn't stir.

Chapter 9

New York City
November 1957

Jackie watched her one-hour-old daughter lying in a crib by her hospital bed, filled to the brim with wonder. The baby had been sleeping, making little snuffly noises, but suddenly she awoke with an involuntary jerk and began to mewl. A nurse appeared, picked her up, and settled her in Jackie's arms.

The little girl had a fine sprinkling of reddish-blond hair, like thistledown. Her nails were tiny perfect ovals. The eyes were screwed tight against the harsh hospital lights, and the toothless mouth made strange shapes, as if she were trying to talk but couldn't figure out how.

Who are you? Jackie wondered. *Who will you become?*

This child would never know how precious she was. Third time lucky indeed! But her arrival was also tinged with sadness because Jackie's father, Black Jack, had not lived to meet her.

He had been diagnosed with liver cancer—the drinker's cancer, everyone said—earlier in the year, but no one had predicted the speed of his decline. Jackie had visited him in the hospital at the end of July and had been shocked to see that the whites of his eyes were a garish yellow. At least his spirit seemed as strong as ever.

"I'll be home in a week or so, they tell me," he said. "Not a moment too soon. These nurses have no sense of humor." He glared at the one within earshot, who was marking something on a chart.

"*Mr.* Bouvier," she said, "we nurses have a right to go about our jobs without the patients manhandling us."

"It was only a kiss," he pleaded, winking at Jackie.

"Oh, Daddy!" she rebuked. "You can't go around kissing nurses. Act your age."

He'd seemed so much himself that afternoon she decided to fly back to Virginia, where she could relax in the relative cool of the countryside. She wasn't riding during this pregnancy—she was taking no chances this time—but it was always soothing to spend time with the horses at her stepfather's stables.

Then a call came on the evening of August 2 to say Black Jack had taken a turn for the worse. Jack drove her to New York first thing the next morning, her chest tight with dread. *Hang on, Daddy. I can't lose you, I just can't,* she repeated over and over in her head, fighting off the panic that threatened to take hold.

When they reached the hospital ward, the matron intercepted them. "I'm so sorry, Mr. and Mrs. Kennedy, but he's gone. It was peaceful at the end."

I don't believe you, Jackie thought. *Black Jack would never have gone peacefully.* But the nurse who had sat with him as he passed confirmed that he had been told Jackie was on her way, whereupon he closed his eyes, seeming content, and never awoke again.

Jack put his arms around her but she didn't want to give in to grief. Not in a hospital. There were things to do, arrangements to be made.

After collecting the few belongings he'd had with him, they went to her daddy's tiny apartment on East Seventy-Fourth Street to await Lee, who was flying in from London. The drapes were closed and the temperature was as hot as an oven, with dust motes dancing and an irritable bluebottle buzzing. She lit a cigarette and wandered around, numb with grief, unable even to cry. Jack started exploring what was left of a man's life: some clothes, a few sticks of furniture, a couple of shelves of books, and a stack of 78-rpm jazz records. "I didn't know he was such a jazz hound," he said, flicking through the sleeves.

You hardly knew him, Jackie mused. *A few alcohol-fueled dinners don't make a close friendship.*

On the dresser there were several framed photos. In pride of place was one of her, aged nine or ten, holding up a gymkhana trophy. There were photos of her and Lee with their mother, then one of Jackie walking precariously atop a stone wall that was far too high. Her daddy always let her take risks, confident she would land on her feet.

The tears came suddenly as she realized she had lost the person who loved her most in the world. There had never been any question that she was her daddy's favorite; he used to tell her as much in front of Lee. It must have been hard for her, growing up with that knowledge. Jackie was the one who did best academically; she was the athletic daughter, who won prizes and commendations; the one who resembled him most. Lee had been more beautiful as a girl, and she got to be her mother's favorite, but Black Jack was the exciting parent, the one they both wanted to impress.

The result of his favoritism had been Lee's fierce competitiveness, although she was four years younger than Jackie and it was natural that she would not have achieved the same milestones. During one summer vacation she practiced the piano relentlessly, staying indoors day after day, so that she would outshine Jackie at the school recital in the fall. On the night of Jackie's coming-out party, Lee tried to upstage her by sauntering out in an off-the-shoulder, skin-tight pink gown, a tart's gown. She was only thirteen and got a mighty telling off from their mother, but she grabbed the attention, just for that fleeting moment.

Lee was determined to be the one to marry first, so she wed her teenage sweetheart, publisher Michael Canfield, while Jackie was still trying to nudge Jack Kennedy toward the altar. Lee and Michael moved to London, where she began attending the Paris shows, befriending the designers, and boasting to Jackie of new acquisitions. She wouldn't dream of being seen in last season's colors or hemlines; Lee was always *au courant*. It sometimes felt as if she had an imaginary scorecard and was trying to prove that she was just as good as, if not better than, her sister.

When she arrived later that afternoon, Lee's eye makeup was smudged, her hair tousled, and her cream Balmain suit creased, with what looked like a red wine stain on the lapel. Jackie wondered if she had been drinking on the plane. It wasn't like her to be less than impeccably turned out.

They all hugged, then Lee began to sob: "I can't believe he's gone. What will we do? How will we manage without him?"

Jackie stroked her hair, feeling a surge of tenderness. "You've got me," she said. "I'm not going anywhere."

She had always been the stronger of the two; Lee could fall apart, but she would cope.

Over the next few weeks, while Lee often collapsed in bouts of noisy sobbing, Jackie's sorrow came and went from one day to the next, sparked by the tiniest things. The scent of Wildroot hair tonic. Plus fours worn with two-tone shoes. The racing reports in the newspaper. She missed that feeling of being understood without having to say a word. She and Lee had it sometimes, a legacy of their shared childhood, but with Black Jack she used to be able to communicate her opinion with an arch of the eyebrow, and be rewarded with his grin.

And now, just over three months later, Black Jack's first granddaughter was lying in her arms. The little girl opened her eyes and looked directly at Jackie, a gaze that startled her because it seemed so knowing. She got the strangest tingling feeling that her daddy was looking back at her. The resemblance was striking.

The door burst open and Jack hurried in.

"Are you alright, honey? Is this her? Oh, my . . ."
He gasped as their daughter turned her head in the direction of his voice, cross-eyed, unfocused now.

"Do you want to hold her?" Jackie asked.

He took a step back. "She's so tiny. What if I drop her?"

She laughed. "You must have held your younger brothers and sisters. Come here. Like this."

She took his hand, pulled his arm into the correct position, then passed the baby to him, sliding her own hand clear so the fuzzy head rested on his palm.

"I wish I had a camera." She laughed. "The look of terror on your face is priceless. You saved the crew of a PT boat from shark-infested waters during the war, and you lambast Republicans in the House, yet you are petrified of a creature who weighs six and a half pounds."

He gave a sheepish grin, and she thought she had never loved him as much as she did at that precise moment.

Chapter 10

Milan
September 1958

"Who was that on the phone?" Maria called over the banister to the hallway two floors below. The dogs had been barking, so she couldn't hear.

"Aristotle Onassis," Battista called back. "He's in Milan next week and wanted to invite us for dinner, but I told him we'll be in America."

"What a shame! That's the third time he's asked and we haven't been free. He'll think we're giving him the brush-off." She was annoyed she hadn't gotten to the phone first. It would have been fun to chat with him.

"I've invited him to the gala concert in Paris in December."

Maria couldn't think that far ahead. She had so many engagements stacked up for the next three months that she felt exhausted just thinking about them: London first, then fourteen concerts in cities across the States and Canada during October and November. To her huge relief, there had been no shortage of offers to fill the gap left by the end of her contract with La Scala, including a long-term commitment to the Met in New York. She had worried that her career might be on the rocks, so it was wonderful to find herself still in demand. But she missed being part of a company, and she was sick to the back teeth of airport departure lounges and anonymous hotel rooms.

That afternoon she was busy helping her maid Bruna pack. It was difficult to plan her wardrobe in the fall because the weather could be so variable, from one extreme to another. At least they had a week in Dallas. Maria had loved Dallas ever since she had first been invited to sing there. The climate in November would be warmer than Milan, she liked the opera house, the hospitality was lavish, and she had good friends in town. One in particular. That part of the tour would be a welcome respite.

"Maria! Over here!"

Her friend Mary Carter was running across the tarmac, skirts flying, as Maria descended the steps of the plane at Dallas's Love Field airport. No one tried to stop Mary; she was statuesque, with an air of authority and a frank, no-nonsense way of speaking that got her backstage at any concert and ushered to the best seat in every restaurant.

"Maria Segunda!" This was the nickname Mary had been given by their Dallas friends because of the similarities between the two women: both tall, both dark, both larger-than-life characters. Maria flung her arms around Mary's waist and squeezed tight. "I've missed you *so much!*" It was true. Mary was one of the few people with whom she could be entirely herself.

Mary pulled back. "You look tired, honey. You're coming to my place for dinner tonight. Put your feet up and let me give you a good ol' southern welcome."

"So long as you're not serving grits, like last time," Maria retorted. "Foul, slimy stuff."

"Gotcha, loud and clear," Mary replied. "No grits."

Battista looked on, no idea what they were talking about. His English had not improved.

Mary's ranch house was a proper home, with couches you sank into, an outdoor dining area surrounded by sycamore trees strung with colored lanterns, and hammocks swinging between the trunks. Maria slipped off her shoes and walked barefoot on the grass, inhaling the scents of honeysuckle and home cooking.

Mary served a heaping platter of fried chicken that they ate with greasy fingers, along with freshly baked cornbread and a bowl of collard greens. There was a pitcher of Maria's favorite root beer for the women, while Battista and Mary's husband, Jack, had bottles of Dixie beer.

After eating, the women went for a stroll around the garden and stopped at a pergola shrouded in bougainvillea with a bench underneath.

"How come you're looking so pinched, gal?" Mary asked, touching her cheek. "You haven't been dieting again, have you? There's not a scrap of flesh on you. Sit down and tell me what's going on in your life."

The women had met only the previous year, after a concert Maria gave in Dallas, but right from the get-go it felt as if they had known each other forever. Mary had bypassed the usual social niceties and dived straight in, asking Maria how she had achieved her famous weight loss back in 1954. The papers had reported all kinds of weird and wonderful stories, from tapeworms to spaghetti diets.

"If there's a secret miracle, you need to share it with me," Mary said, slapping her well-padded haunches. "I'm getting married in a couple of months and can't fit the dress, which is a family heirloom I simply have to wear."

Maria was disarmed by her frankness and gave an

honest answer. "I'm afraid the truth is boring. I cut out all the foods that made me fat in the first place: pasta, pizza, doughnuts, and ice cream . . . basically, I lived on steak and salad for fourteen months."

Mary shuddered. "Weren't you permanently starving? I'd get so hungry, I'd eat my own arm."

Maria thought back. "I had good reasons to lose weight: my size was limiting the roles I could play. No one was going to ask me to sing Cio-Cio-san in *Madama Butterfly*. Can you imagine? A two-hundred-pound Heffalump thundering across the stage, pretending to be the fifteen-year-old Japanese beauty?"

"But you must have extraordinary willpower. I start diets all the time and last a day if I'm lucky. Usually much less."

"I do have willpower," Maria agreed. "I just had to channel it."

She didn't tell Mary that a fertility expert had suggested weight loss might help her get pregnant. That was the greatest motivation of all. She had set herself a goal, visualized the sylphlike shape she wanted, and not stopped till she got there. Every week she measured her hips, thighs, waist, and bust, noting the shrinking measurements, watching a new shape emerge as her excess flesh evaporated.

"I was unhappy being big," she continued. "I started

overeating as a miserable teenager and it got out of hand. But you shouldn't diet. Being curvy suits you. Get a wedding dress you feel comfortable in and help yourself to a big slice of wedding cake. Eat some for me!"

As they sat under the pergola, Maria wondered how to answer Mary's question about her life. She didn't often have time to reflect.

"It's been a tough year," she began. "Trouble with contracts, trouble with the press. Leaving La Scala was horrible. I've got a headache that never seems to go away and my doctor says it's caused by tension, and that I also have low blood pressure. But still the commitments pile up. The Met in New York got me to agree to a whole string of concerts and it seems there's no letup in sight."

"Why doesn't Battista tell the Met to go jump?"

"I'm under contract, so I'm trapped. I just need to find the energy to get through the winter."

Mary took her hand and squeezed it firmly. "You're taking on too much. Promise me you won't sign any more contracts till you've had a good long rest!"

Maria sighed. "We had two months at Lake Garda in the summer, but they sped past and now it's hectic again. Anyway . . ." She shook herself. "Enough about me! Tell me your news. How's Dallas? How many social committees are you bossing around this fall?"

Mary had a soft light in her eyes as she answered. "I've cut back on the committees but I do have some news. It seems I've got a little one on the way . . ." She patted her stomach.

"You're pregnant!" Maria tried to force her lips into a smile but couldn't manage it. Instead, to her horror, tears welled up. She blinked hard and covered her eyes with her fingertips, but emotion got the better of her and a sob slipped out.

"What's wrong? I didn't mean to upset you."

Maria struggled for control, ashamed of her outburst. "It's *magnifico*. I'm happy for you, I really am."

Mary produced a handkerchief from the pocket of her flared skirt. "I believe you . . . although you've got a funny way of showing it." She chuckled. "The baby won't change anything between us, you know. We'll have help, so I can still fly across to visit."

"It's not that," Maria stuttered, dabbing at her eyes. "It's just . . . I wish with all my heart I could be pregnant too. I've wanted a baby for as long as I can remember."

"Make Battista give you one!" Mary chided. "It's his duty."

"It's not that simple," Maria told her, and the story poured out about the specialist telling her she had a malformed uterus and her husband's waning sexual interest. "I bet Elizabeth Taylor doesn't have trouble getting men to perform in bed," she finished.

"I bet that woman has a whole heap of trouble with her men," Mary retorted. "But why didn't you tell me you wanted a baby? I'd have been more tactful about breaking my news if I'd known."

Maria laid her head on Mary's shoulder and looped an arm around her waist. "I sometimes get the strangest sensation that my child is out there waiting to be born. I'm sure she's a girl. If only I could figure out how to make her come to me." She began to cry, softly.

Mary held her close. "It'll be alright," she murmured, stroking her hair. "I'm sure she'll come. I know she will."

Maria threw herself into the production of *La Traviata* in Dallas, while at the same time rehearsing for *Medea*. She loved the ensemble she was working with—the director, the musicians, the other singers—and worked obsessively, trying out new textures and cadenza, figuring out ways to make dramatic use of the set, practicing till she was note perfect. She pushed other worries to the back of her mind and focused on making these her best performances yet. What was the point in treading water? She wanted to improve, and working with a great team gave her a chance to push herself, the way she used to back at La Scala.

On the afternoon of the dress rehearsal for *Medea,* a telegram came from the director at the Met with a schedule for her forthcoming commitments. He wanted her to alternate the roles of Lady Macbeth and Violetta in *La Traviata,* one after the other, with no rest between. The former was a dark, forceful role, the latter a weak, delicate one, and Maria knew that switching between the two would put a huge strain on her voice. It was the words at the end of the telegram that enraged her: "Your confirmation is required by ten tomorrow morning."

"It's like a declaration of war!" she told Battista. "Like the demands Italy made on Greece that forced us into the Second World War."

"It *is* the Met, Maria," he replied. "Perhaps we should agree."

Mary Carter was attending the dress rehearsal, and she took a different line. "Stuff 'em. They can't treat you like that. Make 'em wait."

Maria was at the stage of rehearsals when she was living and breathing the role of Medea, the volatile wife whose husband ran off with a younger woman, stealing their children and leaving her intent on revenge. It was a tempestuous role fraught with tragedy. She couldn't focus sufficiently to devise a way of keeping the Met happy while not compromising her voice.

"They must give me two more days to think about it," she told Battista. "Until after we open here."

The following afternoon another telegram arrived from New York. It read, "Since we did not hear from you by ten this morning, your contract with the Met is hereby terminated."

Maria stared at it in disbelief. "What did you reply yesterday?" she asked Battista, breaking her rule of resting her voice on a performance day.

"I didn't reply," he said. "You didn't tell me what to say."

She clenched her fists, digging her nails into her palms. "I told you to ask for two more days."

"I'll consult our lawyers," Battista said. "I'm sure they can't do this. I'll threaten to sue."

Word came back that the Met were within their rights because a deadline had been missed. Suddenly Maria could feel her entire career slipping away from her. Like a landslide, it began with one or two rocks tumbling off a cliff, then the ground shifted entirely. Rome had gone, Vienna had gone, San Francisco had gone, La Scala had gone—and now the Met? It was a disaster.

But when she took the stage in Dallas a few hours later, she channeled all her fury and despair into *Medea*, giving a performance of such fiery brilliance that she stunned her fellow performers, left the audience enraptured, and even surprised herself.

Chapter 11

Nice, the South of France
August 1958

Lee and Jackie lay sunbathing on a raft anchored a hundred yards off the beach. Both were deeply tanned and wearing two-piece swimsuits with halter necks, the height of fashion in France that year, which would have been considered racy back in the States. Jackie had on a cream swimcap covered in rubber flowers.

She raised herself on an elbow. There was a deep valley between her sister's hipbones and she worried that Lee had gotten too thin again. As teenagers, they'd swapped tips on slimming—eating grapefruit, smoking cigarettes, running in place—but Lee took it too far sometimes. Yet another area where she was competitive with her older sister.

"I can't face going back to tedious old London," Lee

said, without opening her eyes. "The weather changes to fall overnight, bringing gray skies and damp. I've never known such a *damp* city."

"Have you got a case of the blahs?" Jackie asked. It was a phrase they'd used since childhood. "Or is it Michael who's making you crabby?"

Lee and her husband hadn't stopped bickering since they'd arrived at the villa. They couldn't find a civil word for each other. She'd married too young, in Jackie's opinion, without thinking through what she wanted out of a husband, and Michael wasn't strong enough to keep her in line.

Lee sighed. "If only we had children, I think I could bear it. But after five years of trying, the doctors tell us he has a low sperm count. Just my luck."

Jackie sat up and hugged her knees to her chest. She felt so blessed with little Caroline, now nine months old and starting to crawl. When she entered a room, she thumped the floor with her hands to announce her presence: *I'm here!* She had a determined personality, liking blueberries and refusing cheese, with firm favorites among her toys. Jackie marveled that they had created this unique person from scratch.

"Children don't fix a marriage," she said. Jack was a doting father, but that didn't mean he was home any more often. It just meant that, when he was, he lavished attention on his daughter rather than on his wife. "What you and Michael need is money. Serious money. It makes all the difference, not having to worry."

They were both aware of the importance of wealth from their mother's two contrasting marriages: first to a man who'd teetered on the verge of bankruptcy, and then to a millionaire. The girls had grown up knowing they needed to marry money, because nothing but debt would come from Black Jack's estate, while their stepdaddy, Hugh Auchincloss, would leave his Standard Oil fortune to his own children. "Money and power," Janet Auchincloss drummed into them. "That's what you need in a husband."

"Shame Michael and I can't have an allowance from the Kennedy bootlegging fortune," Lee remarked, and Jackie shushed her with a giggle. She didn't ask questions about where Joe Kennedy's fortune had come from but had heard the rumors, like everyone else.

"Did I tell you I've met someone?" Lee ventured, opening one eye to gauge the reaction. "His name's Stas. He's a prince in exile, from Poland. But it's complicated because he's married, I'm married . . ." Her voice wobbled.

"Be careful," Jackie cautioned with a frown. Lee was emotionally precipitous, always had been. "Maybe he won't leave his wife, while you could lose your own marriage if Michael found out."

"Michael would never leave me; he's not the leaving type." Lee sounded dismissive.

"Is *he* faithful?" Jackie asked. She and Lee didn't often get the chance for intimate conversation, but it seemed this was a moment.

"I couldn't care less," Lee said, adding, "but I doubt he'd stray; he's too boring to have a mistress." She rolled onto her side to face Jackie. "How about Jack?"

Jackie blinked, her mind flitting through the blond assistants with pert rears and pointy breasts who were forever scurrying around Jack at conventions. "Who knows?" she replied, then added, "Infidelity isn't the worst thing in a marriage."

Just at that moment, they heard the splashing of someone swimming up to the raft.

"Why, Jack!" Lee cried as his head bobbed up. "What a powerful stroke you have! We were just talking about you."

Jack hauled himself onto the raft to join them, and Jackie admired the muscles of his upper arms. He was in good shape, even though he couldn't exercise as much as he used to because of his bad back.

"Guess where we've been invited tonight?" he asked Jackie.

She shook her head. "Where?"

"Aristotle Onassis's yacht is moored in the harbor and Churchill is one of the guests on board. We've been invited for drinks." He grinned, his teeth white and strong.

"Are you sure it's wise to socialize with Onassis?" Jackie asked. "Is that business over the fraudulent ships all settled?"

"Yeah, we kissed and made up with him back in '55. Technically a U.S. victory but he didn't come out of it too badly."

"Let's go, then," Jackie said. Churchill was one of Jack's great heroes and she knew he would be determined to make an impression.

"Ooh, can I come?" Lee begged.

"I'll call and ask. We've to be there at six-thirty sharp. I think I'll wear black tie. See you later, girls." He stood and executed a perfect dive into the sea.

"Black tie?" Jackie raised an eyebrow at Lee. "I bet the other men won't even be wearing ties. But I guess it's his call . . ."

Jack, Jackie, Lee, and Michael were greeted by Onassis himself at the top of the *Christina*'s gangplank. As Jackie had predicted, he was wearing an open-necked shirt and casual pants. She winked at Lee.

"I'm delighted you could come," Onassis said. "It's an honor to meet you."

The yacht was every bit as swanky as a five-star hotel. Their host led them along the deck to a seating area near a turquoise swimming pool with a mosaic of a minotaur at the bottom.

"It converts into a dance floor for parties," Onassis told them with a wry grin, as if simultaneously boasting and laughing at himself for boasting.

"Is that a helipad I see?" Jack pointed.

"Yes, it's useful when I'm in a hurry." He circled his finger in the air.

The other guests were seated in cushioned rattan chairs, alongside rattan side tables on which to place their drinks. There were around twenty of them, and Jackie memorized the names as Onassis made the introductions. Jack blatantly snaked his way toward Churchill, pulling up a chair so he could sit by him.

"We met before," Jackie said, when it was her turn to be introduced to the old man. "At a Buckingham Palace garden party." She'd been invited there while on a European tour with a school friend and had joined the line to shake hands with Churchill. They'd had only a brief conversation, but it was a cherished memory. She didn't for one moment expect him to remember, but Churchill nodded and said, "Of course. Yes."

Jackie thought he seemed befuddled and wondered how much he'd had to drink before they arrived. She greeted Lady Churchill, then chose a chair from which she could observe the party. She loved people-watching. Onassis was circulating, making sure everyone was comfortably seated and relaying their drink of choice to the hovering waiters.

"I'll have a vodka martini, thanks," she requested when her turn came.

"With an olive?" he asked.

She arched an eyebrow. "Is there any other way?"

He crouched by her chair, holding on to the arm, and she noticed he shaved the backs of his hands. There was something vulpine about him: hairy chest, glinting golden-brown eyes, a flash of teeth.

"Personally, I'm a man of simple tastes: a good bottle of red, then an aged brandy or cask whiskey drunk under the stars. But I believe there are many types of martinis now, and some young women even take theirs with a cocktail onion. Scandalous behavior." He grinned. "Tell me, did your baby daughter accompany you on this trip?"

"She did." Jackie smiled. "But her nanny will right this moment be tucking her into her crib."

Onassis's pretty blond wife, Tina, joined them, asking

questions about Caroline's progress. "My own children are ten and seven," she confided, "and I miss those early years terribly. They were un*bearably* cute babies."

Onassis stood to address another guest and Jackie was left talking to Tina about children, but she watched the rest of the party out of the corner of her eye. Jack was doing his best to charm Churchill, giving him the hundred-watt smile and touching the old man's arm.

"I'll send you a copy of my book, *Profiles in Courage*," she heard him promising, and she cringed on his behalf when Churchill clearly hadn't heard of it, despite the fact that it had won the Pulitzer the previous year.

His wife, Clemmie, whispered something in Churchill's ear, and he nodded and murmured, "How kind." It was then Jackie realized he was a bit senile, and that made her sad. She was a fan of the history books he had written, as well as his stirring rhetoric during the war years, which had galvanized the public in America as well as Britain.

Lee was standing with Onassis by the ship's railing, striking in a white silk Chanel tunic that had cost a king's ransom. She bent toward him like a willow branch, head tilted to one side. Jackie couldn't hear what they were discussing but knew from her sister's posture that she was flirting. She was a born flirt. Michael was engaged in conversation with an English guest and didn't glance up. Jackie feared for Lee. Divorces were always traumatic, and her sister was a fragile creature.

The waiters circulated with little plates of delicacies: mounds of glistening black caviar heaped on melt-in-the-mouth wafers, slivers of sweet orange melon wrapped in salty ham, miniature vol-au-vents with pink prawns balanced on top. As soon as a glass was less than a third full, a waiter silently appeared with a fresh drink. It was extraordinarily civilized. Jackie's mother would have approved; she was a consummate hostess and had coached both her girls in social skills.

It had been daylight when they arrived, but as they walked down the gangplank an hour later it was dark, and the lights of the town twinkled in a giant smile.

Jackie teased Jack about his obvious courting of the former prime minister. "I'm not sure you made much of an impression. If anything, he looked baffled. I think he thought you were the waiter."

Jack grinned. "You were right that I was overdressed in black tie. I never can understand dress codes."

"Why is Churchill cruising with them?" Lee asked. "I wouldn't have thought he and Onassis had much in common."

It was Jack who answered: "Onassis collects celebrities. He's had Garbo, the Grimaldis, all kinds of rich and famous on board, and Churchill is the biggest prize of all. Whoever said money can't buy you friends was a fool."

Jackie linked her arm with his as they walked down the quay toward Chez Palmyre, the restaurant where they had dinner reservations. "I don't think anyone ever said that, darling. It's so patently untrue."

Chapter 12

Paris, France
December 19, 1958

"Are you sure you haven't forgotten anything?" Maria wrote on her notepad, and held it up for Battista to see. Her gala performance at the Paris Opéra was that evening and she felt agitated.

"Of course not." He never had any patience with her pre-performance nerves.

Maria looked at him, sitting with his legs slung over the arm of his chair, reading an Italian newspaper without a care in the world. Her faith in him had sunk to an all-time low after they lost the Met contract. A decent manager would have salvaged the situation, but instead there were denigrating headlines alleging that she had been scared her voice wasn't up to the role of Lady Macbeth. It simply wasn't true—she'd sung it many times. A good publicist could have contradicted them, but it was left to Maria to call radio-show hosts and press contacts to deny it. She felt humiliated at being forced on the defensive.

It was no wonder that she was alarmed about Battista being in charge of so many of the arrangements for the evening's concert, which was to be televised live in nine European countries. The 2,130 seats had sold out overnight despite a steep price of 35,000 francs apiece, and Maria's fee was a record-breaking 5 million francs. Those figures rattled her, increasing the pressure exponentially.

"You've sung to audiences this big before," Battista replied.

He couldn't understand that the more famous she became, the harder it was. What if her top notes weren't there tonight? Sometimes—not often, mercifully—they just refused to come. It happened to all first sopranos, but it would be devastating if it occurred when television viewers across Europe were watching, many of them hearing her for the first time.

She walked through to the bedroom and slammed the door, then poured herself a glass of water. She had to drink lots of water on performance days, served at room temperature, no ice. Standing by the window, with a view of the Paris skyline, she ran through some exercises to relax her throat and jaw, but found it hard to concentrate. No longer feeling that she could trust Battista made it hard to focus. He wasn't any different; the change was within her. She wished there wasn't such a chasm between them and that she didn't feel quite so alone in her marriage.

She heard a knock at the door of their suite and Battista calling "Come in." When she popped her head out, she saw a bellhop carrying a huge bouquet of red roses, at least two dozen of them.

"For Mrs. Callas," he said, placing them on the table.

Maria picked up the card, which was in Greek, and smiled as she read it: "This evening you have one chance to change my mind about opera. Aristo." She inhaled the summery scent of the roses as the bellhop produced a vase in which to display them.

She nudged Battista, hoping he would offer the man a tip, but he didn't look up from his newspaper, so she had to scrabble for a few francs in her own purse.

"How did Aristotle know where we were staying?" she wrote on her notepad.

"He called last week wanting an invitation to the after-show party," her husband replied. "I must have told him then."

Maria was pleased. It was a good night for him to hear her for the first time. She was singing a program of famous arias in the first half, followed by the second act of *Tosca*—all of it easy listening. Maybe Mr. Onassis would even stay awake.

More roses arrived from Aristotle later in the afternoon, but by then Maria was engrossed in her preperformance warmups and paid little attention. By the time they reached the Opéra she had already begun her transformation into her stage alter ego, a figure whom, in her head, she called "La Callas."

She placed the Madonna icon on her dressing table and sipped water as her hair and makeup were done, focusing her mind as she watched her reflection. Two dressers helped her into a champagne satin gown trimmed with sable, and fastened the million dollars' worth of diamonds she had been lent for the night by Van Cleef & Arpels. Their security guard sat outside her dressing room, looking officious, and he would stay in the wings throughout the performance.

Once she was in costume, Maria sang a few trills, reaching F5 with ease. Her throat felt fine. When the time came, she walked to the stage with only the slightest flutter of nerves in her stomach, handed her glasses to the security guard, who happened to be nearby, crossed herself three times, and then stepped out on her right foot.

Time flew, until two hours later she was standing

and shaking with emotion at the jubilant ovations. The French never rose to their feet—*never*—but tonight they were standing and cheering. Bouquets were thrown onto the stage and she stooped to collect an armful. When she tried to leave, she was drawn back for curtain call after curtain call. While she was singing, Maria had forgotten about the television cameras, but now she looked for them, wondering how she had sounded, how she had looked.

It always felt strange after a performance, as if she were returning from a voyage to a distant land. She was disoriented, her ears ringing with the applause, as she walked to the opera house's grand foyer and stepped out to greet the party guests.

In an instant Onassis was at her side, taking her hands in his. "You made me cry," he told her. "Real tears rolled down my cheeks. You were magnificent. Truly."

"I apologize for your distress," she replied. "But I'm glad you enjoyed it."

"There are no words to express how I felt." He looked into her eyes, pressing her fingertips. "I still have goose bumps."

He had been speaking Greek but used the phrase in English, and his pronunciation made her laugh.

"I apologize for them too."

They couldn't talk further because others were hovering nearby, waiting to be introduced. She was dazzled by the turnout of the rich and distinguished, their jewels glinting: the Rothschilds, the Windsors, the Aga Khan, Brigitte Bardot, and Charlie Chaplin. They all greeted her like old friends, which felt phony because she'd never met any of them apart from the Windsors, and they were merely the slightest of acquaintances.

Tables were laid for supper beneath the sparkling chandeliers and ornate gilt-framed ceiling paintings of the foyer. There was a seating chart with place cards, but Onassis swapped his card for Battista's and sat down beside Maria. She laughed at his audaciousness but didn't force him to undo the mischief. Battista looked baffled at first, then shrugged and accepted the new arrangement with good humor.

"You looked as if you were experiencing every emotion onstage," Aristotle said, once they were seated. "How do you get into character, particularly on evenings like this when you have to switch from one role to the next?"

"It's not a conscious process," she admitted. "I immerse myself in the music and feel the emotion coming through the notes. The composer has done the work for me."

"And now you emerge to entertain your adoring public." He was watching her closely. "That must be a difficult transition."

"You're very astute." She smiled. "It can be hard after a particularly dramatic role, but I am fine this evening."

"So I am definitely speaking to Maria, not *Tosca's* Floria?"

"Aha! You read the program!" she quipped.

Aristotle grinned.

"I'm not planning to leap to my death from a parapet before the end of our supper, if that's what you're worried about."

Waiters brought appetizers, and she turned to speak with the director, who was on her left, but by the time the main course was served Onassis had reclaimed her attention.

"I wonder if I could tempt you to come for a cruise on the *Christina* next summer?" he asked. "We will have a distinguished party on board. Winston and Clementine Churchill join us every year. There are Greek musicians and you would not be required to sing a note, but could tour the islands of our homeland, swim, eat, drink—whatever your heart desires."

He was leaning close, his voice lowered, and she could feel lust emanating from him. He wanted her badly, and she had to admit that she was attracted to him too. There was an animal quality she found very sexy. It was flattering to be pursued, but at the same time she sensed it was La Callas he wanted, the creature he had seen onstage, not her; not Maria.

"That's a tempting offer," she replied. "I'll have to check my schedule—and my husband's too. It's our tenth wedding anniversary next year and he may have something planned." She watched his face as she threw in a reminder of her marital status, but he didn't falter.

"I hope he cherishes you," he whispered into her ear, his hand resting on her shoulder and his breath tickling her cheek.

Chapter 13

Hyannis Port
November 1958

Jackie arrived at Rose and Joe Kennedy's house and let herself in. She'd spent the past hour trying to decide what to wear for a television show entitled *At Home with the Kennedys* that was being filmed that afternoon. She wanted to look elegant but not over-dressed. Finally she'd opted for a plain dark-green wool dress with bracelet sleeves, and a string of pearls. Her hair was backcombed but she applied only the subtlest of makeup, her mother's voice ringing in her ears: "Men want to see a pretty face, not a painted mannequin."

As she hesitated in the hall, she heard male voices in the dining room and took a step closer, wondering if Jack was there.

"She's polling as too remote, too upper class, not someone who shares their concerns," said a voice Jackie recognized as belonging to Jack's brother Teddy, and straightaway she knew he was talking about her. It was so unfair. America was a huge country and she was never going to appeal to every demographic.

"What do you want her to do?" Jack replied. "Talk about the brand of soap powder she buys? People might say in polls that they think she's remote but look how many more turn out when she comes to rallies with me."

At least he was standing up for her; that was something.

"You've gotta talk to her about her clothes," someone else said, a voice she couldn't place. "If it's gotta be designer names, ask her to make it homegrown American designers, not fancy French ones."

"I'll try," Jack said. "But don't bank on it. Jackie's got strong views on her clothes."

Jackie looked down. The dress she was wearing was Lanvin. She couldn't remember whether she had any American designer frocks in her closet. And anyway it was too late to change now.

What right did they have to dissect her like this? It was irritating to be discussed behind her back. Her hand hovered over the doorknob as she considered bursting in to remonstrate, but what would it achieve? Instead she walked toward the living room, where she could see the TV crew positioning a huge black camera.

Rose Kennedy and Jack's sisters Eunice and Jean were already sitting on some floral-patterned couches and chairs that had been arranged in a C shape.

"Hi, everybody," she said, smiling at the TV folk and then her in-laws.

"*There* you are," Rose said in a friendly enough voice but without a smile.

Jackie knew she was seen as an interloper by the Kennedy women, but she was tolerated as long as she toed the line and played the role of a politician's ideal wife. Was she late today? She glanced at her watch. Less than five minutes. She sat down by Rose and smoothed her skirt.

"Can I powder your nose, Mrs. Kennedy?" A woman approached her with a powder puff. "Television brings out the shine."

She leaned her head back, inhaling the old-lady scent and hoping she wasn't going to look as if she were coated in flour.

Teddy appeared in the doorway and had a chat with one of the team, perhaps the director, about the running order. Then he turned to her. "Jackie, we're going to start with Rose asking whether you like campaigning, so get your answer ready. You know the kind of thing: Meeting the people your husband represents is a great honor. You'll do whatever you can to support him, but your most important role is making his home comfortable and raising his daughter."

Jackie felt patronized. "And there I was, about to say I hope Jack gets voted out so I never have to attend another rally for the rest of my life."

Rose rolled her eyes, glancing at her daughters.

Teddy cleared his throat. "Can you deepen your voice?" he asked. "It sometimes sounds a bit too high, too breathy."

Jackie was a talented mimic, and she imitated various accents as she asked, "What would you prefer? Flat Boston? A southern drawl? California girl?"

Teddy chuckled. "Just yourself, but a little less patrician."

"Have you been on TV before, Mrs. Kennedy?" one of the crew asked. "Do you know about not looking into the camera? Just pretend we're not here."

She nodded and replied crisply: "I surely will."

Once the camera was rolling, she tried to lower her voice but it felt false. She sounded like a schoolmarm teaching class as she gushed, "I've enjoyed campaigning *so* much . . ."

Jack knew from the start that she came from a society family; that was part of the attraction for him. He liked that she spoke French, Italian, and Spanish and had studied art and literature. He was tickled that she had been "debutante of the year" in 1948 and that her favorite pastimes were horseback riding and reading. If he'd wanted someone more down-home, he should have thought about it way back then.

The first time they met was on a train from Washington to New York, when she was still a student at Vassar College and he was a newly elected congressman from Massachusetts. He leaned across the aisle to introduce himself, and her first impression was that he looked very Irish, with his thick reddish-blond hair, broad face, and arresting gray-green eyes. She felt uncomfortable telling a stranger her name but it would have been rude not to, and, after all, he *was* a congressman.

"You seem fresh and incorruptible in your crisp white frock," he said next, "but I've got a theory about girls like you."

Jackie's hackles rose. "Is that so? You know nothing about me."

He grinned, like a cheeky kid with his fist in the cookie jar. "I bet you are the best kind of kisser. I can always tell."

She thought of opening a book to terminate the conversation, but part of her was intrigued. She and her girlfriends were forever talking about what made men fall in love with one girl over another, and not always going for the prettiest one either, so she decided to use Jack as research.

"Are there many different kinds of kisser in your *vast* experience?" she asked, hoping he caught the sarcasm.

"Four main types, with lots of variations," he said, ticking them off on his fingers. "There's the frigid type with bone-dry lips who give a quick peck then run away scared as chickens; there's the girls who are too busy trying to kiss the way they think they ought to, following advice they've read in some magazine, to actually enjoy themselves; there's the types who scare a guy to death by coming on too strong, all panting, drooling, and desperate eyes; and then there's the ones like you, who relax and surrender to the sensation of lips on lips and just enjoy the kiss for itself."

Jackie willed herself not to blush. "I hope you are not expecting me to prove your theory true, Mr. Kennedy."

"I wouldn't dream of it," he said with a grin. "What kind of a lecher do you take me for?"

When the train pulled in to Penn Station, he tried to persuade her to come to a nearby bar for a drink but disappeared pronto when he heard she was meeting her daddy.

She assumed she would never see him again, but

four years later, in June 1951, her friends Charles and Martha Bartlett invited her for dinner, saying there was a man they thought she might like to meet. She walked into their front room—and there was Jack Kennedy.

"We've already had the pleasure," Jackie interrupted as her hosts began the introductions.

"You're the one who's a great kisser." Jack grinned, and Jackie had to laugh.

She had been eighteen when she'd met him before; now she was twenty-two and far more self-assured. She had traveled around Europe, spent an entire summer in France, and was due to return there the following week for an extended trip with Lee before she took a job as "inquiring photographer" for the *Washington Times-Herald.*

Jack glanced at her left hand. "I had assumed you would be married by now, Miss Bouvier."

"You assumed wrong, Mr. Kennedy."

She'd had dozens of beaus, of course, but they all wanted to turn her into a housewife. They clearly hadn't read her high-school yearbook, where she noted that her ambition was "not to be a housewife." She wanted more; she didn't know what, exactly, but was sure she would find it eventually. And when Jack began talking about politics, her interest was piqued. She admired the fact that he was ambitious and wanted to create social change. She was impressed to hear that he was a war hero. She found him attractive, and maybe she had an inkling that life with a man like that would never be humdrum.

At the end of the evening, he asked if she wanted to go for a nightcap, but Jackie had already arranged to meet a friend and didn't want to let him down.

"In that case, give me a call when you're back from Europe," he suggested.

Jackie thought that was too casual. If he wanted to see her again, he should ask Charles Bartlett to let him know when she returned, and *he* should call *her*. She wasn't the type of girl to chase a man.

In fact, the way things turned out, once they started dating she *did* have to chase Jack Kennedy. It came as a surprise to her when she fell headlong in love with him. Even more of a surprise was that he didn't seem quite as smitten. Before then, Jackie had always possessed the knack of making men fall for her. She would ask all about them and listen attentively, as if they were the most fascinating people she'd ever met; she would laugh at their jokes, no matter how feeble; she would be sassy and funny but never overshadow them. None of those techniques worked on Jack, though. He liked her, sure, but she could tell he wasn't *in love,* and she knew she wasn't the only girl he was dating.

So Jackie stepped up her game. She read tedious books about political theory so that she could discuss them with him; she translated papers from French to help him in his work; she took hot meals to his office on evenings when he was working late; and she charmed his father, old Joe Kennedy, when Jack took her to meet the family at Hyannis Port.

Was it the fact that she couldn't win his heart easily that made her so determined? No, it wasn't just that. He was different from every other man she'd met: unpredictable, brave, witty, clever, and fiercely, burningly ambitious. Politics came first, second, and third on his priority list. It wasn't long before she knew she wanted to marry him, but how could she get him to pop the question? At twenty-three, she was virtually the only one of her college friends who hadn't walked down the aisle.

It was her daddy who told her that she would have to play hard to get if she was ever to make Jack propose.

"Cancel dates at short notice. Be vague about your plans. Whatever you do, don't seem desperate," he advised.

Jack's sister Eunice was getting married in the summer of 1953, and he asked Jackie to accompany him to the wedding, but, following her daddy's advice, she persuaded the *Times-Herald* to send her to London to report on the coronation of Elizabeth II. It was a gamble; perhaps he'd take another girl in her stead, someone who would finagle her way into his affections.

Jack seemed surprised by her decision. "I wanted you to get a chance to meet the wider Kennedy clan," he said. "And there was a question I was planning to ask you beforehand."

He said it in such a casual way that she had no inkling of what would come next. "Oh, yes? And what might that be?"

"I want you to marry me, kid. You know we make a great team." He grinned his naughty-boy grin. "What do you say?"

She was stunned. She'd begun to think he might be a lost cause, especially after a recent magazine article reported that he was dating the actress Audrey Hepburn.

"When did you decide to propose?" she asked, wondering if it was her booking the trip to London that had nudged him into it.

"About a year ago. I decided to wait, but I knew all along you were the one."

She hit him on the arm and exclaimed, "How big of you!" But she couldn't stop smiling as he pulled her in for a kiss.

The biblical quotation "As ye sow, so shall ye reap" came to Jackie's mind as she posed for the television cameras with Caroline on her knee. She'd fallen for a man who put his career first, and that's what she'd gotten. The midterm elections were coming up, and since September 15 she had been on the road with Jack, appearing by his side on platforms throughout the length and breadth of Massachusetts, greeting dignitaries and their identical wives, listening to the same speech over and over with a fixed smile that made her jaw ache.

Her daughter was tired and crotchety that afternoon, with red teething spots on her cheeks. Jackie unfastened her pearls and handed them over to distract her. Jack came to sit beside them, in an attempt to leave voters with a wholesome family image at the end of the documentary. The film crew wanted Caroline to smile, but she was squirming and close to tears.

When at last they'd gotten the shots they wanted, Jackie whispered, "Thank God! That was excruciating."

Jack patted her shoulder quickly but didn't once thank her. It was taken for granted that she would play her part.

"Did Teddy tell you we've got *Time* magazine coming to the house next Wednesday?" he asked. "They're going to interview me and take some photographs."

Jackie sighed. "So that Mrs. Average Voter can check out my taste in drapes?" Caroline was trying to stuff the entire string of pearls into her mouth and squawked loudly when Jackie peeled them from her fist. "I hope they'll stay downstairs and not invade our bedroom, at least."

Jack's mind was already half-engaged elsewhere. He glanced down the hall toward the dining room, where his team was still at work. This wasn't the best time to get picky with him.

"Hell, I would give them a nude shot of you if I thought it would win me a hundred more votes . . ." He leaned over to kiss her cheek, then stood up. "But I guess that's not what Teddy means by 'family values.'"

"I believe you would," Jackie murmured, but he had already gone.

Chapter 14

The Mediterranean
August 1959

Much as she enjoyed Aristotle Onassis's company, Maria didn't plan to accept his renewed offer of a cruise on the *Christina*. Aside from the prospect of paparazzi photographing her in swimwear, she preferred friends who were not in the limelight, loyal ones like Mary Carter. She knew none of her inner circle would talk about her to the press; that was of paramount importance. But she couldn't trust the guests Aristotle might invite.

In the end, though, Battista was insistent that they should accept. He loved mingling with the rich and famous, enjoyed all the accoutrements of real wealth. She wondered if he was aware that Onassis was flirting with her. And, if so, did he even care? As long as it didn't go too far, he might decide it was good publicity.

Aristotle's attentions had become even more apparent at a party he threw for her in London's Dorchester Hotel after she sang at Covent Garden that June. He scarcely left her side all night and they danced together several times. She decided Battista was either oblivious to it or flattered by it—he loved to wallow in the reflected glory of her fame.

At last she let him persuade her to go on the cruise, on the proviso that they could disembark at any time if she felt uncomfortable. She would get her friend Biki to create a cruise wardrobe, with plenty of light cover-ups that she could throw on when they were close to shore. Both their spouses would be present, as would the Churchills and several other guests, so that would stop Aristotle from taking liberties. Not that she would have let him anyway, she told herself.

They boarded the yacht in Monaco and were shown down a grand staircase lined with onyx pillars, then along a corridor to a guest suite that had the name Ithaca on the door. Inside were a sitting room, bedroom, and dressing room, all with wood-paneled walls, solid gold fixtures in the shape of dolphins, Venetian glass screens, and a carpet that her feet sank into. Through wooden doors she found twin marble bathrooms. It was more luxurious than the top hotel suites.

Tina Onassis arrived to give Maria a personal tour of

the facilities: a beauty and hairdressing salon, a library, a laundry, and two kitchens—one for Greek food, one for French.

"We have cocktails on deck at six-thirty, then dinner at eight-fifteen. Earlier in the day, please ask the waiting staff for whatever food and drinks you require," she said.

"It sounds wonderful," Maria replied, relieved she was not required to rise for an early breakfast. She was a night owl and seldom awoke before noon.

Tina opened the door to a sumptuous lounge. "There's a Steinway piano here. I thought you might like to use it when you practice."

"How thoughtful! But I've decided to give myself a break from singing." She pressed Tina's hands between her own. "Frankly, it's been a hectic year, and I just want to relax and rest my voice."

Tina beamed. "We'll make sure you do that, alright."

The two women embraced, and Maria looked at her hostess closely. Her complexion was fresh and there was no hint of a wrinkle, although she had celebrated her thirtieth birthday earlier that year, making her just six years Maria's junior. Tina had never done a day's work in her life: she'd been born into a wealthy Greek ship-owning family, then married Onassis at eighteen, and he'd taken care of her ever since. But who knew? Maybe there were pressures in her life all the same.

Twenty of them sat down to dinner on either side of the long, elegant dining table. Stars twinkled through a skylight and candles flickered in silver holders on the walls. Churchill was the guest of honor, in the middle with Onassis by his side, but Maria was seated opposite, where she could see the great man up close. He was, of course, instantly recognizable, with those jowls and the broad, high forehead, but Maria was puzzled by the vacant look in his blue eyes. He was like a child. His wife, Clemmie, kept glancing across to check on him, but Onassis had taken charge.

"Remind me again: Where are we?" Churchill asked his host, sounding bewildered.

"You're on a summer holiday, on my yacht. We'll be setting sail soon." Onassis spoke with infinite patience.

"Ah, yes. A yacht. That's like a boat, isn't it? I enjoy boating."

As appetizers, there were eight types of caviar served in tiny heaps, with melba toast on the side. Churchill frowned as he tried to decide how to eat it. Finally he scooped some caviar onto a sliver of toast, but when he raised it toward his mouth, the black globules fell into his lap.

Without a word, Onassis shook out the old man's napkin and spoon-fed him caviar directly from his own plate, continuing his conversation without pause, as if it were the most natural thing in the world.

"The forecast is calm so we should have a good night's sleep. But of course you must join me for brandy and cigars on deck after dinner."

"Cigars, yes, of course." Churchill nodded. That was something he remembered.

Maria was moved as she watched them; no son could have been more attentive. Onassis anticipated Churchill's every need and met it without making him feel patronized. She had heard he was a generous host, but this was an unexpected side to his personality.

English was the language spoken around the table, in honor of the Churchills and several other English guests. Tina leaned over to translate for Battista that first evening. Maria was rather quiet at dinner, feeling self-conscious among these people with whom she would spend the next three weeks. She wanted to observe first; there would be time to forge friendships later.

The Churchills retired at eleven, and Battista went to bed at midnight, but Maria was restless. She wandered the decks, looking out at the velvety darkness penetrated occasionally by the blurred lights of a fishing boat. The movement of the yacht was so smooth, you could barely tell you were at sea.

"Come and join us," Onassis called from a doorway in the aft section. "This is what we call Ari's Bar."

He was sitting with a couple of English women whose names Maria had forgotten.

"Don't do the joke, Ari," one said. "I can't *bear* to hear it again."

"What joke is this?" Maria asked, and the women groaned.

Onassis shook his head. "I would never be so uncouth as to repeat it in front of the great Maria Callas."

"But I insist!" Maria clapped her hands.

"Definitely not," he said. "Tell me, what can I offer you to drink?"

"Whatever you're having," she said, and he went to look for a waiter.

One of the women confided, "His barstools are covered in whale foreskin, from his whaling days, and when a woman sits on one he asks, 'Do you realize you are sitting on the largest penis in the world?'"

Maria made a shocked face. "I'm very glad you told me so I can be sure to avoid them."

Onassis returned and handed Maria a glass.

"Napoleon brandy," he said. "The only drink for the small hours."

They toasted the voyage; then he switched to speaking in Greek, since the English women were talking to one another, and asked if Maria planned to base herself at another opera house now she was no longer part of the company at La Scala.

Maria sighed. "No, I think I shall become a gypsy, wandering from place to place with nowhere to call home. Your life must be similar." She took a sip of the brandy, which was smooth and warming.

"My home is the *Christina*," he replied. "It doesn't matter which country's waters we sail in; my toothbrush resides in the same bathroom. But I have read in the newspapers of your troubles with La Scala and the Met. It must make it difficult to focus on the music."

Maria agreed. "I hate that side of things. I'm fed up being misquoted and called names and photographed at odd angles to look ferocious. It's not good for a woman's ego."

"No matter how hard they try, no photographer could make you look less than beautiful," he said.

"Thank you." She felt shy suddenly. *Ridicolo!*

"I had an idea I wished to discuss with you on this

cruise," he continued, "and maybe it is as well to introduce it now, on your first night, so you have time to consider it."

"Please do," she said. She inhaled the exotic aroma of the brandy.

"I don't know if you are aware of my association with His Serene Highness Prince Rainier and the principality of Monaco?"

She nodded. She knew he had a controlling interest in the Société des Bains de Mer, which managed commercial real estate there. Some said he was the true ruler of the principality.

He continued: "I have suggested to Rainier that we create an opera company in Monte Carlo and invite you to be the resident soprano. You could choose how much or how little you sang each year and have a hand in selecting the repertoire. You don't need to make up your mind now but . . ."

Maria loved the idea. She missed working with a team that she knew. Perhaps she could tempt some of her favorite backstage staff from La Scala to join them. And having creative control would suit her to a tee. She interrupted him. "Yes, please. When do I start?"

He laughed. "It's just as well you don't negotiate your own contracts, my dear. You need to drive a much harder bargain. Hold out for an extortionate fee. A penthouse apartment overlooking the harbor. A say in the choice of orchestras and conductors . . ."

"You tell me that *after* plying me with your best brandy." She laughed. "It's a clever tactic. But the answer is still yes."

Onassis called for more brandy, and they clinked glasses to seal the deal.

Chapter 15

Hyannis Port
August 1959

Jackie persuaded Jack to buy a house in Hyannis Port, on a road that ran behind the main house occupied by Rose and Joe, so she wouldn't have to stay with her in-laws anymore. Bobby and Ethel already owned a property just in front of theirs. Jackie spent the summer of 1959 there with Caroline and her nanny, and she invited Lee and her new husband, Prince Stas Radziwill, to join them straight after the birth of their son, Anthony.

The affair Lee had mentioned during their vacation in the South of France had proved irresistible, and both parties had left their spouses so they could be together. Jackie felt sorry for Michael but she warmed to Stas from the start, finding him easy company, with elegant manners. He and Lee seemed well suited, and even looked a bit alike, with their high foreheads, sharp noses, and sculpted cheekbones. It felt as if he was the husband her sister had always been meant to have and that Michael had been an aberration along the way. A baby arriving just five months after the wedding seemed proof of their compatibility, and Jackie was delighted for her sister.

Motherhood mellowed Lee: with Michael she had been carping and never satisfied, but now she had the inner glow of a woman whose emotional needs were being met. In the past, she had been loath to accept her big sister's advice—Lee had to be the one who knew best—but now she was grateful for tips on how to settle little Anthony, or how to burp him. He was an easy baby, and a rather aristocratic-looking one, with jet-black hair and a high brow, reflecting the looks of his father's regal family.

Lee and Stas spent a lot of time in their room and Jackie scarcely had any moments alone with her sister, but she enjoyed their company over dinner each evening. Stas told fascinating tales of the Radziwills' lengthy history in Poland, and he was a voracious reader with a keen appreciation for literature and the arts, so Jackie was in her element; they felt more like her true family than the politics-obsessed Kennedys. Sometimes Jack would join them, sometimes not. He was more distracted than ever that summer, his head bursting with polls and campaign strategies.

"No politics at dinner," Jackie chided. "You'll spoil our appetites."

Most days the weather was too windy to sit on the beach, and a pungent, glutinous mass of seaweed hugged the shoreline. You had to clamber through it to reach open water, but Jackie waded out every day for long solitary swims, floating on her back beneath scudding clouds. She also spent a lot of time with Caroline, who loved to toddle along the shore collecting "treasures" that had washed up—colored sea glass, conch shells, a dead crab. Their porch was fast filling up with souvenirs.

In August, Jack was officially on vacation, but the campaign team turned up most days to hold meetings around the kitchen table. One morning Jackie came down early to make coffee, still in her pale blue nylon negligee, and found half a dozen of them reading the morning papers, like unwelcome houseguests.

"Morning, all!" she said. "Are you waiting for Jack? He'll be down in ten minutes."

They coughed and scraped their chairs, embarrassed by her skimpy attire, as she breezed out again, swallowing her annoyance. Bit by bit her life was being consumed by politics, and it seemed as if the moment when it might have been possible to draw the line had long since passed.

One evening, Jackie went to bed before Jack returned. She read for a while, then turned out the light but couldn't sleep. Her body was tired but her brain was buzzing. The vacation was drawing to a close, and soon they'd be traveling back to Georgetown, where she would see even less of Jack than she did here. They were supposed to be trying for another baby, but she couldn't imagine how that would happen when she was invariably asleep by the time he came to bed, and Caroline woke her early in the morning, running into their room and clambering in for a cuddle.

Jackie got up and walked to the window. The shutters were flung wide; she hated a stuffy bedroom, and the regular shushing of waves in the distance was soothing at night. She heard the strike of a cigarette lighter and, looking out, saw Lee sitting in a deck chair on the lawn. The orange tip of her cigarette floated like a firefly. Jackie was about to call to her when she noticed that Jack's Cadillac was in the drive; she hadn't heard him return.

As her eyes grew accustomed to the dark, she realized he was sitting on the grass by Lee's chair and they were talking in low voices. Jackie strained to hear but could only make out snatches.

"Great guy . . . good one this time." She guessed Jack was saying that he approved of Stas.

Lee replied, her voice harder to follow, but Jackie caught the word *annulment* drifting on the night air. She knew Lee wanted to apply to have her first marriage annulled so that she and Stas could marry in the Catholic Church. Perhaps she was asking Jack's advice on how to go about it.

"Shame we won't be able to have a repeat of our tryst," Jack said—or at least she thought he did. Jackie froze. What did he mean? What tryst?

Lee reached out and touched his shoulder. Jackie felt a stabbing pain in her chest as she tried to make sense of it. Was *tryst* the word he had used? Did it mean that her sister and her husband had *slept* together? They wouldn't, would they?

Lee had always been crazy about Jack, and made no secret of it. She openly embraced him in front of Jackie, and cocked her head to one side in her irritating manner, asking his opinion and giggling disproportionately at his witticisms. That was fine. She was like that with any handsome man. But why was her hand *still* resting on his shoulder? Had they really betrayed her? The two people she was closest to in the world? She clutched her stomach, sick at the thought.

As she watched, Jack stood and said, "Good night." He didn't stoop to kiss Lee, but strode across the grass toward the front door. Jackie shrank behind the shutter so he wouldn't catch her spying, then scuttled to bed, deciding she would pretend to be asleep when he came in. She needed to think.

Her heart was banging in her chest. Was this about Lee's jealousy of her? What a *bitch*! She'd been annoyed that Jackie had married a richer, more ambitious husband. Perhaps that's why she swapped Michael for a Polish prince, albeit one in exile; she was sure to drop her new title into conversation at any opportunity. *Princess Lee.* Had she flirted her way into Jack's bed? It was possible, but Jackie couldn't think of when it might have happened.

What about her husband? Would he do that? She could accept that he was unfaithful with faceless, nameless blondes; them she could ignore. But her own *sister*? Would he be so disloyal? Her throat felt raw at the thought.

Perhaps she had misheard and it was all a mistake. Maybe "tryst" had referred to something else entirely— but she couldn't think what. She heard his feet on the stairs and wondered whether to admit she had overheard the conversation and ask him what it meant. That's what a normal wife would do.

But they didn't have a normal marriage. They had a marriage full of secrets, in which each lived separate lives that overlapped from time to time. He had the Scandinavian blonde in the hot-pink bikini, and all the other women whom he thought she didn't know about, while she held that knowledge hidden in her breast pocket, like a dagger.

"Are you awake, honey?" he whispered as he tiptoed into the bedroom.

She lay very still, slowing her breathing, as she listened to him remove his clothes and fling them on the chair. His belt buckle clattered to the floor; then she heard him curse as he unfastened his fiddly back brace.

The mattress dipped as he sat on his side of the bed to remove his socks, and Jackie pretended to stir.

"Are you alright?" she asked, in a drowsy voice.

"Yeah, we had a good meeting. I'll tell you in the morning. You go back to sleep."

When he climbed under the covers, she rolled toward him for a hug, trying to ignore the fury and hurt that she knew would make her implode if she ever let them.

Chapter 16

The Mediterranean
August 1959

The cruise took them around the boot of Italy and across the Aegean to Piraeus and the Greek islands. Onassis—Ari, as Maria now called him—said he wanted to show his guests the places he loved best.

Maria slept more soundly than she had in years, lulled by the gentle motion of the yacht and drowsy from the expensive brandy she drank with Ari late every evening. On the second night at sea, they began to talk about the war years, and Maria told him she had lived in occupied Athens.

"Mother never thought the war would reach us, and when it did, we were too late to board any ships leaving town," she told him. "I was training at the Conservatoire by day, then in the evenings Mother forced me to date German soldiers and beg them for food and money. It was humiliating. Horrible."

Ari was aghast. "How could she? You were only a teenager. Anything could have happened."

Maria grimaced, remembering one soldier who'd wrestled her to the ground and tried to rape her. She had fought tooth and nail, scratching and biting, until at last he gave up. "A big girl like you should be grateful," he'd said. "No one else will want you." And when she got home, her skirt torn and knees bleeding, her mother assumed she had been raped. There was no maternal sympathy, no words of comfort, just the cold demand: "How much did you get?"

Ari was listening with a compassionate expression. "I don't understand how she could put you in such danger."

Maria shrugged. "I drew the short straw when mothers were handed out. Mine never warmed to me. She had been hoping for a boy and was so disappointed when I emerged from the womb that she couldn't bear to look at me for four days. My sister was the pretty, charming one, and I was a huge disappointment." She smiled as if to brush it off, although it still hurt to say the words.

"But she must be proud of you now? How could any mother not be?"

Maria shook her head. "When my talent was discovered I became her cash cow." She used the phrase in English, unable to think of a Greek equivalent. "As a child I was dragged to radio-station competitions and forced to sing on command for the paltry prizes. Then she brought me to Athens for training at the Conservatoire and as soon as they started paying me a salary she commandeered it."

"I suppose she did you a favor in getting proper voice training," Ari said.

Maria wrinkled her nose. "Perhaps, but it was in her own interest so I would make more money. After I got married, she still demanded half my earnings and I paid up for years, like a good Greek girl. Eventually Battista put his foot down and cut back her allowance, but in retaliation she sold her story to *Time* magazine, telling them what an ungrateful daughter I am."

Ari shook his head. "She sounds appalling. Are you still in touch with her?"

"God, no; not since the *Time* article. I have washed my hands of her at last. It was long overdue. Once in a blue moon I get a letter from my father or sister but I haven't seen them for many years."

"I'm amazed you succeeded despite all those odds stacked against you. I'm sure it's not just your voice; it's your character that got you to the top."

Maria smiled her thanks for the compliment. "I

think you and I both know it's working harder than everyone else that counts. I believe in destiny, but you can't relax and wait for success to happen."

"A woman after my heart. We share the same philosophy."

"So, tell me about you," she said. "I read that you are a self-made man but I don't know anything of your background."

"In my case, my difficult relationship was with my father." He drained his glass before continuing. "He had a tobacco-import business in Smyrna—until September 1922 when the Turkish army came to drive the Greeks out."

Maria knew about this; it was a brutal campaign that quickly turned into a massacre.

"I lost several relatives. My uncle Alexander was hung in the public square in Kasaba." His tone was neutral but a flicker in his eyes betrayed emotion. "My aunt Marie was burned to death with her husband and child in the church in Akhisar. Then my father was jailed and my three sisters sent to evacuation camps. I was just sixteen and entirely alone in a city where the Turks were shooting civilians on sight."

"What about your mother?" Maria asked, aghast.

"She died when I was three. I was raised by a grandmother."

Maria felt a surge of compassion. Ari seemed invulnerable, but his past was filled with so much pain. She'd had no idea that his seemingly charmed life had been built out of such sorrow, and it made her feel close to him. They both shared something—a tragic childhood—and had both succeeded in spite of it.

He signaled for the barman to top up their glasses, but she placed three fingers across the top of hers. She couldn't possibly drink any more.

"I persuaded the Turkish commander who took over my family's home that they needed me alive because I knew how everything worked in the city. I ran errands for them, found them bottles of raki and ouzo, all the while trying to get my father freed." He paused. "Would you mind if we step out on deck so I can smoke a cigar? I don't want to irritate your throat with my smoke."

Maria was touched by his thoughtfulness. So often people lit their cigars or cigarettes without any thought for her voice. "Of course," she said, standing up.

They settled on cushioned chairs in the stern, where the moon lit a path across the yacht's wake. Two of the English guests were in the pool, shrieking as they splashed each other.

Ari continued his story: "The Turks passed a law that meant I would have been sent to a concentration camp as soon as I turned seventeen. That's when I knew

I had to flee. I escaped through the American base and snuck onto a U.S. destroyer that took me to Athens."

Maria realized how lucky she had been to survive the wartime occupation with nothing worse than cuts and bruises from the soldier who'd tried to rape her.

He took a cigar from his breast pocket, cut off the tip, then toasted it with the flame from his lighter before putting it to his mouth to take short puffs until the tip was glowing. Maria could smell the smoke although they were outside; it was fragrant, like freshly cut grass drying in the sun.

"I borrowed money from all my father's friends and business associates and managed to buy his freedom from jail. It seemed the only thing to do. But when he arrived in Athens, he was furious." He was gazing at the horizon as he spoke. "He said he would have won his release anyway and I had thrown good money down the drain."

"I'm sure he wasn't really cross," Maria sympathized.

"He definitely was," Ari insisted. "Our relationship broke down. It's then I decided to sail for Buenos Aires and make my own way in the world. I set off with just sixty dollars in my pocket, and four years later I had made my first million. So you and I both know what it is to struggle in a foreign land. One of many things we have in common."

He reached across to squeeze her hand, just quickly. His skin was warm. She squeezed back, feeling their relationship deepen with the revelations they had shared.

Every morning, the *Christina* was moored in a deserted cove and the younger guests leapt into the water to swim. Ari's son, Alexander, who was eleven, and his daughter, Christina, aged eight, got the lion's share of his attention. Although they were the only children on the cruise, no one seemed to mind their antics. Tina, Ari, and his sister, Artemis, who had joined the cruise party, doted on those youngsters. Maria stayed in bed till noon most days but she heard Ari shouting encouragement as he drove a launch so Alexander could water-ski or lifted Christina in the air and tossed her into the water.

"Throw me higher!" she shrieked. "Do it again!"

In the afternoons Maria sunbathed on deck, watching the pride in Ari's eyes as his son executed a perfect dive or Christina did a silly dance in her pink mermaid swimsuit with its frilled skirt. He clearly adored his children, but she never saw him spend time with Tina. Maria saw no intimate conversations or hugs, no eye contact between them.

Surreptitiously she checked out Ari's figure and saw that he was fit and well muscled. His skin was very tan but it appeared soft, not at all leathery. His chest was covered with a mane of soft, fine hair, and his waist was trim. She realized how strong he must be when Alexander cut his leg during a trip ashore and Ari carried him on his back for the rest of the afternoon, making it look effortless.

Privately, Maria found the children a little spoiled; they ran around on deck, splashing water on the fully clothed elderly guests, but she never heard Tina or Ari chastise them. They beamed with pride at each minor achievement and ignored misdemeanors. Maria envied those children; she had never experienced love like that from a parent.

As the first week came to an end, Maria began to relax more fully. She had daily massages in the yacht's beauty salon, she read books and swam; then in the late afternoons she and Tina often went ashore to explore tiny Greek villages and buy souvenirs, along with some of the English women. Only one thing niggled at her: Battista. He wandered around on his own unless either she or one of the Onassises was available to converse with him in Italian. It irked Maria that he had never taken the trouble to learn another language. He was clever enough; it was sheer laziness that had stopped him.

There was more. She felt embarrassed when he left his shirt hanging open, because his belly was as round as if he were six months pregnant. She cringed at his manners when he reached across his neighbor at dinner to grab the bread basket. These were all minor complaints, but soon he began to get on her nerves no matter what he did. When they were alone in their cabin, she snapped at him for no reason, then felt bad afterward. It had been he who had wanted to come on this cruise, but, as it turned out, he was a fish out of water, while she was in her element.

Every evening when Battista went to bed, Maria would wander along the deck to Ari's Bar. Although Tina retired early, Maria was never entirely alone with Ari, because a few younger members of the English crowd stayed up till the early hours. Ari and Maria usually chatted to each other in Greek, and as the evenings passed they shared more confidences.

One evening he surprised her with a personal question: "Is everything alright with you and Battista? It's just that—forgive me—I thought I sensed tension earlier."

Maria paused, aware she was about to cross a line. "You're right. He drives me crazy sometimes." She tried to make light of it, but her tone was harsher than she had intended.

"I love him, of course," she added, unconvincingly.

Ari nodded and waited for her to continue.

"Marriage is difficult, isn't it?" She felt tears prick her eyes and blinked them away. "I feel very under-appreciated. Because Battista is my manager, our conversations tend to be about contracts and money and I feel as if . . ." She hesitated, took a sip of brandy, then continued. "I feel as if I am the goose that lays the golden eggs, while he just lives off me. He distributes my money to his family as well. It's like my mother all over again—although, of course, he is much kinder."

She bit her lip, feeling that she had gone too far. She should be loyal. He was her husband, after all.

Ari nodded, his expression concerned. "He doesn't earn his own money?"

"He used to when we were first married. He had a brick factory. But he sold it to manage my career. I should be grateful, really." Maria turned her head away. Money wasn't the root of the problem; not really. "I am a firm believer that marriage is for life. I'm sure you are too. It's just that sometimes it feels like a life sentence instead of a love affair."

She shouldn't have drunk so much. The brandy had loosened her tongue. She should stop now.

"Is he unfaithful?" Ari asked quietly.

She shook her head. "No, he's not. But at the same

time I don't think he truly loves me anymore." She felt like crying now the words were out there. She had never said this to anyone else.

Ari's next words surprised her. "Tina is unfaithful to me. Three years ago she had an affair. It got serious and she asked for a divorce but I refused. Same reason as you: because I think marriage should be for life."

Maria wasn't surprised. It explained her earlier observations that Tina never seemed interested in what Ari had to say; there was little communication between them. Instinctively, she reached over and touched his arm in sympathy. He took her hand and squeezed her fingertips.

"If only we had met first," he said, his voice so low she could barely hear it.

Tears sprang to her eyes again. If only.

Chapter 17

The Mediterranean
August 1959

Maria knew she should avoid being alone with Ari after their night of mutual confessions. At last she'd admitted the unthinkable. Ari wasn't just an entertaining new friend; she was falling in love with him. She knew she should disembark with Battista at the next port and fly to Lake Garda. Her husband would be pleased, at least; his face showed his unhappiness as he slunk around the deck all day with no one to talk to.

Yet she didn't suggest it. She danced cheek to cheek with Ari when the orchestra played after dinner each evening, and later, when most other guests had gone to bed, a kind of fatalism led her steps to his bar. The young English guests would be there, sipping nightcaps, playing board games, or splashing in the pool. But even across the room, she could feel Ari's desire burning like the rays of the sun. She was hyperaware every time he glanced at her, knew he was listening closely to every word she said and was watching when she crossed and uncrossed her legs.

Maria couldn't help sneaking glances at him as well, and every day her attraction grew. She adored the musky hint of masculinity that mingled with the smell of his cigars when he leaned over to top up her glass. But, most of all, it was the razor sharpness of his brain she loved—that, combined with the gentleness she saw when he was with his children, or sitting for hours entertaining Churchill. The mixture of flint and honey was irresistible.

In bed, she lay awake imagining . . . what would it be like with him? Would he leave Tina if she left Battista? But it couldn't be. It mustn't be. It was wrong even to think of it.

Sometimes she wondered what would happen if Battista died. He was sixty-three, after all—a whole decade older than Ari. But Tina would still stand in the way. She couldn't break up a marriage with two children involved. It was totally against the teachings of her Church. She was committing a sin even by thinking it. There were so many bad thoughts to confess to God: dreaming of having sexual relations with another man, wishing her husband was out of the way, and, worst of all, letting herself fall in love with someone who could never be hers.

The party went ashore on a remote island one day, and Maria slipped inside a tiny white-painted chapel tucked between tall cypress trees. She knelt at the altar and closed her eyes, praying to God for guidance. *You know what's right.* The words came into her head as if direct from the Almighty himself. But when she emerged into daylight, there was Ari standing a few yards away, watching her from behind his dark sunglasses, and her knees trembled.

They sailed as far as the Turkish coast, and Ari showed them around Smyrna, the town of his youth. He pointed out his family's old house, then the place where he had slipped under the fence onto the American naval base to escape the Turks. Maria translated for Battista. He was her husband, after all, and she hadn't been as kind to him as she should have been, so she made an extra effort that morning.

The next stop was Istanbul, the magnificent city astride the Bosphorus, with glittering minarets rising amid a huddle of multihued buildings. Ari announced that he had arranged for them to have an audience with the Patriarch of the Greek Orthodox Church, who was based there in St. George's Cathedral. Maria gazed at him in wonder. The head of her Church? Was there nothing this man couldn't do?

The English guests said they would rather go shopping in the Grand Bazaar, but seven of the party went to the cathedral around noon—Battista and Maria, Ari and Tina, Artemis and her husband, and the *Christina*'s captain. They stopped to light candles to St. George, and Maria couldn't help noticing that Ari donated a hundred-dollar bill, while Battista only left a few crumpled lire.

Next they were shown into the Patriarch's wood-paneled reception rooms, and he emerged from a doorway, dressed in black robes, with a black stovepipe headdress, long white beard, and straggly white hair. Maria was awestruck. This man was the holiest of the holy. Would he see straight into her sinner's soul?

He sat on his Ecumenical throne and Ari went up to greet him; then the Patriarch beckoned her too. She slipped forward, bowing her head.

He spoke, his baritone resonating in his chest: "I am honored to find Greece's two most famous citizens, the world's finest singer and the greatest mariner since Odysseus, together in my church. Let me say a prayer of blessing."

Ari and Maria knelt side by side in front of him. She clasped her hands in prayer and felt her palms sweating.

"Glory to the Father and the Son and the Holy Ghost, now and forever and to ages of ages," he intoned, and the ancient words of the prayer rang in Maria's head like the most beautiful music, their rhythm lulling her into a trancelike state. She glanced at Ari, and his expression was deadly serious. Their eyes met. It felt as if the supreme head of their Church was giving his blessing to their union—almost as if he were marrying them to each other.

Maria still felt in a dream state when they rose and looked around to see Battista and Tina watching in disbelief. She avoided their eyes, incapable of speaking on the way back to the *Christina*.

The Patriarch was joining them for lunch on board, and a feast of many courses had been prepared. The English crowd returned, and the Patriarch said he would pray for them too. The Churchills had stayed on board, and Winston looked terrified as this strange man in his black robes approached, murmuring in Greek, his silver cross swinging.

Maria's mind was in turmoil. Suddenly, as if a veil had been lifted, she could see where her destiny lay.

She had been looking for a sign—from God or from the universe—and nothing could have been clearer than the word of God's highest representative on earth.

That night, after Battista and Tina had retired to bed, Maria made her way to Ari's Bar. He was waiting for her at the entrance, unsmiling. Without a word, he took her hand and led her to the *Christina*'s lifeboat, which had a small suite of rooms. They tiptoed to the bedroom and had begun to unfasten each other's clothes before their lips touched for the first thrilling time. When they were naked, he pulled her onto the bed, and she tasted salt on his skin, smelled his scent. Their limbs became entangled till it wasn't clear which were his, which hers; then she felt the deep, primal touch of him inside her very core . . .

The bed creaked and a stiff breeze rattled the rigging, but they were quiet, entirely lost in the moment, as they consummated their union with all the desire they had been repressing for the past two weeks.

Afterward Maria cried tears of pure happiness. Ari wrapped her in his arms and held her so tight that it felt as if they were one being.

ACT II

Chapter 18

Washington, D.C.
September 1959

For once, Jackie and Jack were eating breakfast together in the dining room of their Georgetown house, with its striped Regency-style wallpaper and tall sunny windows. Usually he rose before her, dashing off to the Capitol or meeting with his advisors. But this morning he stood at a raised lectern, which was more comfortable for his back, while she sat at the table, with the *Washington Post and Times-Herald* spread in front of her.

They ate different meals. Jack liked poached eggs and broiled bacon with toast and marmalade. He suffered from Addison's disease, a disorder of the adrenal gland, and his weight could plummet if he didn't eat enough. He always had a huge breakfast on top of his other meals—favorite dishes such as fish chowder and baked chicken. Jackie watched her weight and had done so her entire life. Her breakfast was half a grapefruit, followed by a boiled egg and one slice of toast with just a scrape of butter. She was zealous about exercise too, doing sit-ups and push-ups every morning.

"Are you busy today, kid?" Jack asked.

She glanced up. "Why? Do you need me? I don't have anything on the calendar." She'd been hoping to do a spot of shopping; she fancied a fur-lined winter coat and some patent-leather boots, before the weather changed. Lee had sent a picture from a London magazine of exactly the style she wanted.

"Just wondered."

He was looking at her fondly and she smiled back, although it felt false because she was still angry with him. The conversation she had overheard, when he mentioned a "tryst" between him and Lee, stuck in her craw. She'd even obsessively looked up the formal definition in a dictionary and it said, "An agreement, as between lovers, to meet at a certain time or place."

Whenever she tried to convince herself that she was reading too much into a single word, she remembered how her husband and sister had treated it like a private joke between them, and she knew it could be true. How awful that she couldn't trust them. Jack, she knew about, but Lee—she was heartbroken.

Something caught her eye on the front page of the paper and she read it quickly. "It says here that Maria Callas is cruising with Onassis on the *Christina*," she remarked. "I wonder if she will become his latest conquest."

Jack loved gossip and squinted at the black-and-white photo of a group walking down a Greek street, Maria and Onassis in the foreground. "Didn't she used to be a big fat mama?" he asked. "I remember her being built like a tanker." He puffed out his cheeks.

"That was years ago," Jackie told him. "She's very chichi now. She would make an attractive addition to his trophy cabinet. I hope he's good to her." She spoke the last words with a sharpness in her tone, and Jack looked up.

"Is everything alright?"

"Yeah, sure," she replied, but the photograph had struck a chord. "I'm getting used to living in a cage at the zoo, where my looks and clothing choices are criticized by half-baked journalists who can't even tie their own shoelaces. And my daughter is getting used to being paraded around like the new Shirley Temple." She laughed to soften the sarcasm, but the words were heartfelt. "Honestly, sometimes I wonder if it's worth it. You've not declared for the presidency yet. Why not change your mind so we can lead a normal life?"

She was teasing. She knew Jack would never give up his great ambition, but she wished he would appreciate how much it cost her.

He walked around the table and stood behind her, placing his hands on her shoulders and kissing the top of her head. "Politics is the only game worth a candle," he said. "And in the top job, I could really change things. I know you make a lot of sacrifices. Don't think I don't notice. But I believe you would make an excellent First Lady. The best." He began to rub her shoulders.

Jackie closed her eyes, enjoying the sensation, happy to have his undivided attention for once. "So, you don't think I should lower my voice and dumb down and wear frumpy dresses from the Sears catalog?"

"I think the team is wrong about that. The public likes your movie-star glamour and your intelligence. Voters want someone to admire rather than a replica of their next-door neighbor."

She was tickled by the praise. With Jack, compliments were few and far between, so when they came, they meant something. "Before I get anywhere near being First Lady, we've got a tough year ahead. Bobby gave me a list of primaries he wants me to attend and I all but fainted. Caroline won't recognize us."

"The nanny—what's-her-name . . . Mrs. Shaw—can

bring her along to some . . ." He cupped her face in his hands and tilted her head back so that he could kiss her forehead. "Why not stand up so I can kiss you properly?" He couldn't bend far when wearing the back brace.

She rose slowly, stepping around the chair and into his arms. There it was: that special moment when it all became worthwhile. Their bodies fit like magnets, her head at his shoulder, hip against hip. After six years of marriage, she still felt the magical tug of lust. She loved the way he smelled, the solidness of him, the coarseness of that Kennedy hair, the electric touch of his lips. They kissed properly, arms wrapped around each other, lost in the moment, and she felt her mistrust and resentment dissolving, like aspirin in a glass of water. If only there was more of this, she might forget the word *tryst* entirely.

Jack broke away, and she could feel him checking his watch over her shoulder.

"Time for a quick one before the team gets here?" he whispered, his voice husky.

She smiled. "You sure know how to make a girl feel special, Mr. President."

He put a finger to her lips. "Don't call me that. I don't want to jinx anything."

"Come on," she said, taking his hand to pull him toward the door. "Quiet on the stairs in case Caroline hears and wants to come and play."

Jackie lay in bed afterward, Jack's sperm inside her, watching him whistle as he dressed. The front doorbell rang and he grabbed his tie and hurried out, turning in the doorway to give her a lascivious wink.

"Same time next week, Mrs. Kennedy?"

"Sure thing," she called.

She swiveled and rested her feet on the wall above the bed so that her pelvis was tilted. She'd read in a magazine that it was a good way to help the sperm reach the egg. It made sense, when you thought about it.

An image of Lee with Jack flashed into her mind again, but this time it didn't sting so much. Lee had her own family now, and she was happy with Stas, happier than Jackie had ever seen her. If anything had happened between her sister and her husband in a single treacherous moment, it was unlikely to be repeated. She could blink the image away.

Suddenly a memory flashed to mind from a week or so earlier. She and Jack had been driving to a rally. She'd noticed two crows sitting on a fence and recited the rhyme "One for sorrow, two for joy, three for a girl, four for a boy," adding, "So we will have joy today."

"Where does that come from?" he asked.

"It's an old English rhyme," she said. "I think it's supposed to be about magpies, not crows, and it goes right up to ten."

"What does 'four for a boy' mean?" He was concentrating on the road ahead.

"I suppose it means you might be about to meet a boy? Or to get pregnant with a boy?" She wasn't sure. "Five is for silver and six for gold. It must be something that's given to you or comes your way."

"So we just have to find two more crows for a boy, right? Keep your eyes peeled." He peered out across the close-cropped autumnal fields.

Jackie didn't want to tell him they would have had to see four crows sitting together. She joined in the game, and both looked for dark shapes in the sky or sitting on fence posts by the roadside, not quitting until they had spotted two more crows.

"Great! That should do it." Jack grinned. He couldn't have made his wish plainer: he was desperate for a son and heir.

With her feet still resting on the wall, Jackie tried to remember when she'd last had her period. She would love nothing more than a boy. Maybe, just maybe, they had made one today. Maybe he was right this very moment coming into being.

Chapter 19

Milan
September 1959

After she and Ari made love that first time, Maria crept back to her cabin. What had she done? Would Tina guess? Women were sensitive to betrayal. What about Battista? Would he smell sex on her skin? Be suspicious about the way she couldn't stop grinning? She felt a mixture of extraordinary, incandescent joy and gnawing guilt, along with trepidation about what the future might hold.

Before they'd parted, as dawn was beginning to streak the horizon, Ari whispered, "I love you. I've never met anyone like you. I feel as if I've found my soul's twin."

And Maria felt the same. Everything about him—his power, his compassion, his energy, his intellect—made her weak with desire. She was thirty-five years old and in love for the very first time. Thousands of times she had sung about love and acted the part of a lover, but she had only been imagining what it felt like; now she knew.

Over the next few days, they tried to behave normally, especially in front of their spouses. Was she imagining that Tina seemed cooler toward her? When the English women whispered behind their hands, were they discussing her secret? Guilt made her tongue-tied over dinner, and she tried to keep to herself as she lay reading on deck. But every night she and Ari slipped into the lifeboat to make delectable, irresistible love. He made her feel feminine, sexy, and liberated. She wanted to ask what would happen at the end of the week when they docked and she flew back to Milan, but was too anxious about the reply. They had both said they believed in the sanctity of marriage. Then, on their second-to-last night, he brought it up.

"I can't be without you," he said, holding her close. "Not now."

"Nor I," she breathed, and the taut elastic of her anxiety eased a little. It would happen. Their feelings were too strong to be ignored.

It was sad to disembark, but Ari had already promised that he would come to Milan in a few days, and she decided to speak to Battista before then. He had a right to know.

Her husband laughed—a cruel, harsh laugh—when

she told him on the night they arrived back at their town house that she was in love with Ari and he was in love with her.

"Don't flatter yourself," he sneered. "You're just a passing fling for Onassis. If you take it seriously you'll be a laughingstock."

"I hope we can manage this as civilized adults," she continued, ignoring his taunts. "I would like you to move out of the house. You can go to Sirmione and I'll stay in Milan while we work out the arrangements."

He shook his head. "You're fooling yourself. Onassis won't leave his wife. He'd have to give her half his fortune. Wealthy men don't do that."

Maria narrowed her eyes. "Let's wait and see, shall we? In the meantime, I would like you to pack your things and leave today. You can take the car."

She turned and swept from the room, trying hard not to let the doubts that he had sowed take root in her head, like knotweed.

At seven that evening, Ari called, and straightaway he said, "I can't bear this. I feel as if a limb has been severed. I need you, Maria. I'll fly to Milan tomorrow. Tell me where to meet you."

She hugged herself, overcome with joy. "Come to my house," she said, and gave the address. "I'll make sure Battista is gone."

After hanging up, she stormed into the sitting room and unleashed her temper on her husband. She asked why he had not left yet, when she had asked him to, then berated him for losing the Met and La Scala contracts, for spending all her money, and for his embarrassing social skills. He tried to defend himself, but she had worked herself into a rage, and at the climactic moment she hurled a glass bowl across the room so that it shattered in the fireplace with a satisfying crash. Displays of temper always made Battista uncomfortable. She knew he would run away.

"I'll give you a few days to come to your senses," he told her as he scurried off to pack a bag. "You'll soon realize that Onassis only wanted you for one thing."

The following day, Ari arrived and presented her with a black box with BULGARI printed in silver letters on top. She opened it to find a stunning cabochon emerald-and-diamond bangle.

"You suit emeralds," he told her, slipping it onto her wrist. "I think you will suit all the jewels I am going to buy you."

"There's no need for this," she said, turning her arm to admire the bracelet. "I want nothing material from you. No money, no jewels. I only want you."

———

They spent most of the next two days in bed, a tangle of limbs in sheets, lips swollen from kissing. They made love so often that her skin was hypersensitized and she could scarcely bear the separation when he left her to bathe or to talk on the phone. They fed each other delicious morsels scavenged from the kitchen, and sometimes slipped out the back door of her town house to eat in a local taverna, where she knew the owner would be discreet.

It felt as if they were honeymooners; she had no qualms about making love with Ari in her marital bed because it was as if he were the husband she should always have had. Maria had never known such passion was possible; now it was clear that Battista had been a friend and business manager but never a lover. Ari told her that marrying Tina had been a business arrangement with her father, not a love match; not like this.

Most of the time she managed to close her mind to the fact that she and Ari were married to other people, to block out the guilt. She concentrated on the here and now, on learning more about this beautiful man with every moment they spent together. Little details thrilled her: his humming a Greek folk song as he shaved; the fact that he bought an ice cream for the taverna owner's young daughter every time they dined there, making her shriek with delight; the confident way he sat in a chair, inhabiting space, a presence no one could ignore.

But a phone call from Battista snapped her back to reality.

"Have you come to your senses yet?" he asked. "When are you coming to join me?"

"I'm with Ari now," she told him. "I thought I made that clear when we spoke three nights ago."

"In that case, I need to speak with you and Mr. Onassis," he said coldly. "This situation cannot continue."

Maria covered the receiver with her hand while she told Ari, and he agreed that his chauffeur would drive the two of them to Sirmione for a meeting the following evening. Matters had to be dealt with, and at least they would have each other for support.

It was a gloomy, overcast day with intermittent showers. Ari's Rolls-Royce smelled of new leather and cigars. They held hands as they headed north, saying little, staring out at the trees bent double in the gusty wind as if bowing to an imaginary monarch. Maria felt sick with nerves, and she realized that Ari was nervous too when he suggested they stop for a drink at a roadside bar.

"I'll ask for his consent to a divorce," Maria said. "With regard to the financial situation, I'll be as generous as I can afford. I can still earn more when I want but it would be hard for Battista to make a new fortune at his age."

"Don't commit to a figure now," Ari cautioned. "You're too good-natured. Let the lawyers work it out." He downed a brandy in one gulp and raised a finger to indicate to the waiter that he wanted another.

"What if he won't give me a divorce?" What would happen then? What could they do?

Ari dismissed her concern. "Of course he will. Everyone has a price."

She sipped her brandy, feeling it ease the tightness in her diaphragm. Battista knew their marriage had grown cold. Perhaps he would agree they could go their separate ways. Maybe he would find another woman, and they could all be happy.

He greeted them formally at the door of their three-story, yellow-walled villa set on a hillside overlooking the town.

"I was expecting you earlier," he said. "Bruna has prepared supper. I suggest we eat straightaway."

He led them to the dining room, where a chandelier glowed overhead. The shutters were open, offering a view over the lights of the town, all the way to the darkness of Lake Garda.

Ari pulled his chair close to Maria's and spread her

napkin on her lap, making his possession clear. Battista watched, his expression disapproving, as Bruna poured glasses of wine and water.

"Does Tina know about your *affair*?" he asked once Bruna had left the room, his enunciation making the word sound seedy.

"That is between me and my wife," Ari replied.

Battista persevered. "Do you intend to tell her?"

Ari made an impatient gesture. "Of course."

They fell silent again as plates of grilled fish and salad were served. There was no pasta course, no bread, and Maria worried that Ari would be hungry.

"Is this all there is?" she asked.

"This is what you normally eat," Battista replied, eyes cold with anger. He turned to Ari. "Maria has to watch her weight. When I met her she was huge, like a First World War blimp. I'm sure you don't want her slipping back to her old habits."

"Stop it!" Maria snapped. "You are the only person in this room who is overweight."

Ari patted her hand. "The fish is fine. I don't like a heavy meal in the evening."

Battista asked Maria whether she intended to fulfill her singing commitments for the remainder of the year: she had concerts booked in Bilbao, London, Berlin, then Kansas City and Dallas.

"Of course," she said. "You know I don't cancel concerts except on medical advice."

"But you haven't been practicing."

She felt a twinge of panic as she replied, "Leave the singing to me." She knew she had to get back to intensive practice; the Bilbao concert was less than two weeks away and she'd been neglecting her work. That she might not be ready nagged at her, adding to her underlying anxiety.

After dinner they moved to the living room. She found a bottle of brandy and poured each of them a glass, then sat beside Ari on the couch. It was time for business.

Battista preempted her. "I will never give you a divorce," he said. "Never."

She was aghast. "But why not? Ours is a marriage in name only. We haven't been husband and wife for many years."

"In the eyes of the Church we have. And here, in Italy, divorce is not legal." He crossed his arms. He had thought about it, and this was the position he had decided to take.

"Maria could divorce you in America," Ari countered. "She has American citizenship. There are states where consent is not needed if you have been separated long enough."

"But we would still be married as far as the Church is concerned," Battista countered. "I know you understand how much religion matters to Maria. That's why you organized your stunt with the Patriarch performing his mock blessing. It was all to lure her into bed."

"Battista!" Maria rebuked. "If you are implying the head of the Greek Church is corruptible, you're being ridiculous."

"Everyone has their price," Battista said, glaring at Ari.

"Okay, so how much do you want for a divorce?" Ari asked. "Name *your* price."

His words were slightly slurred, and Maria realized he was drunk. Two bottles of wine had been consumed at dinner, and she had barely touched a glass.

Battista crowed. "Is that the only language you speak? Money? For me, our marriage is about loving and cherishing each other, and for you, it's dollars and cents. Your true colors are emerging."

Ari crashed his glass down on a side table. "I am not the one who lives off a woman. You're a kept man. Don't you dare tell me it's not about money for you. Go on, what would it take to give her a divorce? Ten million? Twenty?"

"You are not a man who understands love, are you?" Battista asked quietly.

Ari leapt to his feet and hurled the contents of his brandy glass. It dripped into Battista's eyes and plastered his thinning hair to his scalp, revealing a shiny spot on his pate.

"Stop!" Maria shrieked, jumping up to grab Ari's wrist. "I will not tolerate this."

Ari yanked his hand from her grip and raised his fists like a bare-knuckle fighter. "Let's sort this out like men," he taunted.

"Sit down!" Maria ordered, yanking his arm so fiercely that he had to obey. She desperately wanted this divorce, but she had lived with Battista for many years. He had helped her and guided her career. He didn't deserve to be treated this way, even if he was being a fool.

Ari perched on the edge of his seat, fists still clenched, a wary eye on his opponent.

Battista's shirtfront was stained amber from the brandy and his eyes were reddened. He took out a handkerchief to wipe his face.

Maria stood in the middle of the floor between them.

"Do you really think it's true that he understands love and I do not?" Battista asked, glancing at Ari. "I suspect you will soon find otherwise. I'm going to bed. I can see no point in continuing this discussion. You both know my position."

He stood, clutching his handkerchief.

"We need to talk further," Maria insisted. "Maybe in the morning?"

"I don't want you staying here with *him*. Not under my roof. Spare me that, at least."

He left the room, limping slightly. When had he developed a limp? It wasn't the time to ask. She turned to face Ari.

"I'm sorry," he mumbled. "I handled that badly. It's only because I love you so much."

She sat beside him and kissed him hard on the mouth. "What shall we do now?" she whispered.

"He's not going to budge. Let's go back to Milan and hire you the best lawyer in town."

Maria looked around. She would miss this house, but Battista needed somewhere to live, so it would be best if he kept it. Perhaps she would never return here again.

She went out into the hall and explained to Bruna what was happening. "Please pack all my clothes and jewelry," she said. "Be as quiet as you can, so as not to disturb Battista. I hope you will come to Milan with me."

"Of course," Bruna agreed. She had been Maria's maid for three years and was good at her job, and loyal too.

While she packed, Maria tiptoed around the house, taking a few knickknacks that she was particularly fond of, and a portrait of her painted by an artist friend. She didn't go near the master bedroom, where the light was off; anything in there would have to be left behind.

It was two in the morning when they got into the car, Bruna in front, their luggage piled into the trunk. Ari soon fell asleep as the chauffeur sped through the night, but Maria stayed awake, her thoughts racing, panic in her throat. Dark trees were silhouetted against a starless sky, and the windshield wipers screeched against the glass, with not quite enough rain for them to glide easily. Where did they go from here? What on earth would happen now?

Two mornings later, the entire front page of the newspaper was taken up by a story about her "*adulterio*"—such an ugly word—illustrated with photographs of her trying to hide from photographers, taken some months previously. Maria realized straightaway that it was Battista's revenge. Any sympathy she'd had for him left her in that moment.

"I am devastated," he had told journalists. "I had no idea what was going on behind my back. They have betrayed me."

Maria also knew it would play badly in Catholic

Italy. Thank goodness she was no longer singing at La Scala, where the entire audience would have booed her off the stage.

Ari scanned the words, frowning in concentration.

"Battista knows this is the worst thing he could do to me," Maria said, "and yet he chose to do it. He is dead to me. That's it. *Finito.*"

"It was already *finito*, was it not? After our conversation in Sirmione, there could be no going back. But now I must fly to the *Christina* and see how my wife has taken the news."

"Perhaps she won't have seen the newspapers," Maria suggested, worried for him, and pricked with guilt about the woman who had been such a generous hostess during the cruise.

"Oh, she will have seen," he said, weariness in his tone. "She will definitely have seen. You understand, it is one thing to be unfaithful; it's another to be indiscreet about it."

He got on the telephone, arranging a flight to Athens on one of his own planes, and organizing a connecting seaplane to take him to the *Christina.*

"I'll call when I can," he said, kissing her goodbye. "Never forget that I love you."

Maria was beside herself with anxiety once he left. She hoped Tina would be pleased that she could at last have the divorce she had asked for three years ago—but what if she wasn't? Ari adored his children and wouldn't want them to be hurt, which made everything so much more complicated. She sat in the kitchen and poured out the whole story to Bruna. Who else could she tell?

Bruna listened calmly, nodding, asking few questions. "If it's true love, it will work out," she said. "What's for you won't go by you, my old grandmama used to say."

Maria hugged her. "I hope your old grandmama was right."

It was after eleven that evening when Ari called. Maria grabbed the phone after one ring, gripping the receiver so hard that her nails dug into her palms.

"Tina's gone," Ari said. "She had left before I got here, and she's taken my children. There's no note. I don't even know where they are. They flew to Athens on the helicopter, then disappeared." He sounded distraught.

"She'll be in touch soon," Maria soothed. She felt desperately sorry for him. It was hateful that other people had to be hurt in order for them to be together, but this difficult time would pass. She was one step closer to achieving her heart's desire.

"When can you come?" he pleaded. "I can't bear to be alone."

"Tomorrow morning," she said. "I'll fly to you first thing."

When she got off the phone, she sat for a long time with her face in her hands, thinking about it all and trying to stop herself from trembling.

Chapter 20

West Virginia
Spring 1960

J ackie had never been inside a supermarket in her entire life. There had always been staff to do her grocery shopping, so there had never been a need. Did that make her out of touch? Perhaps, but now she hoped it wouldn't show. She stood for a few moments gazing at the squat brick building with a plate-glass front and FOOD FAIR above it in huge red letters.

"Let's go in," said Randy, one of the younger members of Jack's campaign team. He had been placed in charge of her visit and had arranged for a handful of local journalists to show up.

Inside, harsh lights shone on the aisles of products, and tinny country music played over loudspeakers. Bobby had advised Jack against campaigning in West Virginia, which was 95 percent Protestant and highly unlikely to elect a Catholic, but he insisted. So there she was, being introduced to a store manager with clammy hands, whose name she instantly forgot.

"Wander around and introduce yourself to shoppers," Randy suggested. "Pick up a couple of items for your family. Put 'em in a cart. I'll be right here if you need me."

As soon as she set foot in the first aisle, Jackie realized she was overdressed. The women shopping there wore shapeless and faded garments. Long, straggly hair was the norm, and no one wore makeup. Their children had scuffed knees, runny noses, and clothes of the wrong sizes, probably hand-me-downs from siblings.

She hurried back to give her suit jacket to Randy and unfastened her pearls, shoving them in her handbag, so she was just wearing a gray wool pencil skirt and pale pink sweater. She still stood out, but that was the best she could do.

She picked up a carton of Florida orange juice from a refrigerated shelf, then spoke to a woman standing by the milk.

"Excuse me, I'm the wife of Jack Kennedy, who is standing as Democratic candidate for the presidency. I wondered if you would consider voting for him?" She smiled.

The woman regarded her without expression. "What

good would that do? They're all the same. Prices go up, wages go down. Things only get worse."

"I'm sorry to hear that's your experience. What's your husband's line of work?" Jackie bit her lip, only noticing after she spoke that the woman wasn't wearing a wedding ring, despite the two scrawny kids clinging to her coat hem.

The expression turned to suspicion. "What's it to you?"

"I'm sorry. I didn't mean to pry. Perhaps I can ask what work there is for men around here?"

"Coal. You're either a miner or you work at one of the hospitals where they treat them who's been breathing in coal dust all their lives." The woman had a husky voice and deep lines etched in her face, although the children were only toddlers so she couldn't have been more than about thirty.

"You said that wages go down. Why is that?"

"Depends on the shifts, what seam they're working. It's not steady work. We need the overtime to get by."

The children had been watching with wide eyes, but they were bored now. One shoved the other hard against the metal shelving, and it began to wail. Was it a boy or a girl? Jackie wasn't sure.

"My husband is concerned about getting a decent standard of living for all those who do an honest day's work," Jackie said, aware of how pompous she sounded. "It's families like yours he wants to help."

"Are you sure it's not rich folk, like his daddy?" the woman asked, reaching down to pick up the wailing child and swinging it across her hip.

Jack had been dogged by the notion that he was simply a puppet of Joe Kennedy, who was subsidizing his presidential run. "Jack is his own man," Jackie assured her, "and I guarantee he is a good one."

"Them folks're all the same, you ask me," the woman said, turning her back and walking down the aisle. "Enjoy your *orange juice*," she called over her shoulder, emphasizing the words with sarcasm as if it were some impossible luxury. Perhaps for them it was.

Jackie put the carton back on the shelf, feeling guilty for being so out of touch. She never gave a second thought to the cost of the food served at her table and ordered freely in restaurants, but these people had to budget for every item in their shopping carts.

She wandered down the cereal aisle, trying to make eye contact with shoppers. One woman had six children clustered around her, ranging from a baby in a buggy up to the biggest, who didn't look a day over five.

"My, you have a lot of mouths to feed," Jackie remarked. "How are you finding food prices right now?"

"A million dollars would help," the woman snapped. "Got any spare cash?" She answered her own question— "Nope, didn't think so"—before moving on.

A few conversations were more productive: Jackie heard about a local glassworks that was laying off dozens of men and promised to ask Jack to look into it; she was shocked to hear about the very limited health insurance the mine owners offered their workers' families; and a few said they would vote for Jack because it was high time the younger generation had its say.

Jackie felt like a fraud. She had never been shy or tongue-tied but she was struggling to make conversation with these people, whose lives were so radically different from hers. There were loads of questions on the tip of her tongue. "Why have so many children if you can't afford to feed them?" "Couldn't you get a job to help the family budget?" "Why not move to another town where there's more work?" But the choices they made were none of her business.

Could Jack help any of them? She wasn't sure, but when she looked at the meager contents of their shopping carts she wished she could do something to relieve their poverty. These weren't even the worst off; she knew there were many who couldn't afford to shop in stores and lived off what they could grow or scavenge.

Jack genuinely cared about people like this. That's why he would be a great president.

She was relieved when Randy called her to the checkout so that the local press could take photographs. She helped one young mother load groceries into a brown paper bag while the cameras flashed. She might have won over a couple of voters but knew the next day's story would comment on her "floor-mop hairstyle" and her "fancy clothes" rather than her social conscience—they always did.

As they drove out of town, she asked Randy to look into the glassworks closure and the mine workers' health-insurance policies to see if there was anything that could be done for them. He scribbled in a notebook. He was only twenty-nine but so ambitious he bristled with it, like iron filings under a magnet. Jack was his god. He would have kissed his shoes if asked; would probably kiss hers too if she promised to put in a good word.

She spotted a gas station up ahead and asked, "Could you get me some cigarettes, please? L&Ms Class A."

Randy leapt out of the car, and when he came back with the pack, he took her lighter and sparked a flame as she inhaled. She had been smoking since she was fifteen years old because it helped keep her weight down, but she was careful never to be seen in public with a cigarette. Her mother had drummed into her that it wasn't ladylike.

The driver left her at Merrywood, her stepfather's Virginia estate, which overlooked the Potomac River. The mansion was situated on sprawling grounds with tennis courts and a swimming pool, but it was the stables Jackie was headed for. She called for a groom to saddle Danseur, her favorite mare, changed into her riding clothes, and within ten minutes of arrival was heading off into the woods.

As they cantered along the paths she knew so well, she felt the tension of the day dissolve. Danseur was a chestnut beauty who loved this countryside, especially the long grassy fields where they could gallop at full stretch. The light was fading to apricot on the horizon, and Jackie could sense frost crystals forming, but her cheeks glowed with the exercise. Here was the place where she was most fully herself.

She breathed deeply and noticed her breasts felt tender under her tightly buttoned riding jacket. That had been the first sign of her three previous pregnancies; that, and missed periods, and she was a couple of weeks late. If she was pregnant, it had been a long time coming. All winter she'd ensured that they made love on the fertile days of the month, but with no luck. Now it seemed there might be a chance, but she mustn't get her hopes up. It was early days; too early for a test.

She wasn't seeing Jack till the weekend and tried to remember where they were meeting: somewhere like Milwaukee. If they had private time alone she would tell him her suspicions, but for now she hugged the precious secret to herself.

"Please let me be pregnant," she breathed into the bone-chilling wind. "Please let it be a boy."

Chapter 21

Dallas, Texas
November 1959

M aria flew to Dallas for her concerts, and straight off the plane she took a taxi to Mary Carter's house to meet her baby daughter, Samantha. She'd brought a gift of a floaty lace Dior party frock with matching bootees, and Mary was tickled: "She'll look fancier than her mom."

Maria held the little girl in her arms, a lump in her throat as she examined the porcelain-perfect skin, the sapphire eyes and gummy smile. "She looks like you, Mary. She's a beauty."

Maria handed her over when she began to squawk, then was taken aback when Mary lifted her shirt to feed the little one. She'd always assumed breastfeeding was something you did if you couldn't afford formula.

Mary laughed at her expression. "It's the only way

I'll get her to hush up and give us peace to chat. Now, tell me, is it true what I read in the papers? You've only gone and snared the richest man in the world?"

Maria grinned. "He could be the poorest in the world and I'd still love him. I've never felt like this before, Mary. It's the real thing. I can't wait for you to meet him."

"If you love him, I'm sure I'll love him too."

Mary cupped the baby's head with her hand. "But boy, oh, boy, you sure don't do things by halves."

"I've turned down most offers to sing next year because I just want to be with him," Maria continued. "You of all people know that the backstabbing of the opera world had been getting me down. Now I can sing when I feel like it, for the sheer love of music."

Mary looked thoughtful. "That sounds wise, but I hope you won't give up performing entirely. The world needs Maria Callas. And take it slow and steady with the romance, *dahlin'*. Listen to your old friend."

Nothing could dampen Maria's excitement, though. She and Ari spoke on the phone every day, long, loving calls that neither wanted to end. He sent vast bouquets of flowers to each hotel and concert hall—entire nurseries' worth must have been plucked to create them—and he was waiting at the airport to sweep her into his arms when her plane touched down in Athens at the end of the tour.

———

That December the weather was mild, and she and Ari spent most of their time on the *Christina*. Maria kept her clothes in Ithaca, for the sake of propriety, but she slept every night in her lover's bed. She loved taking care of him: choosing new clothes for him, fussing over his health, planning meals with the chef, even cooking some dishes herself—she loved to cook. She got to know his sister, Artemis, and her doctor husband, Theodore, finding them warm and understanding of their situation, although she knew Artemis had been close to Tina. Her one and only desire was to make him happy.

Ari spent his afternoons on the yacht's telephone, talking to his offices around the world, the captains of his tankers, and the bank managers in tax havens, switching among the seven languages he spoke fluently. He kept all his global contacts in a scruffy address book, with business cards and scribbled notes shoved inside, all held together with rubber bands. Maria teased him, saying that it was not very grand for the world's richest man, and offered to buy him a Cartier address book, but he insisted that everything he needed was right there.

While he worked, she sat reading on deck, huddled in blankets on the chillier days, listening to the sound of his voice in the background. He was sharp with some callers but she never heard him lose his temper. She could tell he had an astonishing facility for mental arithmetic, making complex calculations in seconds and retaining figures in his memory; perhaps part of his talent for business lay there.

In the evenings, after dinner, they sat talking, faces inches apart, sharing minute details of their lives and beliefs, memorizing every new fact about each other. Maria had never been so happy. Her heart was filled to bursting.

One evening during the week before Christmas, Ari suggested they have daiquiris before dinner. After Maria had taken a few sips, her stomach heaved, and without warning she threw up violently on the deck.

Ari rushed to offer his handkerchief and called for a steward to clean up.

Maria was mortified. "I'm sorry. I don't know what came over me." She wiped her mouth, trying to remember what she had eaten earlier in the day, but there had been nothing out of the ordinary. She hoped she hadn't caught a bug.

Ari was scrutinizing her, as if trying to work something out. "When is your time of the month? I can't remember."

Maria had stopped taking note of the dates. There seemed no point anymore. She was thirty-six years old and infertile—or so she thought. Her eyes widened. Was it possible she was pregnant?

"I think you should see a doctor when you are back in Milan," Ari said.

She shivered with excitement. Could she be with child? She glanced at Ari to see if he looked pleased at the prospect, but his expression was unreadable and she was too nervous to ask. It was still early days in their relationship, after all.

He asked the steward to fetch a glass of water for her, then changed the subject to talk of his friend Prince Rainier. The Monaco National Council had bogged down his budget in red tape, so the money for an opera company could not be found just yet, but he was hopeful that the situation would be resolved soon.

Maria didn't care about that anymore. She had a much more exciting prospect in mind.

Before Maria could return to Milan for a pregnancy test, Ari's children came to visit. He told them Maria was his "good friend," but they knew otherwise and scowled, refusing to shake hands until their father insisted.

"Mama told us you stole Papa from her," Alexander said when Ari stepped out of earshot. "That's not nice. You should give him back."

Maria shook her head, flustered. Tina must be furious with her to have said such a thing to her children. "It's not like that at all, I promise . . ."

She felt horribly guilty that Tina blamed her, and she wanted to say more, but she couldn't tell these children that their mother was the one who'd had an affair first. If only she could win them over by telling them they might have a new brother or sister—but that would have to wait.

Throughout their stay, the children refused to engage in conversation. She asked questions about their new home in England and their favorite games, but got no answers, even when Ari snapped at them not to be rude. They sat glumly at the dinner table, picking at their food, and Maria felt awful that grown-ups' actions were responsible for their misery.

"They'll get over it. I'll see they do not lack for anything, and they can visit me in the school holidays. It will work." Ari spoke as if trying to convince himself.

His lawyers were negotiating with Tina's lawyers, and Maria knew he was concerned about how much of his fortune he would have to give away. Battista's warnings—that Ari would never divorce Tina because of the money—rang in her ears.

"I don't want to break up the empire that Alexander

will inherit one day," he explained. "Many of my businesses are interdependent. Tina knows that."

Maria felt it was not her place to comment on Tina's settlement. At least they were moving toward a divorce, while Battista wouldn't even contemplate the idea. He had dug in his heels since their meeting in Sirmione and would not budge on anything, even on returning her lucky Madonna icon, which she'd accidentally left behind there. She'd written, begging Battista to forward it to her, offering to pay whatever he asked, but he refused point-blank.

"Why should I do one single favor for you?" he wrote in his reply. "I can't think of a reason. So the answer is no."

She couldn't help but worry that it was a bad omen.

When Maria's doctor in Milan confirmed her pregnancy, she flushed scarlet with joy.

"Do you have any idea how much I have wanted this?" she breathed, close to tears. "Thank you, from the bottom of my heart."

The doctor explained that they would take special precautions because of her abnormal uterus, and because it was a first pregnancy at her advanced age. The baby would be delivered by Caesarean section, and they'd keep a close eye on her in the final weeks.

She covered her face with her hands, overcome with emotion, silently thanking God for answering her prayers. If only Ari could have come to the appointment. She couldn't wait to rush home and telephone him. He had to be pleased. Surely he would be? Her hand was shaking as she dialed.

"My darling Maria!" he exclaimed, sounding emotional. "To be frank, I didn't think I wanted any more children, but now it has happened I can't wait to meet this baby we have created together. I hope it will be a girl and that she has your voice and your beauty."

"And your intelligence," she added. "It is due on the twenty-sixth of June. Just think . . . I have been pregnant since October without realizing!"

"You know that I will always take care of you and the little one," he said. "No matter what."

A shadow of doubt made her shiver. "It would be wonderful if we could be married before it is born," she ventured. "So that no one could call our child a bastard."

"We are already married in the eyes of God. The Patriarch blessed us, and no two people could be more in love. If we can't manage to get married in law before June, that is of less concern to me."

"But we can try, can't we? The lawyers might find a way."

"Of course we can."

They agreed that Maria would spend the spring months on the *Christina* with him, then both would live in her Milan house for the final weeks before the birth.

When she got off the phone, Maria grabbed Bruna and twirled her around the hall. "We're going to have a little one!" she cried.

"Oh, madame! I couldn't be happier for you." Tears glinted in her eyes. "I'll help you. I looked after all my sister's babies. Such wonderful news!"

Maria clasped a hand over her belly, feeling sure this child was a girl. Her star sign would be Cancer, which meant she would be a loving, sensitive child. Cancer was particularly compatible with her own sign of Sagittarius, so she hoped they would be the best of friends as well as mother and daughter.

Until the birth, she didn't want a hint of her pregnancy leaking to the press. She would hate to see headlines about her getting pregnant out of wedlock, illustrated by unflattering photos of her belly. Ingrid Bergman had been crucified in the media after getting pregnant with the child of director Roberto Rossellini while married to another man. No; it would remain a tightly guarded secret until she and Ari could stand side by side with their child in her arms and make a joint announcement.

Chapter 22

The Mediterranean
April 1960

Maria's nausea had passed and her belly began to swell. Her hair grew thick and glossy and her skin glowed; she'd never felt healthier. She sent Bruna to purchase ever-larger brassieres and swimsuits and loose, exotic kaftans that she could wear on board the *Christina*, plus a chinchilla swing coat that disguised her figure when she went ashore.

"Pregnancy suits you," Ari said, running a finger along her cheekbone. "You look ravishing."

The pregnancy hormones seemed to stimulate her libido as well, because she had never felt such urgent desire for Ari. As she lay beside him on a lounge chair, tanning in the spring sunshine, her skin ached for his touch. Many times a day she reached across to kiss and caress him, then they slipped down to his suite to make love. Unlike Battista, he was always willing.

"I will have to keep you pregnant all the time if it has this effect," he murmured, drowsy in the aftermath of lust. "You were sexy before but now you have turned into an insatiable diva." He grabbed a handful of her backside and bit her shoulder.

They became more adventurous in the bedroom. Whatever Ari wanted to do, Maria agreed, as long as it wouldn't harm the baby. He had told her that his earliest sexual experiences had been with prostitutes, and she sometimes wondered if that was where he learned some of these more advanced techniques. It didn't matter. She wanted to do everything with him that a man and a woman could possibly do together, and she loved it all: every magnificent erotic moment.

The only cloud that spring came when a friend sent a telegram to warn Maria that her mother had written a book about her that was soon to be published by a New York house. Straightaway Ari got his American lawyer to send a threatening letter, telling them to stop publication, but it was too late. The book came out, and the lawyer sent a copy to Maria so she could decide whether she wanted to sue.

"Don't read it," Ari advised. "Don't let her words inside your head. If you sue, it will give the book a publicity boost and it will reach many more readers. Leave it alone and it will disappear by the end of summer."

Maria looked at the cover, bearing the title *My Daughter Maria Callas*, and couldn't stop herself from opening to the first page. Then she sat down and read some more.

According to Evangelia, Maria had been an adorable baby, but she had a personality change after being knocked down by an automobile at the age of five. From a sunny-natured toddler, she became bad tempered and selfish overnight. According to her mother, Maria never appreciated the years of sacrifice that she, Evangelia, had endured, the scrimping and saving to pay for voice lessons, the hardships of the war years in Athens—all of it had been for the sake of her ungrateful daughter.

A decade earlier, when she still yearned for her mother's love, this would have devastated Maria; now that her heart was hardened, it meant nothing. She didn't recognize herself in her mother's words; she knew that was not the child she had been.

After Maria had finished reading, she asked Ari to read it too. "Tell me honestly what you think," she said. "I trust your judgment."

He started laughing before he reached the second page. "I'm sorry," he said. "I know she's your flesh and blood, but any normal reader is going to think she is insane. You clearly made the right decision in cutting her out of your life."

"Are you sure?" Maria had thought the same. The pages were dripping with malice, and full of factual errors too. She would not dignify it with a response, and she would not let it spoil her otherwise idyllic pregnancy. Her mother was her own worst enemy, but she was nothing to Maria now. And she would make sure that, no matter what happened, Evangelia would never meet her grandchild.

Chapter 23

Hyannis Port
Summer 1960

Jackie was coming up on twenty weeks pregnant and did not want to risk traveling cross-country for the Democratic convention in Los Angeles, but she stayed up till two in the morning to watch on television as Jack accepted the presidential nomination. She almost missed it, because the set took ten minutes to warm up; then she had to tinker with the antenna to get rid of fuzzy zigzag lines slashing the picture. Two-year-old Caroline awoke and came downstairs to snuggle sleepily on her lap.

Behind Jack on the stage were the four candidates he had defeated, all of them seasoned politicians. She wondered how they felt about being beaten by a comparative newcomer. Adlai Stevenson would be particularly peeved; he had tried to persuade Jack to run for vice president on his ticket and had now been outrun by him. They looked sincere in their congratulations, but politics was a game for competitive men and no one liked to lose.

Caroline quickly lost interest; to her the distant figure on the TV screen was not her daddy. Jackie felt curiously detached as well, as if he were someone else entirely.

"The New Frontier of which I speak is not a set of promises—it is a set of challenges . . ." Jack announced.

It was grandiose sounding but there was nothing of substance. The policies could wait. For now, it was about making an impression.

Jackie had asked Joan, Teddy's ultraglamorous blond wife, to chaperone Jack on the West Coast. She would be the woman on his arm at formal dinners, the one sitting behind him during the interminable speeches. Jackie had urged her to stay close, hoping the presence of his sister-in-law would curtail Jack's extramarital activities. He had to be careful not to get caught now he was in such a high-profile position.

Jackie was spending the summer at Hyannis Port, reading, painting, and playing with little Caroline. The baby in her womb was much more active than her previous three; she could feel it kicking and rolling around from about eighteen weeks, getting livelier in the evenings, as if having a private party. She was glad for the reassurance that it was alive and thriving; when she realized Arabella had stopped moving inside her, it had been the worst moment of her life.

Jackie's peace was disrupted on the day of the nomination announcement by the press arriving en masse. Low-flying planes buzzed overhead with photographers leaning out to snap pictures, and she had to give several interviews and stand in the sweltering heat, posing for photographs, just when she was feeling her least attractive. No designers made chic clothing for pregnant women. She had some flared cotton sundresses in floral prints that she wore with white, low-heeled pumps, but they were far from the elegant, streamlined look she normally favored. Then her father-in-law insisted on a press conference, held in the living room of Joe and Rose's home.

"I'm so excited," she gushed in answer to the questions fired at her. "Jack would be a wonderful president, who could do so much for this country."

She had hoped the level of interest in her family would die down after an initial frenzy, but, if anything, it increased. Sightseers came to gawk at their house, so she could no longer wander into the yard without being photographed. Some folk leaned over the picket fence and helped themselves to stems of the rambler roses.

If she so much as appeared at a window, the cameras came out.

Is this really the life I wanted? she wondered, thinking back to the six years between her coming-out party and her marriage to Jack, years when she could have chosen a different spouse and changed her fortunes entirely. She had achieved her ambition "not to be a housewife," but was this too much?

While still at school, she had wavered between John Sterling, son of an ambassador, and Bev Corbin, son of an attorney: the former was fiercely intelligent but not sexy enough, and with the latter it had been purely a physical attraction. She had dithered for a while, then decided to hold out for both qualities in one package, and had broken up with both of them before she turned eighteen.

At her coming-out party, she had scrutinized the eligible candidates and decided that none was dynamic enough. Her long summers in France had featured plenty of flirtations and flings, with men who were exciting but not the marrying type. And then there had been John Husted, lovely John, to whom she had been engaged for a few heady months.

John was a handsome stockbroker with a romantic,

poetic side. When she met him at a party, she'd just had her hair cut in the fashionable feather style, which gave her a gamine look.

"You look like a startled deer emerging from a wood and seeing its first ever human being," he said. Those were his first words to her.

"I don't know how to take that," she replied. "Are you offering to protect me in the big, bad world?"

"It would be my pleasure." He smiled and handed her a glass of champagne from the tray of a passing waiter. "Is that a good start?"

He fell in love with her right from the start—head over heels, utterly besotted—and she was swept up in the romance. When he got down on bended knee and asked her to marry him, when they had known each other less than a month, she was bowled over by his impetuosity and said yes straightaway.

Jackie shook her head, remembering her confidence in the face of the shocked reactions of her mother and friends. "When you find the right person, you just *know*," she told them, with a twenty-two-year-old's certainty.

Looking back, she could imagine what life with John would have been like. They would have lived on New York's Upper West Side, where he had his stockbroker practice, and kept a summer home on Nantucket near his family's estate. They would have been members of all the exclusive East Coast clubs and have dined out in New York's top restaurants. There would have been staff, and she would have spent her days shopping and lunching with friends. She knew he wanted children, and she was pretty sure he would have been faithful.

It was meeting John's mother that had shown her how much of a straitjacket that life might prove to be. The Husted matriarch seemed determined to slot her into a preformed, wife-shaped mold: she would have to look a certain way, run her household like a battleship, entertain John's clients in fitting style, and produce exactly the right *sort* of children. His mother had been shocked that Jackie planned to work for the *Washington Times-Herald;* nice girls didn't do *dirty* jobs like journalism.

Jackie knew she could have fought the matriarch and won. John was so much in love he would have let her do as she pleased, but that in itself put her off. She guessed she had wanted more of a challenge—and Jack Kennedy was certainly that.

A few weeks after her engagement to John, she called Jack at his office and asked if she could interview him for her column.

"I was wondering when you would get around to calling, Miss Bouvier," he said with a grin, as his secretary showed her in. "But you didn't need to make work an excuse."

"Actually, work is the only reason," she said, holding out her hand to show him her ring. "I've gotten engaged since we last saw each other."

"Who's the lucky fella?" he asked, and when she told him, he groaned: "Not a stockbroker! Anything but that. He'd be all wrong for you. Let's go for a cocktail and I'll explain to you exactly the type of man you need to marry."

Jackie went for the cocktail but maintained that she was marrying John Husted and that was the end of it. Jack waged an intense campaign to change her mind, and it wasn't long before he captured her heart. With John, she'd been like an Edith Wharton heroine, consumed by romance; now she realized that true love was bigger and sexier and far more dangerous. It was only a matter of weeks before she had returned her engagement ring to John and started dating Jack instead.

Jack Kennedy seldom brought her flowers or surprise gifts—and, if he did, she knew he was feeling guilty and had gotten his secretary to pick them out. He didn't shower her with compliments or ask how her day had been. He didn't often discuss his work with her, because he knew she wasn't interested in the nitty-gritty of politics. But he asked her advice on the people around him, and she found that flattering.

Jackie had been a people watcher as far back as she could remember. She came across as reserved because she didn't dominate conversation in a group but sat back and formed her own opinions, and she considered herself a good judge of character. When Jack brought a TV news reporter to dinner, a man named Bob Merryman, the liquor flowed and the jokes got lewd. Jackie watched Bob and saw a shrewdness in his eyes; he was pretending to be drunker than he really was and attempting to lull Jack into indiscretions.

"Don't trust him," she whispered behind her hand.

She was proved right the following day when Bob said, on air, that Jack Kennedy told "the bluest jokes" he had ever heard. That wasn't the kind of image they wanted to cultivate. From then on, Jackie kept a keen eye on the circle Jack surrounded himself with.

She couldn't imagine him winning the 1960 election. It would mean such an upheaval: a move to the White House, life in the public eye, severe curtailment of her personal freedom. Was she up to the role of First Lady? What if she let him down? Sometimes she secretly hoped he wouldn't win—but of course she would never breathe a word of that.

He arrived in Hyannis Port on the Sunday after receiving the Democratic nomination, trailed by photographers and eager journalists with pens and notebooks poised.

"Where's my favorite girl in the whole wide world?" he cried, swinging little Caroline high in the air but looking directly at Jackie. She loved those moments when they searched each other's eyes and found understanding there. He looked tired, and she knew from his posture that his back was hurting.

"Mrs. Shaw," she asked the nanny, "can you take Caroline down to the beach?" Caroline protested, but Jackie insisted: "There will be time to play with Daddy later. It's grown-up time now."

She took Jack's arm and tugged on it. "Let's go indoors."

She led him to the living room and unfastened his tie, then knelt to untie his shoelaces.

"Thank God for home," he sighed, lowering himself into an armchair. "I feel saner already. Any chance of a beer?"

She had already asked the maid to leave a chilled Budweiser on a side table, and she flipped the top and poured it into a glass, careful not to make too much foam. She liked knowing what he needed and doing it for him. It was a simple thing. The world would never see her behind-the-scenes supporting role, but she knew she was performing it to perfection.

Chapter 24

Milan
June 1960

M aria decorated a nursery at her home in Milan, choosing pale lemon for the walls, hedging her bets, although she was positive the baby was a girl. She bought heaps of toys: a wooden rocking horse with a thick wool mane and leather saddle; a Steiff teddy bear; a music box that played *Swan Lake* and had a revolving silver-skirted ballerina. She hired a nurse, who would come and live in the house straight after the birth and accompany them to the *Christina* later.

She and Ari discussed names, and he accepted her hunch that it was a girl.

"I would like a name from opera," she said. "Perhaps Elvira or Isolde."

"Didn't they all commit suicide or have their hearts

broken?" Ari asked. "Why not a classic Greek name, like Polyxeni or Vassiliki?"

"Vassiliki!" She laughed. "Do you want her to sound like a grandmother?"

"Okay," he conceded. "Perhaps you should choose the name if it is a girl and I will choose for a boy. Do we have a deal?"

Maria was so sure it was a girl that she agreed.

Ari showed her how he shook hands on a business deal, squeezing firmly with his right hand and grasping his associate's elbow with his left.

He had not yet told his children that they were to have a new sibling; he said he feared it would give Tina ammunition in the ongoing divorce negotiations. Maria squirmed when she imagined Tina's reaction to their news.

The legal processes were moving at a snail's pace and it became apparent that they could not be married before the birth, but Maria decided it was only a minor setback. God would forgive them. By wearing her swing coat whenever she left the house, she had succeeded in keeping any hint of her pregnancy out of the press. When the news eventually leaked, as it surely would, she hoped the wedding date would have been set.

As the weeks passed, she marveled at the changes to her body. She had feared she might get fat again, but although her weight rose by twenty pounds, all of it was in her breasts and her belly. The doctor was pleased with her health. The only ill effect she suffered was low blood pressure, which caused occasional dizzy spells, but they passed after a rest and a light snack. She often sang to the baby, hoping to instill a love of music while it was in the womb. Both she and Ari noticed that the little one seemed to stop squirming when it heard her sing, as if it had paused to listen.

On the twenty-sixth of June, the day the baby was to be delivered, Maria traveled to the hospital with Bruna, clutching a bag that contained two of her night-gowns and some newborn-baby clothes, soft and fine as gossamer. Ari would remain at her house until after the Caesarean, then visit mother and child later. He had ordered Montecristo cigars, which he claimed were essential for a proud father—that and some bottles of Maria's favorite vintage of Dom Pérignon.

Maria was nervous as she was prepped for the oper-ation. She didn't like the idea of being unconscious, or the knife that would slit open her belly, but it would all be worthwhile later in the day when she could kiss her child for the first time. She closed her eyes and breathed as instructed when the rubber mask was placed over her mouth and nose, aware of a sickly sweet scent as she went under.

———

When Maria opened her eyes, she was in bed, and Bruna was sitting beside her, fiddling with her rosary beads. She glanced at the window and saw the light outside fading. It must be early evening.

"Where's the baby?" she asked, her voice husky.

Then she noticed that Bruna looked as if she had been crying, and felt a glimmer of fear.

"There's a problem," Bruna said, standing up. "Let me get the doctor."

Maria pushed herself up on her elbows despite the tearing sensation in her belly. "What kind of problem?" she croaked, but Bruna was halfway out the door.

Was there something wrong with the baby? Why wasn't it in the room? She lifted the sheet and saw a dressing on her abdomen. The operation had been carried out. She couldn't feel much when she lay still, so perhaps the anesthetic was still numbing her.

Minutes later Ari came into the room, followed by the doctor, and she knew it was bad news when they couldn't meet her eyes.

"Where is my baby?" she demanded. Ari came to sit beside her and took her hand, but still he wouldn't look at her.

The doctor spoke slowly, as if reluctant to tell her.

"The child—a boy—was delivered at four-thirty this afternoon."

"A boy!" She registered this with surprise.

"But I'm afraid he failed to breathe. It seems the lungs were not developed. We tried to assist him but all our efforts failed and he died twenty minutes later."

"*What?*" She turned to Ari and he nodded, gripping her hand so tightly she thought he would crush the bones.

Maria turned to the doctor again. "My child was alive this morning. I could feel him moving. How can he be dead now?"

"It seems there was a disorder affecting the lungs. We're not sure what."

She couldn't take it in. How could her child have underdeveloped lungs, when hers were so powerful? She would have given the baby one of her own, were such a thing possible.

"Was it my fault?" she asked. She needed to know. "Was it because of my malformed uterus?"

The doctor shook his head. "Not at all. There's nothing anyone could have done differently. It's just nature's way sometimes."

She looked at Ari again. He was fighting back tears. "I'm so sorry," she whispered. "I've let you down."

He made a strangled noise in his throat and shook his head.

There was a ringing sound in Maria's ears, and for a moment she thought this might be a nightmare. Maybe she was still under anesthesia and would awaken to find the baby was fine. Or maybe they had made a mistake, and when they checked again they would find he was breathing.

"Can I see him?" she asked.

They didn't like that idea. The doctor frowned. "We don't encourage it. You might find his appearance up-setting."

"Of course I must see him. I insist!" She knew she would never believe this without seeing him with her own eyes. It was so sudden, so surreal.

The doctor asked a nurse to fetch him and she closed her eyes to pray. *Dear God, please have mercy. Let my baby live. Please don't take away the thing I wanted most in the world.*

The nurse brought in a bundle swaddled in white muslin, and she unwrapped a little so Maria could see tufts of dark hair above a high forehead. Maria reached for him and snuggled the bundle close, finding him heavier than she'd expected. When she pulled back the muslin, there was his face, eyelids shut tight, plump cheeks, lips a little blue. She kissed his forehead and it wasn't cold, but it wasn't warm either.

Ari stood and walked to the window. He couldn't look, but Maria wanted to see everything. She asked Bruna for her glasses, then unwrapped the muslin completely. Her baby was perfectly formed, with funny frog legs, a roll of fat around each thigh, miraculously tiny fingers and toes, a rounded belly with the sprout of cord still attached, dimples in his elbows, a chubby penis. Everything was perfect—everything, except his chest was not moving.

"I want a proper funeral," she told Ari. "With an Orthodox priest. Can that be done even though he was not baptized?"

"I will arrange it," he said, the first words he had uttered in a long time.

"What shall we call him? He is a boy so you must choose."

"Omero," he said straightaway. "After the author of the *Odyssey*."

"Omero." Maria nodded. She liked that name.

She tried to decide which of them he looked like. Was there a hint of Ari's chin? At least he didn't have her big nose. His skin was smooth and as downy as a peach. She kissed him again.

"Let me take him now," the nurse said, reaching out.

Maria shoved her hand away. "Get *off*! You will *not* take him. You will *not*!"

She must have sounded fierce, because the nurse leapt backward.

Grief was beginning to swell within, wild and unfathomable, but she wouldn't let it out, not yet. She wanted to spend time with her little boy and memorize every inch of him before they took him away forever.

The day after she was discharged from the hospital there was a funeral service, attended only by Maria, Ari, Bruna, and a priest. Afterward Maria's legs gave way and she collapsed.

Most of the next days were spent in bed like an invalid, with Ari beside her, cradling her. He murmured words of love and comfort but she was too far away for him to reach. It wasn't the same for him, couldn't possibly be: he had children already; he hadn't carried Omero inside him for nine months.

When the tears came, they were unstoppable. She couldn't speak, couldn't breathe, her entire being consumed by sobbing. Her chest hurt; her throat, nose, and eyes stung; and her heart ached with an intolerable pain.

Ari stroked her hair, kissed her tears, held her close.

"We will try again," he whispered. "We will have another child. I promise."

"A baby was all I ever wanted," she sobbed. "I didn't want to sing. I didn't want to be famous. I wanted a child. How could God be so cruel?"

"I will fix it," he told her. "I promise."

He wanted to feel in control, Maria thought. As if he had a say in this. But there were some things money couldn't fix, and this was one.

Perhaps it was punishment for their sin of breaking up two marriages to be together. If so, it was the harshest punishment imaginable. She felt broken in ways that she knew could never be fixed.

Chapter 25

Hyannis Port
November 8, 1960

Jackie was thirty-four weeks pregnant on Election Day when she went to the polls with Jack to cast her vote. He dropped her at their house, so distracted that he started to pull away while she still had one foot in the car.

"Hey! Stop!" she called, and he paused just long enough for her to catch her balance and slam the door behind her.

She ate lunch with Caroline, read her a story before her afternoon nap, then walked over to Bobby's house, where a command communications center had been set up. Her lower back ached because some unidentified part of the baby—perhaps an elbow or a knee—was pressing against her spine. She could feel it moving lower into her pelvis. Jack teased that she walked like Caroline's windup duck toy.

His campaign team was crammed into a bedroom at Bobby's house: one person on the telephone, others huddled around the radio, yet more watching television news coverage, and they all stopped to discuss each report. The voices were low and serious, nerves etched on their faces. No one paid the slightest attention as Jackie wandered in, listening to disjointed snatches of conversation.

From what she could make out, they were worried about Virginia and Oklahoma, but resigned to losing the Electoral College votes in Florida. She knew they were confident of the African American vote in the southern states, especially since Jack had helped get Martin Luther King released from jail, but the big unknown was how much his Catholicism would count against him. Some Republicans had been spreading the rumor that Jack would have to take orders from the pope if he was elected, and there were bound to be voters who would believe that.

This election was also about which man the electorate trusted to stand up to the Soviets as they developed new long-range missiles. Their satellite, Sputnik, was already in orbit, and who knew what *that* might be used for? Jackie had been convinced when she watched the TV debate with Richard Nixon that her husband would emerge victorious, but the polls were neck and neck. Sitting president Eisenhower had been campaigning hard for Nixon during the past two weeks, and he remained popular at the end of his second term.

Jackie hoped Jack was remembering to eat and to take his medication. She had intended to remind him, but when she spotted him in Bobby's dining room, surrounded by acolytes, she realized she wouldn't get close enough for a private word.

After a while Jackie waddled back to her own house to find that some of the team had commandeered her sitting room and were watching her television and talking on her phone. She would have preferred to have the house to herself, to put her feet up on the sofa and read, but instead she sat in a chair to watch the first exit polls. The CBS computer predicted a Nixon victory, at which there were howls of despair around the room. The baby kicked hard as if in protest.

He can't win, Jackie thought. *Not now. Jack would be devastated.* But then, she supposed Pat Nixon was thinking the exact same thing about her own husband.

Her housekeeper produced bowls of clam chowder for everyone, served with hunks of home-baked bread. Caroline accepted the presence of strangers at her kitchen table without question. Jackie was glad she wasn't a shy child. She was calm and settled, despite the febrile atmosphere.

By mid-evening, the news shows had changed their tunes and were predicting a Kennedy landslide, and when Jack came to the house for a brief moment, Jackie congratulated him.

"Don't tempt fate!" he cried, touching the wooden banister.

The first states to declare were the East Coast ones that were largely Democratic, so Jack was in the lead when Jackie went to bed at eleven P.M., but she knew that the Midwest results would swing things in the other direction. How far? That was the question.

She woke briefly and glanced at the clock when Jack came to bed. It was four-thirty.

"What news?" she whispered.

"Too close to call," he said, and was asleep within minutes of his head hitting the pillow.

When a shaft of daylight snuck around the edge of the shutters, she awoke and checked the clock: seven-thirty. Careful not to disturb Jack, she clambered out of bed, keeping her knees together as she pushed up so that her pelvis wouldn't crunch. She padded to the window, pulling the shutters open just enough to see out.

There were black, shadowy figures on her lawn,

216 · GILL PAUL

loads of them, and they were carrying oversized guns.
Fear gripped her as one looked up at the window and
spotted her. Who were they? Was it a kidnap attempt?
Then the man raised his hand to his temple in a salute
and the truth dawned on her. These were Secret Service men. They were there to protect Jack. It meant her
husband was the thirty-fifth president of the United
States. She shivered. At forty-three years old, he was
the youngest man ever to win the presidency, and the
first Catholic. It was history in the making.

She glanced at Jack, desperate to wake him and share
the news. But no; let him sleep. She didn't know exactly what the day would bring, but there were bound
to be nonstop press conferences and meetings. One
thing was for sure: their lives would never be the same.

The mood was celebratory all morning. The popular
vote had been close, but Jack had a strong lead in the
Electoral College and had long since passed the magical 269 votes needed. All the same, Nixon did not
concede until that afternoon. Jackie watched Jack taking the phone call, filled with pride. He looked presidential already, standing tall, his voice powerful.

Right afterward, she tied a headscarf over her hair
and slipped out for a walk on the beach. It was a blus-
tery day, but the wind and salt spray helped clear a

slight headache that had been nagging at her temples since she awoke. Out of the corner of her eye, she noticed some black-clothed Secret Service agents shadowing her, but they stayed well back.

Is Jack up to the presidency? she wondered. He would soon have his finger on the nuclear button. Would his health suffer with the strain of office? Eisenhower had visibly aged over the past eight years. It would be her job to ensure that Jack got sufficient rest, that he ate healthfully, that he took his daily cortisone to hold the Addison's at bay, and that he looked after his bad back. He had great mental strength, so she was confident he would manage the psychological pressure, but his body had weaknesses the public did not know about.

What about her? How would she cope with the pressures of being First Lady? It was too late to worry about that now. She'd simply have to manage, one way or another, because she couldn't let Jack down.

In January, they would all move into the White House, and after that there would be Secret Service men present wherever they went. She knew she would find it hard not to be able to slip away to go riding or clothes shopping without them, but on the plus side it was bound to be harder for Jack to have affairs. She had no idea if there had been girls on the campaign trail; if there had, he must have been discreet, because she hadn't caught as much as a whiff of scandal.

Lee had managed to get a call through to the house that morning amid the hundreds flooding in. She was still weak after the birth of her second child that summer, a baby girl who remained in intensive care, so she and Stas wouldn't be able to fly over for the inauguration.

"I can't believe we're missing it!" she wailed. "Could you ask Jack to postpone it for us?"

Jackie knew she was joking, but something about her sister's tone grated; it was as if Lee were claiming the victory, although she had contributed precisely nothing to the campaign. Tryst or no tryst, Jack was just her brother-in-law.

"Jackie!" She heard a voice calling her name and turned to see him running across the grass. He slowed as he got close, hands on hips, catching his breath. "We need you for a photo call."

"Come here," she beckoned. It was the first time she'd had him to herself for days, except when he slept beside her.

He stepped closer and looped his arms around her. She reached up to hold his face between her hands, then kissed him on the mouth.

"I'm so proud of you, bunny," she breathed.

"I couldn't have done it without you," he replied, then kissed her again, cupping one hand under her belly. "You've been perfect. The best."

They stood in silence for a few moments, faces touching, until they were interrupted by calls from the other side of the grass. She saw figures waving frantically. Time to go. Before they turned back, their eyes caught and Jack made a face.

"Guess I'd better go and start learning how to be leader of the free world," he said, with a distant expression.

Jackie shivered. She felt a frisson of dread, but shook it away and slipped her arm through his for the walk to the house.

Chapter 26

Washington, D.C.
November 25, 1960

For the next two weeks, Jackie scarcely saw Jack as he flew around the country thanking everyone who had supported his campaign. She was due to give birth by Caesarean section in early December, and most of the time she stayed indoors at their Georgetown home, within reach of the hospital. Jack was midair on a flight to Florida on November 25 when Jackie felt a gush of warm liquid between her legs as she sat in the sitting room with her daughter and Maud Shaw, the nanny.

"Could you take Caroline upstairs?" she asked, keeping her voice level, nodding at the spreading stain on her skirt.

Mrs. Shaw understood immediately, and Jackie heard

her call for the housekeeper as she led Caroline through the hall. Her chest was tight with fear. *It's too early,* she thought. *Only thirty-six weeks.*

An ambulance was called and she lay silent, stiff with terror, as they rushed her to the hospital, siren wailing. The memories of the babies she had lost filled her thoughts. She couldn't lose this one. This was the child of a president.

Her obstetrician was waiting when they arrived at the hospital, and he held her hand as they wheeled her to a private room.

"I can't lose this baby," she whispered, so that he knew.

"We'll do all we can," he promised. "Just stay calm."

She lay back as medical staff buzzed around, peering and poking between her legs, talking in hushed voices. Outside, the sky was already dark. She remembered the comfort of Bobby being there when Arabella had died, but this time Bobby was with Jack and there was no one else she felt like calling.

"We're going to operate," the obstetrician told her. "This baby is ready to be born."

"Jack's on his way," someone said.

It wasn't often that Jackie prayed, but now she whispered, "Pleasegodpleasegod," like a mantra.

When she awoke, the room was dark but a nurse was nearby, her face illuminated in the glow of a monitor.

"What happened?" Jackie asked quickly.

"You have a little boy, Mrs. Kennedy," the woman said in a Scottish burr. "He's in an incubator but that's just a precaution. He's fine. He looks like his daddy."

Jackie covered her face with her hands and cried tears of relief. He would be called John, after his daddy. John Junior.

"Och, dear," the woman said, passing her a tissue. "Try to rest."

Jack came rushing in as dawn was breaking the next day. Her nurse turned on the overhead light, and Jackie noticed tears rolling down his cheeks.

"I saw him through a glass window. He's beautiful." His voice cracked, and for a moment she thought he was going to sob out loud. He pressed his face against hers, then kissed her lips, before whispering, "No one has ever given me a gift as precious as this. I love you, Jacqueline Bouvier Kennedy."

She held his head in her hands, feeling the wetness of his tears on her cheek, his coarse hair between her fingers. This was what she had wanted in her marriage: to feel this loved. At last it felt as if their time had come.

Chapter 27

Milan
November 30, 1960

A couple of weeks after John F. Kennedy's election victory, Ari's oldest friend and business colleague, Costa Gratsos, came for a meeting at Maria's house in Milan and stayed for lunch. Maria liked him. He wasn't flashy, but he was clever, and she could tell he cared for Ari like a brother.

The conversation turned to the new president, and Ari told them he had met him. "He came for cocktails on the *Christina* with his wife and her sister. He's very charismatic."

"What's Mrs. Kennedy like?" Maria asked, sipping a glass of wine. She did everything slowly these days, still feeling like an invalid since Omero's death four and a half months earlier.

"Poised and aloof," Ari replied. "She doesn't give

much away. Lee is the prettier of the two, but Jackie is an enigma. She is clearly intelligent but you never know what she's thinking."

"Why did you invite them?" Costa asked, giving him a knowing look.

Ari chuckled. "I wanted to see if he was as much of a bastard as his brother Bobby."

"Why don't you like Bobby?" Maria interjected, and Costa snorted with laughter.

"Bobby was on the senate subcommittee that had Ari's ships impounded in docks across America back in 1953, then got a warrant for his arrest."

"I spent time in jail," Ari continued. "Me! Locked up with a load of Puerto Rican terrorists. I was furious!"

"What were you charged with?"

Ari spoke with clear exasperation. "America needed cash after the war and they had lots of surplus oil tankers and ships that had been used for troop transport and so forth, so I offered to buy some. They said no, only American companies could own them . . . so I set up American companies, with American CEOs, and bought the damned ships. Then a few years later they realized how much money I was making and regretted selling them. There was a long investigation into all my business interests and in the end the only thing they could find to charge me with was one tiny misdemeanor."

Costa joined in. "Ari played them brilliantly and got off with a small fine. The Americans were the losers because he moved all his shipbuilding back to Europe. But he still holds a grudge."

"You can't hold a grudge against all Americans!" Maria exclaimed. "I'm an American!"

"My children are American," Ari replied. "I made sure Tina gave birth in the U.S. No, my grudge is against the senators who treated me like a crooked dago. I still have scores to settle with them."

"So it's about pride," Maria said.

Costa laughed. "Everything with Ari is about pride. But America is also the world's biggest economy so he would like to sneak back into it."

Maria turned to him. "You already have more money than you could ever spend. Why this constant quest for more?" Ari hesitated and she answered the question herself. "I think I know. It's because you have to be best at everything. The champagne you drink must be the most expensive; you only visit the most exclusive restaurants; you must have the most famous guests on *Christina*. It's not about money, is it? Sometimes I think you are still trying to prove yourself to your late father."

Costa roared with laughter and banged the table. "She's got you there, Ari!"

Ari stared at her for a moment. "That's very perceptive!" He seemed surprised. "As a young man I was desperate to make my father proud, but even when I returned from South America having made a fortune that was greater than his, I got no word of congratulations. That wasn't his style."

"You are a different kind of father," Maria said. "I love the way you are with Alexander: proud, patient, and loving, all at the same time." She felt sadness descend, knowing that was how he would have been with Omero.

"What motivates me now is building my empire and passing it on to Alexander, so that he can bequeath it to *his* son, and the name Onassis will live through generations."

He had a faraway look in his eyes. He had his first-born son and didn't need any more children.

During the summer, Maria had consulted a new fertility doctor, based in Athens, a man with an international reputation. He had persuaded her to wait six months after Omero's death before trying to get pregnant again; in the meantime she was receiving a course of vitamin injections to build her strength. Next year, he said, if a pregnancy did not occur naturally, they would try some hormone treatments to nudge nature along.

Ari had agreed to this—he would do anything to make Maria happy, he said—but he wasn't grieving the loss of their child. She could tell. He slept soundly while she lay awake wondering what kind of boy Omero would have been. Which of them would he have resembled? Would he have been musical? She remembered how he had seemed to listen when she sang.

She knew she would never have pushed him the way her mother had pushed her as a child. He would have had all the things she never did: time to play with friends, trips to the zoo, family days at the beach, a normal childhood. All the love she had wanted to give him was stored up inside, a huge glowing parcel of it, but now there was no one to lavish it on.

One day that fall, Maria was passing through the hall in her Milan home as Bruna accepted a pile of mail from their mailman, and she saw an airmail envelope on top.

"Who's that from?" she asked, squinting at it.

"It's nothing, madame." Bruna tried to bury it under the pile.

"Can I see?" Maria held out her hand and was puzzled when Bruna still hesitated.

"It's from your mother," she confessed at last. "Your husband told me to destroy all her letters as soon as they arrived."

Maria took the airmail envelope, shuddering as she recognized the handwriting. It had a New York postmark, so that meant her mother was still there. She tore it open and began to read: "You have brought nothing but shame on our family from the day you were born but I never dreamed you would become a whore," it began.

For a fleeting moment, Maria felt as if she were once more the unloved child who brought nothing but disappointment. She gulped as she scanned the letter to the end. Evangelia was lambasting her for her extramarital relationship with Ari, which, she said, would see her damned in the eyes of God; yet still she could not resist a plea for money: "You live in sin with the world's richest man while I live on the breadline," she ranted. "Think of your immortal soul and send succor to your flesh and blood in their hour of need."

Ari came into the hall and Maria handed him the letter, watching his face darken as he read.

"Has she written often?" Maria asked Bruna.

Bruna nodded. "At least once a month. I always destroyed them before you saw them."

"I think you should continue doing so," she said, then glanced at Ari. "The last thing I need is her dripping poison in my ear."

There was an expression on his face she had never seen before: naked fury. In that moment, he looked as if he might be capable of anything.

"Part of me wants to tell her she is a monster," he said. "But I'm guessing she would only go to the press. It's best to ignore it." He looped his arms around Maria and pulled her close. "I'm sorry you have such an appalling mother. It makes it all the more extraordinary that you are so sweet natured."

He ripped the letter in two and slipped the pieces into his trouser pocket.

When Alexander and Christina arrived for a visit at Ari's Athens house on Agios Vasilios Day, the first of January, there were towering piles of presents for them to open. Ari had told Maria that his son was crazy about flying so she'd bought him a radio-controlled model aircraft. She could tell when he opened it that he was thrilled. His eyes widened and he began to rip off the packaging.

"Say 'thank you' to Maria," Ari instructed, and the boy stopped in his tracks. He hadn't realized it was from her.

"Thank you," he mumbled, almost inaudibly, then put the plane to one side and picked up another present.

"You're welcome," she said. "Perhaps you and your father can try it out later."

Christina couldn't resist her gift from Maria: a Barbie doll and a dozen different outfits. Launched in America the year before, Barbie had become the most desirable toy for young girls, and Maria had gotten Mary Carter to send this one over from Texas. Christina pulled her from the box, squeaking with excitement, and began dressing her in a nurse's uniform.

"Thank you, Maria," she recited when prompted.

Maria was pleased with her gifts. One way or another, she would win these children over. Who knew? They might even grow to love her.

After lunch, Ari and Alexander went out in the garden to fly the model plane, while Maria sat playing dolls with Christina. Suddenly she heard Ari shouting and rushed out to see what had happened. The plane had crash-landed against a rock and one wing was smashed.

"You did that deliberately," Ari accused Alexander, who stood with his arms folded, looking sullen.

The boy caught Maria's eye for a split second, and she spotted a glint of triumph. She realized Ari was right and felt a burst of fury at this intransigent child, but she quelled it quickly. He was only twelve.

"I'll ask the shop if it can be fixed." She forced herself to smile at Alexander, and he turned his back with a scowl, arms still firmly crossed.

I will be patient, Maria vowed to herself. If only she could have a child of her own, perhaps it would bridge the gap between them. If only.

One night, Ari said he had something he needed to discuss with her, his tone serious. "I've had a message from a man who was working as a hospital porter in Milan last June. He is no longer employed there, but he knows about Omero's birth and says if I don't pay him, he will leak it to the press."

Maria gasped. "No! Please, no!" She couldn't bear that.

"Don't worry. I have ways of dealing with blackmailers. I just had to tell you in case he tries to get in touch with you directly."

His expression frightened her. "You sound like the Mafia. What kind of ways?"

He shrugged. "I pay them or scare them, or both at once. It happens when you're in my position. Every port my ships dock in, there's someone wanting protection money or an official whose palm has to be greased."

After her initial shock, Maria felt fury. "I suppose we should go to the police. He shouldn't get away with this."

"Then the story would come out. Leave it with me. But if you ever receive a letter or call from a man by the name of Gallo, ignore it. I'll tell Bruna to destroy any correspondence, the way she does with your mother's. Promise me you won't worry." He stroked her hair, kissed her cheek.

"I promise." It was reassuring to be with someone who took such good care of her, whom she knew she could trust implicitly.

Chapter 28

Washington, D.C.
January 1961

January brought a glittering round of inauguration events: a party hosted by Frank Sinatra and attended by all the top names in showbiz, Jack's inaugural address and parade, then the all-important inaugural ball, where she and Jack would dance in front of the world's press. Jackie was dog tired after childbirth but determined to find the right outfits for each occasion so that Jack would be proud of her.

She had always loved fashion. As a young girl, when she hadn't felt like going to church her mother would tempt her with clothes—"But you could wear your new cherry-red coat with the white fur muff"—and that would do the trick.

Diana Vreeland, the fashion editor of *Harper's Bazaar*, became a behind-the-scenes advisor, and the inauguration outfits were split between American designer Oleg Cassini and the team at Bergdorf's so no one could accuse her of being unpatriotic. With Diana's help, Jackie designed her own gown for the ball: ivory silk chiffon with silver embroidery and seed pearls, overlaid by a sheer sleeveless blouse. This stunning outfit, along with a Dexedrine energy pill supplied by Jack's doctor, soon helped get her into the party spirit.

As she and Jack ascended the steps of the Armory, huge flakes of snow started to fall. So many flashbulbs were exploding around them, it was as if the entire atmosphere were sparking with electricity. In his inaugural address, Jack had spoken of a new dawn, and she felt thrilled, as if she were quite literally stepping into it.

It took Jackie awhile to learn her way around the White House—which bell to ring if she wanted a cup of coffee, and where all the corridors led—but from the start she had a clear vision of the kind of First Lady she wanted to be. She felt the gaze of previous occupants upon her as she began to restore the décor. The White House had been neglected for so long, it looked as if it had been furnished from discount stores. She planned dinners and soirées to entertain the country's artists and intellectuals, as well as foreign ambassadors and visiting dignitaries.

Her dream was to be at the heart of a hub of creative enterprise and inspiration, such as had existed around enlightened monarchs and rulers in history. There were the masterpieces created during the Italian Renaissance, when Michelangelo and Leonardo da Vinci had popes as their patrons; the Shakespearean era in England, when literature flourished under Elizabeth I; the burgeoning of all the arts in the court of the Sun King, Louis XIV. Now she was in a position to bring creative people together, to introduce them to potential patrons, and she was determined to put her personal cultural stamp on the Kennedy White House years.

Jackie knew from experience that when attending the Eisenhowers' receptions guests first had to line up in unheated rooms, without so much as a drink to ease the tedium, until they were formally greeted by the presidential couple. One of the first changes she initiated was to have cozy fires burning, a fully stocked bar, and ashtrays for smokers on all the tables. At dinner, she made sure there were abundant flower arrangements, and she hired a French chef to improve the quality of the food dramatically, from diner-style fare to Michelin-standard cuisine. Champagne would even be served, for the first time in White House history.

Before Jack became president, they hadn't entertained much as a couple, so he hadn't appreciated the hostessing skills that she had imbibed with the rest of her mother's teachings. She relished the challenge of inviting and seating guests who would get along with one another, choosing menus and themed décor, and guiding the conversation so that everyone was inspired to contribute.

"How come I didn't know you were such a party queen?" Jack asked as they got ready for a dinner in honor of the governor of Puerto Rico. "I thought I was marrying a studious, bookish kind of a gal."

Jackie was sitting at her dressing table, applying lipstick, and she smiled at him in her reflection. "One doesn't preclude the other. But I'm glad you approve."

Jack watched as she placed a tissue between her lips to blot them, then checked her teeth quickly. "So, who's coming tonight apart from the governor?"

Jackie always gave him a rundown before the party began and would step in with prompts if he was introduced to someone and she could tell he had forgotten who they were. "Pablo Casals, the Spanish cellist, is playing Mendelssohn. He's in his eighties now, but still the best in the world. Leonard Bernstein will be there—remember, we went to the premiere of *West Side Story* on Broadway?" She ran through the list of prominent guests, giving him a quick profile of each.

"Are Lee and Stas coming?" he asked. As soon as Lee had recovered from the difficult birth of her second child, she had jumped on a flight to D.C. to check out her sister's new home.

Jackie gave him a loaded look. "Our persistent house guests? Of course. We're going to need a crowbar to lever Lee out of the guest suite. She's fallen in love with the razzmatazz of power."

"Stas wants to get her back to London. He says at least there she doesn't demand a new frock for every single dinner."

Jackie laughed. "Lee's never liked to be seen in the same outfit twice. He'd better step up and earn more if he's to keep her in Chanel."

Jack leaned past her to peer in the mirror. "I look pasty. Can you touch me up?"

She pulled a Max Factor Creme Puff compact from her makeup drawer, where she kept one in a shade of tan that suited Jack's skin tone. "Who are you trying to impress tonight?" she asked as she dabbed foundation on his face, careful to avoid the starched white collar of his shirt.

"You, as always," he murmured.

"I saw you without makeup and I still married you." She tilted his chin so she could blend the color and make sure there was no tideline. "It's supposed to be women who take hours getting ready for parties, but I swear you're vainer than me."

"Nature needs more help in my case." He held out his gold cuff links: "Can you fasten these? And my tie? I have no idea how bachelors manage."

"Poor things, all weak and helpless," Jackie cooed, as she clipped the cuff links into place, tied his bow tie, and brushed a stray hair from his shoulder. "You're all done."

"Are you ready? Shall we make our entrance?" He glanced at his watch.

She pulled a guilty face. "I'll have a quick cigarette, then I'll be right with you."

Jack hated her smoking. He was forever nagging her about it. "Are you sticking to five a day? That was our deal."

"Round about five," she lied. "I've cut down a lot. Give me two minutes."

She smoked her cigarette and slipped a peppermint into her mouth before joining Jack to walk along the hall and down the stairs. There was a large mirror over the staircase and Jackie almost didn't recognize them as she glanced into it. Frozen for an instant, their image looked like a movie still. As they came within sight of the waiting crowd, there was a collective gasp.

This could go to my head if I let it, she thought. But

she wouldn't. It was theirs for eight years at most, and then they would reinvent themselves in a different, much less public life.

Jack was keen to snatch time with his children every day, and he fell into a routine of taking Caroline for a swim in the White House pool at six-thirty. She loved the water, loved having daddy time, so when he did not appear one evening in April there were tears. Jackie couldn't get through on the phone so she decided to walk to the Oval Office to see what was holding him up.

"Is he alone?" she asked the secretary, who nodded and indicated that she could enter.

Jack was sitting at the oversized desk with his head in his hands, and he didn't look up as she crept in. He seemed small against the backdrop of tall windows overlooking the lawn. She could tell from his posture that he was upset. He spoke when she was a couple of feet away.

"I've screwed up," he told her. "Badly."

She walked around the desk, put an arm around him, and kissed his temple. "I'm sure, whatever it is, it won't turn out as bad as it feels right now."

"It will," he said. "It definitely will." He paused. "We sent a force of fourteen hundred CIA-trained men to

Cuba this morning. It was Eisenhower's plan to unseat Castro. The generals told me it was infallible—but already it's falling apart. Some of our ships sank on coral reefs outside Bay of Pigs that for some inexplicable reason no one knew were there; then our paratroopers landed in the wrong place. It was supposed to be a covert operation but now it looks as though the Cubans have been expecting us for days . . ."

"Christ!" Jackie breathed. "Are there any casualties?"

"I don't have figures yet. We used Cuban exiles but Castro knows full well America is behind it. Why did I let my arm be twisted?" He thumped the desk. "This is the last thing I wanted."

"Can't they turn it around? We have the best military in the world." She tried to hide her mounting horror. Jack didn't need to see that.

"It's been botched from start to finish. I should have followed my instincts and said no."

She took a deep breath. "It's not your fault. You were taking your generals' advice and they're the experts. It's they who've failed."

He shook his head. "Like Harry Truman said, the buck stops here. That's the deal with this job."

Jackie rubbed his shoulder, trying to find words to comfort him. "People have short memories in politics," she said. "You've told me that many times. Six months from now, no one will remember the name Bay of Pigs. It will be less than a paragraph in the ten-volume history of your presidency."

The phone rang, and he picked up straightaway. She heard the secretary's voice announce someone, then Jack said, wearily, "Go ahead. Put him through." He covered the mouthpiece with his hand. "This'll be a long one. Say sorry to Caroline and give John a kiss from his daddy. I'll come over as soon as I can but don't wait up."

She looked back before closing the door behind her, and her heart twisted to see how very lonely he looked.

Chapter 29

New York City
May 19, 1962

M aria was surprised and flattered when she was
invited to sing at the forty-fifth-birthday gala
being thrown for President Kennedy at New York City's
Madison Square Garden. The Kennedys were the golden
couple of their era: attractive, articulate, and cultured.
Maria had watched the iconic television footage of them
during their visit to France, appearing fresh and vibrant alongside Europe's antiquated top brass, and been
intrigued by Mrs. Kennedy. It was said she had even
charmed the cantankerous general Charles de Gaulle,
president of France, and Nikita Khrushchev, the bully-
ing Russian premier.

"Who else is appearing?" Ari asked.

"I'm the only opera singer, but the lineup includes
Jack Benny, Judy Garland, Jimmy Durante, and Ella

Fitzgerald. And guess what? Marilyn Monroe will appear—although goodness knows what she will do!"

"The Kennedys like to surround themselves with celebrities, so the glamour rubs off," he commented.

She winked at him. "The pot's calling the kettle black. I've never known a man as obsessed with celebrity friends as you are."

He laughed. "I suppose that's true. And I am the luckiest man in the world because I wake up every morning with the biggest star of them all."

President Kennedy had requested that she sing a couple of arias from *Carmen*—"Habanera" and "Seguidilla." She was accepting very few singing commitments now, because her voice had become unpredictable in its top notes, but *Carmen*'s mezzo-soprano range would be fine. Perhaps with regular practice she could return to form, but it was hard to find the motivation. She had reached the peak of her singing career and was tempted to perform only if it was music she loved, if there was a great director and orchestra involved, and if it was at an opera house where she felt comfortable. She decided she would say yes to President Kennedy, though. The occasion sounded like fun.

Three months earlier, she had started receiving hormone injections from her fertility doctor. A calendar hung in her bathroom with circles around the dates when she and Ari must make love to give her the best chance of conception. Looking back on all the occasions when she had failed to seduce Battista, she felt cross. Ari was willing to give her a child because he loved her; Battista had lost her because he wouldn't even try.

The treatments had unpleasant side effects. Her stomach was permanently bloated, the headaches to which she was prone became more frequent, and she sometimes awoke feeling irritable for no reason—but it would be worthwhile if it worked. Her doctor told her there was a risk of twins or triplets, and she replied that would be wonderful, but she'd be deliriously happy with just one healthy child.

On the first anniversary of Omero's death, she and Ari drove to the cemetery where his little body was buried beneath a white marble gravestone with a carved angel on top. Their names did not appear on it—a decision Maria had made with heavy heart. She couldn't risk a passing journalist spotting it and making inquiries. They brought a lavish bouquet of white roses, a Greek cake called *revani* with a single candle on top, and some champagne to toast his short life. He would have been crawling by the age of one, and speaking baby words. Maria cried, and Ari comforted her.

"Can we come every year on this date?" she asked.

"No matter what is going on, I want us to spend time with our son on his birthday."

"Of course we will," he said. "Of course."

Maria flew to New York two weeks before the Madison Square Garden concert and checked into a suite Ari kept at the Pierre Hotel, overlooking Central Park. She shopped for a new gown, choosing a full-skirted, metallic-sheened one that seemed sufficiently ostentatious for a president's birthday.

Ten days before the concert, her manager called the suite.

"I'm sorry to be the bearer of bad news," he told Maria, "but it seems your mother is in Roosevelt Hospital after trying to kill herself. I've got the hospital number for you."

Maria was stunned. Suicide? That didn't sound like Evangelia's style, unless it was attention-seeking behavior or a new bid to get money from Maria, who she must have realized was in New York.

She wrote down the number, then phoned Ari. "I'd better call," she told him, a sudden heaviness descending.

"Let me do it," he offered. "I don't want her upsetting you."

She shook her head. "I should make the call. But I won't talk to her directly."

"Be sure you don't," he cautioned.

She was put through to a doctor, who explained that her mother had taken an overdose of sleeping pills.

"She keeps asking for you," the doctor said. "She's not entirely coherent, though. Sometimes she claims that men have threatened to kill her if she contacts you."

"That's odd." Maria frowned. "Could the overdose have caused delusions?"

"It's hard to say, but she will need extended psychiatric care as she recovers."

"Is my father with her?" She couldn't remember when she'd last heard from him.

"She says your father has gone back to Athens. I don't know if that's true, but she certainly hasn't had any visitors since she's been here."

Maria was surprised to hear her father was in Athens. Did that mean his marriage was finally over, or was it a temporary break? Eleven years had gone by since she'd last seen Evangelia, years in which the bitter *Time* magazine article had appeared and her mother's book about her had been published. The thought of a reunion filled her with dread. "Is she going to pull through?" she asked.

"She's responding to treatment," the doctor said, "but she is very weak. She left a note addressed to you. I don't know if you would like me to forward it?"

Maria shuddered. "Do you have it there? What does it say?"

Almost immediately she regretted asking as the doctor opened the note and read: "I am sure you will shed no tears for the woman who gave you life and sacrificed her own so that you might one day be famous . . ." It went on in the same vein and finished by saying that she would only forgive Maria if she came to see her "dying mother."

"Can I tell her you will visit?" the doctor asked.

"I don't know. I'll have to think about it." She thought she had grown used to the ways her mother tried to manipulate her emotions, making her feel guilty for being "the bad daughter," but the letter still stung.

"Do you have a message for her?" he persisted.

"No. No message."

"I have to ask . . . I'm afraid there's the small matter of her medical bills. She told us you would pay them."

Maria sighed out loud. "That figures. Send them addressed to me at the Pierre Hotel." She hung up and called Ari.

"Don't visit," he advised. "Remember how much her book upset you. Remember this is the woman who forced you to date German soldiers in wartime."

An image came into Maria's mind of the cold expression on Evangelia's face when she thought her daughter had been raped and all she cared about was the money.

"But she's on her own and it sounds as though she is going senile." The old emotions bubbled to the surface: the little girl who was desperate for her mother's love but could never win it; the feeling that she was unlovable.

"What would it achieve?" Ari persisted. "If you visit, she will be back in your life and she will have more ammunition to sell stories to the press, calling you a whore and whatever else."

Maria pursed her lips. "But I know the way her mind works. If I don't visit, she'll tell journalists I wouldn't even come to her bedside when she was dying. She's already told the hospital to send me her medical bills."

"We can counter that if we get in first. Your manager can release a statement saying that despite your mother's vile treatment of you, and the awful book she wrote, you telephoned as soon as you heard of her suicide attempt and have agreed to cover her medical bills. It will make a positive story for a change. Remind me: Which hospital is it?"

Maria told him. He was right: she wouldn't visit, because she couldn't let Evangelia back into her life. She was capable of doing too much harm.

On May 19, the performers gathered backstage, sequins sparkling and sticky clouds of hairspray wafting from every dressing room. Maria nodded in greeting to the familiar faces from stage and screen but did not stop to chat, because she didn't want to tire her voice. She went through her normal warm-up routines, although the two arias she was singing were undemanding compared to a full operatic production.

When her cue came, she walked onstage, right foot first. As she waited for the orchestra to play the jaunty opening bars of "Habanera," she smiled mischievously at the audience, inhabiting the role of Carmen, the fiery gypsy who broke men's hearts. Her voice was strong and dark as she launched into the opening bars: "Love is a rebellious bird that nobody can tame . . ."

The applause after her second number was uproarious, although she did not for one moment suppose this crowd was opera lovers. President Kennedy was sitting in the first row, just beyond the orchestra, but she was disappointed not to spot Mrs. Kennedy by his side. She was curious about the chic First Lady.

As she walked back to her dressing room, she bumped into the unforgettable vision of Marilyn Monroe, with her iconic bleached hair, wearing a gown so revealing that Maria couldn't think where to look. It was made of flesh-colored fabric studded with rhinestones and was completely molded to her curvaceous figure, making it clear she was not wearing a scrap of underwear.

Without introducing herself, Marilyn put a hand on Maria's arm, saying, "I wish I could sing like you. I'm on later and I'm terribly nervous." She was blinking rapidly, her lips quivering and her pupils huge.

"No one expects you to be note-perfect. I'm sure you'll bring your many other talents to the performance." Maria smiled, so it didn't sound like a criticism.

"Is there nothing you can suggest? I *have* to do a great job."

She looked so scared that Maria decided to demonstrate an exercise to calm her nerves. "Blow out the air to empty your lungs completely," she instructed, and did it herself. "Can you feel the diaphragm muscle engage?" She placed her hand on top of her own diaphragm.

Marilyn tried, pouting her lips and blowing hard.

"Now breathe in fully," Maria said. "Try to sing from there and not from your throat. You'll find you have more breath."

Marilyn stood, practicing intently, in and out. She smelled as if she hadn't bathed that day. It wasn't an unpleasant odor, but it was intimate, somehow conveying more than Maria wanted to know.

She excused herself to return to her dressing room

and freshen up, but she couldn't resist hovering in the wings when Marilyn was due to take the stage for the finale. She looked terrified in the moments before she stepped out, then in a split second her posture straightened, her expression changed, and she became the star everyone knew. Maria recognized the transformation: she did the same herself, going from simple Maria to La Callas.

She watched as Marilyn sang "Happy Birthday"—whispering entirely from her throat, barely singing at all. The suggestive hip movements, the heavy breathing, and the pouting lips were excruciating. Maria glanced around at the other performers who were watching from the wings: many were openmouthed.

"How was I?" Marilyn whispered as she tottered off the stage, smelling more strongly than before.

"Extraordinary," Maria told her. "The audience loved you."

"Do you think the president liked it?" she asked, lip quivering, and Maria assured her that he must have.

At the after-show party, President Kennedy came to thank Maria in person.

"I was awestruck by your performance, Mrs. Callos," he said, mispronouncing her surname. "My wife is a big fan and plays your recordings at home, so I knew your voice, but I'm delighted to finally hear you in person."

"Is your wife here tonight?" Maria asked, glancing over his shoulder. Perhaps she had been sitting elsewhere in the auditorium.

"No, she had a prior commitment. Something to do with horses, I believe. I often think she prefers horses to human beings. But she will be very jealous when she hears that I have met you. It's a great honor that you flew all the way from Europe."

"My goodness, the honor is all mine," she replied. "I hope you've had a wonderful birthday." She noticed a smear of beige makeup on his shirt collar and wondered how it got there.

"How could I do otherwise with so many beautiful women singing for me?" He grinned, his impossibly white teeth gleaming as he gestured around the room. "Look at this crowd: I'm completely starstruck. It's so much *fun* being president. I love that I can pick up the phone and call anyone in the world and they take my calls."

"I rather imagine everyone here is starstruck on meeting you," she replied.

"You're very kind. I hope we can tempt you to come to one of our state dinners in the White House? My wife loves to bring together the leading lights of the arts."

"It would be my pleasure," she said, meaning it.

"I'll pass that on. It might win me a marital merit badge."

"Are you in need of one?" Maria teased.

"Always. You women are terribly difficult to please."

He didn't linger for long, because there were many other guests to talk to, but Maria had already decided she liked him. He was warm and personable.

As he moved on, she glanced across the room and saw that Marilyn's puppy eyes never once left the president. It looked as if she had an overwhelming crush. Maria wondered if they had met before, or if Marilyn was simply overcome with awe.

When she got back to the hotel, she called Ari, even though it was the middle of the night in Europe. He'd made her promise she would.

"You were right about Kennedy being charismatic," she said. "I think Miss Monroe has fallen under his spell. She only had eyes for him."

"Yes, she's sleeping with him," Ari said matter-of-factly. "Bobby too. They pass her between them."

"What? Surely not!" Maria was astounded. "What makes you say that?"

"My publicist knows everything that happens in Hollywood, and he reports back to me. Information is useful, especially when it concerns the president of a country that impounded my ships."

"I hope you're not going to use the information. Poor Marilyn is the victim in all of this." She remembered reading in the papers that Marilyn was single again after her unlikely marriage to playwright Arthur Miller had broken down.

"It's an insurance policy," he said. "That's all. Was Mrs. Kennedy there?"

"No, I hear she had a prior commitment with some horses."

Ari laughed: "Yeah, I bet she did!"

After they hung up, Maria couldn't sleep, going over the events of the evening in her head and worrying about poor, vulnerable, childlike Marilyn Monroe. She felt protective toward her.

Chapter 30

Virginia
May 19, 1962

Jackie sat down to watch Jack's birthday gala on television. She was spending the weekend at Glen Ora, an estate they rented in Virginia, where she'd been attending the Loudoun County Horse Show. She'd decided to go there in protest after she heard Marilyn Monroe was included in the lineup. It was idiotic of Jack to invite a woman whose name was synonymous with sex. What's more, Jackie had heard that Marilyn was obsessed with her husband; Arthur Miller had told her as much when he'd dined at the White House ten days earlier. She was determined not to be photographed alongside, or even in the same room as, that woman.

As she watched the show's finale, with Marilyn breathing the words "Happy birthday, Mr. President" and writhing as though making love to him, Jackie felt acid flood her throat. Did Jack think the public was stupid? How could he allow such disrespect toward her? Fierce rage took hold. She wanted to slap him, scream at him, tear his hair. She clenched her fists hard.

Was he sleeping with Marilyn? On the evidence, it looked likely. And if he wasn't before, she was sure he would after watching that performance. He never could resist flattery from a pretty girl. But Marilyn was exactly the type who would run to the press with her story when he cooled things off. Had Jack considered that?

Every time Jackie reckoned she could deal with his infidelities, another one came along that was worse than the last. She, Caroline, and John Junior were due to drive back to Washington the following day, but she decided they would stay in Virginia for another few days, and she'd not be available to take Jack's calls either. It was perfect weather for riding. She would remain there until she had calmed down enough to speak civilly to him, without unleashing her rage. That way, they could maintain the façade on which their marriage depended.

Less than a month later, Jackie answered the telephone in the Residence one afternoon to hear the operator announce, "Mrs. Kennedy, I have Marilyn Monroe on the phone for you."

It caught Jackie unawares, although part of her wasn't surprised. "Put the call through to my bedroom," she instructed.

She fetched her cigarettes, then sat in an armchair and picked up the receiver.

"This is Mrs. Kennedy speaking," she said.

"Is it really you?" The breathy voice was unmistakable. "I wasn't sure if you would talk to me." She was slurring the words, as if she were drunk or doped up.

"How can I help you, Miss Monroe?" Jackie asked, then lit an L&M and inhaled, feeling concerned. By all accounts, the actress was volatile and unpredictable. Was she going to confess to an affair with Jack? If so, how should she respond?

"I just . . . I wanted to ask what it's like living in the White House. Is it very beautiful?"

Jackie blew out smoke. "The original building is lovely but it has been much added to over the years, with some extensions more elegant than others. But I can't imagine you called me to discuss architecture."

"No, you're right . . . I wanted to ask . . . is it nice being the president's wife?"

Jackie squinted against the smoke. Where was this

conversation going? "Your freedom is limited when you are in the public eye—but I imagine you know all about that."

"You're so glamorous!" Marilyn exclaimed. "I loved it on your trip to France when Jack said, 'I am the man who accompanied Jacqueline Kennedy to Paris.' Wasn't that gallant?"

Jackie remembered it well. He had used it to begin his speech at the Palais de Chaillot and had been rewarded with universal laughter. "It was humorous," she replied. "A joke."

"Was it?" Marilyn sounded crestfallen. Her mood switched from moment to moment, making it impossible for Jackie to judge the purpose of the call. And then it came. "Do you think you will ever divorce him?" Marilyn asked, plaintive now. "He must be a terrible husband."

Jackie gave a short laugh. "Why? Would you like to take my place?"

There was silence on the other end of the line, then a hiccup.

"You'd be welcome to all the problems that come with being First Lady," Jackie continued. "But the public would be very disappointed if you retired from movies."

There was a rustling sound, as if Marilyn was moving some papers and muttering to herself. Jackie made out the words "should never have called," and suddenly the line went dead. Marilyn had hung up.

Jackie was alarmed. Marilyn was either a drunk or she was unhinged. Deep in thought, she ground out her cigarette. She had to tell someone about this call, but if she confronted Jack she would be forced to look into his eyes while he lied to the back teeth about their relationship. Instead she walked down to Bobby's office in the West Wing and tapped on the door.

He looked up from some paperwork and gave her a bright smile. "Come in. Sit down. Distract me! This is a day of abject tedium."

"I won't stop," Jackie said, "but I thought you should know that I just took a call from Marilyn Monroe. She wanted to ask if I was considering divorcing Jack. She's a liability, Bobby. I don't know what he was thinking of, having her perform at that gala."

Bobby's face was inscrutable. "I'm sorry she bothered you. I'll ask the operators not to put through her calls."

"It's not *that* I'm worried about. I can deal with her. But what if she starts talking to the press?" She considered sitting down but decided against it. Better to keep it brief. "Have you met her? What's your opinion?"

There was a flicker of a twitch of Bobby's upper lip, and Jackie knew not just that he had met her, but that he was already doing his best to protect Jack, because protection was sorely needed. "I'll deal with it," he said.

"Thank you. I'll leave you to your tedium." She turned and swept back toward the Residence, arms swinging and lips pursed. She never swore out loud, but some choice curse words took shape in her head as she contemplated the effect that Jack's "trysts" with Miss Monroe could have on his legacy—and, by extension, hers.

Jackie and the children were in New York on August 5, getting ready to fly to Italy for a vacation with Lee, Stas, and their two children, Anthony and baby Tina. Immediately after breakfast, Bobby rang to tell her that Marilyn Monroe had been found dead at her Brentwood home.

"It's a probable suicide," he said. "There were empty pill bottles strewn around. You may be asked to comment, so have something ready."

Jackie was shaken but, after a moment's reflection, not surprised. "That poor woman! She was clearly fragile. Why did no one help her?"

"She had a therapist," Bobby said. "It seems there was a history of overdoses."

"If that's the case, 'people' should have been more careful around her," Jackie remarked, her voice steely.

As she read the press coverage the next morning, she felt irritated with the so-called friends who were rushing to sell their stories, grabbing a quick buck before Marilyn was even buried, but most of all she felt angry with Jack. He had given a vulnerable young woman hope, and that was unforgivable. She was glad to be absent from the White House so she did not have to discuss it with him face-to-face.

When a journalist spotted her at the airport and asked what she thought about Marilyn's death, she replied, "I'm sure her name will live on."

Lee was curious, asking outright, "Do you think Jack ever slept with Marilyn? I wondered, after that outrageous birthday gala performance."

"Of course he didn't!" Jackie snapped, closing the subject with her icy tone. Lee was the last person she would discuss it with. But there was no doubt in her mind that he had.

Their marriage went in cycles, she mused. It seemed she was either furiously angry and barely speaking to him, or she was madly in love with him, with no calm, in-between times. It was exhausting. She was sure he didn't experience the roller coaster of emotions that she did; he got on with the daily life of being a president, oblivious to her moods.

Their vacation villa in Ravello was beautiful. Every morning she climbed down a steep cliff path to swim off the rocks in the clear, azure water. In the afternoons she read one of the tottering pile of books she'd brought with her and played with the children in their villa's pool; then they dined out in local trattorias in the evenings. One afternoon they were invited onto Fiat car manufacturer Gianni Agnelli's yacht, and she glanced at the photographers snapping them as they boarded, worrying about how it would play in the American press. Then she shrugged: her children had a right to a vacation, no matter who their daddy was. *She* had a right.

By the end of the month, her rage at Jack had subsided and she began to miss him. They'd spoken on the phone several times, but the calls had been practical rather than romantic. Lee and Stas were usually within earshot, and Jackie hadn't been in the mood for sweet talk.

After they were driven home from the airport in D.C., she headed straight to the Oval Office, but Jack's secretary told her he was in conference and couldn't be disturbed. He didn't come to the Residence for dinner, and it was ten at night before he appeared, looking haggard.

"What's up, bunny?" Jackie asked, embracing him. "You look as if you've been through the wars."

He shook his head. "I can't tell you. But it's not good. I've got my hands full."

She didn't press him when he refused to talk about the job. Instead she relayed some anecdotes from their vacation—Caroline's first attempts at waterskiing, John's funny mispronounced words—but could tell he wasn't listening.

It was only over the next few weeks that Jackie heard from other White House staffers that Soviet nuclear missiles had been photographed on Cuba, just ninety miles off the Florida coast. She was horrified. When she'd sat next to Khrushchev at dinner in Paris, he'd been full of wisecracks, a regular Abbott-and-Costello type; he had even sent a puppy as a gift for her children, after they shared a joke about Laika, the space dog. Yet now it looked as if he were willing to plunge the world into a nuclear war that could wipe out a third of the human race.

The physical toll on Jack was soon apparent. A furrow was etched between his brows as if with a chisel, and the bags under his eyes grew heavier, almost folding over on themselves. His back was flaring up, and he swallowed handfuls of painkillers and God only knew what else. When he got to the Residence in the evening, he didn't want to discuss the crisis. Jackie mixed him a stiff daiquiri and urged him to relax, but he was often interrupted by phone calls till the early hours. She was weighed down by anxiety but hid it, so as not to spread alarm to the staff and the children.

As she watched Jack's October 22 television address to the American people, the weight grew heavier. "Our goal is not the victory of might, but the vindication of right," he said, after listing all the countries that the Cuban missiles could strike in an act of "sudden mass destruction." He announced an immediate blockade of Cuba to prevent any more missiles reaching the island, and they waited to see how Khrushchev would respond.

"Maybe you should take the children to Europe," he suggested that night. "Washington is likely to be targeted in a first strike."

"We're not leaving you," she insisted, although her throat was so tight with nerves it was as if a fist were gripping it.

"But there's only limited space in the White House bomb shelter and so many folk to fit," he argued.

Jackie was adamant. "I'd rather die here with you than live without you. I'm staying, and that's that."

He accepted her decision, and didn't ask again. She had no regrets, but she wished she could help in some way other than mixing daiquiris and offering back rubs.

Her feet often led her to the West Wing, where she hoped to hear the latest developments from staffers. Everyone was in a hurry, few had time to stop, but she learned about the challenge to the American blockade on October 25, about the American pilot who went missing over Soviet airspace and was only rescued in the nick of time, of Khrushchev's offer on the twenty-seventh to remove his missiles from Cuba if America removed theirs from Turkey. . . . It was an impossible dilemma for Jack, because America could not be seen to back down in the face of threats. She knew he was seeking former president Eisenhower's advice by telephone, and she was glad of that; he needed all the wise counsel he could get if he was to resolve this without starting the war that could end all wars.

On the twenty-eighth, agreement was reached but still there was much that could go wrong. "Reds Back Down on Cuba" read the headlines, but Jackie knew it wasn't that simple. The agreement still had to be implemented. As far as the rest of the world was concerned, the missile crisis lasted thirteen days. For Jack—and for her—the pressure went on a lot longer.

Many nights during that period Jackie suffered from

insomnia, and she raised herself on one elbow to watch Jack sleep. He always lay on his side, his cheek sagging into the pillow. He made no sound, no grunts or snores, and his expression was peaceful. She marveled that he could sleep so soundly when the world had come within a hairsbreadth of nuclear war on his watch, and she prayed he would always have that ability.

From feeling so upset with him over Marilyn Monroe, she'd turned 180 degrees to feeling freshly in love with him again.

Chapter 31

Athens, Greece
Spring 1963

Shortly after her mother's suicide attempt, Maria tracked down her father through relatives in Athens and sent him a note, asking if he would like to meet for lunch. She wanted to find out why her parents were no longer living together, and perhaps discover what had driven her mother to take such a drastic step, but at the same time she was apprehensive about where any reunion might lead. She'd managed just fine without her family all these years.

George Callas was a quiet-spoken man, whose life had not been a happy one. Never the successful businessman whom Evangelia had wished for in a husband, he had teetered on the edge of bankruptcy several times.

He wrote back to Maria, saying he would be happy

to have lunch with her and asking if he could bring her sister, Jacinthy, as well.

Maria was curious to see Jacinthy. They'd never been close—their seven-year age difference, combined with their mother's blatant favoritism, had seen to that—but they had shared a childhood, and that had to mean something.

Maria's busy schedule meant it wasn't possible to meet them until early in 1963; she chose Vassilenas, an old restaurant with a pretty rooftop garden near the port of Piraeus. When a waiter showed Maria to the table, Jacinthy rose to greet her. Slim and pretty, with scarcely a wrinkle, her hair expensively colored and set in a shoulder-length style, she looked every bit the upper-class Athens socialite. When they embraced, Maria felt a warmth from her sister that surprised her. Then she hugged her father. He had aged: nothing she could put her finger on, but his face had drooped like melted candlewax and his hair was thinner. She felt a wave of compassion.

Maria asked where both were living and was pleased to hear they were not far from each other in the city. Her father explained that he was separated from her mother, although not divorced. Jacinthy had been living with a wealthy shipowner's son, Milton Embiricos, since before the war. They had never married because of his family's objections to the match but had been lovers for over two decades, until he had died of cancer the previous year.

"I hope his family are treating you with the respect due to his widow," Maria said, after expressing her condolences.

"Hardly." She glanced off into the distance, and Maria could tell it was a sore subject that she did not want to discuss. "How about you? Do you still live in Milan?"

"I'm selling my house there, since I scarcely use it, and renting an apartment in Paris." Maria didn't add that her Paris apartment was around the corner from Ari's. "But we spend most of the summer on Ari's yacht, the *Christina*."

"Would you not consider returning to Athens?" her father asked.

Maria shook her head. At the end of the war, thanks to her mother's forcing her to date the enemy, the Conservatoire had sacked her. She worried that there were Athenians with long memories who still thought of her as a collaborator. It had colored her attitude to the city.

"Ari has a villa in Glyfada where we stay if we're in town," she said. "And he is buying the Ionian island of Skorpios. We want to create our dream home there."

It felt good to say that. After almost four years together, she felt secure in the relationship, happy to plan a future, and still hopeful that fertility treatments would one day result in the longed-for baby, although so far there was no sign. Every month she felt downcast when the bleeding started. She glanced at Jacinthy and wondered if she had wanted children. They weren't the kind of questions she could ask when they hadn't seen each other in—what was it?—almost eighteen years.

The conversation continued, polite and general. They commented on the food, which was top-notch. They talked of their plans for the remainder of the year. Maria told them of the singing engagements she had committed to, in Germany, London, Copenhagen, and Paris. None of them mentioned Evangelia until after the plates had been cleared, when Maria asked her father whether she had fully recovered from her suicide attempt.

Jacinthy and her father looked at each other, and her father spoke. "To be frank, I don't know. She is furious with me for leaving New York, so her letters at the moment are not very civil."

"I don't blame you for leaving," Maria said. "No one could. Her suicide note says it was my fault for being such a terrible daughter, but I don't accept that. She's just an impossible woman."

"I know what you went through with her," Jacinthy

said, "and I have never blamed you for cutting her out of your life. I still correspond with her, but I sometimes wish I had your courage. She can be vile."

"I'm paying for her psychiatric treatment and I hope she's getting the help she needs. But I don't hold out any hope for a personality transplant." Maria wondered what her mother was living on, but assumed her father must be sending an allowance.

The waiter brought the bill and Maria paid, then asked if they would like to come for coffee on the *Christina*. They glanced at each other before agreeing. People were always curious to meet Ari.

There was no missing the *Christina*, which was so long it took up an entire pontoon by itself. When they approached, Ari came to the top of the gangplank to greet them. First he backslapped her father in Greek fashion, then he greeted Jacinthy, kissing her hand. A bottle of champagne was opened, toasts were proposed, and Ari played the convivial host meeting his in-laws.

Maria watched them chatting, feeling strangely detached. Her father and Jacinthy were like acquaintances from a distant past. She was happy that Ari welcomed them as if they were close family, but it wasn't true. They were all acting a part.

When they rose to leave an hour later, promises were made about keeping in touch, about having lunch again soon, but Maria knew she would not be in a rush to arrange the next meeting. She had nothing in common with them anymore. It made her feel a little melancholy.

"What did you think of them?" she asked Ari. She always enjoyed hearing his views on people they met.

He considered before he spoke. "Your father is a decent man to whom life has dealt an unfair hand. And Jacinthy? She seemed guarded. You told me you were jealous of her as a child, but now it appears the shoe is on the other foot. You are far more beautiful, and far more successful, and I could see her swallowing that knowledge with every sip of champagne."

"Really? You think she is jealous of me?"

"Of course she is." Ari joked, "She must be mad with jealousy that you have me as your lover."

Maria laughed and mock-punched his arm. "Isn't it strange that my sister and I are both religious women who ended up living with men to whom we are not married? She waited two whole decades for a ring on her finger and never got one. I'm giving you fair warning that I don't have her patience."

Marriage was a subject that came up from time to time, but it never seemed pressing. Ari was divorced from Tina, and she had immediately remarried an English aristocrat, but Maria had reached a stalemate in her attempts to divorce Battista. Their legal separation had been agreed at a court in Brescia, but that settled only their estate; it didn't mean she could remarry. If she could have claimed that he had been unfaithful, she could have divorced him in America on those grounds, but she was sure he had never strayed. She could have asked for a divorce on the grounds of "emotional cruelty" but she would have struggled to provide evidence in court. It would have been embarrassing and untrue. And neither reason would be accepted by the Orthodox Church, so if she and Ari were to wed it would still not be recognized where it mattered to her the most.

"Are we not happy as we are?" he asked, reaching out to take her hand, pulling gently on her fingers.

"We are." She smiled. "But if I get pregnant, I want us to be married before the child is born. Take note."

"Duly noted," he said; then his expression changed. "I wish we could get Alexander to be more civil to you. I'm sure his mother is behind the rudeness. When he grows up, he will understand that love is complicated."

Christina had accepted her presence, and even let Maria paint her nails and style her hair, but Alexander remained hostile. He refused point-blank to sit down for dinner at the same table as Maria, and when his father was out of earshot he called her *Kolou,* meaning "big ass." It was only with difficulty that she refrained from slapping him.

"Perhaps it's time for you to be stricter with him," Maria ventured. "He is fifteen—old enough to know better. If you spent a tenth of the time explaining our relationship to him as you do discussing the finer points of the shipping business, he would have accepted me."

Ari shrugged. "It's difficult for men to discuss such things. If we leave it, he will come round eventually."

Maria didn't agree but felt she was on shaky ground telling him how to behave with his own children. She wasn't an official stepmother, just their father's mistress.

"There's something I wanted to ask you," she said. "Have you been intercepting letters from my mother? She is living alone in New York so I'm astonished her demands for money have not resumed. Even now I've left Milan, it's not hard to reach me. All she needs to do is read the papers."

Ari looked her straight in the eye as he replied: "I'm not aware of any letters, my love. Forget about her. She's not your problem anymore."

Chapter 32

The Mediterranean
Spring 1963

Maria loved playing hostess on the *Christina*. She discussed menus with the chefs, chose flower arrangements, and, if guests were staying overnight, ensured their suites were prepared with every comfort. She had entertained all of Ari's closest friends: Prince Rainier and Princess Grace; Costa Gratsos and his wife, Anastasia; business associate Panaghis Vergottis; Baron van Zuylen and his wife, Maggie, a witty, warm woman of Syrian descent; Artemis and Theodore; and Stas Radziwill, a Polish prince in exile, with whom Ari enjoyed long boozy lunches at Claridge's hotel whenever he found himself in London.

Stas had married Jackie Kennedy's sister, Lee, and sometimes Maria and Ari had dinner with the Radziwills, but Maria found Lee difficult to talk to. She held her cards close to her chest and never volunteered information, meaning that conversations were hard work. Maria assumed she had to be discreet because of her famous sister and brother-in-law.

When Ari announced that he had invited the couple for a cruise in May, she made careful preparations, hoping she and Lee could at last become friends. It would make things much smoother, because their menfolk got along so well.

The Radziwills arrived at the *Christina* on a blazing hot afternoon, with porters dragging six huge leather suitcases behind them. Maria was surprised because she had thought they were staying only a few days.

Lee was wearing a chic cotton dress with a hem several inches above the knee, and her legs were slender as a foal's. Maria knew that short dresses were in vogue but would not adopt the style herself, because even after the weight loss her legs had remained sturdy and definitely not her best feature.

"Welcome aboard!" she cried, with her broadest smile.

Lee air-kissed her with a lip smile that didn't reach her eyes. Stas was more fulsome in his greeting, saying, "Thank you for arranging such glorious weather."

"Glorious? I'm *roasting* alive," Lee complained. "I simply must have a dip in the pool to cool off. Which is our cabin?"

"Let me show you," Maria said. "Have you been on the *Christina* before?"

"I came for drinks with *Ja-ackie* and *Ja-ack* a few years ago. When the Churchills were here." She had a strange mid-Atlantic accent, placing an emphasis on *ah* sounds.

"By coincidence, I received a letter from your sister yesterday," Maria told her as they walked down the main stairs to the cabins. "She wants me to sing at a White House reception for Emperor Haile Selassie of Ethiopia, but sadly I am in the recording studio on that date so won't be able to make it."

"Jackie throws the most wonderful *pa*-arties," Lee drawled. "She's a *ma*-arvelous hostess."

Maria felt as if a gauntlet had been thrown down: would her hostessing skills match up? She opened the door of the cabin and Lee swept in, surveying the room as if looking for flaws.

"Do let me know if there's anything you need," Maria urged.

"I just need a swim to cool down, then I'll be human again," Lee said. "My dress is positively *stuck* to me."

"I'll see you by the pool, in that case," Maria replied, closing the door.

When Lee emerged, she was wearing the tiniest bikini Maria had ever seen, in burnt orange with a white-and-green swirling pattern. The top was like a low-cut brassiere and the bottoms had suggestive little ties at the sides. She was even thinner than Maria had imagined, with a figure that was lithe and toned, like a teenage boy's.

Maria had never stopped feeling insecure about her appearance, despite all the compliments that Ari lavished on her. She still hated her big nose, her chunky legs, and the dark hair that sprouted in the wrong places and required strict taming. Vanity meant that she seldom wore her glasses, even though anything more than ten feet away was a blur. And she wasn't sure about the new, shorter hairstyle Ari had talked her into earlier that year; it felt less feminine than her longer tresses.

As she watched Lee execute a perfect dive into the pool, Maria tucked her sarong around her ankles, feeling elephantine. It was exactly the way she used to feel alongside Jacinthy when they were children. Strange how the ghosts of childhood insecurities lingered in adult life.

After Lee emerged from the pool, hair sleek as an otter's, she spread her towel on a sunbed and lay on her back, sunglasses masking her face.

A steward approached to ask, "Would you like a drink, ma'am?" and she glowered at him.

"I am a princess and expect to be addressed as such."

"My apologies, Your Highness." He bowed.

"I'll have a vodka and lime."

The steward left to get the drink and Maria came to sit by Lee, meaning to start a conversation.

"What ages are your children now?" she began, reasoning that all mothers liked to talk about their children.

Lee paused before replying, as if trying to remember. "Anthony is three and Tina two."

"I love toddlers! They're so cute," Maria said. "You should have brought them with you." She wondered how Lee could leave them. If she had children, she would never have gone anywhere without them.

As if sensing criticism, Lee replied, "Everyone needs a break from their kids. They drive you insane otherwise."

Maria gave a little laugh, assuming she was joking, but Lee's expression behind the glasses was stony. "You've lived in London for a while, I believe," Maria persevered. "Do you like the city? Is it a good place to raise children?"

"Of course it is. Otherwise we would move." Lee turned to lie facedown, reaching behind her to unfasten her bikini top. Maria caught a glimpse of the side of her left breast.

She decided to give up. Striving to make conversation was clearly fruitless. Instead she lay back and closed her eyes. Lee did not attempt any further communication, so after a while Maria rose to see what the men were doing.

"Do you find Lee rude, or is it just me?" she asked Ari in their suite later.

"She's reserved," he said. "It takes her awhile to relax with new people."

"She's never asked a single question about me. I think she reckons I'm not grand enough to merit her acquaintance."

Ari chuckled. "I'm the son of a tobacco importer. That's hardly grand, yet she's perfectly friendly to me."

"I'm afraid it's nothing to do with class in your case, darling. You can bet your bottom dollar she wouldn't give you the time of day if it weren't for the size of your bank balance."

"I'm well aware of that, my love. Of all my friends, only you and Costa would stand by me if I was broke."

Over cocktails that evening, Maria tried once more to befriend Lee but her questions were met with monosyllabic answers that verged on rudeness. Her efforts weren't helped by the fact that Lee and Stas were big drinkers and Ari matched them, glass for glass, while Maria couldn't keep up. She had a low tolerance for alcohol at the best of times, and it made her nauseated if she drank more than a couple of glasses of wine while taking the fertility drugs. It meant she felt excluded when they laughed themselves silly at jokes that were not remotely funny, or played card games in which the loser had to down a shot of vodka, but that soon became the evening routine.

After the Radziwills had been on board for a week, Maria had to fly to Germany to sing three concerts, followed by one in London and another in Paris. While packing, she couldn't find her sleeping pills and opened one of Ari's drawers to see if they had been put there by accident. Inside she saw a scarlet-and-gold Cartier jewelry box and couldn't resist opening it. There was a pretty diamond bangle nestling on red velvet inside, and a note in Ari's handwriting that read, "To my dearest, my sweetest love."

Maria smiled. He must be planning to give it to her for her name day in August. She would have to pretend to be surprised.

When Maria arrived back at the *Christina* in early June, Ari was on the telephone, ensconced in a complex financial discussion with some unknown colleague. She kissed him on the cheek and he held up a finger to indicate that he had to finish the call.

She wandered down to her cabin to change, joyful to be there again with a whole summer of relaxation stretching in front of her, apart from a Copenhagen concert in early July, which she needn't think about yet. She took off her traveling clothes and tied a sarong over her favorite swimsuit, then wandered along the corridors to Ari's suite. The door was open and she went inside and lay on his bed. An idea came to her: it always aroused him if she reclined naked, adorned in jewelry that he had bought her. Perhaps she would surprise him by donning some jewels and waiting for him to come and find her.

She sat up, planning to go to the safe to retrieve a necklace and some bracelets—perhaps the emerald-and-diamond ones—and it was then she saw the merest scrap of fabric wedged in a tight space between the edge of the bed and the wall, barely visible. She broke a fingernail prizing it out. The fabric was orange, with a green-and-white pattern. Maria instantly recognized a tie from Lee's bikini bottoms.

Cold fingers gripped her heart, followed by a wave of acid rage. "*Ari-sto!*" she screamed, so loudly that she strained her throat.

She was trembling as she charged up to the boat deck, clutching the piece of fabric. He was still on the phone and looked puzzled at her approach. A beer sat on a nearby table and she picked it up and hurled it at his head, glass and all.

"Holy Christo!" he exclaimed, swerving to avoid it. "I'll call you back," he said into the receiver, just as Maria launched herself at him, punching him in the chest. "What is it? Stop, damn you!" He held up his arms to shield his face.

"You bastard! I trusted you!" Maria kicked his shin with her bare foot, hurting her toe, then swung at his head with her fist.

"What on earth are you talking about?" he demanded, grabbing her wrists and restraining her.

Maria sank her teeth into his forearm, causing him to yelp and leap backward. "This!" She flung the fabric tie at him.

He looked bemused. "What is it?"

"Part of Lee's bikini. It was in your bedroom. Down the side of your bed. The bed where you and I make love. I *hate* you for this, Ari. I will never forgive you." Tears were coming but she refused to give in to them. She needed him to feel the force of her rage.

"Stop, Maria. There must be some mistake. I have no idea how it got there. None." He held out his hands, all wounded innocence.

She paused, scrutinizing him. "You're lying."

"I swear it's true. I wouldn't lie to you." He took off his sunglasses so she could see into his eyes.

"How could the tie of Lee's bikini get down the side of your bed? There's no other explanation."

He shrugged, seeming mystified. "Maybe one of the maids dropped it. Perhaps it got caught up in the sheets at the laundry. Please, darling. I hate to see this jealous side. It's not worthy of you."

Am I going mad? Maria wondered. But she could feel the truth in her heart. That's why Lee wouldn't be friends with her—because she had decided to seduce Ari. Maybe they had already slept together before the cruise. Ari had invited Stas to become a director of Olympic Airways some months earlier. Was that a quid pro quo for sleeping with his wife?

"How long has it been going on?" she demanded. "Weeks? Months?"

"Nothing is going on," he insisted. Reassured that her rage had subsided a little, he stepped forward and wrapped his arms around her. "Please don't be jealous. You've got the wrong end of the stick. These past three weeks, I have been lonely in my bed and pining for you. Here." He guided her hand to a swelling in his shorts. "All this passion has made me want you, badly. Let's go to bed."

Maria allowed him to lead her down to his cabin. She was still trembling with fury, but lust took over and the sex was wild and violent. She scratched his back, leaving long bloody trails, and bit him till he yelled for her to stop; he pushed inside her hard, forcing her legs over her shoulders so he could dominate entirely.

Afterward, as she lay with her head on his chest, both of them slick with sweat because they had not stopped to switch on the air conditioner, reality engulfed her once more.

"I thought you loved me as much as I loved you," she said, in a voice that was small and sad. "But you don't. It would never occur to me to be unfaithful to you. If any man tried to seduce me I would tell him not to be so ridiculous. But I left you here with a rude, haughty woman who happens to have a famous sister, and you couldn't resist. I'm disappointed in you. Disappointed and deeply hurt."

Ari was quiet at that; then he spoke softly. "You have to believe me that it meant nothing."

"It means everything to me."

"The last thing I wanted was to hurt you." He stroked her hair.

"I'm sure that's true. You hoped I would never find out." Her heart ached, as if it had been punched. "How many times did it happen?"

"Once. Only once," he said quickly. "She appeared at my door in that bikini and threw herself at me. I was weak, and I'm sorry. Believe me, it will never happen again."

Maria nodded, then peeled herself away from him and rose. "I need a drink," she said. "And some time on my own. I'll see you at dinner."

She called for a glass of champagne, then went to her cabin and closed the door, sitting down in an armchair and taking a sip. When she thought of the effort she had put into entertaining Lee and Stas on the *Christina,* she was infuriated by Lee's betrayal. Did she hope to lure him away? What did Stas think of it all? But most of all, how could Ari do that? She couldn't bear to think of him touching that bony body, so tiny and birdlike compared to hers.

And then she realized that she had betrayed Tina in the same way. Even though Ari's first marriage had grown cold, she should never have slept with him while they were both married to other people. It had been wrong of her.

He was in the wrong too—of course he was—but she had no choice but to forgive him. He was her entire life. She couldn't imagine being without him. So she would forgive—but she would never forget. And she would never leave him alone with Lee again. Not ever.

Chapter 33

Squaw Island, Massachusetts
Early August 1963

Jackie lay on a lounge chair outside the weatherboard house they had rented on Squaw Island, so heavily pregnant that she had trouble hauling herself to her feet when she needed to go to the bathroom—as she often did. She'd been staying there with the children right through June and July—swimming, catching up on the latest novels, painting watercolors, and thinking. Jack had gone on an official trip to Europe—back to his family's roots in Ireland, then via London to the divided city of Berlin—and Lee was accompanying him.

It had been his suggestion. Drew Pearson, a *Washington Post* journalist, had hinted that Lee might be having an affair with Aristotle Onassis, and Jack wanted to find out if it was true. If so, it could be hugely embarrassing for him politically. Jackie had gone to great lengths to persuade the Vatican to annul Lee's first marriage so that she could marry Stas in the Catholic Church. If they now divorced, it would make them both look bad—and, in the worst-case scenario, Jack could end up being brother-in-law to the controversial Greek tycoon.

"I don't believe it," Jackie said straightaway. "She's happy with Stas! Onassis is short and hairy and not at all her type."

"Don't forget how much Lee likes money," Jack reminded her. "It's the great aphrodisiac."

"Stas is an old friend of Onassis," Jackie said firmly. "If she was going to stray, she wouldn't do it with his friend."

"I called Drew Pearson and he says they were all over each other at the opening-night party for the Hilton Hotel in Athens."

Jackie's eyebrows shot up. "Really?" She considered it, then screwed up her nose. "I'm sure he's got it wrong. Lee was probably just flirting. But go ahead and ask her yourself."

She didn't feel remotely worried about Jack and Lee traveling together. If there had ever been a moment of indiscretion between her husband and her sister, a so-called tryst, it was ancient history now.

The children were adorable that summer, just perfect. At five years old, Caroline was a strong swimmer and a keen horseback rider, who reminded Jackie of herself at that age. John was two and a chatterbox, who liked to entertain the crowd. A neighbor had some puppies, and they loved rolling around on the grass with them, squealing with laughter at their antics.

As she watched, Jackie stroked her swollen belly and wondered what this baby would be. Boy or girl? Calm and thoughtful like Caroline, or the life and soul of the party like John? Three was a lucky number. She felt very blessed with her family.

After he returned from Europe, Jack came to Squaw Island on the weekends, but every Sunday night his presidential limo swept him back to Washington, where the Oval Office awaited. His European tour had been a great success, he said. Ireland had claimed him as one of her own, with huge crowds lining the streets to watch the motorcade pass, and the speech he delivered while overlooking the Berlin Wall was hailed by the press as the strongest anti-Communist statement yet and a watershed in the Cold War between East and West.

Jack said that Lee had performed her social duties admirably, but, when asked, she had denied any affair with Onassis.

"See? I told you so," Jackie replied, and Jack grunted, unconvinced.

On Wednesday, August 7, she took the children pony riding and watched their excitement as they trotted around the paddock. She was determined that they grow up to share her love of horses. Suddenly she felt a sharp cramp in her womb and turned to grab the hand of Mrs. Shaw.

"I think that might have been a contraction. But it's six weeks early. That's too soon." She told herself that she mustn't panic. John had been early, and he'd turned out just fine. But fear consumed her as she remembered that Arabella hadn't been fine. She didn't know how she could stand it if she lost this child.

Mrs. Shaw got her to sit down on a grassy bank, just as another contraction came. Then another. They were only a couple of minutes apart.

"Call Dr. Walsh," Jackie said, extracting a card with his telephone number from her purse. "Ask him what I should do."

Mrs. Shaw ran to the farmhouse to borrow their phone, and Jackie sat, clutching her belly, waving as the children rode past, teeth gritted against the next contraction.

The nanny returned five minutes later. "He wants us

to go straight to Otis Air Force Base," she said. "He'll meet us there."

Jackie shivered, cold despite the heat of the day.

There was a hospital on the base. Dr. Walsh was already there when they drove up, and he examined her straightaway.

"Are they false contractions?" she asked.

"No. You're in labor, as you thought, so I'm going to operate without delay."

"Please get Jack. I need him." She felt shaky and tearful, and desperately in need of Jack's reassuring solidity.

"I'll send word," the doctor promised.

Mrs. Shaw said she would take the children home. Jackie overheard her promising them a trip to the beach later, and some chocolate-chip cookies after their swim. She lay back, trying to breathe calmly. Dr. Walsh had delivered John. He knew what he was doing.

When Jackie came to after the operation, Jack was at her side.

"Where's the baby?" she asked, noticing straightaway that he wasn't smiling.

"It's a boy," he said, his voice serious. "He's beauti-

ful, but he's having trouble breathing, so they're helping him out."

"How much trouble?" She bit her lip.

Jack hesitated a moment too long. "They want to
transfer him to Boston Children's Hospital. I asked
them to fetch a chaplain first so we can christen him. Is
that okay?"

"Patrick Bouvier," Jackie whispered. Names from
both sides of the family. They'd already agreed.

The christening took place as Patrick lay in an incubator at her bedside. Her arms ached to hold him, to
kiss that little face, but all she could do was stretch a
hand inside to stroke his fluffy brown hair and slip her
finger into his palm. He didn't open his eyes, although
she sensed he was awake. He looked very sick.

"You go to Boston with him," Jackie instructed.
"Patrick needs you more than I do." She knew she had
to be strong and that she had to let Jack go.

Jack looked so upset when he left that she wondered
if the doctors had told him more than they were telling her. But then, he had always been the more openly
emotional of the two of them. He got tears in his eyes
at the sight of little John throwing a baseball or when
Caroline first read a sentence to him from her school-
book. Jackie couldn't remember when she had last cried,

even in private. She kept a tight rein on her emotions. She had to.

Jack called after they arrived in Boston to say that the specialist had put Patrick in something called a hyperbaric chamber filled with oxygen, where he lay sound asleep, with drips feeding into his arms.

"He looks like a little peanut surrounded by all those machines," he told her. "Now it's just a question of keeping him stable and hoping his lungs start working by themselves."

Jackie gripped the phone. "Do they think they will? Don't leave him, Jack. I don't want him to be alone."

"There's not a lot I can do, but he's in the best of hands. The specialist is world renowned."

All the following day, Jackie lay in bed, chewed up with anxiety, waiting for Jack's calls. In the morning, he reported they were pleased with Patrick's heart function and blood pressure, but by the afternoon he said they'd had to insert a breathing tube to force air in and out of his lungs. She thought of that rosebud mouth with a rubber tube strapped into it and covered her face with her hands. Poor little mite.

Lee arrived from Europe, clutching a teddy bear she'd brought as a baby gift, and was crestfallen when she heard the news. "I'm sure he'll be fine," she soothed, unconvincingly. "Look at Tina. We didn't think she'd make it, after all those months in intensive care, but now she's full of life."

That evening Jackie couldn't sleep. She had a feeling of impending doom that nothing could shift, so at 1:00 A.M. the doctor gave her a sedative to help her get some rest.

When she awoke the following morning, leaden limbed, Dr. Walsh was sitting by the bed, and she knew before he spoke.

"He didn't make it, I'm afraid. He fought so hard, but it wasn't to be."

She clutched her throat, feeling as if there weren't enough air in the room.

"He died at four this morning. I'm so sorry. Jack is on his way."

When Jack came into the room, he was already sobbing. Jackie took his hand and pulled him toward her so that she could reach his face. She wiped his tears with her fingertips, saying, "Shush, now," as if she were comforting one of the children after a fall. He leaned his head on her shoulder, and she felt the tears soaking her nightdress. He was shaking with grief.

Jackie felt as if her jaw were locked. She should be crying too. How strange that she wasn't. She couldn't react, couldn't think straight, because none of it seemed real. It was as if it were happening to someone else entirely.

Chapter 34

Squaw Island
August 1963

J ack and Lee flew to Boston for Patrick's funeral, but Jackie was too ill to get out of bed. She still felt numb, as if she were under anesthetic and hadn't quite come around.

When she was well enough to return to the house on Squaw Island, Jack took a week off to join her. They sat watching John and Caroline play with the puppies, or paddling off the seashore that was just at the end of the garden. Jack had to stay near the house in case he was needed on the hotline, but Jackie didn't want to leave anyway. She couldn't bear to bump into anyone who might offer sympathy.

Around and around the thoughts swirled. Now she had lost two fully formed children—Arabella and Patrick—as well as the little one who never made it past the first trimester. Was it her fault? Was it because of her smoking, as Rose had rather unkindly hinted? Why was she so bad at childbearing compared to the other Kennedy women? Rose had nine, and Ethel had given birth to her eighth just a month earlier. It was as if they were taunting Jackie.

What would Patrick and Arabella have been like? What kind of lives would they have led? She wished she could believe they would find each other in heaven. That would have been comforting. But how would they even recognize each other?

Jack had to return to the White House in mid-August but Jackie stayed on as summer trailed to an end. At first she needed a wrap to sit out on the porch in the evening. Then the winds picked up, sandblasting her face when she took solitary walks along the shore. Purply gray clouds gusted in and rain came in short squalls. She couldn't face winter: the darkness, the days trapped indoors by the weather, the children getting fractious, the dark skeletal trees against a gray sky. It was too much.

And then Lee phoned one evening. "Why don't you come to Europe for a cruise on Aristotle's yacht in October?" she suggested. "It's still hot and sunny in Greece then. You'll love it."

"Weren't you just there in May?" Jackie asked, surprised.

"Yeah." Lee's tone was airy. "He's invited me again, and suggested I ask you. What do you think?"

It sounded enticing. Bright sunshine and blue skies, swimming in a warm sea . . . she had always enjoyed vacations with Lee, from the time when they spent a summer touring Europe together in 1951. They moved at the same pace, had the same interests. "I'll have to ask Jack," she said. "I'll get back to you."

"What's she doing issuing invitations in Onassis's name?" Jack responded immediately. "I told you they were having an affair."

Jackie shook her head, dismissing it, although a doubt had crept into her mind. "I could use a change of scene, Jack. Once I'm there I could assess the situation and report back."

Still Jack hesitated over the course of a week, and she knew his advisors were rallying against it. It could put him in a compromising position, raising conflict-of-interest issues. It didn't look good for Jackie to be vacationing with a man who had been charged with conspiracy to defraud the U.S. government, even though he had been found guilty only of a lesser charge. But on the other hand, he wanted to cheer her up.

"You haven't smiled since Patrick died," he told her. "You barely talk. You sit, still and inscrutable, and I can't reach you. So if this trip will help you to feel better, then you should go. But we'll send chaperones along, people who are beyond reproach. And Stas must be there too."

"Thank you," Jackie said, bowing her head. "It means a lot."

He leaned over and kissed her. "Tell Lee that if she plans to marry Onassis, there is to be no announcement till after the '64 election and he mustn't set foot in the U.S. before then. Warn her I won't be responsible for my actions if she costs me a second term."

"It won't come to that," Jackie promised. "I'll talk to her."

Chapter 35

The Mediterranean
August 1963

"I'm having dinner with Stas in Monte Carlo this evening," Ari told Maria, "and he's bringing Lee. Would you like to come?"

Maria couldn't imagine how she would cope with seeing Lee face-to-face without clawing her eyes out. "Do you have to go?" she asked.

"I'm afraid so. He's a director of my airline, and we have matters to discuss."

"In that case, I'll come." She certainly wasn't going to let him see Lee without her.

Maria dressed with care, in a new black-and-white asymmetric evening gown, which she accessorized with diamonds. They arrived early at the Hôtel de Paris and Ari ordered champagne for their table, which was on the top-floor roof terrace, with a view of the Mediterranean. It was a sultry evening, but large fans cooled the wealthy clientele.

When Lee and Stas arrived, Maria rose to greet them with cheek kisses, but, as soon as Lee sat down, Maria's eye was caught by the bracelet jangling on her wrist. She was almost positive it was the Cartier bangle from Ari's drawer. She felt sick. What had that note said? *To my dearest, my sweetest love?*

The men were talking about an incident on an Olympic flight that day. Lee sat back and lit a cigarette, regarding Maria's dress with a critical expression.

"Who designed your gown?" she asked.

"Biki of Milan," Maria replied. "She's a friend who makes a lot of clothes for me."

"*Rah–lly,*" Lee drawled, with a disparaging sniff.

Maria couldn't let her get away with that, so she hit back. "Are you on holiday without your children again? They're so young, they must scarcely recognize you."

She knew from the sharp intake of breath that she had scored a bull's-eye. The atmosphere between them was barely civil for the rest of the evening.

"You eat bread, I see," Lee remarked. "How very brave of you not to worry about your figure."

"I'm careful not to drink too much alcohol," Maria replied. "There's nothing quite so undignified as a drunk woman." She looked meaningfully at Lee's wineglass, which was nearly empty again, minutes after a waiter had topped it up.

Stas seemed puzzled by all the veiled barbs and hostile glances, but Ari knew what was going on. Maria suspected he was secretly enjoying it.

As soon as they got back to the *Christina*, she hurried down to his suite to check the drawer. The Cartier box was still there but empty. He had given the bracelet to Lee. How could he? She slammed the drawer shut. Should she confront him? Admit she'd been snooping? Jealousy was an unattractive, destructive quality. It was better to take the high road. She was the woman he chose to be with, after all.

She didn't mention the bracelet but, from then on, insecurity raged whenever Ari made a trip ashore. She tried to sound nonchalant as she asked whom he was dining with and which friends he planned to see. If she could have had him tailed twenty-four hours a day, she would have, but that was no way to conduct a love affair.

In mid-September, Ari announced, "I've invited Mrs. Kennedy for a cruise to help her recover after the loss of her baby."

Maria had felt sympathetic when she read of the death of the Kennedy baby. She knew all too well what it was like to lose a child straight after its birth, because Omero still haunted her thoughts. But she was instantly wary about the cruise.

"Who's coming with her?" she asked, trying to keep her tone from sounding inquisitorial.

Ari listed the guests: "American congressman Franklin Roosevelt Jr. and his wife; Princess Irene Galitzine and her husband; Stas and Lee; my sister, Artemis, and her husband . . ." He'd slipped Lee's name into the middle, as if trying to gloss over her presence.

"And what dates are they coming?"

"We sail on the fourth of October, from Athens."

Maria tapped her fingernail on the tabletop. "I told you I have to be in Paris during the first week of October. I'm meeting Zeffirelli to discuss a production of *Tosca*."

"Of course you are!" he exclaimed, clapping his forehead as if he had only just remembered. Maria was not fooled for a moment. "But perhaps it's just as well," he continued. "You haven't met the First Lady and she will not be in the mood for socializing with strangers. I understand she is a very private person."

"She hasn't met Artemis either, has she? She's a stranger to her."

"Artemis will stay out of her way, as will I. I don't plan to impose myself on the party. In fact, I offered to let them borrow the *Christina* and cruise without me, but Mrs. Kennedy insisted I should be there." He shrugged, as if to say, *What else could I do?*

"Perhaps I will join you on the tenth," Maria persevered. "You could send the helicopter to collect me from Athens."

"It's probably best not to, my love," he said. "Give Mrs. Kennedy her privacy and I'll fly to meet you in Paris as soon as they leave."

"What about Princess Lee?" she asked, her tone hardening. "What if she strolls into your cabin in her skimpy bikini? Will you be able to resist this time?"

He pulled her toward him, kissing her with tenderness. "I will resist," he said, then drew his head back so she could see the flecks of gold in his irises. "I promise I will send her packing."

She turned away so he would not see the emotion on her face. She hated Lee now, with her affected, breathy voice and the expensive clothes draped over that bony frame. What was she good for? She didn't have any talents, except betrayal.

Chapter 36

The Mediterranean
October 1963

Jackie felt so ill during the eleven-hour flight from New York to Athens that she had to ask a stewardess for an oxygen mask. Her whole body felt broken, every bone and joint aching, and her head fuzzy with exhaustion. Franklin Roosevelt Jr. and his wife, Sue, were worried and offered to call a doctor when they landed, but Jackie refused. She just wanted to get there. A chauffeur-driven Rolls-Royce was waiting to collect them at the airport, and they were whisked to Piraeus and straight onto the Onassis yacht, which towered over the others in the port.

As they boarded, she saw that the railings were decorated with roses and gladioli, and a lavish cocktail party was underway, with a live band and a barman in black tie mixing cocktails in a shaker. Jackie was not in the mood. She made her excuses and slipped down to her cabin, where she climbed into bed and slept for fourteen hours straight. The sheets were finely woven, the mattress sublime, and the wood-paneled walls seemed to hold the warmth of summer.

On waking the next morning, she pressed a bell set in the wall, and a maid appeared, who took her order for orange juice, tea, and toast. Through a porthole, she could see white sun glinting off the turquoise Aegean Sea, and there was not a cloud in the sky. Jackie felt stiff from sleeping so long, but she could also feel the release of some of the tension she had been holding in her body since Patrick died. The change of scene helped.

That first day, she lay in the sun, an unopened book by her side, and every now and then she dove off a diving board into the sea, which was as warm as bathwater. They docked in Istanbul that evening, but she did not feel like going ashore and ate dinner alone before an early night.

The next day they sailed to the island of Lesbos, and Jackie swam far out from the shore, till the *Christina* was a mere dot on the horizon. There, where no one could see, at last she let her tears for Patrick flow freely; they mingled with the salt water stinging her eyes and became part of the vast ocean. It felt cathartic.

That evening, all the guests dined on board. An orchestra played on deck after the meal and Lee got up to dance, drifting around the floor on her own: "showing off," their mother would have called it. Still their host had not made an appearance. It seemed he had his own quarters on the yacht and was giving them their privacy. They were to dock at Smyrna the next day, and Jackie sent Franklin to request that Onassis join them, because she knew this was the place of his birth.

Their host appeared the following morning and gave them a guided tour of Smyrna, explaining the background of the Turks' decision to drive out the Greeks in 1922 and the complex enmity between the neighboring nations.

"You're a talented raconteur," Jackie complimented him. "I wish you could be our guide during the rest of the cruise. I've always wanted to explore this area and learn about its history and mythology."

"It would be my honor," he said, with a slight bow. "If you're sure I'm not intruding."

He had an old-fashioned charm, she decided, as if he came from a more genteel prewar generation. "I read an article that called you the modern-day Odysseus," she probed. "Is that true? And, if so, where is the Ithaca you are searching for?"

Onassis gestured toward his yacht: "The *Christina* is my Ithaca, the place I call home."

"I was hoping Maria Callas might be here," Jackie continued. "Will she join us later? My husband has already met her and he is not remotely an opera fan, whereas I love it, so it doesn't seem fair."

Onassis seemed uncomfortable with the question. "Unfortunately Maria had to go to Paris on business," he said, before changing the subject abruptly. "Shall we head back now? Cocktail hour is fast approaching and I seem to remember that you favor a vodka martini, *with* an olive."

"Well remembered, Mr. Onassis." She smiled.

"Please—call me Aristotle."

"Only if you call me Jacqueline," she replied.

The day after their jaunt into Smyrna, Ari called Jackie up to the boat deck, which served as his office. "There's a call for you," he said. "From your husband."

"Isn't modern technology extraordinary?" she exclaimed as she took the receiver. Aristotle left the area to give her privacy. An Oval Office secretary was on the line, and she put the call through.

"Is everything alright?" Jackie asked straightaway.

"The kids are fine," he said, the line crackly, with a ghostlike echo. "But some photos of you with Onassis made a big splash in the papers this morning. You even appear to be holding hands in one of them."

"Really?" She couldn't remember that.

"Anyway, I'm glad you're having a good time but you need to be more discreet. Stay away from photographers."

"I'll try, but it's not easy. They're sneaky critters. How are you?"

"You know," he said. "Tired. Sad. I miss you."

"I miss you too, bunny." Her heart ached for him suddenly. What was she doing so far away? Jack had lost a baby too. She kept forgetting that. "I'll write every evening. We'll be back in ten days, no time at all."

"I hope this trip helps. I really do. I have to go now, kid."

The line cut off when she was in the middle of saying goodbye, and she sat clutching the receiver, aching with missing him.

"Need a drink?" Aristotle asked, appearing in a doorway.

She shook her head and forced a smile. "Another swim, I think," she replied. "But thank you."

Chapter 37

Paris
October 1963

The day after Maria arrived in Paris she had lunch at Maxim's with Ari's old friend Maggie van Zuylen. There were pictures of Lee and Jackie all over the newspapers and Maggie wasted no time in questioning her about the *Christina* cruise.

"Why are you not with them?" she asked, her brown eyes full of concern.

Maria had trusted Maggie from their first meeting, and she told her the story of Ari's infidelity with Lee and the way that he had arranged the cruise for a period when he knew she had to be in Paris.

Maggie leaned back, looking thoughtful. She was an astute, raven-haired beauty who had suffered her share of setbacks in life. She had fallen madly in love with the son of Baron van Zuylen, but his parents refused to countenance the match and disinherited him when he married her against their wishes. For the next three years, it was only Maggie's exceptional poker skills that kept them from penury. When she finally found a way to meet the old baron, she was able to wrap him around her little finger and have his son reinstated to the succession—and to his inheritance.

"Ari adores you," Maggie said now. "He talks of you as if you are a goddess. But perhaps he has become a little too sure of your devotion. He's been a naughty boy and needs to—what do the English say?—he needs to pull his socks up."

"What do you suggest?" Maria asked, sipping a glass of Bollinger. She was scared of losing Ari to the president's scrawny sister-in-law, so Maggie's reassurance was very welcome.

Maggie's eyes twinkled. "We both know that Ari enjoys conquest: signing a new deal, outsmarting business rivals, or getting a prestigious new guest on board the *Christina*. With you, perhaps he feels he has already pulled off the deal and there is no challenge left. Do you catch my drift?"

"Ye-es," Maria answered, unsure of where this was heading.

"So perhaps you should drop a hint that the deal is not impregnable." She lifted her glass and clinked it against Maria's. "Then you are a challenge again."

Maria was baffled. "A hint? You mean like him finding an item of men's swimwear in my cabin?"

"No. Much more subtle." She looked around the grand dining room, decorated with curling art nouveau tendrils painted on glass panels. "Have dinner with a gentleman friend. Someone young and handsome, whom Ari will not recognize. Come here, or to another prominent restaurant. Let me know the evening it will happen and I will mention it to a photographer friend and—lo and behold—Ari will get a shock when he peruses his morning papers. You and I know he can't resist the society pages."

Maria wasn't sure. "Isn't that a dangerous game? I don't want to encourage tit-for-tat infidelities."

"Of course not." Maggie shook her head slowly. "Your dinner will be completely innocent. And when he telephones—as he surely will—you can assure him of that. But for a short while he will be worried, and it will focus his mind. *I* know you would never be capable of infidelity, but *he* doesn't know that. Lotharios make the most suspicious lovers, because they judge everyone by their own standards."

"Is he a lothario?" Maria felt exhausted at the thought.

She knew there had been affairs during his marriage to Tina but had expected them to stop once he was with her. How naive she had been.

"He is not the worst. But make him woo you. Be a little mysterious. Don't always rush for the phone when he calls. You two will be fine. I can feel it in my gambler's bones." She finished her champagne and signaled for a waiter to bring two more glasses. "To love!" she toasted.

"To love," Maria echoed.

Maria wasted no time in inviting Zeffirelli for dinner at Maxim's. He was roughly her age, with Italian good looks—a high brow, winning smile, year-round tan, and elegant clothes. There was no flirtation in their relationship, but they shared many interests and had an amusing evening. When she spotted Maggie's photographer friend wielding his camera, Maria leaned in close, as if keen not to miss a word that her companion was uttering.

A photograph appeared in *Paris Match* the following morning, along with a caption mentioning that Maria Callas had dined with a "mystery escort." Maggie called, laughing her pretty trill of a laugh.

"Darling, when I suggested you ask a man for dinner, I meant one who likes women!"

Maria was puzzled. "What do you mean?"

"Zeffirelli is a homosexual."

"Really? I had no idea." Maria giggled. "I wondered why he didn't mention a wife or girlfriend. I must be very slow on the uptake."

There were dozens of homosexual men in the world of opera. Sodomy was illegal in many countries, so few men openly broadcast their preferences, but word got around. Sometimes it was widely known, but at other times, such as this, she was one of the last to find out.

Ari called a couple of hours later, and she greeted him cheerfully. "Hello, darling. How are your famous guests?"

He got straight to the point. "Who did you have dinner with last night and why is your picture in the newspaper?"

"Is it?" Maria asked, disingenuous. "I can't think why. Zeffirelli and I had a meal yesterday to talk about our *Tosca*."

"Did he try to seduce you?"

Maria paused, as if considering the question. "He was very sweet but I don't think he meant to seduce me. Perhaps . . ." She let her voice trail off, teasing.

"Perhaps what?" he barked.

"Oh, nothing. I am sure it was innocent."

"You don't understand men," he told her. "You have

only known Battista and me. You don't realize the way men think."

Maria didn't mention that she had spent her working life in the company of men and had learned how to rebuff those who behaved inappropriately. "I'm sure his intentions were honorable," she replied. "Don't give it a second thought."

Before Ari hung up, he asked about her itinerary for the next few days. She told him she was flying to London to try to persuade the management at Covent Garden that her *Tosca* should be staged as soon as possible. She loved Zeffirelli's ideas and wanted to strike while the iron was hot. Ari demanded to know where she would be staying, whom she planned to see, and what day she would arrive back in Paris. She gave him the information, chuckling to herself. Maggie was a genius. She must ask her advice more often.

While in London Maria caught up with several old friends, and she took the opportunity to ask more about Lee Radziwill. She learned that as well as their London town house at 4 Buckingham Place, the Radziwills owned a country house called Turville Grange outside Henley-on-Thames. She learned that Lee had been on the previous year's best-dressed list and was friends with a number of Paris designers, who gave her the first pick of their collections. And she was told that Lee's adoption of the title *Princess* was considered rather outré in London society. She and Stas should have asked permission of the reigning monarch, Queen Elizabeth II, to use their royal titles; such permission had not been sought, so legally they were just Mr. and Mrs. Radziwill.

Maria knew that both had been married previously, and she asked how they had obtained their divorces and still managed to have their union blessed by the Catholic Church. This was a question close to her own heart. The answer came that Mrs. Kennedy had personally intervened at the Vatican to help Lee get an annulment of her first marriage, thus making the second acceptable to the Church. *Was that ethical?* Maria wondered. *Didn't presidents' wives have better things to do with their time?*

She didn't know what she would do with the information she collected, but it felt important that she understand her enemy. And she was under no illusion: Lee was most definitely an enemy.

Chapter 38

The Greek Islands
October 1963

The *Christina* sailed to a new Greek island each day. After breakfast, anyone who wished to could take the launch ashore to wander around seaside villages, shop for souvenirs, or stroll along the beach. Jackie made sure to stand near Lee or Sue Roosevelt rather than any of the men, so that if she was photographed there could be no adverse media coverage. Usually there was a group of passengers on these excursions, but one day Jackie and Lee were the only two to disembark, and, after they had poked around the only two shops in the village, Jackie suggested they have an early lunch at a beachfront taverna.

They ordered glasses of retsina and Greek salads and began chatting about their fellow guests.

"I love the silk palazzo pajamas Princess Irene Galit-zine wears," Jackie said. "I must get a pair. They look so stylish." The princess was a fashion designer who catered to the European aristocracy.

"I've got loads of them," Lee said. "She brought them out in 1960. I guess they haven't reached America yet—although I'm sure I've seen Audrey Hepburn in a pair."

Jackie took a sip of retsina, remembering that Jack used to date the actress—but that was a long time ago. "What do you make of Aristotle?" she asked. "He's hospitable but I find it hard to get a sense of the real man." She noticed that Lee's cheeks flushed slightly at her words. Her sister began fiddling with her napkin as she answered.

"He's a generous host . . . still, I suppose he can afford to be." She looked up. "What is it? Why are you looking at me like that?"

"You like him, don't you?" Jackie took a cigarette from her pack and offered Lee one, then sparked her lighter. "Are the rumors true?"

"What rumors?" Lee asked, sucking in smoke as if it had been days since her last cigarette, not just half an hour.

"The *Washington Post* hinted that a certain Greek

tycoon might be hoping to become the brother-in-law of the American president." Jackie smiled, encouraging disclosure. "Go on, tell all."

"Who wouldn't want to marry him?" Lee shrugged. "All that money is hugely erotic."

"But you're married already. And you love Stas!" Jackie tried to hide her annoyance. It was hard, but if she remonstrated with her sister she knew that Lee would clam up.

"Stas and I haven't had sex since Tina was born." She flicked ash to the ground and took another drag, exhaling slowly. "I love him but I'm not attracted to him anymore."

"Oh, for crying out loud!" Jackie clattered her glass on the table, losing patience. "You can't change husbands every time desire fades a bit. After giving birth, sex is the last thing you feel like but it will come back, I promise."

Lee wrinkled her nose. "Keep your hair on. It's not as if we're getting divorced or anything."

"I should hope not," Jackie rebuked, "because I certainly won't pull strings to get you an annulment next time." She bit her tongue. This wasn't how she had meant to broach the subject. "So tell me . . . what's Aristotle like in bed?"

"Surprisingly talented," Lee admitted with a coy expression. "You'd be amazed."

Jackie sat openmouthed. "So it's true! You *are* sleeping with him." She leaned back in her chair to regard her younger sister. "Isn't he hairy as a gorilla?"

"Not like a gorilla. The hair is very silky and fine. And he has the most beautiful smell." Her tone was soft. It sounded as if she was smitten.

"What about Maria Callas?" Jackie asked. "He's still with her."

Lee's expression darkened. "Wasn't it a Greek who said 'All's fair in love and war'?"

"No, it was the English writer John Lyly," Jackie replied tartly. Fidelity clearly wasn't part of Lee's moral code. This was the woman who might have slept with Jack and who was being unfaithful to Stas, so why would she worry about Ari's long-term mistress? "Does Stas know?"

"We haven't discussed it," Lee said. "But he has affairs too." She tilted her head girlishly. "Are you cross with me? Please don't be cross."

Jackie stubbed out her cigarette in a glass ashtray. The breeze instantly picked it up and blew it to the sandy floor. "I need you to promise that if you get divorced, and you and Aristotle decide to make it official, you wait till after November next year so it doesn't interfere with Jack's reelection chances. And in the meantime, you keep it out of the papers. Can you do that?"

Lee shrugged. "It's not just up to me."

"Shall I make Aristotle promise as well?" Jackie asked, pushing away her untouched salad.

"No!" Lee reacted quickly. "Don't say anything to him. I'll have a word."

One balmy evening, as they sat out on deck, Sue Roosevelt asked Jackie about Patrick. She shook her head. She couldn't talk about him. Another time, Aristotle expressed his condolences, and she thanked him and said she was feeling much better for being on the cruise.

It was only with Jack that she told the truth. Every night, she wrote him a letter, telling him what they had done during the day, telling him how much she missed him, and telling him that she carried Patrick in her heart wherever she went.

The letters grew more romantic as the days went by. "It is too long to be away from you," she wrote halfway through the vacation. "I wish you could have come with me, to relax without any pressure, but I know that's impossible.

Do you ever look backwards to the coincidences that brought us together? Meeting on the train— then that funny old evening at the Bartletts'? Isn't it strange that I had been looking for you all my life, then I didn't recognize you when I found you? Not straightaway, at any rate. I wonder how long it was before you knew I was the one. A while, if I remember correctly. Thank God we did—before it was too late.

We've had our share of sadnesses—more than our share—and you know I haven't been crazy about life in the political zoo, but if I could have my time over, whether in this lifetime or another, I would always choose you.

Your loving Jacqueline

Every morning she handed her letter to the maid who brought her breakfast, and by the time she appeared on deck it had been dispatched by Onassis's staff.

Jackie flew back to New York on October 17, then transferred for the short flight to D.C., expecting that there would be a driver waiting to take her to the White House. Instead, as she arrived at Washington National Airport, there were Jack and the children, holding a banner that read WELCOME HOME, MOMMY. She ran into Jack's arms, not caring who was watching. His face was puffy, a side effect of the steroids he took for his Addison's disease, and he looked more tired than she had ever seen him.

"I'll never leave you again," she whispered before turning to hug the children, who were tugging on her coat and squealing for her attention.

Chapter 39

Paris
October 20, 1963

Ari arrived at Maria's Paris apartment on October 20, while she was still asleep. She awoke with a start to find him sitting on the edge of the bed, watching her. Bruna must have let him in. Without saying a word, he pulled a jewelry box from his coat pocket and placed it in the palm of her hand, wrapping her fingers around it.

Maria opened the box and saw a pair of earrings, but the light was too gloomy with the shutters drawn to make out any detail. She switched on her bedside lamp and found that they were drop style, with pinkish, pear-shaped rubies set in stems of diamonds. Art deco, if she wasn't mistaken. Ari knew she loved deco. They were beautiful, but to her the gift smacked of a guilty conscience. She closed the box and put it on the bedside table.

"Thank you," she said, without smiling.

He leaned in to kiss her on the lips, tentatively. She didn't turn her head away but didn't reciprocate either.

"Your guests have gone, I assume?" she asked.

"They have. I think Mrs. Kennedy enjoyed her holiday," he said. "At first she only wanted to swim, read books, and sleep, but by the last few days she seemed relaxed."

Maria nodded. "And Lee? Was she relaxed too?"

She watched him closely, but his eyes looked sincere as he replied: "I think so, but I didn't spend any time alone with her—with either of them."

Maria nodded, a lump in her throat. She'd had to ask.

"I need your help," he told her, lifting her hand and linking his fingers through hers. "I'm having an architect draw up plans for the building work on Skorpios. I'm dredging a harbor for *Christina,* building roads, and importing sand for a beach, but the main villa and guest cottages need a woman's touch. I want you to look at the ideas. Will you help?"

Maria closed her eyes. She would love for them to build a home together, to create a cozy nest. Although she was mistress of the *Christina* when she was on board, it wasn't hers and never would be. But before she agreed, there was another matter that had been preying on her mind.

"I would be happy to help, but there is something I want from you in return." She took a deep breath. "I am going to be forty in December, and I want us to be married by then. I don't care what form of ceremony, but forty is too old for a woman to remain unwed."

He looked startled. "But the Church won't recognize it."

"That is less important to me than you making an announcement to the world that I am your wife." She tried to read his expression, but his face wasn't giving much away.

"Is this about Lee?" he asked. "Because you have no reason to be jealous of her."

"Not just Lee; there will be other women who come creeping around, trying to win your affections. I don't want to be just another of your conquests. You say I am the most important person in your life; you say you have never loved anyone as much as me. Now is the time to prove it."

Ari rose and walked to the window, drawing back a shutter to look out at the gray, overcast sky and the rain-soaked street below. "When the time is right we will marry, I promise. Until then, can't we simply enjoy each other? You are the only woman who truly knows me. You're my great love, my best friend. Why change all that?"

"It's a question of respect, Ari. I don't want to be your mistress anymore." She had been giving it a lot of thought. A ring on her finger might not stop him from being unfaithful, but it would make him think twice about leaving her for another woman. "Your divorce from Tina was finalized long ago, so you're a free agent. What will it take for 'the time' to be 'right,' as far as you're concerned?"

He crossed his arms, leaning against the wall. "Under Italian law, you are still married to Battista."

"What does that matter? Neither of us lives in Italy." She silently cursed her ex-husband.

Ari continued: "More to the point, I always hoped Alexander would come to accept you, but he remains as prickly as ever. He would hate us getting married and I don't want to upset him at such a difficult age."

Maria tutted. "Is that your strongest argument? We can't have our happiness dictated by a fifteen-year-old. He would accept our marriage in the end." She paused, then said something that was very hard for her. "If Omero had lived, I know you would have married me. Have you changed your mind because it doesn't look as though I am capable of bearing you a child?"

"Of *course* not," he said with feeling. "I am sad for your sake, but it doesn't change my wariness about marriage."

Maria closed her eyes to stop the tears from coming. She had recently agreed with her fertility doctor that there was no point in continuing the hormone treatments. It seemed her womb was what he termed "inhospitable"; eggs were being fertilized but not implanting. Every monthly bleed could mean another little death. Every month she mourned for the child that she hadn't been able to bring into being.

"I am not saying it is impossible," the doctor told her. "I often find my patients get pregnant the moment they stop trying."

Maria clung to his words. Pray God that would be the case with her. She hadn't been trying when she got pregnant with Omero—but she was four years older now and knew that would count against her.

Ari came back to sit on the bed and took both her hands between his, kissing the palm of one, then the other. "Would you like to adopt a child? We can do that if it would make you happy."

Maria shook her head. She was touched that he would offer, but the whole point was to see their genes passed on. Besides, an adopted child would be a second-class citizen compared to Ari's children with Tina; he would never feel the same emotional attachment and she might end up raising it on her own. "Thank you, but no," she said, squeezing his fingers.

He leaned in to kiss her properly, pushing her back on the pillow, pinning her wrists above her head, letting his kisses stray down to her breasts. She succumbed to his touch, let him slide the nightgown over her head and start making love to her. They knew many little ways to please each other now. For her, the sex was sublime, but she sometimes worried that her body held no surprises for him and he might lose interest.

At least there was no sign of it yet. They made love for many hours that day, opening a bottle of Dom Pérignon and licking it off each other's skin, ringing for Bruna to bring food when they got hungry.

"I won't be able to sit down for a week," Maria told him, giggling.

"That's as it should be," he replied, smacking her hard on the backside.

After eating, they lay with their faces close together, and she smoothed his eyebrows with her finger, her brain fuzzy with lust. She loved this man with all the passion in her soul. Perhaps she loved him too much. He was the center of her universe, her overriding preoccupation, the one person who could make her happy—or miserable. Somehow she needed to feel more secure in the relationship, so she would not give up on getting him to the altar, but she vowed not to turn into a nag. Little by little, she would work on him until she got her way.

"Where shall we go for dinner this evening?" she asked, after a long scented bath in which she soaked her bruised flesh.

"Maxim's?"

"How about Café de la Paix?" he called through the bathroom door.

"I thought you were a creature of habit!" She laughed. "Wherever we go, it has to be your usual restaurant: Maxim's in Paris, the Hôtel de Paris in Monte Carlo, the Negresco in Nice."

He popped his head around the door. "That's true, but tonight I am glad there is peace between us, so Café de la Paix seems a good omen."

"I'm all for good omens," she replied, flicking him with bathwater.

She dressed in a chic black evening gown, very low cut and fitted to emphasize her curves, and accessorized it with the new ruby-and-diamond earrings. The effect was stunning. He had a gift for choosing jewelry.

Before they left for the restaurant, she had a quiet word with Bruna. "Could you call Maggie van Zuylen?

Ask her to tell her photographer friend that I will be dining with Ari at Café de la Paix."

Bruna nodded. "Of course, madame." She never asked questions.

As they dined on seafood under the café's grand gilt ceilings, Maria noticed that the photographer had arrived. Laughing, she leaned across the table to feed Ari an oyster, tilting the shell so that it slid down his throat. He leaned his head back, eyes closed, surrendering to the sensation.

Maria held the pose for a few seconds to give the man time to get the shot. Let Princess Lee see that in her newspaper tomorrow morning. Let her understand that although she might have been able to seduce Ari once, or even twice, this was a war she was never going to win.

Chapter 40

Washington, D.C.
November 1963

Jackie had not been home long when she realized how much Jack had been coping with in her absence: growing tension in Vietnam under the much-hated anti-Communist leader Ngo Dinh Diem; seemingly impassable opposition to the civil rights legislation that was so close to his heart; the Soviets crowing about putting the first woman in space and claiming to be a more egalitarian society than America. On top of that, Jack had faced fierce popular criticism for letting her vacation with Onassis. She should never have put him in that position.

She felt guilty as she fingered the parting gift Aristotle had given her—an extravagant art deco diamond-and-ruby necklace that must have cost a king's ransom. Lee was furious, because he gave her only three little diamond bracelets: "The sort of thing Caroline might wear," she scoffed. Secretly Jackie hoped it signaled a cooling of her sister's relationship with Onassis. That was an additional problem Jack could do without.

"So, is she Onassis's lover?" he had asked on the evening of her return. "Did you find out?"

"I think there may have been a tryst." Jackie watched him but there was no reaction to her deliberate choice of the word. "But it appears to be over now, as far as I can make out. At least I hope it is."

"I hope so too." He shook his head. "Lee's charming but she can be a liability."

"She's back in London now, out of harm's way."

Jack was peering at a schedule his secretary had given him. "I don't suppose I can persuade you to come on that trip to Texas from November twenty-first to twenty-third? It's just pressing the flesh, a few lunches, nothing taxing. I need to smooth things out between a congressman and the governor, who've gotten themselves in a spat."

Jackie sighed. She hated that kind of thing, and she knew there was a lot of opposition to the Democrats in Texas so they would be in for a rough ride. But if Jack thought she could be of use . . . well, maybe this was the time for her to show up and do her bit.

"You don't have to. I could go without you," he said as she hesitated.

"No, of course I'll come," she said. "I owe you."

Jackie asked her staff to check the weather forecast for Texas and they said it would be cool, so she packed accordingly—but they stepped off the plane in Houston into an inferno. It felt as if it was at least eighty degrees, and the humidity was dreadful. Jackie was perspiring before they reached the limo and cursing that she had brought entirely the wrong wardrobe for their three-day trip.

That evening she delivered a speech in Spanish at a meeting with the Hispanic community, and it was a pressure she could have done without. She hadn't used her Spanish for years and was sure her accent was rusty. But, to her relief, it seemed she had done a good job.

Jack was delighted with her effort and paid tribute to her at the dinner afterward: "Wasn't Jackie sensational?" he asked anyone who would listen. "Did you see her ovation?" She liked making him proud. It gave her a warm glow.

Fortunately it was the only time on the trip that she had to speak in public; her main role was trying to charm the warring parties behind the scenes. Everyone knew she wasn't one to discuss the nuances of politics, so they found different topics of conversation when she was around and steered clear of controversy.

Back at their hotel that evening, Jack was preoccupied. "We're off to nut country tomorrow," he said, referring to Dallas, where the opposition to his presidency was particularly heated. "I've got some early meetings but I'll catch up with you for the breakfast event at nine-fifteen. Then we'll hop on the plane to Dallas."

Jackie laid out her clothes for the morning: a pink suit, navy blouse, and pink pillbox hat. Two more nights away from home, then she could get back to her children and sleep in her own bed.

Air Force One landed at Dallas Love Field just after 11:30. Jack was heading off to give a speech at the Trade Mart, while Jackie was going to a luncheon with the local political wives. Jack had instructed her to "charm their socks off," and the phrase rang in her head. She suspected these would be ultraglamorous society ladies who hadn't worn socks since the passing of girlhood.

"How do you like campaigning, Mrs. Kennedy?" a reporter called as they got off the plane, and she gave her stock answer: "It's wonderful!" The lie came naturally now.

She was handed a bunch of red roses, curiously lacking in scent, and they got into a waiting Lincoln. She and Jack sat in the backseat behind Governor Connally and his wife, Nellie, who were in the seats behind the driver. All around them were cars and motorbikes with Secret Service men in black, murmuring into walkie-talkies. Their motorcade was to drive slowly through the streets from Love Field to the Trade Mart. It would take about forty-five minutes, giving Dallas citizens plenty of time to see their president and First Lady up close.

"Zoo time," she whispered to Jack as they set off, and he grinned.

"Smile and wave, kid. Give them their ten cents' worth."

She turned to wave at the crowds on the left side of the limo. "Mr. President! Mrs. Kennedy!" they were shouting, frantically trying to catch her attention for a split second. Some were holding hand-lettered placards, but although the car was crawling along, it was hard to read them. There were groups of high-school kids, who must have been allowed a morning off, and lots of women—many more women than men.

Whenever they reached a section of the route without any crowds, the car sped up and she donned her sunglasses to shield her eyes from the diamond-sharp November sun.

"Take off the glasses," Jack said to her as they rounded a corner, and she slipped them back onto her lap before repinning the smile on her face and turning to wave at the crowd to her left.

"We're almost through," Nellie Connally called over her shoulder. "It's just beyond that." She pointed to an underpass up ahead.

Suddenly there was a noise like a car backfiring, and Jackie turned to see Jack clutching his head with a quizzical expression.

"What is it?" she started to ask.

Their car slowed down, and at the same moment there was a deafening explosion and part of Jack's head blew off. She saw it fly in an arc through the air and land on the back of the car; flesh colored, with a piece of white bone inside.

Jackie opened her mouth to scream but no sound came. A steel band tightened around her chest and panic took over, making her mind go blank. Seconds later, someone was pushing her into her seat. How had she gotten out of it? The Lincoln was speeding up, and the acceleration jolted her backward. Jack toppled sideways onto her and she cradled his head in her lap. *His dear head.*

"I love you," she whispered in his ear, bending over so that her lips were close. There was a slight wheezing sound, and his chest moved. He was breathing, she was sure of it. Hope stirred for a second, then she looked at the awful wound. Brains glistened through a mess of bloody hair. He couldn't possibly survive.

"I love you, darling." Could he hear? She stroked the undamaged part of his head, running her fingers through his hair the way he liked, her white gloves scarlet with his blood. There was a rhythmic thumping, like a drum, and she wondered where it was coming from, then realized it was her heartbeat.

The world went into shadow as they entered the underpass. She was distantly aware of moans coming from the front seat but all her attention was on Jack. "I'm here, bunny," she whispered. "I love you so much. Hang on."

When they emerged from the tunnel, the heat of the sun struck her like an assault. There was a metal taste in her mouth and the salty smell of blood in her nostrils. "Jack, please don't go," she whispered. "Please stay." Her whole body was shaking, the blood pulsing, white noise in her head. Why was it taking so long? Where was the damn hospital? They were driving fast but time was standing still.

And then they pulled up outside some glass doors and she saw white-coated medics rushing toward them with a gurney. Someone opened the door on her side and took her arm to pull her from the car but she wouldn't let go of Jack's head. What if more of his brains fell out through that gaping hole? She clung to him, not letting go.

Someone leaned in from the other side, eased her arm away, and wrapped a jacket around the wound.

"We need to take him inside," a man's voice said, and she nodded. Of course they did.

Jack was lifted onto the gurney and she gripped the edge, running to keep up as they pushed him down a corridor. She had to let go when they reached some swinging doors and a nurse took her arm, forcing her to halt.

"Sit here, please, Mrs. Kennedy. Let the doctors do their work."

She sat on a hard chair, feeling cool firmness beneath her legs. People were talking to her but a strange thing had happened that meant she couldn't hear them. Odd words filtered through. "Operate." "Speed." "The issue." None of them made sense.

Why was she there? Why wasn't she with Jack? None of these people loved him. He needed her more than he had ever needed her. She must be by his side when he died.

Suddenly she made a decision, stood up, and pushed through the swinging doors. No one stopped her this time. Inside she saw Jack lying on a narrow bed, wearing only blue boxer shorts. Tan lines from the summer marked his legs and arms. There was bandaging around his head and his eyes were closed.

The doctors turned but didn't stop her from approaching. Jack didn't look himself anymore. She had often watched his face in sleep, when the frown lines softened and his jaw relaxed, but this was different. His features were tightening as death took hold.

She bent and kissed him on the lips, and he didn't kiss back.

"A priest is coming, Mrs. Kennedy," someone said, but she knew it was too late. Jack had gone. She wasn't sure of the exact moment when his spirit had risen out of his body, but she knew he wasn't there now.

She slipped off her wedding ring and pushed it onto his little finger. Was there still a realm in which he could sense her presence? Was his spirit in the room, watching them?

The priest arrived, very somber, and made the sign of the cross over Jack, anointing him with holy oil and murmuring about forgiveness of sins and eternal blessing. There should have been some comfort in the words. Wasn't that the point of religion? But there was none.

"Bring him back!" she wanted to scream. Jesus had

raised Lazarus. Why couldn't one of the learned men in this room perform a miracle?

Instead they formally pronounced him dead, citing the time of death as 1:00 P.M. exactly.

There was a lump in her throat, as if a rock were lodged there, but she didn't cry. She felt frozen, trapped in the horror of the moment.

She took Jack's hand, lacing her fingers through his. It was the saddest thing in the world to hold the hand of the person you loved and not feel any response at all, not even the tiniest flicker of a muscle.

There was only one person she wanted to tell about this, and he had gone forever. She was alone.

ACT III

Chapter 41

Paris
November 22, 1963

Maria was dining with Maggie van Zuylen and two other friends at Le Train Bleu, a smart restaurant above the Gare de Lyon, when the maître d' made an announcement.

"Mesdames *et* messieurs," he called out. "Terrible news from America. President Kennedy has been shot dead."

The murmur of chatter stopped, and forks clattered onto plates as a shockwave traveled around the restaurant. For a few seconds there was silence. Maria looked at her companions, suddenly petrified.

"Can it be true?" Maggie asked. "I don't believe it."

"He had a lot of enemies," a man at the next table said, leaning over. "It could have been the Russians."

"Or the Mafia," someone else suggested.

"No, the Mafia would hit Bobby Kennedy if they were going for anyone. He's the one who's been locking them up."

"What about the Ku Klux Klan? Could it be them?"

"You met him, didn't you?" Maggie asked Maria, and all heads in the vicinity turned toward her.

"I did. He was charming. I can't take it in." She shivered as if someone had walked over her grave, and she wrapped her arms around her shoulders. Suddenly she felt an urgent need to get back to her apartment. She wanted to be safely within her own four walls and she wanted to talk to Ari. "I'm going home." She scraped her chair back and stood.

"You've hardly touched your meal," Maggie protested. "Let's finish, then we can leave together. It might not even be true. You know how false rumors spread."

"I want to go home and check if it's on the television news," Maria said. "Don't worry about me. I'll hail a taxi."

She picked up her purse and raced for the door. Several other customers had also decided to leave and there was a line at the cloakroom, but as soon as she exited the doorman found her a cab. She felt panicky as the city lights flashed past. It took her right back to the campaign of intimidation against her at La Scala.

When you were in the public eye, you were always vulnerable. It just took one crazy person with a gun, and your life could be over.

She dashed into the apartment, and before taking off her shoes or coat, she dialed the number of the hotel in Hamburg where Ari was staying while he supervised work on a new oil tanker.

"I'm afraid his line is engaged," the receptionist said. "Do you want to hold?"

"Yes, please."

She sat down at the telephone table, phone in hand. Bruna came into the hall.

"Did Ari ring when I was out?" Maria asked, covering the mouthpiece with her hand.

"No, madame, not since you spoke to him earlier. Can I get you anything?"

"A brandy," she said. "Please."

She sat waiting, listening to the clicks and a hint of indistinct voices speaking German at a telephone exchange hundreds of miles away.

"I'm putting you through," the receptionist said after almost ten minutes.

"You heard the news?" Maria began as soon as his voice came on the line.

"It's shocking. I can hardly believe it."

"Nor I. Is it definitely true? Is he really dead?"

"He is," Ari said. "They got him to the hospital within minutes but he was declared dead half an hour later. Lyndon Johnson was sworn in as president on board Air Force One."

She could hear a television in the background and guessed that was where he was getting his information. "Who did it? Do they have any idea?"

"The newscaster is saying that a policeman was shot and killed trying to apprehend a man who fled the scene. I hope they'll catch him soon. It's a terrible day for the world."

"Are you alright, darling?" she asked.

"I'm fine. How about you?"

She told him about the announcement in the restaurant and the nervous chatter as everyone speculated on who could have done it and why. "I couldn't stay. It was too upsetting."

"I wish I could be with you," he said. "At times like this, you feel you should be with your loved ones, holding them close."

"I wish that too. Is it too late for me to jump on a plane to Hamburg?" She glanced at the clock, only half-joking.

"We need a time machine," he replied. "It could bring you to me instantly, whenever I need you, and it could also go back in time and have someone shoot the man who assassinated Kennedy before he could open fire."

Neither wanted to hang up; they said "I love you" many times and whispered goodbye, then held on longer, listening to each other's breathing along the telephone wires.

Maria sat up watching television till she couldn't keep her eyes open any longer, and the next morning she turned on her radio as soon as she awoke, feeling she had to hear every last detail. Only then could she begin to make sense of it. France Inter had nonstop coverage, and Maria learned that a man called Lee Harvey Oswald had been arrested and charged with shooting the president. The name meant nothing to her.

When the morning papers arrived, most featured a front-page picture of Mrs. Kennedy standing by Lyndon Johnson as he was sworn in. She was gaunt, eyes round and staring, clearly in shock, with smears of her husband's blood on her suit. Maria's heart went out to her. It was inhuman that she was being photographed straight after such an appalling trauma. Why was no one protecting her?

Mrs. Kennedy was said to be in the White House, planning her husband's funeral. Bobby Kennedy had met her when the plane landed in Washington. Maria guessed Lee would fly out to join her. She was probably on her way.

Details were sparse, so the newscasters kept repeating the same story, finding eyewitnesses to give their accounts. It was only in repetition that Maria could begin to feel it had really happened. She invited Bruna to join her in listening to the radio, and they discussed the minutiae. Where had the president's protection officers been? Why were they traveling in an open car? Presidents had been assassinated before—these things happened in America—but somehow this killing felt earth-shattering. He'd been so young, so eloquent, so good-looking.

At six that evening—the time they always spoke when they were apart—Maria rang Ari's hotel.

"I'm afraid he's checked out," the receptionist told her.

That was odd. He hadn't said he was leaving Hamburg. And then it occurred to her that he might be on his way to Paris. Perhaps he would arrive that evening. She smiled, with a quiver of excitement.

"What's for dinner?" she called to Bruna. "Is there enough if we have an unexpected guest?"

She touched up her makeup, just in case, but Ari had not arrived by dinnertime. She opened a bottle of champagne and sipped one glass, then another, while watching television, but when Ari had not arrived by midnight, she started to get anxious. They always spoke in the evening, no matter what. Had something happened to stop him?

She couldn't sleep for worrying that he had been in an accident. Perhaps he was dead too. The idea took root in her head and she obsessed through the early hours, tossing and turning till the sheets were tangled in knots.

She must have dozed off toward dawn but was awakened a couple of hours later by the sound of the telephone. Straightaway she leapt out of bed and rushed to the hall to take the receiver from Bruna, bracing herself for bad news.

"Oh, thank God!" she cried when she heard Ari's voice. "Where are you?"

"I'm in Washington, D.C. I flew out to see if I could be of any help to the Kennedy family. My plane landed just a couple of hours ago."

Maria was stunned. It made no sense. "Surely they'll want privacy at a time like this. You can't just walk in offering your services . . ."

"I was invited," Ari said. "I'm staying in the White House. That's where I'm calling from."

Maria frowned. "But you hardly know Mrs. Kennedy. You spent two weeks with her, and suddenly you are a close confidant?" She paused, and then the truth dawned on her. "Did Lee invite you? You're still sleeping with her. That's it, isn't it?"

"No, Maria, no." His voice was soothing. "Lee and Jacqueline are friends of mine so I'm here to support them in their hour of need. I was surprised when they invited me but it would have been bad manners to refuse."

"Friends?" She raised her eyebrows. "Are you sure about that?"

She couldn't shake off her suspicions about Lee, but a transatlantic telephone call was no place to argue with him. They probably taped calls at the White House. Perhaps the FBI listened in.

"I wish you had called me last night," she said instead. "I've been worried sick."

"I know, I'm sorry I missed our call but when the invitation came I rushed to catch the first flight. I'll call you again this evening at six your time. It's nighttime here so I must try to get some sleep. It's been a long day."

His voice was gravelly with tiredness. She was reluctant to hang up, though. Then she would have to wait nine hours till she spoke to him again.

"Have you seen your room?" she asked. "What's it like?"

"It's adequate. Simple decoration and a rather too-firm mattress. But I could sleep on a plank of wood right now if I had to."

"When will you be back? When will I see you?" she asked, hating herself for sounding desperate.

"I'll come to Paris straight after the funeral," he promised. "I miss you. I love you so much."

When he hung up, she tried to feel reassured by those last words, but they weren't enough to quell the sickening anxiety she felt at the thought of him staying in the White House, with Lee wandering around in an emotional state, seeking comfort . . . it felt as if he were slipping away from her and into the arms of the Radziwill woman, and there was no way she was going to sit back and let that happen. She would fight it with every bone in her body. But how?

Chapter 42

Washington, D.C.
November 25, 1963

Jackie lay wide awake, despite the Amytal the doctor had injected into a vein in her elbow. Her head was woolly with tiredness, her limbs leaden, but her brain was on full alert and would not let her doze off. Obsessive thoughts flickered like an old black-and-white movie, and her heart raced like a metronome. There was so much to be done. She had to find a new home for herself and the children as soon as possible, because, although the Johnsons had been the soul of kindness, they needed her to vacate the White House. Before she could start house hunting, though, she had to keep a firm grip on every detail of the funeral plans.

Everyone—even Bobby—had tried to talk her out of walking behind Jack's casket, saying it was too great a security risk, but she wasn't going to be deterred.

It was imperative that this funeral be as magnificent as that of Lincoln, the other truly great American president who had been assassinated. She gave little thought to Lee Harvey Oswald, the assassin, who had been shot and killed the previous day while in police custody. It had infuriated her when she'd heard that her beloved husband had been killed by a silly little Communist; if he had to die, she wished it could have been because of a great issue, such as his civil rights bill. But he was gone, and nothing could bring him back.

She looked at the clock: 3:20 A.M. This was the worst time of night. At one o'clock, she could tell herself some folks were still out at parties; at five, some were getting up for work. But between two and five were the dead hours, when she felt like the only person in the world who was awake.

She could have asked Lee, or Stas, or Bobby, or even her mother (God forbid), to sit with her. But the only person she wanted was Jack, and she was burying him the next day.

Details of their last conversations ran through her head, all of them inconsequential. What time they were meeting; what she was wearing; him wanting her to charm the ladies at luncheon; and then that last instruction to take her glasses off. His final words should have been profound, about world peace or racial equality, not about sunglasses.

Last words. Tears filled her eyes. She would never hear his voice again, never hear him teasing her or saying he loved her. *Last* meant last.

Mrs. Shaw brought Caroline and John to her room, so smart in their pale blue coats and shiny shoes that it made her want to weep. They'd been little angels since their daddy died. John was too young to understand, but Caroline knew. She kept trying to comfort her mother, clinging to her arm like a koala bear. It was tragic that she would grow up without a daddy. Black Jack had been a flawed father in many respects, but he was the lodestar that Jackie's young life was shaped by. Her childhood would have been less joyous without him; she'd have been less confident.

She found it hard to speak now, her throat tight with nerves. Others addressed her, their words floating over her head but not entering her brain. There was still an overwhelming sense of unreality. How could it be that Jack, who had been so full of life—the most *dynamic* person she had ever known—was gone?

When Bobby said it was time, she walked out of the White House, gripping a child's hand in each of hers.

There were hordes of photographers and television cameras recording each moment as they went to the Capitol to see Jack's coffin lying in state, but she didn't acknowledge them. Her mother had raised her to retain her dignity in public no matter what, and Jackie knew she would have to call on every ounce of that training. She was determined not to break down, because, if she did, that would be the photograph emblazoned on tomorrow's front pages. Today should be about Jack, not her.

As she followed the flag-draped casket to the cathedral, she did not glance around at all the heads of state she knew were following, or at the military bands or the thousands of spectators—not even at the Kennedy brothers on either side of her. She didn't worry about someone taking a potshot at her, but kept her eyes firmly fixed on the caisson that was transporting Jack's body and concentrated on putting one foot in front of the other. It felt like the last time she could be with him, the last service she could do for him, and that was in the forefront of her mind.

Thank God there was a degree of privacy inside the cathedral. She could huddle in the midst of the black-clad Kennedy tribe, each one grieving their own version of Jack while milling around to protect her, like an invisible shield. There was comfort to be had in large

families, she'd learned. After years of her feeling somewhat of an outsider, they'd all made it very clear that
she was a Kennedy now and they would look after her.
Bobby had been like her shadow from the moment Air
Force One had landed back in Washington. Today he
stood so close their arms were touching.

She kept her dignity during the eulogies, but as Luigi
Vena sang "Pie Jesu," the emotion welled up suddenly,
like a pot of milk on the boil. That perfect music soar-
ing around the nave and up to the cupola penetrated
her defenses, and a sob burst out. Bobby put a protective arm around her and Caroline squeezed her hand
hard. She was strong, her daughter; thank God for her
strength.

After they left the cathedral, she prompted John
to salute his father's casket and heard the clack-clack-
clack of hundreds of flashbulbs. That most private of
moments—a son bidding farewell to his father—could
not remain unphotographed. It was awful; just awful.

The children were taken back to the White House
while she continued to Arlington for the burial, and
now she felt as if her legs might give way at any second. Who would catch her if she fell? Probably Bobby.
He was right there, as he had been all day. But she
wouldn't collapse; she mustn't.

The Irish cadets were unbearably moving as they performed their silent drill. She had invited them in deference to the heritage Jack had been so proud of. He had loved his visit to Ireland that summer—just five months earlier—and Jackie wished with all her heart she had gone with him despite her pregnancy. She had Irish blood on her mother's side, and they'd always planned to visit together. Of course, they'd assumed they had decades in front of them. Now she would never see the land of their fathers by Jack's side.

It was her moment to step forward and light the eternal flame. She took the torch, but her hand was shaking badly and she couldn't touch flame to wick. The one thing she had to do, and she couldn't manage it. Her resilience was running close to empty and she almost burst into tears. But she mustn't; she wouldn't. She clutched her wrist with the other hand to steady it and finally managed to get the wick to light.

Soon she would be back at the White House, where she would close the doors, kick off her shoes, light a cigarette, and gulp down a vodka. She had done what was required of her; she had given Jack a send-off befitting a great world leader. The greatest. Now she just had to find a way to live without him.

Chapter 43

Paris
November 25, 1963

Maria watched the coverage of President Kennedy's funeral on French television and was moved beyond words by the austere dignity of the former First Lady, rake thin and fragile behind her black veil, two tiny children clutching her hands. It had been only three days since her husband was shot as he sat in a car beside her. How could she get out of bed, never mind parade in front of the world's television cameras? She must have nerves of steel.

Maria scanned the images, looking for Lee, but couldn't spot her. Today was all about the Kennedys.

She was surprised when Ari called at six o'clock, because she'd thought he would still be with the mourners.

"I didn't go to the funeral, but I had dinner with

the extended family last night," he said. "You wouldn't believe the amount of alcohol that was consumed, and the jokes turning the air blue." He chuckled. "Bobby Kennedy's face was a picture when he came into the room and spotted me. I thought he was going to choke, but instead he started needling me, calling me an ex-convict."

"That was uncalled for." She was annoyed on his behalf.

"He was trying to make me lose my temper, and I was determined not to give him the satisfaction. Then he disappeared and came back with a document that said I promised to give half my wealth to the poor of Latin America and invited me to sign it. I signed but added a few codicils in Greek to make it unenforceable."

"You'd best get your lawyers to check," Maria cautioned. "As America's attorney general, I imagine he knows a few tricks."

"Don't worry—he wouldn't try to use it."

"What makes you so sure?"

"Because he knows that I know about him and Jack and Marilyn Monroe. The minute he took any action against me, the story of their sordid little threesome would appear in the press." He sounded cocky, but Maria was alarmed by his lack of scruples and the risk he was taking.

"No wonder Bobby hates you!"

"Yes, the feeling is entirely mutual. Later in the evening he took me aside and told me not to show my face at the funeral. He said it would attract adverse coverage. I decided it wasn't the time to argue."

She could tell he was pleased with himself all the same, flattered to have been a guest in the White House, delighted that Bobby was not able to get the better of him. But surely it was odd that Ari, who had met the president only once or twice, should be present at such a close family gathering?

"Was Mrs. Kennedy there?" she asked. Somehow she couldn't imagine the grieving widow being part of such tomfoolery.

"No. I've hardly seen her," he replied. "She's keeping to her private rooms. I telephoned her to express my condolences but we didn't speak for long."

So was it Lee who'd invited him? Maria wondered. It must have been. She wouldn't ask, though. He'd be back in Paris soon. That's when she would try to find out what was happening with her rival and figure out how she was going to put a stop to it once and for all.

After lunch, she sat down to write a letter of condolence to Mrs. Kennedy, but it was hard to find the words. She started many times, then crumpled the paper into a ball. She knew there would be many thousands of such letters and Mrs. Kennedy would probably not even see hers, but, still, it should be right.

"I met your husband only once," she wrote, "after his birthday celebration at Madison Square Garden, but in the space of our short conversation I could sense his integrity, his warmth and his humor." She paused, then continued: "I knew he would do great things for his country and felt reassured that the peace of our planet rested in his hands. It is unbearably cruel that he had so little time to achieve his aims, and yet I hope you can take some comfort from the knowledge that the world is a better place because of him."

She didn't follow politics closely, but she knew President Kennedy had persuaded the Soviet leader, Khrushchev, to limit nuclear-weapons testing; she'd read that he was responsible for the Equal Pay Act in America and had signed an order stating that employees should be treated equally regardless of race, creed, or color; he had also established the Peace Corps to help the needy in foreign lands.

She concluded the letter by saying that she was praying for Mrs. Kennedy and her children. She knew the former First Lady was Roman Catholic but hoped she would accept some Greek Orthodox prayers sent with her most heartfelt sympathy.

Maria reread the pages and frowned. Words alone were inadequate, but it was the sentiment that counted. She felt very emotional about John F. Kennedy's death—for more reasons than one.

A week later, on the morning of her fortieth birthday, Maria awoke to the clatter of Ari bringing her a tray on which sat a glass of champagne, a perfectly turned omelette, and a vase containing a single dark-pink rose. After she had eaten, he ran her bath, pouring in a generous glug of jasmine oil, and as she reclined in the water he presented her with her first gift: a Van Cleef & Arpels sapphire-and-diamond necklace.

"Ari! It's divine," she exclaimed. "You're so good at choosing jewelry!"

"Why not try it on?" he suggested, and helped her fasten it around her neck. "Beautiful!" he declared, standing back to appreciate the effect. "Might I join you in your bath?"

"Of course," she said with a seductive smile, curling her legs to make room.

He stripped off his dressing gown, climbed into the claw-foot tub, and made love to her slowly and sensually, the oil making their skin slippery, the water sloshing over the edge.

"My only worry," he said afterward, "is that now I will spend the rest of the day smelling like a homosexual."

Maria laughed: "You need have no worries on that score. I'll give you a glowing reference."

At lunchtime there was another gift: a glorious nineteenth-century gold-leaf mirror adorned with sirens. Then midafternoon a bouquet arrived that was six feet tall and bursting with rare tropical blooms in shades of dark pink, white, and green. She felt thoroughly spoiled.

The celebration continued that evening, when Ari hosted a birthday dinner at Maxim's for twenty close friends and stood to toast her: "To a woman who is as talented in love and friendship as she is in music," he declared. "I wish for your next forty years to be filled with joy."

Maria clinked glasses with the guests, smiling and playing the role of birthday girl, but deep down she was not happy about this milestone. She hated the fine lines that were etched at the corners of her eyes and the way her face was succumbing to gravity. How could she compete with Lee Radziwill, who was a decade younger? She was unhappy with the instability of her voice in its higher registers, and the way it did not always behave as she wanted it to. And she still felt profound sadness that she did not have a child, someone to give her a sense of purpose for the future.

"When is your *Tosca* at the Royal Opera House?" Maggie van Zuylen asked, breaking her train of thought.

"Next month," Maria replied with a smile. "Zeffirelli's production is very modern. He's quite the genius."

"Am I invited?" Ari asked. "I've heard so much about it I feel I must see it."

Maggie gave Maria a subtle wink, but she felt uneasy. Was Ari jealous of Zeffirelli because of her dinner with him? Or did he hope to arrange a clandestine meeting with Lee once he was in London?

"Of course you're invited," she told him, hating the way jealousy gnawed at her, spoiling the moment.

In the car on the way back to his apartment, she confessed to feeling nervous about *Tosca*. "I'm not sure my voice is up to the challenge."

Ari squeezed her knee. "Even if there is a slight wobble, audiences feel privileged to have seen you perform. Your acting is better than ever, your voice miles superior to any other singer. You always give value for money."

"I am not the best any longer," she said, thinking of all the new young stars emerging.

"Audiences want to be able to say, 'I heard Maria

Callas,'" he continued. "And I am the happiest man in the world because I can say, 'I fuck Maria Callas.'" He ran his hand up her thigh. "I fuck her a lot."

Maria laughed. In the early days she used to chastise him for swearing, but she had long since given up. "What about 'I love Maria Callas'?"

He kissed her passionately, then held her face between his hands and looked deep into her eyes as he said, "I will *always* love Maria Callas."

That should be enough for me, Maria thought. But it wasn't. He had been very generous but he hadn't given her the one birthday present she yearned for more than any other—a date for their wedding. It was beginning to feel as if he never would.

Chapter 44

Palm Beach, Florida
December 25, 1963

The glittery, bauble-strewn Christmas tree in the front hall of the Kennedy's Palm Beach home bothered Jackie. It felt wrong to celebrate just four weeks after Jack's death, but the children needed some normality; it wouldn't be fair to cancel Christmas.

Lee and Stas were there with their two children, and Ethel and Bobby brought their ever-expanding brood, all of them shoehorned into the mansion's eleven bedrooms. The children soon went feral, rushing around and whooping in extended games with no apparent rules that lasted from breakfast till dinner. Caroline and John joined in, but they were quieter than usual. John normally liked to be in the center of the action when his big cousins were around, but now he hung back, shadowing his sister.

Jackie watched them for signs of grief, but during the day she saw just their unusual quietness. Only at bedtime, when she tucked them in, did the questions come pouring out.

"Why did that man shoot Daddy?" Caroline asked on Christmas night, after the gifts had been opened, the wrapping paper tossed in the trash, and the ham carved to the bone.

"There are bad people in the world," Jackie told her. "Just a few. Your daddy was a target because he was president and he wanted to make things better for everyone: rich and poor, black and white. Some people didn't like that."

"Why not?" Caroline persisted.

"I don't know," Jackie admitted. "Maybe one day when they finish investigating, someone will explain it to us."

Her children were sharing a double bed in the room next to hers. She slipped off her shoes and crawled between them so that she could put an arm around each.

"When is he coming back?" John asked, fighting to keep his eyes open.

"Who do you mean? The bad man?" Jackie combed her fingers through his hair. "He's not coming back."

"Not him," John said. "When is Daddy coming back?"

Jackie took a deep breath to control herself. "He's in heaven now, sweetheart. But he will always be in our hearts."

She could feel Caroline crying, her little frame quivering, and she pulled their heads to her shoulders, holding them tight until she felt their muscles relax and they slid into sleep.

She was haunted by memories of the previous Christmas. They had all been together in the White House and everything had been perfect: a huge tree, tasteful white and silver decorations, beautifully wrapped presents. The best years of their marriage were spent in that house. How could it be that last Christmas had been Jack's final one?

And then she realized that for the past twelve months he had been living each date for the last time, and no one knew. His last birthday, his last swim in the ocean, last cocktail, last time he tucked his children into bed, last time they made love. Their last kiss, on the morning he died, just after they'd landed in Dallas.

"Thanks for coming to Texas," he'd said. "It means a lot." Then he'd kissed her.

Downstairs, Jackie poured herself a large vodka on the rocks and sat sipping it while the other grown-ups chatted. They were trying to avoid mentioning Jack, as if worried it would remind her—which was laughable. How could she ever forget, even for a second?

"How's the new house?" Ethel asked.

Jackie had moved to a town house in Georgetown, on loan from friends. "It's spacious," she said, "but too close to the road. Crowds of sightseers stand outside with cameras waiting for a glimpse of me or the kids." She wrinkled her nose. "What kind of people would do that?"

Lee shook her head in disgust. "I've seen them having picnics right there on the sidewalk. They throw sandwich wrappers and pop bottles onto the front lawn, and when the protection officers go over to remonstrate, they just take photos of them."

Jackie couldn't bear the sound of cameras now, especially the ones with flashbulbs. The explosions and the flash made her rigid with fear. Any one of those sightseers could have a concealed gun. One day a woman had leapt toward her as she walked to the car and managed to touch her hair before a Secret Service agent stopped her. Why would she do that? What made her think it was okay?

Anything unexpected took Jackie straight back to the car in Dallas, so viscerally it was as if she were still there. Earlier that day, one of Ethel's indistinguishable children had jumped through a doorway waving a toy pistol, and Jackie got such a fright she screamed over and over. A stranger coming to the front door made her panic. She was constantly scared that she or one of her children would be killed by a random lunatic, and the raucous atmosphere of a Kennedy family Christmas wasn't helping.

"I guess folks will have an interest in you for some time to come," Ethel said, not unkindly. "But finding a house set back off the road would help. Do you want me to view some for you?"

"Thanks, Ethel, but I think you have enough on your plate." Ethel had given birth to her eighth child that summer. *How did she even remember their names?* Jackie wondered.

"Will you stay in Washington?" Bobby asked. "That's the first decision."

Jackie looked at him. He knew better than anyone that she was having trouble making decisions. It felt as if her brain wasn't working properly, as if the neurons were misfiring.

"I don't know," she said, and was grateful when Lee changed the subject. Her sister had been wonderful these past weeks. She was always on hand, sensitive to her needs, bringing drinks, ashtrays, and fresh handkerchiefs as required. On the night of the funeral she'd left a note on Jackie's pillow that read, "Good night, my darling Jacks—the bravest and noblest of all." But Jackie didn't confide in her. That wasn't the way their relationship worked. She was the one who had always looked out for Lee, and they couldn't switch roles overnight.

Only Bobby shared the immensity of her grief. He was broken by Jack's death. Shattered. Like her, he was crawling through the days, barely managing to get by. That's why he was the only person she could talk to. She could tell him the raw truth without censoring herself the way she had to around others.

After he had rushed to collect her from Air Force One on the day of Jack's death, she told him every gruesome detail, omitting nothing. It poured out in a torrent. Still did, whenever they were alone. She couldn't help repeating it. Maybe she should hold back so as not to upset him, but the words came of their own volition.

That afternoon, they had walked along the beach in the Florida sunshine, waves washing over their bare toes, the shrieks of children in their ears, and she had told him the list of what she called the "if onlys." She had gone over them so many times in her head that she thought she would go mad if she didn't share them.

"If only we had persuaded Jack not to go to Texas. We all knew he had enemies there. Why did he not make the governor come to Washington to resolve that stupid argument . . ."

"There's no point thinking that way," Bobby interrupted.

"But there is," she said. "I need to pin it down. If only we hadn't been in an open motorcade. If only I had been watching out of his side of the car and seen the shooter take aim. If only I had realized that sound like a car backfiring was actually a gunshot. I should have pulled him down to the floor and shielded him."

"It was up to the Secret Service to protect him. They're the ones who failed. Not you. You did all you could." He took her hand, squeezed it.

Jackie kept walking in silence. Nothing he said could dispel the feeling that she had let Jack down when he needed her most.

A gale of laughter rose from the adult family members sitting near where the children were playing, and Jackie felt so furious that she could have punched them all. How could they laugh when Jack was dead? How could anyone laugh again?

In the first months after Jack died, Jackie often went to Arlington Cemetery alone, to sit by his grave. The winter skies were the color of gunmetal, and a hard frost made the clods of earth sparkle. It was unbearable to think he was there, beneath the soil, yet she couldn't see him, couldn't touch him. Her Secret Service men hovered at a respectful distance.

One day after visiting the grave she went to pray in St. Matthew's Cathedral, and the bishop came to sit with her, crossing his hands in his lap, his round face solemn.

"You must have many questions," he said. "I want you to know that I am always here for you."

"Yes, I have a question: What kind of God let this happen?" Jackie challenged him. "What possible reason could there be, when Jack had so much to give to the world?"

"It is not always for us to know the reason why," he replied, "but we must have faith that everything happens according to God's plan. Remember that this world is not the last. There is another beyond, where you and Jack will be reunited once more."

Jackie felt furiously angry with him, sitting there as if he were the font of all knowledge, yet speaking to her in platitudes. "Answer me this," she demanded. "If I kill myself now, would I go to the same heaven as Jack? Because, quite frankly, I don't want to be here anymore. I only want to be with him." She put her hand over her mouth to stifle a sob.

The bishop regarded her in silence for a moment, as

if formulating a profound theological answer, but when he spoke he was practical: "Who would bring up your living children? Who would look after Caroline and John?"

And Jackie knew she couldn't kill herself, because whether it was Lee or Ethel who raised them, no one would love her children the way she loved them. She was trapped on this earth because of them, and she had to find a way to be a good enough mother to make up for the fact that their father was gone forever.

Chapter 45

Paris
March 1964

"The baron and I had dinner with Lee and Stas," Maggie van Zuylen told Maria over afternoon tea, "and I guarantee you've got nothing to fear from Lee. She has no interesting conversation and her personality can best be described as brittle."

"Yes, but her sister is the world's most famous grieving widow, and Ari positively salivates in the presence of fame." Maria stirred her tea, pressing the back of her teaspoon against the slice of lemon.

"Do you think the affair is still going on?"

Maria shrugged. "I haven't caught them in flagrante. As far as I'm aware, he hasn't seen her since JFK's funeral. When he came to London with me recently, her name wasn't mentioned."

Maggie looked thoughtful. "He's the kind of man

who loves the pursuit and gets bored after conquest. He had his one-night stand with Lee and paid her with a bracelet. 'Dearest, sweetest love' is what you say to a favorite niece, not a lover."

"Do you really think so?"

"I never told you this," Maggie continued, "but Ari once paid Eva Perón ten thousand dollars to spend the night with him. That's all he wanted—just to be able to say he'd had her."

To Maria the story was sleazy. She didn't like to hear about that side of him.

Maggie touched her arm. "Ari told me the other day that he thinks he has finally been accepted by European society through being with you. For a long time they held him at arm's length because of his business reputation, but you bring him class, he said."

"Did he really?" Maria flushed. She would treasure that compliment.

"So, what are you singing next?" Maggie asked. "And when can I come and hear you?"

"Zeffirelli has asked me to sing *Norma* at the Paris Opéra in May . . ."

"How exciting!" Maggie cried.

Maria made a face. "I haven't given him my answer yet. It's more technically challenging than *Tosca* and, frankly, I don't know if my voice is up to it. I've had an operation on my sinuses since the last time I sang *Norma* and it's affected my resonance. Besides, I haven't been practicing as much as I should."

"You are the woman who learned Wagner's Isolde in two months," Maggie remonstrated. "And you've sung *Norma* many times before."

"You sound like Ari," she said. "He wants me to accept so he can invite all our Parisian friends to watch."

"It's a good plan," Maggie said. "Hammer home that you are a much bigger trophy than Lee. Remind him how proud he should be to have you on his arm."

Maria launched herself into a program of intensive practice and sessions with vocal coaches to get ready for *Norma*. She would nail this. She had to!

Rehearsals began in April, and she loved Zeffirelli's design for the enchanted forest, which changed color as the seasons progressed. She loved her multicolored costumes in flowing silk and chiffon that swayed like leaves in a breeze. And she adored the child performers, feeling a maternal protectiveness toward them. She made sure they were given plenty of rest breaks, and always kept a stock of candy and soft drinks in her dressing room, remembering how tough it had been when she was forced to perform at their age.

All that was fine, but vocally she was still struggling in her upper register as opening night drew near.

"Skip some of the high notes," Zeffirelli advised. "Few in the audience will be any the wiser."

"I can't do that. It would be cheating." She would never compromise her art if she could help it. Instead she worked harder than ever, pushing herself to control the pulsation on her top notes, practicing long hours every day.

Ari decided to invite their friends to the fourth night, once the critics had attended and the production had settled into its stride. He asked Princess Grace, the Aga Khan, Charlie and Oona Chaplin, the Duke and Duchess of Windsor, Maggie van Zuylen and her husband, and many others. He arranged a champagne reception for the intermission, and his excitement mounted as the evening drew near.

On opening night, Maria managed all the high notes and cadenzas, but without the power she used to bring to the role of the Druid priestess. She knew the critics realized this, but their reviews were kind, commenting on her "sublime" acting and the "subtlety" of her musical phrasing. The second and third nights followed the same pattern, but she awoke on the morning of the fourth feeling nervous about Ari's high expectations. Her throat was a little constricted, perhaps because of nerves, so she spent the day doing relaxation exercises and focusing on the music, before going through her preperformance rituals.

The applause was thunderous when she stepped on-stage, but from the opening notes she knew she was going to struggle. The vocal cords were not responding cleanly. She had no choice but to skip some high notes and give a softer, toned-down performance. All that would have been acceptable—just—but in the final scene she reached for C5 and her voice cracked on the note. There was no disguising it, even for those who were not opera fans; her failure was clear.

A few audience members hissed their disapproval, and the hisses were soon accompanied by a scattering of boos. Maria raised her arm to the conductor, indicating that she wanted to try again. There was a pause, the orchestra returned to the start of the aria, and Maria summoned all her vocal training to sing a perfectly placed, sustained C5. Most of the crowd applauded, but there was still some grumbling, and she felt humiliated. Why tonight, of all nights?

At the end, she took a few cursory curtain calls, then rushed to her dressing room, where she slammed the door, wishing she could be invisible. She felt terrible for letting Ari down. He had been dying for the evening to be a success.

The dressing-room door opened and he burst in with a bottle of champagne.

"*Magnifico!*" he cried. "I have never been prouder of you than I was when you sang that high note the second time. That's my Maria! That's what I love about you: you never accept defeat."

She shook her head. "I was terrible. Of all nights for my top C to desert me!"

"Your friends are singing your praises. They're in the restaurant now. Come and join us. Shall I open this bottle to get you in the mood?"

"I can't face anyone." She shook her head firmly. "I couldn't bear to listen to their tactfully worded congratulations. You go if you like, but I'm heading home."

"You were splendid and everyone loved you," he said. "But if you want to go home, then I will accompany you."

His Rolls-Royce whisked them back to the Avenue Foch apartment, where his chef prepared a light supper, but Maria couldn't eat. She sipped a glass of Dom Pérignon, still overcome with humiliation.

"I can't sing onstage anymore," she announced. "That's it. It's not fair to risk letting down my fellow musicians and my audiences." Thank goodness Ari's attempts to make her the figurehead of a Monte Carlo opera company had foundered. She wasn't worthy of the honor.

"I don't think you let anyone down," Ari insisted. "But if you don't want the pressure of performing, perhaps you could concentrate on films and recordings."

"Perhaps . . ."

She couldn't think about that tonight. There were only four more performances in Paris, and then they would fly to Athens to board the *Christina* for a long summer cruise. They'd go to Milan for the fourth anniversary of Omero's birth in June, then the rest of the summer would be about swimming, sunbathing, and resting, trying to scrub the memory of tonight's performance from her mind.

So much for showing Ari that she was a more glittering prize than Lee. That plan had backfired spectacularly.

Chapter 46

New York City
Fall 1964

Protecting Jack's legacy became a full-time job for Jackie in the first year after his death. There had been an early, ill-judged interview with a *Life* magazine journalist just a week after the shooting, when she was still so traumatized she scarcely knew what she was saying. She hadn't been altogether happy with the article, which in retrospect sounded too sentimental, but at least she had managed to introduce the idea of Jack's presidency being like the Camelot of Arthurian legend, a time of exceptional brilliance that would be remembered through the ages.

In January she had been interviewed by the Warren Commission, set up to investigate Jack's death, and that was harrowing. How many shots had there been? She thought she recalled two, but everything was a blur.

When, much later, she saw a home movie of the shooting made by a Dallas resident named Abraham Zapruder, she was stunned to see herself clambering onto the back of the car. She had no recollection of doing so— but there she was, in her pink suit and pillbox hat. It felt as if it had happened to someone else, as if that hadn't been her sitting there cradling Jack's bloodied head in her lap, trying to keep his brains inside his skull.

She had spent hours talking with author and historian Arthur Schlesinger, sessions that would serve as a record for the John F. Kennedy Presidential Library, and, once he had finished, William Manchester, the man she had chosen to be Jack's official biographer, began his interviews. There were also lengthy meetings with John Warnecke, the architect designing Jack's gravestone, and she was overseeing a memorial edition of *Look* magazine that would come out on the first anniversary of his death. She had a desperate need to control every detail, every single word written about him, so that the world would understand what a great president Jack had been, and how much he achieved in just two years, ten months, and two days.

By day she held herself together, her mother's training coming to the fore. *Think before you speak; if you don't have anything useful to say, don't say anything at all.* Most women tended to gabble, to fill silences, but

Jackie found that remaining silent could be more powerful, forcing your interlocutor to speak instead.

To all but a tiny handful of observers, she must have appeared to be coping well. Only a few saw the reality—Bobby, more than anyone else. Maybe it wasn't fair to unload her grief on him. He was gray and stooped, forever marked by the tragedy. Like her, he was throwing himself into work to get through the days, but he always made time if she called his office to ask his opinion, or to discuss what was on her mind. She leaned on Bobby, mentally, emotionally, and physically too, often wrapping her arms around his neck and pressing her body against his. He was only a little shorter than Jack, with the same wavy Kennedy hair, but his build was slighter, less solid, and he smelled less earthy. Hugging him helped at the time, but it left her feeling lonelier afterward because it emphasized the absence.

In the evenings, after the children went to bed, was when Jackie let her guard down. The first vodka took the edge off; the second gave her a mellow fuzziness; the third made her weep. There was often a fourth and a fifth, and sometimes they provoked ugly moments that she remembered in snatches the following morning: screaming at the children's nanny, sobbing uncontrollably on her private secretary's shoulder, hurling an ashtray across the room.

But vodka plus sleeping pills was a nightly ritual through which she sought the oblivion that would help her drop off to sleep. Otherwise, gunshots and blood and horror kept her eyes wide open, staring into the darkness, as she relived the moments in Dallas over and over again.

"I can't talk to women," Jackie told Father Richard McSorley, a Jesuit priest with whom she had begun playing tennis. "They say inane things, like 'Time is a great healer.'" She mimicked her mother's voice—for it was she who had come out with that phrase only the day before, after chiding Jackie that she must be a role model for widows everywhere. "Frankly, from where I'm sitting, grief only gets worse over time."

He looked up from lacing his tennis shoes, his hazel eyes full of kindness. "Yet, I'm sure you can see that ten years from now the pain will not be so acute and overwhelming. Everyone around you means well."

"This morning, when I woke up, for a moment I couldn't remember Jack's face. Can you imagine? That was one of the lowest points yet." She fingered the strings of her racquet, biting back tears. "I can't bear it that other people are moving on and he is becoming history."

Father McSorley stood up. He was several inches

taller than she, with white hair and a slim physique. "Don't forget that Jack is part of the future too. His influence is all around, with his civil rights reforms and the other great work he did. He will live on, not just in you and the children but worldwide."

"So *why* did it happen?" she cried, hitting the ground with her racquet in a burst of fury. "*Why* did God take him away if he was doing so much good? It will never make sense to me."

"I've brought you some books," he said, nodding at a bag he had left at the side of the court. "I'll give them to you later. There are insights into the beliefs of different cultures regarding tragedy and death: Buddhism, atheism, Islam. I thought you might find them interesting."

"If you want me to believe that Jack will be reincarnated as a beetle or a frog, I warn you in advance, I don't buy it."

He laughed. "Jack would be a lion or a golden eagle, at the very least. Come, let's play. We can talk after."

He was a good tennis player, who had been coaching Ethel and Bobby's children. Sometimes Jackie won, sometimes he did, but for an hour or so she could focus on the simple task of hitting a ball across a net. It helped.

Talking to Father McSorley helped in many ways.

She told him about her recurring guilt that she hadn't been able to save Jack, her suicidal urges, and the vivid dreams that made her wake abruptly, soaked in sweat and trembling in terror.

Late in the summer, Father McSorley helped her make the decision to leave Washington and return to New York's Upper East Side, where she had spent her childhood. She hoped she could be anonymous there, away from political circles. They could get an apartment on an upper floor where no sightseers could peer in the windows and a doorman would prevent intruders from gaining entry. She loved the cultural richness of New York, the unparalleled shopping, and the fact that it was a cosmopolitan city, where folk would scarcely bat an eye when they passed a celebrity in the street. Most of all, the city reminded her of her daddy, Black Jack, and the happy times they had spent there.

She viewed a few properties before making an offer for a fifteen-room penthouse apartment at 1040 Fifth Avenue, overlooking Central Park, just seven blocks north of a place Lee and Stas had bought. It was a relief to get away from Georgetown, where it was permanently "zoo time," but the first evening they spent there, she sobbed on the telephone to Bobby for over an hour.

"It feels as though I am leaving him," she cried.

"People will say I'm moving on, but you know I'm not, don't you?"

"Of course you're not," Bobby replied. In the background she could hear Ethel shouting at their kids to get to bed. "Trust me. Jack would think you'd done the right thing."

Among the books Father McSorley had lent her was one called *The Greek Way,* in which a classicist named Edith Hamilton described the thinking of fifth-century Athenians as they tried to make sense of the universe. Jackie was struck in particular by a chapter in which the author explained the Greek belief that tragedy could be caused by sins committed by one's forebears, which they had to expiate, or because of a family curse, or hubris. The Kennedy family certainly seemed cursed, she mused. Jack's eldest brother, Joe, had died in the war, and his sister Kick had been killed in a plane crash in 1948. Another sister, Rosemary, was said to be mentally incapacitated and had spent her adult life in an institution. And now Jack. To lose four out of eight children before they reached middle age seemed more than bad luck. Joe Kennedy Sr. had been no angel in his younger years and must have made some enemies.

When Lee mentioned that Aristotle Onassis was in

New York on a business trip, Jackie decided to invite him to a brunch she was planning so she could quiz him about Greek beliefs. She called and left an invitation with his personal secretary, which was relayed to him.

The secretary called back to confirm that Mr. Onassis would be delighted to attend, then added, "He is in town with Maria Callas and wondered if you might consider including her in the group?"

Jackie hesitated. She was a fan of Maria Callas's singing but it might be awkward to meet her because of Lee's affair with Onassis. She wasn't sure if it was still going on, because Lee clammed up whenever his name was mentioned; nor was she sure whether Maria knew about it. The situation was complicated, and she couldn't face a scene. Besides, she was not in the right frame of mind for meeting new people. "Please tell Mr. Onassis that unfortunately I only have one spare place at my table," she replied.

In fact, she had designed the guest list carefully to comprise some of the most intelligent men of her acquaintance: among them were Father McSorley; David Ormsby-Gore, British ambassador to the United States; and Kenneth Galbraith, the economist. Nine men altogether, and herself. Women would bring emotion to the table, and she wanted a discussion that was entirely unsentimental.

She served ham and eggs accompanied by Bloody Marys and, as they ate, she questioned them all about their belief systems, stimulating discussion of some of the themes she had been reading about in Father Mc-Sorley's books. It was a meeting of the minds that she felt privileged to witness.

"Do you believe in curses, Mr. Onassis?" she asked, turning to him. "They say one was placed on the Grimaldi royal family of Monaco back in the Middle Ages, and it accounts for all the unhappy marriages and premature deaths suffered by that dynasty."

"Any large family has its share of misfortune," he replied. "As Mr. Galbraith would no doubt explain, it is statistical. Besides, dying young was commonplace before the advent of modern medicine, and the children of unhappy marriages do not have a good example set them in youth, so may be more likely to enter an unhappy marriage themselves. This seems a more likely explanation than any superstition."

Jackie regarded him. "My parents had an unhappy marriage. Does that mean I am doomed to repeat their example?"

"I would argue that intelligence also plays a part in our relationship choices, so you have a higher chance of success than most." He smiled.

She accepted the compliment with a nod. It was interesting to watch Mr. Onassis in the midst of these men. They were better read and more educated, but he was not intimidated by the conversation. She caught a glimpse of why Lee was so obsessed with him. He was the type of man who would rescue you from a burning building, not with brute strength but by using his cool rationality to figure the best way out.

Chapter 47

New York City
Fall 1964

By October 1964, Maria and Ari had been lovers for five years, so she was stunned when Mrs. Kennedy invited him to brunch without including her. Was Lee going to be present? She urged him to refuse the invitation but he insisted on going, leaving Maria to stew in jealous anxiety all afternoon.

When Ari returned to their hotel suite in the early evening, he told her it had just been a bunch of men talking philosophy while Mrs. Kennedy presided regally at the head of the table.

"It was a very odd occasion," he said. "And I'm not sure why I was included. She is trying to find a rational explanation for her husband's death, but it is unlikely we will ever learn why it happened since Lee Harvey Oswald did not explain his motives."

"That must be hard for her," Maria sympathized, her mood lightening with the realization that the brunch hadn't been a pretext for Ari and Lee to get together. She was wary where any Kennedys or Radziwills were concerned.

That fall Maria made a recording of *Tosca,* which was so successful that it made her reconsider her decision to give up performing. She missed the stage, the buzz of knowing that you were holding an audience's attention, the applause, the drama of it all. If she was careful about the roles she chose, surely there could be more years of performing ahead of her?

Tosca suited her new, lower range and she had always loved Puccini's music, so she decided to undertake a limited tour of the production. After a few months of intensive work with voice coaches, she sang it at the Paris Opéra in February 1965, and the reviews were ecstatic. It boosted her confidence and she agreed the production could transfer to the New York Met, her first performance there in seven years.

The prospect of singing for a New York audience again was daunting. She wasn't sure what reception to expect, but as her limousine approached the building on the first day of rehearsals, she saw a huge banner across the front that read WELCOME HOME MARIA. A line of people huddled in sleeping bags snaked around the block.

"What are they queuing for?" she asked her driver.

"For you, of course." He grinned. "The first fifty-odd on line camped out overnight."

She shook her head in amazement. Not bad for a middle-aged has-been! In her hotel that evening, she switched on the television news and was touched to hear some fans being interviewed: "It would have been a crime to miss Maria Callas," one young man said. "She is undoubtedly the greatest singer of this century."

Another, who had been camping out since the previous afternoon, told the interviewer, "Only for Maria would I do this. Nobody else."

Ari had not accompanied her because of business back in Athens. She had a niggling worry that he might be seeing Lee but pushed it out of her mind to focus on her performance. The voice had to be top-notch for opening night.

When she stepped out onto the Met's stage, right foot first, she was greeted by a full six minutes of applause. She clasped her hands to her face, overcome by the rapturous reception. Who would have thought it? She felt humbled by their warmth and it took awhile before she could compose herself sufficiently to smile and gesture her thanks by applauding the audience in return.

In her own estimation, her voice was smaller and less sure than it had been when last she sang there, but you wouldn't think it to read the reviews after opening night: "One of the most remarkable vocal achievements in my memory," a prominent critic wrote. What's more, her return to the city was front-page news and not just a paragraph in the arts section.

Maria felt giddy with joy. She read the critics' comments over the phone to Ari and he was so proud he sounded fit to burst.

"I'll ask my New York secretary to buy dozens of copies of every single newspaper so I can send them to our friends," he declared.

"Don't you think that's a little boastful?" Maria chided, amused.

"Not at all," he replied. "They will want to share in our triumph."

She smiled at his use of the word *our*. It was the kind of thing a husband might say, and she liked that. She liked it a lot.

Chapter 48

New York City
March 25, 1965

Maria's second performance of *Tosca* at the Met received yet another ecstatic reception from the New York audience. Afterward, as she sat in her dressing room removing her heavy stage makeup, she was stunned when the manager came to the door and asked if Mrs. Jacqueline Kennedy might visit her.

"Of course!" she replied after just a moment's hesitation, far too curious to refuse. She wiped the cold cream from her face and gave her hair a quick brushing, noticing that her hand was trembling. *What did Mrs. Kennedy want? Was this about Ari and Lee?*

Jackie knocked, then entered timidly, looking slighter than Maria had imagined. She was dressed like royalty in a white ermine stole over a white-satin ankle-length gown, and her hair was backcombed and lacquered into the famous style that flipped up at her shoulders. She hung back, as if uncertain whether to approach.

"I don't want to take your time," she breathed. "You must be exhausted . . ."

"Not at all." Maria rose to shake her hand and indicated a chair, saying, "Please—sit down." A wave of expensive scent reached her. Mrs. Kennedy was prettier in real life than in photos, and Maria wished she'd had time to reapply some makeup. She felt exposed, her face shiny from the cold cream.

"I had to call in a lot of favors to get a ticket for tonight," Jackie began, her voice a little croaky, "but I'm so glad I did. You were wonderful." She smoothed her skirt beneath her, fidgeted with her evening bag.

Was this really the visit of a fan? If so, it was very brave of her, under the circumstances. "I'm honored that you came. Next time please ask and I will send tickets to save you the trouble."

"Why, *tha-a-nk* you," Jackie said. Her accent was New England one moment, then almost upper-class British the next, as if she couldn't quite decide who she was. Like Lee's, her words had a prolonged *ah* sound, and she dropped her *r*s. "I've long been a fan. In fact, I heard you sing *Norma* here back in 1956. It was unforgettable."

Maria smiled. "I love *Norma*. I'm very glad you enjoyed it." That had been the year before she met Ari. The production had been marred for her by the critical *Time* magazine article in which her mother denounced her as selfish and heartless, but she knew her voice had been at its peak and was pleased Jackie had heard it then.

"I wanted to apologize," Jackie said next.

She paused and Maria frowned, wondering what the apology was for. Mrs. Kennedy spoke slowly, leaving long gaps between sentences, and Maria's mind leapt through a handful of possibilities. Was she apologizing for her sister's affair with Ari?

Jackie continued: "I should have invited you to brunch with Mr. Onassis last fall but I was not very good at meeting new people back then. I am slowly getting better, I hope."

So that was it. "Please. Don't apologize," Maria said.

"Oh, but I must. I was ashamed of myself, especially since you had written such a beautiful letter after Jack died. I remember it most particularly." Her voice softened at the mention of his name.

She's nice, Maria realized. *Nothing like her sister.* There was sincerity in her expression, alongside vulnerability. "I was so saddened by your husband's death I had to write. It felt important to let you know that the world was mourning with you."

Jackie reached across suddenly and took Maria's hand, her voice so low it was almost a whisper. "No one can explain it to me. I don't think they ever will. Yet opera is full of tragedy. It is part of the universal human experience, is it not?"

Maria nodded. "All of us know loss at some time in our lives, but not of the magnitude of yours. Thankfully that is rare." She paused and chose her words with care. She didn't want to upset someone who seemed so fragile, but she couldn't miss this opportunity to make her position clear. "Your dignity since then has moved me greatly, and Ari feels the same way. I know I can speak for him in saying you and your children would be welcome to come for a cruise on the *Christina* whenever you like. It's a good way to vacation without the world's media photographing you at every turn."

She looked Jackie in the eye and hoped she had gotten the message across: Ari was hers; she was the hostess on the *Christina*. Lee's name was not mentioned, but it was the clear subtext.

Jackie blinked and pulled her hand away. "I have the warmest memories of our cruise in 1963. That was in October, just before . . ." She stumbled over her words. "Jack was alive then. I should never have gone. I could have had two more weeks with him." For a moment her composure slipped. "I regret every moment we spent apart. What I wouldn't give . . ." She clasped a hand over her mouth, seeming close to tears.

"Can I get you a drink?" Maria asked quickly. "A glass of water? Champagne?"

Jackie shook her head. "I think I must go before I make a fool of myself."

She rose to her feet and turned to look back at the chair as if worried she had left something behind.

"Please don't rush . . ." Maria began, but Jackie spoke over her: "Thank you again for moving me so greatly with your music. It has been an honor to meet you."

"The honor is all mine," Maria said, rising. "Please— stay for a drink."

Jackie shook her head with a wan smile. "I can't."

She slipped out the door, leaving Maria staring after her, openmouthed. The former First Lady was much more childlike than she had imagined, with her big eyes and little girl's voice, but how brave of her to come and apologize over that brunch. What guts that must have taken. She might seem fragile on the surface, but she had a core of steel.

The encounter had been fleeting, yet at the same time it felt momentous, and Maria was shaken afterward. She wondered what Jackie had made of her. The former First Lady was regal, Maria decided. Formal. She held herself at a distance and didn't give much away.

Maria liked her, but even if circumstances had been different, she couldn't imagine them being friends.

Chapter 49

Long Island, New York
April 1965

Jackie had invited Lee and Stas to spend Easter break with her on Long Island, but she regretted it almost as soon as they arrived.

"Why are you so clumsy? You've bruised my shin with that suitcase," Lee snapped at Stas, rubbing her stockinged leg as he bundled their luggage into the hallway.

Stas apologized but it wasn't enough.

"And you've probably broken most of my cosmetics, the way you're swinging that vanity case around."

"Give him a break." Jackie laughed, hugging her. "Leave the bags, Stas. I'll get my housekeeper to see to them."

"Any chance of a beer?" Stas asked. "I'm parched."

"There you go, drinking before lunchtime. What

kind of example is that to set for our kids?" Lee moaned.

"Help yourself from the refrigerator," Jackie said, waving an arm toward the kitchen. "Lee, come sit on the veranda. Put your feet up. Relax."

Lee's foul mood was not alleviated by the spring sunshine and fresh sea breeze. The children ran down to play on the beach with their nannies supervising, so the adults had time to sit in the sun, reading and chatting, but still Lee was grouchy. Stas seemed to irritate her simply by being in her vicinity.

"Why are you breathing so noisily?" she snapped, and Jackie had to laugh.

"Poor guy! Do you want him to hold his breath?"

"Don't worry. I'm going for a drive," Stas replied, getting to his feet, pulling the car keys from his pocket. "I can tell where I'm not welcome."

"What's up with you two?" Jackie asked, as soon as he was out of earshot. "You haven't said a civil word to him since you arrived."

"You always take his side," Lee complained. "Why don't you ever stick up for me?"

"Because I don't see what he's done wrong. He's a good father, he makes decent money, and he's been kind to me since Jack died. I don't want you two ending up in the divorce courts."

Lee grunted. "The way things are going, I don't think there's any chance of avoiding that . . ."

"Oh, Lee!" Jackie was distressed. "Think of the children! Try to mend things if you possibly can. All marriages go through sticky patches." She thought back to her own doubts about Jack in the early years, when she'd found it so hard to accept his affairs. She remembered the conversation with her daddy over lunch, when he advised her not to leave her marriage. A suspicion leapt into her mind. "Is this because of your affair with Aristotle Onassis?" she asked. "Are you still seeing him?"

Lee nodded, her cheeks flushing. "When I can." She was trying to sound nonchalant, but Jackie knew her better than that.

"Are you in love with him? You're not holding out for him to marry you, are you?" Jackie searched her face.

Lee turned to gaze out to sea. "I'd love to marry him. But I don't think it's in the cards."

Jackie pursed her lips. "He's still with Maria Callas. I met her last month and she invited me to join them for a cruise on the *Christina*."

Lee jerked forward. "What? Where the hell did you meet her?"

"I heard her sing *Tosca* at the Met. It was a spectac-

JACKIE AND MARIA · 407

ular performance so I went backstage to congratulate her. She seemed friendly and generous, nothing like the persona invented by the media. I liked her." In fact, it had made her feel even more disapproving of Lee's affair with Aristotle. Maria didn't deserve that.

"Personally, I find her voice rather ugly. It's got a strange edge to it, like a knife scraping on glass. I'm glad you went out, though. It's about time you ended your self-imposed purdah." Jackie gasped, but Lee continued in a self-righteous tone, as if punishing her sister for praising her rival. "Well, it's true. You mope around, drink your own body weight in vodka, then complain that you can't sleep. Next morning you moan you've got a headache—actually, it's what we call a hangover! The time is coming when you should stop feeling so eternally sorry for yourself."

Jackie felt as if she had been assaulted, and her reaction was pure instinct. She jumped up from her chair, drew back her hand, and slapped Lee hard across the face: once with her palm, then again with the back of her hand, the way their mother used to slap them as children.

"How could you?" she breathed. "I thought you understood. You of all people know what it's been like for me."

Lee clutched her cheeks, eyes wide with surprise.

She opened her mouth to speak but Jackie wouldn't give her the chance.

"Don't say another word. Just get away from me."

She charged out into the hall, grabbed a wrap, and opened the front door, stepping out into the yard. She badly needed to be alone.

Jackie swerved through the marram grass that fringed the beach, heading in the opposite direction from where the children were playing. She stomped along the sand, feeling the ache in her calves, trying to drown out the noise in her head.

So, Lee thinks I'm wallowing in grief? That I'm drinking too much?

Well, the last accusation was true. She had started keeping a bottle of vodka in her bedroom closet so she could drink herself to sleep. There was a stage she reached when everything blurred in her head and the pain lessened, just for a while. That's when it was safe to lie down and close her eyes.

She often awoke in the early hours, her mouth as dry as sandpaper, a headache nagging at her temples, and her heart fluttering. Nightmares came regularly: violent, terrifying ones in which she had to protect the children from unknown evil. Jack was rarely there, just occasionally, as a distant ghostly presence she could never reach. Some folk thought the dead could speak to you in dreams, but Jack never spoke to her. She wished he would, but it seemed he had no voice anymore.

Her eyes were watering from the wind whipping her face. She wiped them with her sleeve.

Was she wallowing in misery? It had been only seventeen months since Dallas. Father McSorley had said that grief "takes as long as it takes," and that it could come and go without the logic of tides or seasons. She had better days and worse days, but mostly worse. A few things helped distract her for a time: music, books, and exercise. She loved going for long walks. Once the water was warm enough, she would start swimming again, because that had helped after Patrick died. But most days, she dragged herself through the motions: forcing herself to eat, wash, and dress, play with the children, run a household. Should she be better by now?

She remembered how her sister had fallen apart after Black Jack died, forcing Jackie to be the strong one. Surely Lee could remember the awful vertiginous chasm of bereavement, made so much worse in Jack's case by the shocking manner of his death. What she had seen would never be erased from her memory.

Jackie had expected to spend several more decades with him, and instead he was snatched in an instant.

Could Lee not understand that her wound was still raw? It hadn't even begun to heal. Maybe it never would.

Lee was used to Jackie being the steady, responsible one. Maybe that was why she couldn't accept this new fragile person and wanted her back the way she used to be. Sure, she'd shown up when Jackie's babies died, she'd attended Jack's funeral, but she didn't understand. Not really. They never talked about Dallas. If asked, Jackie would have said that Lee was her closest female friend, but they weren't intimate—not the way she was with Bobby or Father McSorley.

Was it her fault? Looking back, she had always preferred talking with men rather than women. Perhaps her closeness with her daddy had influenced that. She and Lee could chatter for hours, but mainly they talked about fashion, or mutual acquaintances, or their children; nothing profound.

She remembered Jack laughing one day when he told her he had watched her engaged in an intense conversation with Lee that lasted over twenty minutes. They were huddled, heads close together, chatting away. Keen to hear what was of such great import, he crept up behind them, only to discover that they were talking about gloves: when to wear them and what length.

"Wake up, ladies!" he had mocked. "We're in the

1960s now! You two sound like you're straight out of Miss Spence's finishing school circa 1920."

She had a sudden memory of Jack's expression when he was teasing her: the creases at the corners of his eyes, the affectionate twinkle. She missed him so badly that she had to stop and bend double with the pain.

What would he say about Lee's current irritability? She slumped down on the sand and tried to look at it logically.

It seemed she was in love with Onassis, but if her love were reciprocated, surely he'd have done something about it by now? He wasn't married to Maria Callas. He could easily have left her for Lee. But instead she had let herself be relegated to the role of his "bit on the side." Their mother had warned them repeatedly not to have sex before marriage: "Manhandled goods don't fetch such a high price." It would never work with Onassis. Lee needed to forget him and focus on her husband and children.

Suddenly Jackie felt a rush of sympathy. Her sister had never been satisfied with her lot. Always she imagined there was some better life out there. But Stas was a great husband: smart, funny, handsome, and good with kids. Lee should count her blessings.

I'll apologize for hitting her, Jackie decided. *And I'll try to steer her away from her Onassis obsession.*

As for herself, perhaps Lee had a point. Maybe she should socialize more and keep her grief behind closed doors. People were getting bored with it.

That fall, Jackie forced herself to accept invitations, and she even threw a party at Sign of the Dove, a favorite restaurant on the Upper East Side. She visited a couple of discotheques, went to the theater and ballet, and dined out at least once a week. It seemed to make people happy: "You're doing so *well*," they cooed, as if she were a child learning to use cutlery.

The press hated her socializing, though. "From Mourner to Swinger" read the *National Enquirer* headline. They wanted her dressed in black and veiled at all times, preferably on the verge of tears. Perhaps they'd have been content only if she'd immolated herself on Jack's funeral pyre, as Indian widows used to do.

She always had a Secret Service officer close by for protection, but it was still terrifying when she was spotted in public. During the intermission at the theater one night, a female audience member noticed her and came over.

"How are you doing, Mrs. Kennedy? Our hearts just went out to you with what happened in Dallas an' all . . ."

"Thank you." Jackie nodded and bowed her head, trying to end the exchange.

"You're very brave, coming to the theater, but life goes on, doesn't it?"

When Jackie didn't answer, she called to a friend— "Look who it is!"—whereupon others in the vicinity turned to scrutinize her. Soon a dozen or so had gathered in a semicircle to watch.

Jackie turned to speak to Joan Thring, the friend who'd accompanied her, but the questions continued.

"What do you think of the play, Jackie?" one man asked.

Her protection officer stepped in: "Please, could you leave Mrs. Kennedy in peace? She's here in a private capacity."

A few of them dispersed, but the rest just stepped back a pace or so and kept on staring. Eventually Jackie stood, picked up her purse, and walked out.

The same scene played out many times: in the street, in Central Park, in airports and department stores. Even knowing that her Secret Service officer was close by, it could be terrifying. What if someone in the crowd had a gun? What if they attacked her or her children? And Lee wondered why she lived in self-imposed purdah? Let her step into her sister's shoes for just one afternoon.

She had to spend her days pretending to cope, pretending she was recovering. Only she knew that she still couldn't get to sleep without pills and vodka, that she shook with terror every time she left home, that she lived in dread of something awful happening to her children—and that she missed Jack every single minute of every single day.

Chapter 50

Athens
Spring 1966

One afternoon, Ari left his battered address book on deck close to the lounge chair where Maria was sunning herself. Glancing up to make sure he wasn't watching, she flicked through it to the letter *R*. "Radziwill, Stas," the entry read, before listing his telephone numbers in London and at Turville Grange. Lee's name was not mentioned.

She scanned the deck again but there was no sign of Ari. Using the stub of pencil attached to the address book by a piece of string, she scribbled both numbers in the back of the novel she was reading, *Valley of the Dolls* by Jacqueline Susann. Next she turned to *K* and wrote down Jackie Kennedy's Manhattan number. She would transfer them into her address book later. You never knew when they might come in handy.

And then she had another idea. There was a 3 in Lee's London number and, with a couple of tiny pencil touches, she turned it into an 8. In the Turville Grange number, she used a quick stroke to turn a 1 into a 7, then closed the book and put it back where she had found it, adjusting the angle so it looked as if it were out of her reach. Leaning back, she carried on reading her novel, smiling to herself. She hadn't planned that; it had come to her on the spur of the moment. Perhaps she should have done it sooner.

When Ari returned, he said he'd been on the phone to Alexander, who was now approaching his eighteenth birthday and worked at his father's office in Monaco. He was dating an Englishwoman named Fiona Thyssen, who had been a fashion model before her marriage to a Dutch baron.

"He could have any woman in the world and he chooses a divorcée in her midthirties," Ari complained. "A dinosaur! I told him she will have the change of life soon and her breasts will be dangling around her kneecaps."

"Hey!" Maria rebuked, flicking his leg with her novel. "I'm forty-two, remember?"

"Your bosom is magnificent," he said quickly. "But why doesn't Alexander pick a girl his own age, without skeletons in the closet? This Fiona Thyssen has two young children. My son's not ready to be a father—he's only a child himself."

Maria shrugged. "It was inevitable that Alexander would choose a beautiful woman: he has grown up around them on his father's yacht."

"I want my grandchildren to be born to a Greek girl from a good family, not some international socialite."

"Would you have let your father choose who you married?"

He snorted. "God, no. I arranged my marriage to Tina directly with her family. It made good business sense."

"Alexander is young," Maria advised. "I think so long as you don't interfere, this relationship will run its course. He will see his friends out partying every night and realize he is too young to be tied down. But if you protest, he will stay with Fiona to defy you."

How the tables have turned, she thought. Who would have believed she would end up defending Alexander? He still refused to sit down to dinner with her.

"He's got no sense of responsibility. He spends his time in casinos and clubs and barely shows up to work."

"You were planning to get him involved with Olympic Airways, weren't you?" Maria asked. "Why not bring him over to Athens now? See if Fiona is willing to follow him . . ." She nodded, thinking it through.

"He's always been obsessed with flying. Maybe once he has a job he enjoys, you'll find him more devoted to work. And he would be traveling a lot, spending time away from home. You might find that puts a strain on his great love affair."

Ari removed his sunglasses and gave her an admiring smile. "You have a devious mind. I like it!"

"Did your divorce from Battista go through yet?" Maggie van Zuylen asked Maria over lunch one day.

Maria shook her head. "Just a legal separation. He won't consent to divorce."

Maggie tapped the rim of her glass with a fingernail. "I heard about a Greek friend who managed to divorce her domineering husband against his will. I can't remember the exact details but she says that any marriage since 1946 that did not take place in the Greek Orthodox Church is not legal in Greece. Something like that. It could be worth looking into."

Maria raised her eyebrows. "It certainly could. At least it would remove one of Ari's excuses for not marrying me."

"Let me get the name of her lawyer," Maggie offered.

Maria visited the lawyer's Athens office for a consultation and learned that what Maggie had said was true. The only problem was that it did not apply to her, because she was an American citizen.

"It would be a simple matter to renounce your American citizenship and become Greek," the lawyer told her. "We have a department that could take care of it."

Maria didn't tell Ari straightaway. Frankly, she didn't care which nationality appeared on her passport. She'd been born in New York, spent her teenage years in Athens, lived in Italy during her first marriage, and now lived either in Paris or on the *Christina,* so she was a citizen of the world. She consulted her accountants about the tax situation, and they said that it could be beneficial to have Greek citizenship. She didn't plan to live in America again, so there seemed to be no drawbacks.

She shared her plans with Ari over dinner.

"You can't renounce your American citizenship," he insisted straightaway. "All over the world people are desperate to become U.S. citizens. It would be crazy to throw that away."

"I don't need it," she said. "I don't want to live there and I'll never have a problem getting a visa to visit."

"What about your investments?" he argued. "Your status will change. There would be all sorts of legal and financial complications you haven't considered. It could have implications for our deal with Vergottis, for a start."

The previous year, Ari had persuaded Maria to invest in a ship, along with him and his friend Panaghis Vergottis. He'd promised there would be good returns stretching into the decades ahead when she was no longer singing. They'd named their joint venture Operation Prima Donna in her honor.

"My lawyers have looked into every aspect and don't think there will be a problem," she countered.

"What lawyers? Have you been paying some shysters? Why didn't you use my team?" He crashed his drink down on the table.

Maria was irritated by his patronizing tone. "I didn't want to bother you. It's a way I can finally get free of my marriage to Battista and I intend to do it. I don't need your permission."

"Is this part of a plan to make me marry you?" he snapped. "Because it won't work. You're more useful to me with American citizenship than without."

A switch flipped and Maria's temper flared. She picked up a bowl of salad and hurled it at him. It was a good throw. The wooden bowl glanced off his head, and the cubes of cucumber and tomato, slick with oil, slithered down his shirt.

Ari leapt to his feet and tossed the contents of a bowl of *gigantes,* broad beans in tomato sauce, in her direction. Maria ducked, but some of them clung to her hair.

"You bastard!" she cried and rushed at him, fists swinging.

Artemis had been in the kitchen, but she rushed into the dining room upon hearing the commotion. "Stop!" she screamed. "What are you doing?"

Maria slipped on the sauce-covered floor and pulled Ari to the ground with her, still trying to punch him. He pinned her shoulders, making her madder than ever.

"You never planned to marry me, did you? You just wanted me as your whore!" She was screaming now, straining her voice.

Ari slapped her. "You certainly have the manners of a whore."

Maria tried to bite his arm and kicked out with her legs. "In your head, you're still married to Tina. You can't bear it that she left you. That's what this is all about."

"No, it's about your ridiculous insecurity," he countered. "Just grow up, Maria."

She got one leg free and kneed him in his testicles, not hard but enough to make him yelp. When he leapt back to protect himself, Maria wriggled free.

"Don't you dare tell me to grow up!" she yelled. "You're the insecure one who needs to collect famous friends in order to feel he measures up to his daddy."

A maid appeared with a brush and dustpan, and

Maria took them from her and began to sweep the floor.

"Maria," Ari said, too quietly. "We need to talk."

Cold fear twisted her insides. What was he going to say? She wished she had handled this with more dignity, but it was a conversation that was long overdue.

By the time they were seated in the garden behind Ari's house, brandies in hand, the atmosphere had changed, as if between the acts of an opera. Maria spoke first.

"I don't understand why you reacted so strongly to me trying to get free of my marriage to Battista. If you're not planning to marry me, surely it's nothing to you?"

"I've always said we will marry someday, when the time is right. I just don't like you trying to force my hand." He wouldn't look at her, his eyes following a giant moth that was fluttering around a lantern, bashing against the glass.

Maria scoffed. "That old excuse again—the time isn't right. Can't you think of an original one?"

He ignored her. "And when we do marry, it will be more useful to me if you have American citizenship. I'm cross that you would think of doing this without consulting me."

"What's behind your obsession with America? Is it because they rejected you and now you are determined to impress them, the way you tried to impress your father?" She could tell he was annoyed from a stiffening of his posture.

"It's the richest economy in the world. Why do I need another reason? With an American wife I could operate freely in their markets."

"So you might decide to marry me for commercial reasons? How romantic!"

He shook his head. "You're twisting my words, Maria." He took out a cigar, and she watched as he went through the ritual of trimming it, running a flame over it, and puffing till it glowed. She loved him too much and he knew it; that was her problem. If she had loved him less, he would have pursued her more. She could see that now.

"I should have insisted you marry me back in 1960 when I was pregnant," she said. "You would have done it then. Now you're used to me, like an old stick of furniture."

"That's not true." He turned to her with a sad smile. "Other women soon bore me, but you continue to surprise and delight me as the years pass. How long is it now?"

424 · GILL PAUL

"Almost seven years," she said, and the Marilyn Monroe comedy *The Seven Year Itch* came to mind.

"You and I are the same," he told her. "That's why it works. We both like our independence. The only difference is that you worry what other people think. That's not a good reason to get married."

Maria snapped, "Another difference is that I am faithful."

He puffed on his cigar. "In my heart I am always faithful to you. No legal ceremony would change that. You are the only woman I want to spend my life with."

"If you want to spend your life with me, why do we not have a home of our own?" she asked. He started to interrupt but she raised her hand. "No, let me finish. I know you say that Skorpios is to be our home, but— let's face it—the building work has barely started. I may act as hostess on the *Christina* when it suits you, but it will always be your domain. And I rent an apartment round the corner from yours in Paris, like a mistress, not a wife. None of them are my home. I want to be the woman who takes care of you as you get older. How can I do that if you keep me at arm's length?"

"Let me think about this," he said, his tone soft. "I will see what I can do."

They sat in the dark for a while sipping their drinks; then, with a surge of affection, Maria reached across and stroked his head. "I didn't hurt you with that salad bowl, did I?"

He shook his head, stubbed his cigar in an ashtray, and said, "Let's go to bed."

It was where all their arguments ended.

Chapter 51

Paris
May 1966

A few weeks after their fight, Maria and Ari had lunch in Paris. Afterward, he had his driver stop outside a grand building on Avenue Georges Mandel, close to the Trocadéro, saying, "I've got a surprise for you. Come inside."

He produced a set of keys and opened the street door, then led her through the vestibule and up the stairs to an empty apartment on the second floor. It had high ceilings, spacious rooms, art deco fixtures, and tall windows looking out into the topmost branches of a chestnut tree.

"Why are we here?" she asked, giving him a quizzical look.

"Do you like it?"

"Of course I do. It's beautiful." She loved the sunlight flickering on the walls, the grandeur.

"Good," he said. "Because it's yours. I bought it for you."

"You did what?" She was astonished. "But why?"

"You said you didn't have a home. Now you do!" He stretched out his arms, pleased with himself.

So, that's the part of the argument you chose to remember, Maria thought to herself. *Very clever.* But at the same time, the apartment was so *magnifico* that she was not about to turn it down. If she made it welcoming and beautiful, she hoped it would become a home for both of them.

Maria threw herself into decorating the new apartment. For the Grand Salon she chose dark-green brocade wallpaper, Renaissance paintings, and Louis XV furniture. She found some eighteenth-century Venetian hand-painted doors and renovated the art deco marble fireplace. There was also a Salon Rouge, which she decorated in chinoiserie, and a Louis XVI dining room, with a table that would seat twelve comfortably. In the bedroom, she installed the eighteenth-century bed she had bought while married to Battista, with its pretty carved headboard painted with flowers. And the adjoining bathroom became her private sanctuary, in pink-and-white marble, with gold taps and lush hanging plants. As well as a large bath, it contained a rose-velvet sofa and matching armchair, a telephone, and a record player, and everywhere there were mirrors, reflecting the light and shimmering with the movement of leaves outside the window.

"It's like an opera set," Ari said when invited to survey the finished effect. "Perfect for a prima donna."

"And stylish enough for an international tycoon, I hope," she said. "We can entertain your business colleagues here."

But although Ari had a closet for clothes there, and he often dined and stayed overnight, he still kept most of his belongings at the Avenue Foch apartment.

Later in the year, Maria was stunned when Vergottis refused to hand over her shares in the ship they had bought jointly in Operation Prima Donna. She had always liked Ari's close friend and business colleague and was bewildered when it appeared he was trying to cheat her. It didn't make sense, unless it was part of some private battle between him and Ari that he was not telling her about.

She couldn't afford to lose her investment, so she asked Ari to get it back for her.

"We'll sue you and we'll win!" Ari yelled at Vergottis on the phone, but Vergottis countered by saying that if they did he would make sure details of their private life were dragged through the courts.

"That's blackmail!" Maria was distressed by the prospect. "What should we do?"

Ari shrugged. "I'll get my lawyers to file a suit and we'll bankrupt him. No one double-crosses me."

"But I don't want us to be headline news. Couldn't we settle out of court?"

"Absolutely not. It would send the wrong signals to my other business partners worldwide and encourage them to cheat me. That's not the way I operate."

Throughout the second half of 1966 and into '67, the impending trial loomed over Maria, and anxiety affected her health. Her blood pressure, always on the low side, dipped alarmingly, and she became prone to painful and unsightly swelling of her legs, as well as persistent headaches. She wished she could send a written testimony to the court in London rather than appear in person, but Ari's lawyers insisted they must both be there. Worse than that, they advised the couple to describe themselves as "good friends" rather than lovers, and not admit to any possibility that they would one day marry.

"They're asking us to lie in court?" She was dismayed. "Surely that can't be ethical?"

"It seems that if we went into the deal as a couple, it changes the nature of the legal contract. It's a technicality Vergottis would use to his advantage."

"But I don't want to lie in court! I refuse."

"I hope it won't arise," Ari soothed her. "Our affair is our own business, no one else's. Let's keep it that way."

But in court, Vergottis's lawyer homed in on their personal life during the early part of his questioning. "Since you are both separated from your spouses," he asked Ari, "do you regard Miss Callas as being in a position equivalent to a wife?"

"No," Ari replied. "If I wanted a wife, Maria and I would have had no problems in marrying. We have no obligations to each other except those of friendship."

Maria kept her expression masklike, but the words stung. When her turn came, the lawyer tried to pin her down about the nature of her separation from Battista.

"Do you regard yourself as a single woman?" he asked.

Maria paused for a long time, glancing over to where Ari sat. He nodded almost imperceptibly.

She had gone ahead and renounced her American citizenship so was now officially divorced under Greek law, yet in Italy she was still bound by her marriage to Battista. "In Italy, no," she replied. "Elsewhere, yes."

The last two words were almost a whisper. It was excruciating to announce to the world that she had spent the last eight years with a man who now described her as nothing more than a friend. She and Ari knew the truth, of course, but it made her look a fool. And it gave a green light to any other women who decided to pursue him. She prayed that Lee Radziwill wouldn't be following the story in the press—but was almost certain she would.

Chapter 52

Ireland
June 1967

When Jackie heard that Sissy, the wife of David Ormsby-Gore, had been killed in a car accident, she was determined to fly to the U.K. for the funeral. As British ambassador, David had been a close ally of Jack's, and he had proven a good friend to her since Jack's death. She decided she would take her children on a vacation to Ireland afterward: now aged nine and six respectively, Caroline and John were old enough to learn about their Irish heritage.

Their nanny and the usual retinue of Secret Service officers would have to accompany them. Rather than lessening as time went on, the public's interest in her appeared only to intensify. Random strangers tried to start conversations in the street as she hurried along, head down, shielded by the largest sunglasses she could find. Some even reached out to touch her, which sparked such panic that she got chest pains and found it hard to breathe. Those were the moments she was grateful for John Walsh and the rest of the team, who would step in and ask the interloper to back off.

But when she was standing in Saks Fifth Avenue, trying to choose pantyhose or a new lipstick, she could see the officer of the day out of the corner of her eye and felt like a prisoner. They knew what she ate and drank, whom she met for coffee, how she spent her waking hours. It was like being spied on in a police state, and it acted as a constant reminder of all that had happened to her over the past four years. Her life would never be normal again.

Jackie would have liked to disappear from the spotlight entirely, but the Kennedys still insisted on wheeling her out at political rallies. Bobby had decided on a run for the presidency in 1968—a decision that left her paralyzed with fear.

"Are you sure about this?" she probed on one of their long walks. "The Kennedys have so many enemies. Why raise your head above the parapet to give them an easy target?"

"You can't give in to these people. I want to carry on the work that Jack started, to fulfill his legacy. But I promise I'll avoid open motorcades."

She was filled with dread when he first asked her to appear onstage at a fund-raiser. She didn't have to speak, he assured her, just show up to demonstrate that she approved of him running.

"Do it for Jack," Bobby urged. "You know he would want you to."

Yes, he would, Jackie agreed. He had often expressed the hope that Bobby would follow him to the White House. They had expected him to run in '68—only after Jack had served two terms himself.

The other reason she felt she had to do as the Kennedys wished was unstated, but it hung over her like a raincloud. Since Jack's death they had subsidized her with a monthly allowance to top up Jack's government pension, which she could never have lived on. It meant she didn't have to worry too much about money—at least, not as long as she remained one of the Kennedy clan.

Sissy's funeral took place in a Catholic church in Oswestry, near the Welsh border. Jackie was grateful that Bobby accompanied her, but it was upsetting to be filmed and photographed by newsmen the moment she stepped off the plane. They even hid behind trees in the churchyard to capture her comforting David as his wife was lowered into the ground.

The trip to Ireland was much more private. They stayed with some old friends in County Waterford, in the midst of sweeping countryside that was perfect for horseback riding and close to a deserted sandy beach. Jackie had one official meeting, with President Eamonn de Valera, and a more personal visit to some Kennedy relatives in the little town of Dunganstown, but otherwise it was a proper vacation, characterized by plenty of fresh air and Irish hospitality.

Late one afternoon, while the children were picnicking with their nanny, Jackie slipped off for a solitary swim. About half a mile down the beach she had found a channel, with a headland on the other side. There and back was just the right distance for a proper swim that would leave her muscles aching pleasantly, and the views were spectacular. The fields that lined the cliffs were such an exaggerated emerald color, the sky so brilliantly blue, that it almost felt as if she were in a Technicolor movie.

She slid into the sea, leaving her towel on the shore, reckoning that the water must be between sixty and sixty-five degrees: refreshingly cool but not too cold. She swam out into the channel, slicing through the waves, then stopped halfway and flipped onto her back to float awhile and gaze up at the vast sky.

The ache of missing Jack was always there; he would

have loved this beach and relished the moments of privacy. Unable to subdue his Kennedy competitiveness,
he'd probably have struck out for the far side ahead of
her, then turned to egg her on. A sense memory came
to her of kissing him while treading water in the ocean
off Hyannis Port: she recalled the saltiness, the touch
of his lips, his sturdy body pressing against her. Would
there ever be another man with whom she could share
such pleasures?

She knew there was gossip in Washington about her
closeness with Bobby. Perhaps Ethel had heard it, because she had been unusually curt at recent meetings,
but in truth Jackie loved him as a brother. It would have
felt incestuous to kiss him, although they often hugged
and he was still the first person she turned to for advice
or comfort.

She had dined with a few men in the years since Jack
had died but none who could begin to fill his shoes.
John Warnecke, who designed his headstone, had distracted her for a while. Ros Gilpatric, who was both
glamorous and intellectual, had been flirting openly,
and they were talking about taking a vacation together.
David Ormsby-Gore took her for dinner whenever he
was in New York, and so did Aristotle Onassis, who
always brought gifts for her and the children. She had

started calling him Telis, a contraction of his full Greek name of Aristotelis.

Now, there was an interesting situation. She had read in the newspapers that he and Maria Callas were no longer a couple, and Ari had confirmed it when she asked him. Lee never mentioned him anymore; it seemed their affair, which Ari had insisted was only a brief fling, was long finished. Jackie could sense that Ari would like his friendly relationship with her to become something deeper, but he never put any pressure on her.

Bobby would have a conniption if she started dating Ari. He had a deep-seated hatred for the man, which appeared to date back to his indictment over a shipping technicality in the 1950s, but she could never fathom why Bobby still held a grudge. Jack had thought him nothing worse than a rogue, but in Jackie's opinion he had a keen mind, old-fashioned manners, and a generous nature. He'd bought her several exquisite pieces of jewelry for birthdays, and on the third anniversary of Jack's death a diamond bracelet arrived that she particularly cherished. He also sent gifts for her children, which were both expensive and well chosen.

She liked that he was a good listener. So many men were just waiting for a pause in conversation so that they could butt in with their own opinions, but Ari paid attention and asked questions. The next time they'd meet, he'd remember what they'd been talking about before and ask how it was going. She liked that. Sometimes she found herself almost flirting with him.

A gust of wind ruffled the surface of the water, and Jackie suddenly realized that she was drifting out too far. She was going to miss the headland on the other side of the channel and risked getting pulled into the twelve-mile-long bay. She rolled onto her stomach and began to swim against the tide, straining for the opposite shore, but the water was choppy now and her arms soon tired. If she stopped swimming for a moment, the headland drifted farther away, but even her most determined crawl was not bringing it any closer.

A wave broke over her head and she coughed and spluttered, panic gripping her as saltwater burned her throat. Was she to die here, all on her own? On one hand, the idea had a certain appeal: at least she would be free; perhaps she could join Jack in heaven—if it existed. All she had to do was stop struggling, just let go. But she couldn't leave the children, couldn't let them become the eleventh and twelfth children of Bobby and Ethel.

Something Jack had told her came into her head: in riptides, you should swim parallel to the shore until the current weakens enough for you to head inland. She struck out again, trying to follow his advice, but the cold was beginning to penetrate her bones, making her shiver. Another wave crashed over her.

How stupid I am, she thought. *How unutterably stupid!* You should never swim alone in unfamiliar waters. Jack would have been furious. It was a rookie error and it looked as if it might be her last, because the coast was impossibly far off now.

Suddenly a head bobbed up in the water close by, startling her. It was John Walsh, one of her Secret Service officers.

"Lie on your back," he ordered.

Drained of all strength, she obeyed. John placed one arm under her chin and began to swim with the other, his solid stroke soon making headway against the current.

Jackie lay back, looking up at the clouds, her heart hammering like a pneumatic drill. Only when they got closer to shore and the riptide lessened was she able to turn and swim shoulder to shoulder with him.

He helped her up onto the beach, then her legs gave way and she began to vomit in the sand.

It had been a close call, she knew; the second time in her life she had come within a hairsbreadth of dying.

Chapter 53

Paris
November 1967

M aria was in her salon, drinking coffee and reading the papers as the morning sun streamed through the tall windows, when Bruna came in, twisting her apron.

"Madame, you asked me to let you know if I heard that Mr. Onassis received any female visitors."

"Yes?" Bruna was close to Eleni, the housekeeper at Ari's Avenue Foch apartment, and sometimes got information from her.

"Eleni says Mrs. Kennedy dined there last night." She bit her lip as if there was more she wanted to say.

"Are you sure it was Mrs. Kennedy?" Maria was instantly alert. "Not Princess Radziwill? They have a similar look."

"Eleni said it was definitely Mrs. Kennedy. She heard him call her Jacqueline."

She frowned. "Who else was present?"

"No one. Just the two of them."

That was very odd. She'd have thought Jackie would be too concerned about her reputation to dine alone with a man in his apartment. Maria hadn't realized they had gotten so friendly. Could it have something to do with Lee? Some message she was passing on? She was determined to find out, so, when Ari came for dinner, she kept her voice deliberately casual as she asked, "I hear Mrs. Kennedy is in Paris. Have you seen her?"

Ari didn't miss a beat. "No, I didn't know she was here."

There was a sinking feeling in her gut. "Why would you lie to me, Ari? I know she dined with you last night."

He was startled, and Maria could tell he was about to lie again but thought better of it. "If I was less than honest, it's only because of your ridiculous jealousy. I can't tell you when I see women friends in case crockery gets smashed."

"That's because I don't believe friendship between the sexes is possible. There's always one party who wants it to become something more—unless, of course, they are homosexual."

"What a cynic you are!" he replied. "I hate to disappoint you, but Mrs. Kennedy and I talk about philosophy and religion. She seems to find my company restful and sometimes she confides in me. At the moment she is weary of the pressure the Kennedy family put on her to promote Bobby's career."

It *sounded* plausible, but Maria didn't trust him. This was a man who collected celebrity notches on his bedpost. She had more faith in Mrs. Kennedy. Surely she had too much class to sleep with someone who had a long-term partner, a man who had slept with her sister.

"What do you know about friendship?" she sniped. "Last time I looked, you had fallen out with all of yours."

The High Court had found in their favor in the case against Vergottis, and he'd been ordered to pay staggering legal costs, which looked likely to bankrupt him. Ari had no remorse: it was the price of crossing him, he said. He'd also fallen out with Prince Rainier and had sold his shares in the Société des Bains de Mer, so she would never sing at the opera house there.

"That's not true. I would never fall out with Costa," he countered.

"Yes, but only because you can't afford to; he knows where the bodies are buried."

Ari laughed, knowing the truth of it.

"And I hope I will never fall out with you either."

"You'd better not!" she warned. "I also could locate plenty of skeletons."

Ari was in a playful mood that autumn, probably because business was going well: he had lots of new schemes under his hat, which he boasted to her about. There had been a military coup in Greece and he was talking to the colonels in charge of the government about a massive project to build an oil refinery and an aluminum smelter outside of Athens. Project Omega, he called it. He'd made investments in South American gold and oil, in Manhattan property, in Persian chemicals, in tourism—Maria lost count of all the countries he had business interests in. The Onassis empire seemed to expand every time he drew breath, and she was proud of his success.

They went dancing one night that November, at Chez Régine, a fashionable nightclub in the Latin Quarter. They both drank too much and danced cheek to cheek to the latest hits: Gene Pitney's "Something's Gotten Hold of my Heart" and Frank Sinatra's "Somethin' Stupid."

As they were leaving the club at two in the morning, both of them giggling and unsteady on their feet, there was the usual clutch of photographers outside, snapping away.

"Any truth in the rumors you two are getting married soon?" one called.

Maria turned to Ari, letting him answer.

"You're too late," he replied. "We got married fifteen days ago. It was a wonderful thing."

The questions came thick and fast then, the camera shutters clicking like crazy.

Ari's driver pulled up and they climbed into the backseat without further comment.

"They'll be rushing off to search the marriage registers," he said, smirking. "That will keep them busy."

Maria wasn't sure of how she felt about his flippant comment. To her, it was no laughing matter, but she played along. "Perhaps you should buy me a ring to confuse them further."

"Perhaps I will," he said, sliding his hand beneath her dress.

After a damp and freezing winter in Paris, Maria and Ari flew to the Caribbean to board the *Christina* for a two-month cruise. They'd both had lingering colds, but, descending the steps of the plane into the vibrant color and warmth of Port of Spain, she felt instantly healthier. Milky turquoise water, pale gold sand, and skies full of birdsong: she breathed in the tropical scents.

The plan was to sail up through the Windward Islands to Haiti, where Ari had some business to attend to, then on to Jamaica. Maria planned to shed some weight and to work on her voice. She'd brought a tape recorder and would record herself, then adjust her delivery till she achieved a sound she was happy with.

She also planned to encourage Ari to cut back on the cigars and booze but knew it would have to be done with subtlety; he didn't take orders gladly. Healthful food, swimming, and sun on their skin would do them both a world of good.

Less than a couple of weeks into the cruise, Ari got word that a rival Greek shipping millionaire, Stavros Niarchos, had presented the colonels running the country with a counterproposal to Project Omega, and his face went purple with rage. For a moment Maria feared apoplexy.

"How did you find out?" she asked.

"I have spies in Niarchos's household. He can't sneeze without me hearing about it."

"Does he know about Project Omega? Maybe the government is trying to push up the level of your investment by bringing in competition."

Ari was concentrating. "I'm not sure. His bid concerns bringing oil from the Middle East, mine from Russia. They're not the same, but I have financial backers while he is putting up his own money. So if he fails, he could go bust."

Maria could almost hear the cogs whirring in his brain. "Are you planning to sabotage his bid?"

"I need to fly to New York," he said, then caught her disappointed expression. "Don't worry—I'll be back before you notice I'm gone."

"Do you want me to come?" she asked, and was relieved when he said no. She was enjoying the Caribbean weather too much to exchange it for the snowstorm she'd read was hitting the Eastern Seaboard.

It was only after Ari left that Maria began to worry. In their last conversation about her "jealousy," he had promised to tell her the truth whenever he dined with other women, in return for which she promised she would not throw a fit, but the agreement had yet to be tested.

After he returned, she waited a few hours before asking, in a casual tone, "Did you see Lee in New York?"

"No, but I gave Jacqueline and her children a lift to Palm Beach on my jet," he replied. "You've got no idea how badly she is pestered if she takes a commercial flight. People approach her for autographs and photograph the children. She was grateful for my help."

"I bet she was."

He poked her in the ribs. "Is Maria jealous?"

"Not at all," she replied, with dignity.

"Good," he said. "Because I've invited Jacqueline to the *Christina* for a few days in May, after you fly back to Paris."

This came as a hammer blow and she struggled to control herself. "Ari, why didn't you invite her while I was here? I'd have loved to get to know her better. Why all the sneaking around?"

"She's a very private person. Besides, she's my friend, not yours." He took out a cigar and began toasting it. Maria had hidden the ones he kept on board but guessed he must have brought more back with him.

She was upset that he clearly wanted to keep her and Mrs. Kennedy apart. The fact that he had told her should alleviate suspicion, but was he playing a game with both of them? "*Should* I be jealous?" she asked, watching his expression closely.

"Do as you wish," he replied. "I'll never understand women."

"No, you probably won't. Your entire knowledge of our sex comes from a Van Cleef & Arpels catalog."

He laughed out loud and raised his glass to clink with hers. Maria wondered if she should be hurling glasses at his head and slinging punches, but there was no point; it wouldn't stop him from doing exactly what he wanted to do.

She caught the Paris flight on May 20 and sobbed as the plane lifted off the tarmac. For two months she and Ari had felt as close as they ever had: talking, sunbathing, dancing, and making love under the stars—yet he could still invite another woman to join him as soon as she left. He'd be in Paris in a few weeks—he was sailing across on *Christina*—but already she missed him so badly that it was as if a hole had been punched right through her.

She knew Ari would make love to Mrs. Kennedy given half a chance, and she was sure he'd try. He thrived on conquest, and she would be a particularly eminent one. All her hopes were pinned on Mrs. Kennedy turning him down. Was there anything she could do to influence her?

By the time the plane landed in Paris, Maria had decided to make sure that Jackie knew the lay of the land. As soon as she got to Avenue Georges Mandel, she looked up the Fifth Avenue number—the number she'd never used before—in her address book and placed a call.

"Mrs. Kennedy?" she asked, upon hearing the famous voice on the other end of the line. "It's Maria Callas."

"Oh! Hello." Jackie sounded wary.

Maria launched into the speech she had prepared. "I wanted to say how sorry I am to miss your visit to the *Christina*. I had to fly back to Paris but I told Ari that next time he simply must invite you while I'm there so we can get acquainted. We love entertaining together and—between ourselves—I think I'm rather better than him at planning menus. I warned him not to serve you steak every single night."

There was a long pause, and she could hear Mrs. Kennedy's breathing over the hisses and crackles of the transatlantic line before she answered: "I'm sure the food will be fine."

"If you are able to pass a pharmacy before you leave, could you please take Ari some liver salts? I noticed he had run out and he does rely on them." She smiled to herself. Ari would be mad at her for having passed that on.

"Of course." She was clearly a woman of few words.

"I hope we meet again soon, Mrs. Kennedy. I'm sure we'd have a lot to talk about."

"Yes. Thank you for calling."

Afterward Maria had no regrets. If Jackie told Ari about the call, he'd be tickled by the idea of the two of them fighting over him. And if Mrs. Kennedy had any scruples, she would back down now she realized that Maria was still the woman in his life.

But if she decided to go ahead and sleep with him anyway, she hoped Ari would hurry up and mark that notch on his bedpost so that Mrs. Kennedy could be filed away, just like Eva Perón.

Chapter 54

New York City
May 22, 1968

After she hung up, Jackie sat for several minutes, shaken by the call. Ari must have told Maria of her forthcoming visit to the *Christina*. Her tone had been friendly but the subtext was a clear warning to back off. Perhaps she was still in love with him.

She felt bad for Maria, but Ari had been very clear that they were just good friends and hadn't been lovers for a while. Maybe she hoped to win him back, but that was no reason for Jackie to change her mind about the cruise. It was only for four days, and there would be others present: his sister, Artemis, and Jackie's friend Joan Thring. For some time she'd felt as if Ari had been edging toward making a move, but he'd have to be on his best behavior with the others around.

Jackie flew to St. Thomas on May 25 and slipped on

board, a scarf covering her hair and huge sunglasses shielding her face.

"I mustn't be photographed here," she told Ari. "Bobby would kill me!"

"I understand," he said. "We'll raise anchor and set sail without delay."

After dinner that evening, when the other guests had gone to bed, they sat on deck with nightcaps. The moon lit a path across the water, and the only sound was the lapping of waves against the bow. Jackie sipped her vodka. She hadn't drunk enough yet to blot out the anxiety that chipped away at her brain.

"I'm so shaken about Martin Luther King," she told him, a quiver in her voice. The popular civil rights leader had been assassinated in Memphis the previous month. "It seems America has gone mad. Anyone can buy a gun and take potshots at public figures. And now there are race riots everywhere. So much discontent, I can't bear it."

Ari swirled his brandy. "It's true there are lunatics in the world, but fewer than you would think from reading the newspapers."

Jackie shuddered. "It only takes one. The FBI tells me there's been a surge of threats to kidnap or kill my children since King was shot. My *children*!"

"I don't want to be unduly alarmist, but I would

advise you to get more protection for them. An extra layer of security on top of what the government provides would make sense."

Jackie hugged her knees to her chest. "That costs money. The Kennedys don't give me enough to cover an expense like that."

Ari waved his arm dismissively. "It's not so much. I have a permanent team I could assign to you while the threat level is high. And you know you are always welcome to use my private jets, or to holiday on the *Christina* or Skorpios. No one sets foot there but my employees."

"It's very tempting," Jackie said. "I'd love to escape for a while, but the world's press would find out where I was and the Kennedys would be furious. It could harm Bobby's election campaign. They might even cut off my allowance."

"Don't let money stand in the way of your happiness." His eyes never left her. His meaning was clear.

"It's not only money. They're my children's family. *My* family."

"The real question is whether you want to escape from the Kennedys and make a life of your own," he said, shifting his chair till he was so close she could feel the heat emanating from his skin. "Whether you are ready to love someone new."

Jackie turned away. She had to admit she was attracted to him. She had always been attracted to powerful men, particularly rich ones; she couldn't afford
to fall for a pauper. Ari wasn't Jack, but no man would
ever match up to Jack. She was thirty-eight years old
and fed up with being alone. It wasn't sex she missed; it
was the connection with another human being. Having
someone care what she was doing with her day; someone to comfort her when the nightmares came; someone to have fun with. And Ari knew how to have fun.
Life was never dull with him around.

"I can't have affairs in my position. I'm the nation's
grieving widow. I need to behave with 'moral probity.'"
She tapped a cigarette from her pack and Ari leaned
over to light it, his arm brushing hers.

"Do you really care what anyone else thinks?" he
asked. "I'm surprised you give it a second thought."

"I don't want to become a hate figure," she said.
That reminded her: "By the way, Maria Callas telephoned me in Manhattan last week. She seems to believe you two are still an item." Jackie inhaled deeply
and held the smoke in her lungs as she waited for his
reaction.

"Did she? I wonder how she got your number." His
brow creased as he tried to figure it out. "Well, no mat-

ter. I can't be responsible for what Maria says. She's a strong-minded woman. But I know my own position."

He leaned close as if to kiss her, but Jackie pulled away. "I can't just jump into bed with anyone, Telis. These things have a way of reaching the papers no matter how careful I am. I'd be accused of betraying Jack's memory . . ."

"What would it take for you to let yourself love again?" he asked, stroking her shoulder with a finger.

She considered for a long time, then stubbed out her cigarette before answering. "I think the only way would be if I remarried. And even then I would be reviled in the States."

"Married?" Onassis recoiled. The idea clearly hadn't occurred to him. Jackie watched as he wrestled with his feelings. "I'm sure you will remarry one day," he said at last. "But why wait? This is the 1960s, not the Dark Ages."

Could she trust him? The problem was, he had nothing to lose, whereas for her everything was on the line.

"That's the only way it could work for me," she said, stubbing out her cigarette and rising to her feet. "All or nothing."

She'd made the terms clear. Now the ball was in his court. He liked her, but how far would he go to woo her?

When Jackie returned to New York, there was a message asking her to call Bobby. He was on the campaign trail, sleeping in a different state most nights and attending rallies or visiting schools and factories during the days. She had to call his office to find out where he would be that evening, and it was late when they finally managed to speak.

"How's it going?" she asked.

"It's a disaster," he said. "I lost Oregon. The California primary is on Tuesday and if I lose that too, I'm going to pull out."

"Don't make any hasty decisions," she cautioned. "Think of all the states you've won. You're well ahead in the race."

"I wouldn't be so sure." He sounded dog tired. "But I rang because I have something rather awkward to discuss. I keep hearing whispers about you and Aristotle Onassis. Please tell me they're not true."

Jackie hesitated. "He does seem rather keen on me."

Bobby sighed heavily. "And you?"

"I haven't committed to anything."

"For crying out loud, don't let yourself be pictured with him in the press. You've got no idea how corrupt the man is."

Jackie was irritated at being told whom she could

and could not date. "Presumably he's operating within the law, or he would have been charged with whatever crime you suspect him of."

"There could well be charges down the line . . ." When Jackie didn't reply, he continued, "Seriously, Jackie. If you ever trusted my judgment, trust me on this. He's not one of the world's good guys."

"I'm an adult and I'll make up my own mind about that."

"I've got enough to worry about," Bobby said sharply. "Make this go away."

He hung up abruptly, leaving her seething. She felt like a teenager being told off by her mother. But for Jack's sake, for the sake of the Kennedys, she would not make any decisions till after the election. Ari could wait.

Chapter 55

New York City
June 4, 1968

J ackie went to bed the night of June 4 feeling pleased
for her brother-in-law. There was good news for
Bobby's campaign team that day: he had won both
the South Dakota and the California primaries. The
momentum seemed to have shifted again in his favor.
Jackie had been at a rally that evening, and the cheering had raised the roof when word of the victories came
through. She hadn't wanted him to run, but now he was
in the race she was rooting for him.

Just a few hours later she was awakened from deep
sleep by the sound of the telephone. She grabbed the
receiver, hoping it hadn't disturbed the children.

"Jackie? It's Stas. How is he?" His tone was urgent.
Ominous.

"How's who?" She wondered why Stas was calling so late. Had Lee done something stupid?

"Bobby."

"It's good news!" she said, yawning. "He won the California primary."

There was a pause. "I'm so sorry, I thought you would have heard. Bobby's been shot. In a hotel in Los Angeles. They've rushed him to the hospital."

A scream burst out of her: "Oh, God, no!" Her whole body started trembling as she wailed "No, no, no!" It was as if a mist came down and she couldn't think, couldn't breathe.

Stas's voice cut through her panic. "He's alive, Jackie. We need to go there. I'm in London but I'll catch the first flight to New York. Pack a bag and we'll fly to L.A. together."

When he hung up, she rocked backward and forward, arms wrapped around her shoulders, so shocked that she couldn't think or speak. It felt like Dallas all over again: the explosion, the slice of scalp flying through the air, the heat, the salty smell of blood.

Her housekeeper came rushing into the room in her dressing gown, and Jackie realized she had been moaning out loud.

"I'll get you some tea," the housekeeper said. "Hot sweet tea."

Jackie shook her head. She didn't want tea. Hands shaking so violently that it was hard to dial, she called Hyannis Port and Rose answered.

"He's still with us," Rose reported, "but he was shot in the head and chest. Ted and Ethel are at his bedside at the Good Samaritan hospital. All we can do is pray."

There was a crushing pain in Jackie's chest. *In the head. Like Jack. How could he possibly survive?*

She couldn't decide what to pack, so the housekeeper helped her throw a few outfits into an overnight bag. Caroline and John got up for school and she joined them as they ate breakfast, trying to still the trembling of her hands and sound vaguely normal. Should she keep them home from school? Yet again, she couldn't decide. Perhaps they should go—but what if they heard about the shooting there? She had to say something.

"Your uncle Bobby has been in an accident," she told them at last. "I'm flying out to visit him so I won't be here this evening, but I'll be back soon."

Kids being kids, they took it in their stride and barely asked any questions before setting off for school with their Secret Service officer. It was a wrench to watch them leave. What if a maniac attacked them? She wanted to wrap them in blankets and snuggle with them on the couch, but that wasn't an option.

A friend of Ros Gilpatric's offered to lend her his

private plane, so she didn't have to worry about the public trying to photograph her. She took a cab to La-Guardia and met Stas there, grasping his arm tightly as they hurried through to the departure gate.

"He was shot in the head," she told Stas once they were strapped into their seats. "Just like Jack."

Stas squeezed her hand. "I heard they operated this morning for more than three hours. They wouldn't have done that if there was no hope. Bobby's tough. If anyone can pull through, he can."

"Where's Lee? Does she know?"

He winced. "Lee's distraught. She wasn't in any fit state to fly out with me today but she'll come tomorrow."

Jackie asked the stewardess for a vodka, but instead of acting as an anesthetic it seemed to heighten her anxiety. Her mind was full of vivid memories of the moments after Jack had been shot: his puzzled expression, the flying piece of skull, his brains spilling out. She started to describe it all to Stas; then the tears came and she realized she had gotten muddled. It wasn't Jack who had been shot; it was Bobby. The names kept getting mixed up in her head.

Stas held her hand very tightly and murmured words of comfort, but it was clear he didn't have a clue what to do with her.

They had to push through a barrage of reporters out-side the hospital, then a nurse led them up to the floor where Bobby was fighting for his life. Secret Service agents dressed in black lined the corridors.

Inside the room, Ethel sat in a chair, three months pregnant, her eyes red and her face glistening with tears. Teddy got up to hug Jackie, and she glanced over his shoulder at Bobby, lying in the bed amid a tangle of tubes and wires, with bandaging over his head and his eyes closed. There was a ventilator tube in his throat and it made an eerie hissing noise as air was pumped in and sucked out. A drip was plugged into a port in his arm, and various other wires linked him to monitors that beeped steadily, lights flashing. Everywhere there were reminders of Jack lying in the emergency room in Dallas. She blinked to try to clear them.

"How is he?" she asked in a whisper.

Teddy struggled to compose himself. "Not good."

"Will he make it?"

Teddy glanced around at Ethel before shaking his head slightly. "They are concerned about his failure to improve. There's a possibility his brain isn't function-ing anymore."

Jackie covered her mouth with her hands, tears

springing to her eyes. She mustn't break down here; she must be strong.

She walked to the bedside and took Bobby's hand in hers, careful not to disturb the wires. His face looked peaceful, as if he were merely in a very deep sleep.

"Bobby, it's Jacqueline. Can you hear me? Let me know if you can hear me." She squeezed his hand, hoping he might move his fingers in response, but there wasn't so much as a twitch. At least the regular rise and fall of his chest meant he was alive, but a machine was causing that, not him. "Bobby, you have to wake up. It's time. Come on."

"We've all tried," Ethel told her. "Nothing."

"Did you get a second opinion?" Stas asked, and everyone looked up. It seemed they hadn't thought of that. "I'll go and find someone. It's worth a try."

Their eyes followed him, and Jackie felt a glimmer of hope. Teddy fell to his knees at the foot of the bed and started to pray under his breath.

A team of doctors arrived shortly afterward and asked that everyone leave the room while they did some tests. The family was shown to a private waiting area, where each member sat alone, space between them. No one spoke. A nurse wheeled in a cart with coffee and sandwiches, but it was vodka that Jackie craved and she knew she couldn't get it there, in a hospital. She badly wanted to smoke but Ethel would go crazy, and if she slipped outside, she would be engulfed by the press.

Hours passed, or so it felt. Stas came back. It grew dark outside. Jackie felt as if she were in a trance. The door opened and they all looked up, desperate for news, but it was a press spokesman wanting to know what he should say in his next bulletin. Journalists were hungry for information.

And then a doctor came, and Jackie could tell by the way he addressed them that he was in charge.

"We've tried everything but I'm afraid we can find no sign of brain activity," he said. "The damage caused by the bullet that entered his skull was catastrophic. I'm very sorry, but I suggest you say your goodbyes and, when you are ready, we advise withdrawing life support."

That meant they were going to switch him off. What a bizarre way for a life to end, like turning off a television set so the picture shrank into a little gray dot, then went blank.

"Where is the priest?" Ethel cried. "He must have the last rites."

"The priest is here. Whenever you are ready."

They rose and hurried to Bobby's room. Nothing

had changed. The ventilator hissed, the screens blinked, and he lay pale and unresponsive. There, but not there.

As the last rites were administered, it was exactly like Jack's extreme unction in Dallas. The room was the same: clinical and metallic, with glaring overhead lights and a chemical smell. Jackie wanted to scream at the top of her voice, to smash windows, to punch walls. How could this be happening again? *Why?*

Stas gripped her arm as if he sensed her derailment. Ethel was sobbing quietly, and Teddy looked as if the spine had been ripped out of him so he could barely stand upright.

One by one, they leaned close to Bobby's face and whispered their goodbyes, kissing his forehead, his cheek, any bit of skin not covered by medical para-phernalia. When it was Jackie's turn, she whispered, "Thank you for everything. I love you so much. Please give my love to Jack."

Stepping away from the bed was almost too much. Her legs would have given way if Stas hadn't propped her up.

"Are you ready, or do you need more time?" the doctor asked.

Suddenly Jackie couldn't bear to be in that room a minute longer. "We're ready," she said. No one disagreed. There was a consent form to sign and she did it, her signature little more than a scrawl.

One by one the machines were switched off, the lights on monitors disappearing. When the ventilator tube was removed, Bobby's body gave a shudder. The doctor had said he might keep breathing for up to an hour but it was much less than that, not long at all. The doctor held a finger to his throat to feel the last flutter of exhalation before uttering the words to pronounce him dead. It was 1:44 A.M.

Jackie tore away from Stas's grip and rushed from the room. She ran down a corridor past the nurses' station and sank onto a plastic chair, where she bent double, her face in her arms.

What could she do? They were killing Kennedys, picking them off one by one. She was a Kennedy; her children were Kennedys. She would never be safe in America. At any time, some random stranger might pull a gun.

"Excuse me, Mrs. Kennedy," a young woman's voice said.

She looked up. A nurse was holding out a telegram.

"This arrived for you."

She took it and tore it open. "I'm on my way," it said. It was signed "Telis."

Chapter 56

New York City
June 6, 1968

Maria was taking her late-morning bath when the phone rang. She stretched to grab it, dripping water on the carpet.

"Bobby Kennedy's dead," Maggie van Zuylen said straightaway. "They just announced it on the radio."

"Oh, my God!" Maria was horrified. "But the news last night said he was conscious after the shooting. I thought he was going to make it."

"It seems not. Where's Ari? Does he know?"

"As far as I'm aware he's on the *Christina*, half-way across the Atlantic." A weight descended on her. Ari was bound to go to the States for the funeral. He wouldn't miss another chance to hobnob with the Kennedy clan.

She was dying to see him, and particularly keen to

leave Paris and fly to Skorpios. Student riots had flared up across the city: roads were blocked, university buildings were occupied, and it seemed everyone was on strike, making demands that were muddled and unrealistic. She didn't dare leave the apartment for fear of being caught up in a protest.

A terrible thought struck her. What if Ari didn't get back in time to visit Omero's grave with her on the twenty-sixth? It would have been their son's eighth birthday. She had a picture of him in her mind's eye: dark haired and strong boned, with his father's golden eyes. Would he have had Ari's flair with numbers or her talent for music? Surely his father would come back by the twenty-sixth; he knew how much their annual pilgrimage meant to her.

After climbing out of the bath, she tipped a couple of pills the doctor had prescribed into the palm of her hand and swallowed them with a swig of water. Valium: the new anti-anxiety medicine everyone was talking about. She hoped it would start working soon, because everything seemed to be piling on top of her lately.

Ari phoned later that day. As she had guessed, he was flying straight to New York to support Mrs. Kennedy. Maria tried to still the nerves in her voice as she asked when he would be back.

"I'll meet you in Milan on the twenty-sixth," he promised. "I couldn't miss that."

It was less than three weeks, she told herself. She could hold on. But the days dragged. Few friends were in Paris, and those who were did not want to travel across the city. Although the riots had slowly petered out, some student buildings were still occupied, and the anarchist graffiti scrawled everywhere made her shudder: il est interdit d'interdire—"It is forbidden to forbid." So naive! How could one live in a lawless society?

Ari called most days, but the times of his calls varied. She had expected him to stay at the suite he kept at the Pierre Hotel, but if she called, more often than not the receptionist said he wasn't there. One weekend she didn't manage to speak to him at all, and that left her in a panic.

"I was invited to Rose and Joe Kennedy's place at Hyannis Port," he told her when she finally caught up with him. "It's a funny old house—not at all grand—with flaking paintwork, a battered weatherboard exterior, and scruffy basketwork furniture on the porch. Joe Kennedy can't speak since his stroke, but Rose is a formidable woman."

"Why were you invited there?" she asked, her guts in knots.

"As a friend of the family," he replied airily, then added, "I'm going to Rhode Island to meet Jacqueline's mother and stepfather tomorrow. Somehow I think their property will be rather better maintained."

"What's behind all this meeting-the-family business?" she asked. "Why do they want to meet *you*?"

"It's normal to meet your friends' families. We're all concerned about Jacqueline and we're pulling together to help her."

Maria accepted that with a sniff. "How *is* Mrs. Kennedy?"

"In a dreadful state, frankly. She is terrified that she or her children will be targeted next. I think she's still in shock. She and Bobby were very close."

Maria felt no sympathy. She'd made it plain to Mrs. Kennedy that Ari was her partner, yet she was dragging him around, introducing him to her relatives, and monopolizing his time. Either she was rude and self-centered, or she was trying to steal him and using the death of her brother-in-law as a pretext. She was a predatory bitch, just like Lee. It must run in the family.

When Ari called to say that he wouldn't be back by the twenty-sixth after all, Maria fell silent. She felt chilled. Numb.

"I'll only be a few days late," he promised. "On the first of July, we can meet in Milan and then fly to

Greece. Omero will forgive me this once—and I hope his mother will as well."

"Don't count on it," she said. "You're pushing me too far, Ari."

For once she didn't tell him she loved him before hanging up. He said it, and she simply replied, "Good-bye, Ari."

There were no further postponements and Ari arrived in Milan as promised, clutching a glossy black sable coat.

"This is for you," he said, holding it up so she could see the style.

Instinctively she reached out to touch the fur. It was silkier, plusher, than any coat she had ever owned, and cut to the fashionable midcalf length.

"Have you been outside recently?" she asked. "We're in the midst of a heat wave."

His eyes met hers, and she was surprised to see uncertainty. He knew she was upset with him and wasn't sure what reception to expect.

Maria was still hurt and angry, but she was so happy to see him that she stifled her feelings. She didn't want to sulk or argue; she wanted him in her arms.

"Put it down," she said, "and come here."

Once she could smell the familiar Ari scent and feel

the heat of his body, her anxiety melted at the edges. They kissed, then she pulled back.

"I'm still cross with you, by the way," she said. Forgiveness would take longer.

"I know. And I'm sorry."

She didn't ask what he was sorry for. Some things were better left unsaid.

After their trip to Omero's grave, they flew straight to Skorpios. The pink-walled, marble-floored main villa was set on a hillside surrounded by trees, and its lush, shady garden caught refreshing sea breezes. They swam in the mornings, then snoozed after lunch, shutters drawn, while outside the vicious sun scorched the land. Every evening they dined on the terrace, accompanied by the chirping melody of cicadas and the rhythmic shushing of waves, then sat up late, drinking and talking, while the dark shadows of bats flitted past, silhouetted against the moon.

It was a few days before Maria felt brave enough to ask the questions that had been haunting her for the past weeks. "Tell me about you and Mrs. Kennedy. I need to know the truth: are you sleeping with her?"

"No, I'm not," he said, and from his tone she believed him.

"But you would like to?"

He hesitated. "Perhaps. But I hope you know that you are the only woman I love."

"Are you not in love with her too? A little bit?"

He shook his head. "Jackie doesn't let anyone get to know her. Always there is a barrier. Sure, she tells me some things. I know that Bobby was like a brother to her after Jack died. I know she still has nightmares about what happened in Dallas, and she hates the media attention she attracts because of it. I know she is terrified when members of the public approach her in the street . . . but I don't feel as if I know who she truly is. She's a mystery, perhaps even to herself."

Maria nodded, trying to understand. "And you want to solve the mystery?"

"I want to help. You should see her: she's like a bird with a broken wing. If it wasn't for her children, I'm not sure she would carry on."

"Do you mean she would commit suicide?" Maria was surprised. She had imagined her tougher than that. Suicide was for self-centered people, like her mother, or mentally frail ones like Marilyn Monroe.

"Perhaps." He refilled their glasses from the brandy bottle on the floor by his feet.

"It must be flattering that she has chosen you to be the one to fix her. Is that why she took you to meet her family?" Her tone was sharp.

He pulled his chair closer so he could kiss her bare shoulder. "I understand how hurt you feel that I am spending time with another woman, but you need to have more faith in us. You and I understand each other so well. I hope you know that no matter what happens, I will always come back to you."

She was silent, drinking in the implications. So he did want to have an affair with Jackie. It was as if he were asking for her blessing.

She spoke with all the dignity she could muster. "Please don't humiliate me, Ari. I deserve better."

"I won't," he said. "Of course you do."

Chapter 57

Skorpios, Greece
July 1968

The month of July was glorious. Maria and Ari went sea fishing together and he taught her how to cast a rod. She couldn't bring herself to kill the fish she reeled in on deck, so Ari had to do it for her with a swift blow to the head. She started a collection of the most beautiful seashells that washed up on the shores of the island, arranging them in a stone fireplace inside the villa. They snorkeled together and sailed and ate and drank and made love all over the island, cushioned by cypress needles or the soft, golden sand he had imported.

And then one evening toward the end of July, as they sat on the terrace, Ari said, "I have something to tell you that you are not going to like."

Instantly she stiffened, feeling a chill on her arms.

"Mrs. Kennedy is coming here for a couple of weeks in August and I need you to go back to Paris."

Maria hurled the glass she was holding to the ground, where it shattered into thousands of pin-sharp splinters.

"Absolutely not! I am not leaving and you can't make me."

He had clearly expected a battle and had a stack of arguments prepared. "Mrs. Kennedy needs peace. She is very unstable right now and particularly nervous about meeting you since your phone call to her. Besides, it's not for long."

"No one goes to Paris in August, Ari. That's absurd. I will stay and I will be charm personified with Mrs. Kennedy. I can help you to look after her." Her cheeks blazed with fury. She would not stand for this. She couldn't. Otherwise, where would it lead?

"Maria, this is not up for discussion. She is coming here and I want you to give us time alone." He stood and paced to the end of the terrace, then turned to face her. "I'm not asking, I'm telling you."

She rose to her feet, fists clenched. "You told me Skorpios is my home too. But how can it be my home when you can dismiss me with a click of your fingers? Will you throw me out of Avenue Georges Mandel, like a tenant who is behind on the rent?"

"Of course not." He folded his arms and leaned

back against a wall, as if bracing himself to ward off an attack. "The Paris flat is yours."

"But not Skorpios. I am just a guest here. I wish you had made that clear before I helped you to plan the building work. How odd I got the wrong impression." Her voice was thick with sarcasm.

"I'm not asking the impossible," he said. "I want to spend a couple of weeks with Mrs. Kennedy, without interruptions."

"Just the two of you?"

"No, Teddy Kennedy will be here. Her children are coming . . ."

"Won't that get in the way of you *fucking* her?" Maria never swore, and the word sounded shocking coming from her lips.

"This is not about me fucking her."

"Of course it is. You want the world to know you have seduced John F. Kennedy's widow. You think it will help you conquer the American market. You don't care that it is humiliating and excruciating for me, the woman who has stood by you for almost nine years. You turned up late for our son's birthday this year and now you are planning to play host to Mrs. Kennedy's children. Do you realize her son, John, is the same age Omero would have been? It doesn't even occur to you how much that tortures me." She took a step toward him, ignoring the splinters of glass that jabbed her bare feet. "If you truly loved me, you wouldn't do this. That's what it boils down to."

"Of course I love you. I wouldn't have been with you all this time if I didn't. I still love you, but I want you to let me be a friend to a grieving widow. You're being unreasonable."

Maria considered this. Was she unreasonable? She shook herself. Her brain was foggy from the wine and brandy they'd consumed. What would Maggie advise if she were here? Or Mary Carter?

But it was her decision now, and she sensed danger in his obsession with the Kennedy woman. She could smell it a mile off. She had to take a stand or this would keep happening, time and again.

"It is not unreasonable for me to want to meet your friends and to entertain them by your side. You're treating me like dirt and I won't have it. I will stay here to meet your guests from America and that's final . . ." She paused, considering the dangerous words that were on the tip of her tongue, rolling them around awhile before she said them: "Otherwise our relationship is over. Be very sure you know what you are doing because if you let me go now, you will never see me again. Not ever."

It was the only card she had left, the finale. She held

her breath. Ari turned his back on her and was silent for a few minutes. She took a step toward him, heart thumping, then thought better of it.

When he turned around, his jaw was set with determination, his expression ice-cold. "I will not give in to blackmail, Maria. You know that."

She opened her mouth to speak, but he raised a hand to silence her.

"I'm going to bed. I'll send the housekeeper out with a first-aid kit to bandage your feet." He pointed. "You're bleeding."

He disappeared inside. Maria wanted to run after him, but her wounds were oozing all over the tiles, leaving carmine smears. Besides, she knew she had to stick to her guns. Let him think about it overnight. Maybe he would be more reasonable when he awoke in the morning. Maybe by then she would have thought of some other way to persuade him.

She rose late and found Ari in his study. He looked haggard, unshaven, and didn't smile when she came in.

"How are your feet?" he asked.

"They're okay." She searched his face, looking for some compassion, but it was a closed book. There was a brandy bottle beside him and a near-empty glass. It wasn't like him to drink in the morning.

"The seaplane is ready. It will take you to Athens as soon as you have packed." He was slurring his words, with sibilant s's, and she knew he was drunker than she had seen him in a long time. Had he stayed up drinking all night?

Part of her wanted to take care of him, and part of her wanted to smash that bottle over his stupid, stubborn head. But she had her pride, so she turned and swept upstairs to start packing. She threw clothes into cases any old way, her heart hammering, hot tears trying to squeeze out of the corners of her eyes. What else could she do? No fresh ideas came to her.

She charged noisily through the villa's main rooms, picking up books and records that were hers and throwing them into bags. In an opera, there would have been drumrolls, cymbals crashing. The door to Ari's study was open, and she knew he could hear. She hesitated over her seashells but decided they would likely break in transit, so she wrapped just a few favorites and put them in her handbag.

Next, she applied makeup, drawing her trademark black Cleopatra lines around her eyes. Now she couldn't cry or they would smudge. She was determined not to cry. She fixed her hair, called for the gardener to carry her suitcases, and walked downstairs, head held high.

Ari rose and came toward her but she held up her

hand to stop him. She couldn't bear his embrace, one of goodbye. If he did that, she would break down.

"Don't touch me," she hissed. "I hate you." She walked out to the jeep in which she would be driven down to the jetty without once looking back.

The journey was agony, but Maria kept her composure, tipping porters, smiling at stewardesses, asking her Paris taxi driver about the aftermath of the riots. When she got to Avenue Georges Mandel, Bruna was out.

Maria took a bottle of champagne from the refrigerator, found her favorite crystal glass, and retreated to the bathroom. The sun was setting outside as she popped the champagne cork and poured herself a glass, using it to wash down a Nembutal sleeping pill. Then she drank another glass, and another. She wanted to reach a state in which it didn't hurt anymore.

At one point she tried to call Maggie van Zuylen but there was no reply. She must be on vacation. Next she got the operator to place a call to Mary Carter in Texas.

"It's all over," she lisped when Mary answered. Her tongue felt too big for her mouth. "Ari and me. Finished. Almost nine years down the drain."

"What are you talking about?" Mary asked. "What happened?"

"He chose Mrs. Kennedy. That's what happened." Tears came, and great sobs that tore at her throat.

"Oh, my *dahlin'*, I'm so, *so* sorry."

Maria couldn't bear her sympathy. It made things worse. "I can't talk about it," she said. "I thought I could but I can't. I'll phone back tomorrow."

She hung up and refilled her glass. If only she could sleep. The Nembutal wasn't working, but the doctor had warned her not to take more than one. Maybe if she had a couple of Valium as well, that would do the trick. She tipped them into her hand and swallowed them. The phone was ringing but she ignored it. Instead she lay on her rose velvet sofa, drinking and crying until she drifted into unconsciousness.

Chapter 58

The Greek Islands
August 1968

Jackie lay on a lounge chair on the deck of the *Christina,* as if in a trance. Fierce sun was roasting her shins but she couldn't find the energy to move. Her bones had sunk into the cushions like dead weights.

She could hear shrieks of excitement coming from the sea alongside. Ari was teaching John to water-ski, patiently demonstrating how to position his skis, bending his knees as if sitting on a chair and keeping his arms straight as he held the towrope. Every time he fell over with a yell of frustration, Ari turned the launch to help him try again. He was kind to her children; that was reassuring.

When he had swept into town after Bobby died, offering to marry her, she said yes straightaway. What else could she do? She wasn't safe, her children weren't safe, and he was the only person who could protect them.

Since then she hadn't slept more than a couple of hours a night. Her body was exhausted, but when she lay down in bed her brain stayed on full alert, memories of Jack's and Bobby's murders playing like gruesome silent-movie footage in her head. The piece of skull arcing through the air; Jack's unseeing eyes in the hospital emergency room; the blank expression on Bobby's face that told her he was no longer there. How many days could a human being survive without sleep? It was hard to concentrate now. Her brain felt like a television set stuck between channels, full of zigzag lines and emitting a buzzing sound.

Teddy was talking to someone on the telephone, his tone impatient. He was annoyed with her. Suddenly the job of being head of the Kennedy clan had landed in his lap, while he was still floored by grief for his brother. There were legal issues, financial issues, political issues to deal with. The last thing he needed was to be here, cruising in the Greek islands, negotiating the terms of her marriage to a man he didn't like or trust. He'd made his views very plain: he thought Jackie had gone stark, staring mad.

"What do you have in common? Nothing. You're an

intellectual and he's a heathen. He doesn't even read books."

"He has a broad general knowledge," Jackie replied. "Besides, there are different kinds of intelligence."

"You haven't even thought about where you will live. It's not fair to take your children out of school to attend some backwater establishment in Athens."

"We'll work it out."

In truth, Jackie couldn't envisage how it would work.

"Have you thought about what the American press will say?" Teddy closed his eyes and shook his head briefly.

"I don't give a damn. I'm fed up being their sacred widow. I can't wait to be toppled from that particular pedestal." She yearned to leave America and be a stranger in a strange land. She wanted to leave the Kennedys too; she'd had enough of them telling her whom to talk to and how to act.

She'd gotten support, though, from an unexpected source: Rose Kennedy had taken to Ari during their Hyannis Port visit. "He has a good sense of humor and a pleasant manner," she said. "You marry him if you like, dear. I just want you to be happy."

But Ethel had made her disapproval plain, and Jackie's mother was strongly against the match. It turned out that Janet Auchincloss had known about his affair with Lee all along. "I walked in on them!" She shuddered. "She was staying with him in Claridge's a couple of years ago. Disgusting little man!" She shook her head as if to expunge the memory. "Does Lee know what you are planning? How do you think she will feel about you jumping into bed with her ex? It's unsavory, to say the least."

"That's ancient history, Mother," Jackie said uncertainly. She was too fragile to talk to Lee. She couldn't face conflict. It took all her strength just to get through each day.

Ari had disappeared into her stepfather's study for over an hour, and the two men emerged only when dinner was served. Jackie hoped that was a good sign. Hugh Auchincloss was tight-lipped when she asked what they had discussed, but she assumed it must have something to do with business. That's all they had in common.

One evening, as Jackie and Ari sat on the deck of the *Christina,* enjoying a "sundowner"—vodka for her, whiskey for him—she raised the subject of her sister. He was holding her hand loosely, stroking between her fingers.

"I haven't told Lee about us yet. Do you think she will mind?"

"I'm sure she just wants you to be happy," Ari replied.

Jackie gave a throaty laugh. "No, she doesn't. She's fiercely competitive with me, always has been."

"Does it matter what she thinks? The only two people who should have a say in our relationship are you and me."

"I don't want to alienate her. I want her to come to our wedding." Her voice trembled. She was worried about Lee but couldn't face calling her in person.

Ari pulled his hand away and picked up his brandy glass. "Why are women so sentimental about weddings? As far as I'm concerned, it's just a scrap of paper, nothing more. I've agreed with Teddy that I will provide for you and the children. That's settled. We don't need a ceremony."

Jackie took out a cigarette, and Ari leaned over to light it for her.

"I may not be a practicing Catholic, but all that guilt about fornication and sin makes its mark," she told him. "Don't you ever worry about your immortal soul?"

He guffawed. "My soul is beyond redemption."

"Really? Are you as corrupt as they say?"

"Who says I'm corrupt? Give me their names and I'll sue." He sat back to watch her.

"I need a wedding, Telis," she said softly, thinking of a conversation she had overheard the previous evening.

Some Greek musicians had been invited on board to play for them. The children were whirling each other in giddy circles. Teddy and Ari were talking quietly halfway down the deck, but somehow their words drifted through the night air, audible over the music.

Ari had said, "Which other market would force me to commit to the purchase without testing the goods first? Especially a purchase that is quite so expensive."

And Teddy replied, "That's between you and Jacqueline. I'm not going to negotiate your sex life for you as well."

It chilled Jackie to the bone, but in the next moment she decided to ignore it. Men would be men. It hadn't been meant for her ears.

"Is there a rush to get married?" he asked now. "Might it not be seen as distasteful so soon after Bobby's murder? We could be together discreetly and keep it under the radar so the press doesn't catch on."

"Are you kidding?" she asked. "Try walking a day in my shoes. News of this trip has already leaked."

"Has it?" he asked, acting surprised, but she could tell he knew.

What am I doing? she wondered. She had no touchstone anymore, no moral compass. First there had been her daddy, then Jack, then Bobby, but now there was no one whose opinion she could trust. She was entirely on her own and her brain wasn't functioning properly. All she could think was that she wasn't safe, she needed help, and Ari would protect her.

He cared about her. She was sure that was genuine. She loved his thoughtfulness and all the layers of protection his wealth could buy. He was already advising on her personal finances, buying shares and making investments in her name. She would never have to worry about money again.

"I don't care what anyone else says," she told him. "I'm looking forward to being your wife, to love and to cherish from this day forward . . ." She stopped, remembering the end of the quotation—"Till death do us part." Ari was twenty-three years older than she was. She didn't think she could cope with another bereavement. She was already so smashed up she was barely functioning.

Chapter 59

Paris
August 1968

Maria awoke slowly, aware of a familiar voice saying, "She's coming round."

She opened her eyes a slit. Bright sunlight was reflecting off white sheets and white walls, and there, with a halo of light around her head, was Bruna, along with a nurse.

"What happened . . . ?" she croaked, then stopped. Her throat felt raw and she didn't want to strain it.

Bruna rushed to explain: "I couldn't rouse you last night and there were open pill bottles on the floor so I rang an ambulance. You're fine, though. They think you were just in a deep sleep."

"Please don't tell Ari," Maria whispered. She would hate for him to hear of it.

"Of course not," Bruna promised.

"I didn't try to kill myself." Memories filtered back of the night before, and she knew she had just wanted the pain to stop. It hadn't been a suicide attempt; not like her mother's.

"Mary Carter rang while I was waiting for the ambulance and I've rung back to tell her that you're fine."

Maria vaguely recalled telephoning Mary but had no idea what she had said.

"As soon as the doctor discharges you, Mary wants you to pack a case and fly to the States. She is going to take you on a road trip through the American South. An adventure, she said, to take your mind off everything."

Maria considered this. "What if Ari is trying to find me?"

"If there is anything urgent, I will take a message." Bruna's tone was cold, judgmental. She had turned against him.

Maria lay back on her pillows. It sounded like a plan. At least it would be better than sitting in Avenue Georges Mandel waiting for him to call. Anything would be better than that.

Once she was well enough, Maria flew to Kansas City, where Mary Carter met her, and they began a crazy six-week tour in a rented Cadillac DeVille that took them to Colorado Springs, Santa Fe, Las Vegas, L.A., and San Francisco, followed by a flight to Cuernavaca in Mexico, then back to Dallas. They stayed in motels and with friends, ate in diners and fancy restaurants, shopped in dime stores and designer boutiques, and the whole time Maria talked and talked.

"All my life I've been undefended," she told Mary. "My mother didn't love me, didn't even like me, and my father was too weak to take my side. Battista was a pimp, only interested in hiring me out for cash. The press turned against me. The audience at La Scala booed me. And now Ari has abandoned me . . . it is my fate. Some people are born to be happy but I was not one of them. I am destined always to be the tragic heroine."

"Don't talk nonsense. You have so much going for you," Mary argued. "You have the greatest voice of our time, and you have dozens of good friends. Loyal friends."

"I am not loveable. I'm too irascible, and I upset people by speaking home truths."

"That's not true. *I* love you. All your friends love you."

Maria ignored that. "Nine years I gave him. Nine years! I neglected my career and let my voice deteriorate—all for him! I left my marriage for him. I looked after him better than any wife and put him on a pedestal, even when I knew he was being disloyal. I was always honest with him. He said he loved me so many times, Mary. All lies. I've got no child, no ring on my finger, nothing to show for it, nothing to look forward to. Just lonely middle age, and then death."

A vivid memory came back of their first meeting in the Hotel Danieli, when he had said, "If I make you a promise, I will always keep it." Had he broken promises to her? He'd said, "When the time is right, we will marry," but presumably he would argue that the time had never been right. She should have paid more attention to the fine print before committing herself so wholeheartedly.

"You could go back to singing," Mary suggested. "Directors would jump at the chance to have Maria Callas perform again. You could choose a repertoire that suits you. Promise you'll think about it."

Maria felt exhausted at the thought. She would have to practice slavishly for months to get her voice back to performance level. But it would be a way of regaining her dignity. She could show Ari what he was missing. At least she had talent; what did Mrs. Kennedy have except a famous dead husband?

———————

Every morning, wherever they were staying, Maria called Bruna in Paris to find out if Ari had phoned. Always she replied that there had been no word. Maria agonized. Where was he now? He'd told her Mrs. Kennedy was visiting only for a couple of weeks. She called Maggie and a few other friends in Paris, but no one had any news.

"Forget about him," Mary urged.

"I'm not going to forget him in a few short weeks . . ."

"But promise me you'll do your best, honey."

Maria couldn't tell her that she fantasized about Ari calling to say he couldn't live without her and begging her to come back. It was all she thought about. A love as great as theirs couldn't simply be over; it was unthinkable. They'd had two passionate months in the Caribbean that spring, and a romantic month on Skorpios in July. How could love evaporate so quickly?

She knew she had made a tactical error. Ari was not the type of man to whom she should have issued an ultimatum. It had driven him away, leaving the field clear for Mrs. Kennedy. If she had not lost her temper, she could have been back on Skorpios with him by the end of August. She bitterly regretted that final argument, but she had reached her limit. She couldn't continue letting him push her aside every time Mrs. Kennedy lifted her little finger and beckoned. She had to keep some dignity.

Maria did her best to put on a brave face for Mary, to chat gaily with all the friends they visited, to discuss her operatic "comeback," to paint on her black eyeliner, dress up, and venture into the world, but beneath the mask she was bruised and bloodied. As the days passed, then the weeks, the pain got worse, not better.

Where was he? What was he doing? Did he miss her even a fraction as much as she missed him?

In mid-September, they returned to Mary's Dallas home, where Maria learned from a newspaper that Ari was in his Pierre Hotel suite in New York. That was encouraging. Surely if he and Mrs. Kennedy were a couple, he would have stayed at her apartment? It had been over six weeks since she had spoken to him, and she couldn't tolerate the silence any longer. She had to hear his voice.

She waited until Mary was driving her daughter to school before dialing the number, feeling sick with nerves. She had to give her name before the operator would connect the call. Would he even accept it?

"Hello, Maria," he said when he picked up. She couldn't detect any warmth in his tone.

"How are you, Ari?"

"Fine. And you?"

"Also fine." She told him about her road trip, and of her decision to go back to professional performance.

"Good," he said. "I'm glad." That was all.

"What brings you to New York?" she asked, then bit her lip, hoping he wouldn't say that it was Mrs. Kennedy.

"Business," he replied.

"Are you staying for long? I'm coming up for some meetings next week." She held her breath, hoping he would suggest that they see each other.

"I will be gone by then," he told her. "But I hope your meetings go well. Good luck with your return to the stage."

"Good luck with your business."

"Goodbye, Maria," he said, and scarcely gave her a chance to say her goodbye before he hung up the phone.

She threw herself on the bed and sobbed out loud, gasping for breath. How could he be so cold? He hadn't sounded angry. Worse than that, he had sounded like a polite acquaintance, someone she used to know long ago. And he had sounded as if he couldn't wait to get off the phone.

When Mary returned, she took note of the swollen red eyes, the puffy face and hoarse voice and, without asking questions, enfolded Maria in a hug.

"I'm flying to Paris," Maria told her. "You're right: I need to start talking to directors. I need to be busy." She quelled the frisson of panic she felt at the thought.

Back at Avenue Georges Mandel, Maria helped Bruna pack all the possessions Ari had left there—his clothes, his bottle of brilliantine, the spare pairs of sunglasses, his humidor, even his old toothbrush—and dispatch them to Avenue Foch. She packed away all the photographs of him, even her favorite one of them standing hand in hand on the deck of the *Christina,* which she had always kept on her night table. Next she called her old voice coach and arranged an appointment. She began testing her voice, sitting at the piano to accompany herself to see what felt comfortable. She called her Paris friends to put lunch and dinner dates on the calendar, so that she could stay as busy as possible. It was an effort, and she was weighed down by sadness, but at least she knew since the phone conversation that Ari had truly gone. It didn't make sense, but she had no choice but to accept it.

On the evening of October 16, the telephone rang and Bruna came into the salon, her tone disapproving as she said, "It's him—Mr. Onassis."

Maria leapt to her feet and rushed to take it in her private bathroom, waiting till Bruna had hung up the hall phone before speaking. "Hello, Ari," she said, trying to keep her tone *tranquillo*.

"Maria, help me! I'm begging you!" He sounded distraught, not like himself at all.

"What's happened?"

There was a pause. "I can't tell you but I need you to come and save me from myself." He generally held his drink well, but she detected a slowing of his speech and the careful diction he used when trying to disguise inebriation.

"Where are you?"

"I'm on Skorpios, but it's all a mistake. I don't want to be here."

"If you don't want to be there, then leave." She frowned. "Get on the *Christina* and sail away."

"You don't understand," he said. "You're the only one who can stop this happening. Please come."

She was silent for a moment. Every fiber of her being wanted to rush to the airport and fly to him, but she mustn't. She summoned what inner strength she could muster. "Ari, you sent me away, remember? I'm not going to come running now. If you want to see me, fly to Paris."

"You don't understand," he said again. "It will be too late. Oh, hell . . ." Then he hung up abruptly and there was a whining tone on the line, followed by nothingness.

Too late for what? Maria wondered. Should she have said she would go? No, of course not. She couldn't.

All the same, a flicker of hope was lit within her. Ari was in some kind of trouble, and he turned to her. Perhaps he would accept her invitation and travel to Paris. She had made it clear she would see him if he did. That was as far as she could go, under the circumstances.

The following evening, Mary Carter called from Dallas. "Maria, dahlin', I need you to sit down. I have bad news."

"What is it?" Maria's heart lurched as she sat in the telephone chair in the hall.

"The *Boston Herald* announced that Ari is going to marry Mrs. Kennedy within the week. They haven't said where. I thought you needed to know before you hear it from someone else."

There was a ringing sound in Maria's ears and she clapped a hand over her mouth to stop herself from crying out. When she could gather her thoughts to speak, she breathed, "*Marry?* Are you *sure?*"

"All the TV channels are reporting it. I double-checked before calling you. I'm so sorry, honey."

There was a stabbing pain in her diaphragm. Maria bent double. Would he *marry* the Kennedy woman? After all the excuses he had made not to marry *her*? Yes, she believed he would.

"He is a vile, evil man," she said. Words did not seem strong enough to express her fury. "I am glad he is out of my life. She's welcome to him."

"Are you sure you're okay? I don't want you to be alone after this news."

Maria knew Mary was a good friend, and was grateful for her concern, but she felt an urgent need to get off the phone. "Don't worry. I won't do anything foolish. I have dozens of friends in Paris, and I have work plans I need to prepare for, so I have to go now. But . . . thank you for telling me."

As soon as she hung up, she collapsed onto the floor and curled into a ball. It felt as if she had been hit hard over the head with a mallet and couldn't catch her breath.

Chapter 60

Skorpios
October 19, 1968

The guests had hardly any notice, but the day before the wedding they began to arrive on Skorpios. While they got settled into their accommodations, Jackie and Ari went for a walk along the coast. The skies were overcast, and the neighboring islands were blurred in mist and fringed by gray choppy seas. They didn't talk for a while, focusing on clambering over rocks and down needle-clad slopes, but when they came to a sheltered clearing in the woods, Ari suggested that they rest.

Jackie sat, hugging her jeans-clad knees to her chest. "I hope it won't rain tomorrow. It seems like a bad omen," she said, then laughed as if to imply that of course she didn't believe in such things.

"It was sunny when I married Jack, but my daddy spoiled the day by getting too drunk the night before and not turning up to give me away. Nice, huh?"

Ari turned to her, his face serious. "We don't have to go through with it tomorrow. We could wait awhile. Choose a sunny day next spring. I'm worried that you are still in shock from Bobby dying and you are rushing into this for the wrong reasons. I don't want to take advantage."

Jackie felt hysteria bubbling up. It was always there, ready to engulf her at a moment's notice. "You don't want to get married tomorrow?"

"It doesn't feel right, does it? For me, the romance has been tarnished by all the negotiations with lawyers. It's as if I am leasing an oil tanker rather than taking a new bride." He shifted to put his arm around her shoulders. "At a spring wedding we could have orange blossom and sunshine. We would know each other better and feel more relaxed."

"You don't feel relaxed?" Jackie couldn't understand what he was saying. "We can't cancel now simply because you are not relaxed. My mother and stepfather have flown across the ocean, my children are here—and you said Lee is coming. She is, isn't she?" Jackie hadn't spoken to Lee directly, couldn't face it.

"Yes, Lee and Stas are flying in later. We could still

have a celebration tomorrow, but get married next year when the time feels right."

He's trying to back out, Jackie thought. *What can I do? I can't cope.* Tears welled up and she turned her head away.

"Are you crying? Please don't cry. I didn't mean to upset you." He wrapped both arms around her, kissing her cheek, nuzzling her neck.

"I need this," she whispered.

"But you've already got me. I'm right here. I'm not going anywhere."

"I need to marry you tomorrow," she said, her voice trembling.

Ari was silent for a few moments, before saying in a low voice, "Okay. Then that's what we will do."

The next morning, Jackie slipped on the ivory lace Valentino minidress she had chosen and sat at her dressing table, winding ivory ribbons through her hair. Lee was supposed to be her matron of honor, but she had avoided being alone with Jackie since her arrival the previous evening.

The children came in, looking grown-up in their wedding outfits: seven-year-old John in a blue suit and bow tie, and ten-year-old Caroline in a white dress with tan piping.

"Where is your auntie Lee?" Jackie asked them. "Could you please ask her to come and help me?"

Her hands shook and her nerves fluttered as she waited. Several minutes passed before Lee floated in without smiling, leaving the door flung wide.

"Shut the door," Jackie gestured. "I can't have the groom see me before the ceremony."

Lee slammed it so hard the noise echoed. "What did you want?"

"To see you, of course. I haven't seen you in months. And I wondered if you could tie a ribbon right in the center back of my hair. I can't reach."

Lee walked over and took the ribbon Jackie was holding without a word.

"I'm sorry I didn't tell you about this myself," Jackie began. "It's been . . ." Her voice trailed off as she searched for a word to describe the four months since Bobby's funeral.

"Is that all you are sorry about? Not the fact that you knew I loved him and you went ahead and stole him. What does that say about you?" Lee tugged hard on a strand of hair and Jackie winced.

"I didn't . . ." Jackie was flustered. "I thought your affair was over years ago. Ari told me it was just a brief fling."

"You didn't think to ask me, your own sister?" Lee

finished tying the ribbon and walked to the window before whirling to face her. "It would have been common courtesy."

"You didn't ever want to talk about him. You kept changing the subject . . . and he was photographed in the papers with Maria Callas. I assumed your affair was all in the past. Is it not?"

Lee glowered. "Our affair lasted right up till last year when you started fluttering your eyelashes in his direction and he dropped me like a hot potato. Story of my life. Jackie always comes first."

Jackie bent her head. "I'm sorry. I had no idea."

Had she, though? She remembered that row on Long Island, the time she had slapped Lee. She knew then that her sister was smitten but decided it wasn't going to work out between them and it would be better for her to get over it. And when Ari began courting her, she conveniently forgot. How could she? Lee had a point.

"And now? Would you walk away if I asked you to?" Lee answered her own question: "No, I thought not."

"I wish you could be happy for me," Jackie whispered. "I need this so badly."

"What Jackie wants, Jackie gets," Lee said, with spite in her voice. "Just be careful what you wish for, big sis."

She strode out of the room, leaving the door flung wide.

Shortly afterward, while Jackie was still shaken by the confrontation, her mother came in and sat on the end of the bed.

"You don't have to go through with this," she began, in a matter-of-fact tone. "We don't mind if you decide to pull out at this late hour. In fact, Hughdie and I think you should. We don't trust the man. You'll be making a big mistake if you marry him."

Jackie stared at her in consternation. "I can't possibly pull out, Mother. What else would I do?"

Outside, the rain was persistent, the clouds dark and low. The sea was dotted with dozens of fishing boats filled with photographers and journalists, and when she stepped out of the villa she heard they were calling her name—"Jackie!" Bulbs flashed as they tried to capture long-range shots. She had hoped for peace and privacy but it seemed that was impossible, even on this remote dot on the map. How had they known the ceremony was today? Had there been a leak?

She was driven by jeep the short distance to the island's tiny Greek Orthodox chapel and hurried inside to get out of the rain. It looked eerie in flickering candlelight, and the choking scent of incense tickled the back of her throat. Jackie looked around. Of her twenty-one wedding guests, Lee wasn't talking to her; Ari's children, Christina and Alexander, hated her; her mother and stepfather were horrified by the whole affair; and Teddy Kennedy had made excuses not to attend, leaving grim-faced Pat and Eunice to represent the Kennedy family. It wasn't an auspicious start.

The black-bearded priest in long gold brocade robes was solemn as he began to recite the words of the ceremony. He said them in Greek first, then translated them into English, in a singsong chant: "Servant of God, Aristotle Onassis, is wedlocked to the servant of God, Jacqueline, in the name of the Father, Son, and the Holy Ghost." He draped ribbons over their linked hands, gold rings were exchanged, they walked around the altar three times, then were pronounced man and wife—it seemed to be over in a heartbeat.

Jackie did as she was instructed, but her thoughts kept straying back to her wedding to Jack fifteen years earlier. She had been fluttery with nerves that morning, then distraught at the news that her daddy wouldn't be able to walk her down the aisle. But when Jack grinned at her as she approached the altar, and laced his fingers through hers, she felt a powerful surge of joy. He was the focal point in any room, the person everyone wanted to impress, and she was filled with pride that he had chosen her.

When they emerged from the chapel, the journalists started calling her name again. Ari drove down to the shore to negotiate with them, and came back saying he had agreed that there would be one photo opportunity, in return for which they would be left in peace for the remainder of the day.

Jackie was horrified, but didn't say so. She had hoped to keep this ceremony secret, but now it would be splashed across every front page worldwide.

Ari welcomed the photographers ashore as if they were invited guests, then beckoned her forward to the edge of the swimming pool, near the fountain that spilled into it. Someone held an umbrella over her head, and Ari slipped his arm around her waist. She forced her lips into a smile, then suddenly the flashbulbs went off all at once.

"Give him a kiss, Jackie!" "Smile, Jackie!" "Over here, Jackie!": it was like the feeding frenzy when you threw crumbs for a flock of pigeons. Every instinct screamed at her to turn and run.

"Are you cold?" Ari whispered. "You're trembling."

He had no idea how much this kind of attention terrified her. In contrast, he seemed to relish it.

Once the journalists had left, the evening entertainment began. There was a wedding feast complete with plate smashing, and a bouzouki band playing classic Greek songs. They all formed a circle, arms on their neighbors' shoulders, and danced the *sirtaki*. Ari had taught Caroline and John the steps—starting slowly and speeding up to a breakneck pace before slowing down again—and they shrieked with delight.

Jackie felt removed from it all, as if watching from behind a veil. She smiled and danced and drank from a loving cup and did all that was required of her, but the contrast with her first wedding was never far from her thoughts. She had been wildly, giddily in love with Jack, and she did not love Ari in the same way. He offered her an escape route from a life that had become intolerable, and that's why she had gone through with it. Besides, there had been no turning back once her family arrived. There had seemed no other option. Lee's words—*Be careful what you wish for*—rang in her head, but at least Ari was kind; she knew that much.

When they made love that night in the villa's master bedroom, she found him tender and considerate. That was a relief.

After he fell asleep, she lay awake, a lump in her

throat, listening to the shushing of the waves outside and the wind rattling the shutters.

This was her life now. The decision had been made, the marriage certificate signed. It was up to her to make the best of it.

ACT IV

Chapter 61

Paris
October 21, 1968

Maria examined the wedding photos on the front page of her newspaper. To her, the smiles were fake. Ari was clutching a glass of something, probably whiskey, as if he needed it to get through the day. Mrs. Kennedy looked toothy, as if someone had yelled "Say cheese!" a second earlier. She read the story, then crumpled the paper and threw it to the floor. It would be better if he had died; then she could have mourned. Instead she would have to get used to seeing pictures of them in the press: welcoming guests on the *Christina* or attending premières or balls. These were not as bad as the images in her imagination: Mrs. Kennedy sleeping in Ari's bed, having massages alongside him on the *Christina,* and dining with him on the terrace at Skorpios that *she* had designed.

She felt like an invalid. Her bones ached, her head hurt, she was feverish and low, but she forced herself to socialize. The previous evening, while the wedding was under way, she had attended the première of Feydeau's *A Flea in Her Ear*, starring Rex Harrison and Rachel Roberts. Richard Burton and Elizabeth Taylor had made a fuss over her, and afterward they'd all gone dancing at Les Ambassadeurs until the small hours. That evening she planned to go to the seventy-fifth anniversary of the opening of Maxim's with a crowd of Parisian friends, and she would paste on a smile every bit as false as Mrs. Kennedy's. She wanted Ari to see *her* picture in the papers and think she was having the time of her life. He mustn't know that he had destroyed her.

Three days after the wedding, a bouquet of red roses was delivered to Avenue Georges Mandel. When Bruna carried it into the salon, Maria didn't have a clue who they could be from. Richard and Elizabeth, perhaps? They were being kind.

No. The card read, "I'm sorry. I miss you. Ari."

With a scream, Maria hurled the flowers into her fireplace. The brown paper that they were wrapped in caught fire, and flames shot out; then the stems began to crackle and steam. She tore the card in half, then tossed it on top of the fire. How *dare* he? She clenched her fists, trying to contain her rage.

The mail had brought condolence letters from friends. "He is a madman," Zeffirelli wrote. "No other woman will do all that you did for him." Princess Grace wrote, "You are a beautiful woman and I know that life has another great love in store for you." Her sister, Jacinthy, wrote, saying that she would always be welcome at her home in Athens. Maggie van Zuylen called to say, "He has lost his mind. I no longer recognize him." Even Costa Gratsos, Ari's oldest friend, called, saying, "I warned him not to do this. He is making the biggest mistake of his life. It should have been you." Her friends invited her to dinners, lunches, parties, and other gatherings. She was touched by the affection showered on her.

The following day, there were more letters in a similar vein, and a package. She slit open the latter and gasped: inside was her Madonna icon, the one she used to pray to before performing. She hugged it to her chest, then read the note that accompanied it, recognizing Battista's writing straightaway.

"My dear Maria, I am glad that you must by now have realized Mr. Onassis's true colors but at the same time I am sorry for your very public humiliation." Maria exhaled loudly as her eyes skimmed the page, then she turned it over. "I recognize my own part in the failure of our marriage," he wrote. "I should have appreciated you more and not allowed the flame of romance to be extinguished by the demands of business." Near the end of the letter, he said, "I still love you, Maria. I am here for you should you want to get in touch." She had to laugh out loud at that.

"Bruna?" she called, wanting to share her mirth.

Bruna hurried into the room.

"Battista wants me to return to him now that Ari has married someone else. Can you believe the arrogance of the man?"

Bruna's eyebrows shot up. "How long has it been? Nine years?"

Maria shook her head in disbelief. "I'm glad to have my Madonna icon returned, but I don't think I will dignify his letter with a reply."

She would never forgive him for selling his story to the press. In her book, that was the death knell for a relationship. At least Ari hadn't done that.

On November 15, the buzzer rang in the apartment and Bruna answered, then came into the salon, looking worried.

"Madame, it is Mr. Onassis. What shall I tell him?"

Maria's heart lurched and her mouth felt dry. "Tell him to go away. I have nothing to say to him."

She stood in the doorway to listen as Bruna passed on the message. Ari was clearly arguing with her, because she had to repeat her refusal several times.

When Bruna hung up the intercom, Maria hurried to the window and hid behind the shutter, planning to watch him walk away—but he didn't. Instead, he stood in the street and began whistling a simple four-note tune that all the boys in Athens used to whistle when they wanted to attract the attention of the girls. He whistled, then called, "Ma-*ri*-a!," then started whistling again.

"Oh, for goodness' sake," Maria grumbled. "This is a polite neighborhood. He can't do that."

Far from giving up, Ari was increasing the volume of his shouting. "Ma-*ria*, I need to talk to you! Let me in!"

She tutted. He was stubborn and wouldn't give up when he knew she was there. She would have to see him.

She checked her appearance. Fortunately, she was dressed, coiffed, and made up for going out to dine later. She added a slick of lipstick and patted her hair, then called to Bruna: "You had better press the buzzer or he'll turn the entire 16th arrondissement against me."

She sat in an armchair in the salon, where the light was flattering. He hesitated in the doorway, unsure of whether to embrace her, so she spoke first to make it clear that was not an option.

"It's only three weeks since your wedding. I thought you'd be on your honeymoon. Or has the Widow given you time off for good behavior?"

Ari sat on the sofa opposite. "I need to explain why I got married, and why I couldn't tell you before. Please, will you listen?"

Maria looked at her watch. "Make it quick. I have dinner plans."

"You know me, Maria. You know better than anyone that I had no desire to marry again. The Kennedys trapped me into it."

Maria shook her head in disgust. "That's nonsense. You'll have to do better than that."

"It's true! I confess that I wanted to sleep with Jacqueline." He spoke quickly, in Greek. "But she wouldn't consider it unless we were married . . ."

"Oh, you poor thing," Maria interrupted, with sarcasm. "So you kept me around to satisfy your carnal urges while you were trying and failing to seduce her?"

"No, it wasn't like that. I never meant to lose you, Maria. I . . ."

At least he seemed upset, she thought. Good.

"I admit I miscalculated. I thought I could persuade you to accept me having an affair with Jacqueline and we could carry on as we were." His expression was pleading. "It's true I asked her to marry me but I never meant it to go ahead. I thought she would sleep with me once we were engaged and I could keep delaying the wedding indefinitely. But when I tried to pull out of marrying her, the Kennedys forced my hand by announcing it to the press. Do you remember that day I phoned you and asked you to save me? If you had come then, I swear I wouldn't have gone through with it."

"Don't you dare blame me for this," Maria blazed. "You've made your bed and chosen as bedfellow a woman who only wants you for your money. You've behaved with hubris and we both know what plans the gods have in these circumstances."

Ari jumped up from the sofa and came to kneel at her feet, hands clasped in prayer. "I am begging you . . . please try to understand. You know my weakness. You know I can't resist a conquest. I thought you loved me despite that."

"And I thought you loved me too," she retorted. "But you clearly don't or you wouldn't treat me with such callousness. Do you really think you can discard me, then woo me back? Would you discard me again as soon as the Widow beckoned?" She was gesticulating for emphasis. *It's almost like the plot in an opera,* she thought. *But in real life Ari would find there was no encore.*

"I can't bear to think how much I have hurt you." He leaned his forehead on her knees, but she shoved him away.

"Don't touch me!"

"If you could find it in your heart to forgive me, I swear I will make it up to you."

Maria shook her head. "How? By buying me diamonds? Another fur coat? It's too late for that. I want you to leave now. Please don't come here again."

He argued hard. He talked of all they had gone through together, the son they had lost, the illnesses and setbacks they had supported each other through.

"We are family, Maria. I want us to be family forever. Why let a simple marriage certificate get in the way when you are the one I love?"

Maria willed herself to turn to stone. La Callas would never return to Ari and neither would she.

"I am leaving for my dinner engagement now," she said, standing up and stepping around him. "Let yourself out. And please don't contact me anymore."

She walked through to her bathroom and locked the door, listening until she could hear the click of the front door closing behind him.

What it boiled down to was that she could have him back if she was prepared to be his mistress—but Jackie would always take precedence as the wife. She had already been through that before, when he was married to Tina. No matter how much she missed him, she could never accept a subordinate position in the hierarchy of his women. She couldn't believe he had asked her to. She was Maria Callas. She had far too much pride.

Chapter 62

Skorpios
November 15, 1968

Although summer had turned to autumn and there was a chill in the air, Jackie continued to swim each morning in the warm waters off Skorpios. She had found a local Greek-language tutor, and arranged for him to come over on a launch from the mainland at eleven in the morning every second day. She had also hired a team of interior designers to redesign the main villa, and they visited once a week for discussions.

She liked the pale pink exterior walls, whose color changed throughout the day as the sun moved through the sky; they were pale and silvery at dawn but by dusk they would catch the last rays and take on a warm salmon hue. The interior was decorated in traditional style, with white walls, and she planned to have them repainted in pastel shades that would enhance the light in each of the rooms. She also decided to expand the guesthouses, so she could invite plenty of visitors, and she designed a little one-story cottage that she called the "taverna," where lunch could be served at the beach.

Caroline and John had flown back to New York two days after the wedding and were staying in her apartment, looked after by her mother, so they did not miss too much school. No decision had yet been made about where they would be educated the following year; there was time for that. For now, she called them every day, but their physical absence caused a sense of loss and disorientation, a feeling of being permanently out of sorts.

On top of that, less than three weeks after the wedding, Ari announced he was going on a business trip, so she was left entirely alone on Skorpios, apart from the staff. She had understood that he would sometimes commute to Athens for the day, but now he announced that he'd be absent for almost a week, and the island was lonely.

This is the life I chose, she told herself. *I have to find ways to occupy myself.* Several boxes of her books had arrived from New York, and she spent hours reading every day, but she still had too much time on her hands—too much time to think.

Ari had been furious at the newspaper coverage of

their wedding. She had overheard him on the telephone with his American lawyer, asking if there were grounds to sue. He warned her not to look, but she knew he kept a pile of the offending newspapers in his office. Once he was gone, she peeked at the headlines, and they were worse than she had imagined. "How Could You, Jackie?" one read. "Jack Kennedy Dies for a Second Time Today," read another. "Jackie Marries Blank Check," said a third.

She could see why Ari was angry at the implication that he had nothing to offer but money, like a sad old sugar daddy. It was insulting to her too, but nothing the press could say surprised her.

She wandered around the villa, pausing in each room, deciding how she wanted to rearrange things. Her clothes were still hanging in the guest room she had occupied before the wedding, but she planned to move them into the master bedroom, so she opened the closets to check the space. At the back of one, she found a dressing gown of pearly silk, the lightest, flimsiest, softest gown ever. There was delicate floral embroidery on the back and a sash around the waist.

She took it out, frowning. Whose could this be?

And then the answer came to her: Maria Callas. She was the previous female occupant of that room.

Jackie searched the pockets and found a lace-trimmed

handkerchief with the letter *M* embroidered at the corner.

Finding such an intimate item in Ari's bedroom brought home to Jackie how big a part of his life Maria had been—and how recent. It seemed he hadn't been telling the truth when he assured her the affair was long over. If she was "just a close friend," why was her robe in his closet? There were echoes of Maria everywhere. Jackie had tried to throw out the seashells cluttering the fireplace, only to have Ari admonish her: "Leave them alone. That was Maria's collection." There was a crate of Dom Pérignon in the cellar, which he said was Maria's favorite. It was disconcerting to find the footprints of a woman she had met only once, briefly, but who had put her stamp throughout what was now supposed to be *her* home.

She wondered what to do with the dressing gown. She didn't want to give Ari an excuse to get in touch with Maria. Sending it herself was out of the question, and anyway she suspected Maria would find the act patronizing. In truth, she felt intimidated by the world-renowned soprano who had been her predecessor, and nervous about inviting any contact.

Outside, the gardener was burning some eucalyptus branches he had pruned. Pungent woodsmoke rose in a spiraling column and the smell permeated the house.

Jackie crumpled the gown into a ball, hurried outside, and tossed it onto the fire. It was consumed by flames, and soon all that was left was a pale powdery ash.

The day before Ari was due back from his business trip, Jackie had nothing planned. The endless hours stretched in front of her and she was too restless to read. She asked Konstantinos, the long-haired Greek boy who drove the launch, if he would take her to the nearest town for some shopping.

"Lefkada Town is nearest," he said. "I will prepare the launch."

The day was cloudy but the sea was flat calm, and it wasn't long before she was disembarking in a harbor where fishing boats tugged at their moorings, their masts clanking. Jackie set off along the shopping street that Konstantinos pointed out. Many of the stores were boarded up for winter, but she spotted a bookshop and went inside to browse. All the books were in Greek, but she found one illustrated with images of Greek antiquities and bought it, thinking she could use it to help her learn the language. The shopkeeper regarded her with interest, and she could tell he recognized her despite her oversized sunglasses.

In another shop she bought a length of lace—*reticella,* the shopkeeper told her, pointing to the ornate geometric pattern, and miming sewing to indicate that it was handmade.

"You made it?" Jackie asked, pointing at her.

The woman nodded, with a proud smile, and Jackie kissed her fingertips to show how much she loved it.

The lace shop was at the edge of a town square, and she stopped to watch the locals going about their business: women carrying baskets bulging with vegetables, a priest in black robes, a three-legged dog.

Suddenly a hunched old woman appeared directly in front of her. Jackie took a step back. The woman's expression appeared hostile, but perhaps that was because her face drooped on one side, as if from a stroke. The left eye was filmed with a cataract, and only the right moved.

The woman began to say something in Greek, but Jackie couldn't catch a word of it. She was speaking rapidly, leaning close, jabbing the air with her finger, her breath reeking of stale garlic.

"*Den katalavaíno*," Jackie said—"I don't understand."

The woman was angry about something. She kept repeating an emphatic phrase that sounded like "*kako mati.*"

Jackie looked around to see the shopkeeper watching, an expression of horror on her face. Something wasn't right. Clutching her roll of lace, Jackie turned and sprinted down the street toward the harbor. Konstantinos was outside a café, talking to a friend, and he rushed to intercept her.

"Are you okay?" he asked.

Jackie was trembling in panic, her heart hammering. She bent double to catch her breath. "There was an old woman yelling at me. I don't know what she said. Something like '*kako mati.*' She was clearly deranged."

Konstantinos was alarmed. "Are you sure she said '*kako mati*'?"

"Yes. Why?"

"Oh, God, the boss is going to kill me. I should have stayed with you. Please don't tell him I left you alone."

"What does it mean?"

He didn't want to say, and it took some persuasion before he finally admitted, "It's the evil eye."

"*What?* Has she put a curse on me? For crying out loud, why would she do that?" It was terrifying to think a stranger bore her so much ill will.

He shook his head unhappily. "I don't know."

"The lace seller heard everything. Can you ask her, please?"

They walked back to the lace shop. Jackie peered around, scared in case the old woman was still nearby.

Konstantinos spoke to the shopkeeper in rapid Greek, and translated her reply for Jackie.

"She says that old woman doesn't like Americans. She was saying you should not have taken Onassis from Maria Callas, who is revered by Greek people. That's why she put a curse on you."

Jackie clutched her throat. It felt as if there was no air.

The shopkeeper said something else and Konstantinos translated. "She advises you to see a priest as soon as possible to get the curse overturned."

The woman reached under the counter and handed Jackie a tiny ceramic medallion with concentric circles on it: dark blue on the outside, then white, then pale blue, and a black dot in the middle, like an eerie kind of eye. It was strung on a leather cord, and she indicated that Jackie should wear it around her neck.

"This will protect you until you see the priest," Konstantinos explained.

Jackie slipped it over her hair and opened her purse to offer money, but the woman shook her head.

As she sat in the launch motoring back to Skorpios, Jackie fingered the medallion, shivering, trying to still the panic that threatened to overwhelm her. Would *all* Greeks blame her for taking Ari from Maria? Was this the kind of reception she could expect elsewhere? She was a stranger in their country, and had hoped to find a safe haven. Now she realized she could try to assimilate by learning the language and customs, but she would never be one of them.

What would Ari think about the curse? She imagined he would laugh and call it an ignorant peasant superstition, then tease her for giving it a second thought. She should banish it from her mind.

But instead she decided that she would consult the priest who had married them at the next opportunity. And she would keep the medallion with her—just in case.

Chapter 63

Paris
November 30, 1968

Whenever Maria set foot in a public place that month, photographers and journalists yelled the same question: How did she feel about Ari marrying Mrs. Kennedy? She kept a smile pinned to her face, because she didn't want them to catch her with an expression their caption writers could interpret as angry or jealous. Only once did she reply, hinting at the twenty-three-year age difference between the newlyweds: "It's nice that Mrs. Kennedy has found a new grandfather for her children." Words she knew would annoy Ari if he read them.

She put the message out that she might consider a return to the stage, and offers flooded in, although she got cold feet at the suggestion that she sing *La Traviata* at the Paris Opéra. The truth was that she was nervous about performing; could her voice handle it? She was so out of practice, and she feared failure as much as she missed the music. And then the Italian director Pier Paolo Pasolini called to see if she would play Medea in a film he was making of the great tragedy. There would be no operatic singing; this was an acting role, and it could pave the way for a whole new career in the movies. She accepted straightaway and began to prepare for filming the following spring.

But she still had to get through the long days of winter, so when Maggie van Zuylen called to invite her to a dinner party, she accepted.

Maggie's dinners tended to be grand affairs, so Maria dressed in a full-length, décolleté scarlet evening gown and a diamond-and-ruby necklace that Ari had given her, with matching earrings. She had a hairdresser come to the apartment and took special care with her makeup, drawing the trademark thick black lines around her eyes and applying a pale lipstick, the current fashion. Maggie had assured her that the other guests were friends who were unanimously scathing about Ari's precipitous marriage.

When she arrived at Maggie's apartment, her hostess rushed out to the hall to greet her. "I'm so sorry," she said, kissing Maria on both cheeks, "but Ari is here."

Maria was startled. "How . . . ?"

"He came earlier to talk to the baron, noticed we were expecting company, found out you were one of the guests, and promptly invited himself. I told him we didn't have space at the table, but he said he would perch on the arm of my chair . . . we simply couldn't get rid of him. I tried calling you, but Bruna said you'd already left." Maggie looked harassed.

"Is Mrs. Kennedy with him?" Maria was ready to turn on her heel if the answer were yes.

"Oh, God, no! I wouldn't subject you to that. The question is, can you cope with seeing him?"

Maria's legs had turned to jelly, but she was damned if she was going to slink off home again just because that man had gate-crashed the party. "I'll stay," she said, "but please seat me at the opposite end of the table."

Ari rose when she entered Maggie's drawing room, with its smart, wood-paneled walls and Aubusson carpet. "Maria, how are you?" He stepped forward as if to embrace her, but she snubbed him with a curt nod and turned to kiss another guest. She could feel all eyes on the pair of them, and acted as if she didn't have a care in the world.

"Maria is becoming a movie star," Maggie told the assembled company, and the questions poured in: What was the film about, who was directing, where were they shooting, who were the costars?

Maria answered, pleased that Ari could hear of her triumph. He congratulated her and she met his eyes briefly, as she replied with a cool "Thank you."

Maggie's dining table had been set for sixteen, and Maria noticed that she had hurriedly added an extra place setting for Ari as far from hers as possible. The huge Régence bronze gilt mirrors that lined the walls meant she had a good view of him, though—as he did of her.

It was hard to be in the same company and not be with him. She thought of all the dinners when they had been seated side by side and he'd slid his hand up her skirt under the cover of the tablecloth, or she'd held his crotch with one hand while conversing with other guests about opera. Their eyes met in the mirror, and she wondered if he was remembering the same thing. She looked away first.

Over the foie gras starter, Maria spoke with her neighbors on either side about movies they had enjoyed recently. Maria said she had been disappointed by Zeffirelli's *Romeo and Juliet* but mesmerized by *2001: A Space Odyssey*, which had little dialogue but used classical music to great effect.

As the main course of *filet de boeuf aux truffes* was served, the talk around the table turned to politics. All felt that President de Gaulle should step down in the wake of the student riots, most were alarmed by Nixon's victory in the American presidential elections, and they applauded the anti–Vietnam War protesters in the States.

"Of course, it would have been very different if Bobby Kennedy hadn't died," one guest remarked. "He would have won the election and pulled American troops out of Vietnam."

There was moment's silence when they remembered that the new husband of Bobby's sister-in-law was sitting at the table.

"I feel for Rose Kennedy," Maggie said. "She's lost three sons and one daughter, with another incarcerated in a mental hospital. I don't know how any woman copes with that."

"Did you hear they are talking about the Kennedys being cursed?" another female guest added. "It seems odd for so much ill fortune to follow one family."

"Superstitious nonsense!" Ari interjected crossly.

Maria caught his eye in the mirror. "Why such a vehement tone, Ari? Are you afraid you might be jinxed by your association with them?"

"I thought you were more intelligent than that," he replied.

"And I thought you were more intelligent than to marry a gold digger," Maria shot back. "But men's egos lead them into all kinds of unsavory beds."

For a moment, she thought Ari was going to lose his temper. He scraped his chair back and stood, then walked around the table toward her. A few of the male guests half rose from their seats as if unsure of whether to stop him. Was he going to assault her? Maria kept her composure, a faint smile on her lips. The guests collectively held their breath.

When he reached her, Ari grabbed Maria's face between his hands, bent her head back, and kissed her hard on the lips; then he whispered in her ear, "But it's you I love."

She flushed bright scarlet and raised her napkin to her face to give her time to compose herself, while Ari returned to his seat.

Maggie mouthed, "Are you okay?"

Maria managed to nod, but she was far from okay. The touch of his lips, the smell of him, had shaken her badly. It stirred a yearning deep in the pit of her stomach. She felt like crying. This was too cruel.

For the rest of the evening, she avoided looking at him, and spoke only with her immediate neighbors. She sipped a glass of wine and then accepted a brandy when the gentlemen were lighting their cigars. As early as she could without seeming rude, she made her apologies to Maggie and said she had to leave.

"I understand, *ma cherie*." Maggie embraced her. "My doorman will hail a taxi for you."

Ari appeared beside them. "No. I will give Maria a ride home. We are going in the same direction."

Maria opened her mouth to protest, but Ari was holding her coat—the black sable he had bought her. Her resistance crumbled.

"Are you sure?" Maggie asked, her eyes blazing warnings.

Maria nodded. "I'll be fine."

She climbed into the backseat of the Rolls-Royce and scooted over to the window so there was plenty of space between them. Her apartment wasn't far. She just had to get there without losing her composure.

"I'm delighted to hear about the film you're making," Ari began. "Have you worked with Pasolini before?"

"No, but I admire his work. He won a Silver Lion at the Venice Film Festival with his St. Matthew movie. He has an original vision."

She asked about Project Omega, his deal with the colonels, and he said there was no progress. "There are too many levels of bureaucracy. I get approval at one level, then someone on a different echelon overrules it. And Niarchos is still hanging around like a bad smell."

"I am sure you will prevail," she said, watching a few raindrops meander sideways along the outside of the window.

When they pulled up outside her apartment, Maria reached for the door handle but Ari stretched out an arm to restrain her.

"Can't we talk awhile longer?"

"What did you want to talk about? Your marriage vows?"

He sighed. "I know I have no right to say this but I miss you. I can't sleep, can't think straight. I wish things could be different." His hand was still resting on her arm and she shook it off.

"I am not going to flatter your ego by spelling out how badly you have hurt me, but I think you know. You can't continue to play with my feelings now you are married. Go home to your wife."

He shook his head. "She has flown to New York for her children's birthdays."

"Why don't you go with her as their new . . . what are you? Their stepfather?"

Ari smiled. "I hear you called me their grandfather."

"You can see my point, given that you are in your

sixties and they must be—what—around seven and ten?" She closed her eyes. Omero would have been seven too. It killed her to think that he had been replaced by Jackie's son. She couldn't bear to imagine Ari playing in the sea with John, all gentle and patient, the way he used to be with Alexander.

"I don't want to talk about Jacqueline, or her children. I wish . . ." He spoke wistfully. "I wish we could be friends again."

"You don't treat friends the way you treated me."

"Actually, I take that back. I don't want to be your friend. I want you as my lover, my wise counsel, my sparring partner—all of that." He took her hand, and turned it over, raising it to his mouth to give the palm a lingering kiss. "I hoped—I suppose it is foolish—but I wish you could ignore the fact that I am married and we could carry on as we were."

She tried to summon rage. What he said was arrogant, insensitive, selfish . . . but instead she could feel tears coming. She sniffed them back.

Ari put his arms around her. "I'm so sorry," he murmured. "I'm so very sorry."

With her head on his chest, Maria's tears began to slide down her cheeks. She spoke with profound sadness. "When we got together, the thing that meant most to me was feeling truly loved. No one had ever loved me before. Not my family, not Battista. You made me feel I was the center of your universe."

"You still are," he whispered, and a sob burst from her.

"I don't believe you. Not now. It makes me question whether you ever loved me at all, or if you pulled the wool over my eyes for nine years."

He made a strange noise in his throat and she raised her head to look at his face. He was crying too. "I always loved you and I always will," he said. "My poor, beautiful, precious Maria. I have done a terrible thing and I wish I could undo it. I miss you every minute of every day."

She had never seen him cry, not properly, and she watched in wonder. Greek men didn't cry. She glanced at the driver, sitting on the other side of the glass partition, eyes straight ahead. He shouldn't see his boss like this.

"You had better come upstairs," she said. "Just for a nightcap."

Bruna was in bed, so Maria found glasses and a bottle of Napoleon brandy and they sat on the couch in the salon, arms around each other, and carried on talking. She drank more than she knew she should; she would have a raging hangover in the morning, but how else could she deal with the tidal wave of emotion?

They began to kiss, tentatively at first, like teenagers. Very slowly they began to caress each other, to strip off clothes, and then to make love. It was poignant and more beautiful than ever; everything about it felt right. Afterward, they crept to the bedroom, and he fell asleep with his arms wrapped tightly around her as if scared someone might steal her in the night.

Maria lay awake, listening to his breathing, a headache beginning to jab her temples. There was no going back now. She couldn't throw him out in the morning and tell him this had been a one-off. It was meant to be. Destiny was destiny.

A tiny part of her felt triumphant. Mrs. Kennedy might have his ring on her finger, but she clearly didn't have his heart.

Chapter 64

New York City
Winter 1968

After the *kako mati* experience, Jackie was scared to stay alone on Skorpios. She felt rattled by the old woman's words, even after a priest performed an incomprehensible ceremony with holy water. It was horrible to feel that anyone in her adopted homeland was hostile toward her. She had thought she would be safe on a private Mediterranean island, but it seemed danger followed wherever she went.

It began to rain every day, and the sea became rough and uninviting for swimming. The ache of missing her children was all-consuming; she hugged pillows to her chest as a comfort and had to down a stiff drink when she got off the telephone with them each evening. It was with immense relief that she flew to New York for their birthdays and Thanksgiving at the end of November, then persuaded Ari to join them for a snowy Manhattan Christmas. She invited her mother and stepfather to celebrate with them but received the stony reply that they had "made other arrangements."

Lee didn't bother to return her calls, and that hurt. She had no idea how to build bridges with her sister and didn't have the strength to try.

"Can't we live in New York during the school year and spend vacations in Greece?" she asked Ari. The days she had been alone on Skorpios had been enough to show her that she couldn't spend the winter there.

"You want me to make deals with the Greek colonels on crackly international telephone lines?" he teased. "I have a talent for persuasion but that might be pushing it."

"We could fly back when you need to be in Europe, but base ourselves here till spring, so I can be with the children," she pleaded. Why hadn't she negotiated this with him before they were married? She hadn't been thinking straight.

"There are wonderful international boarding schools in Switzerland," he replied. "If they go there, you could fly from Athens in a couple of hours. I'll even lend you a plane!"

Jackie hated the idea of boarding school. It wasn't right for her kids. Their friends and family were in

New York, and they were getting a world-class education there.

The discussion was good-natured, but no resolution was reached before Ari had to fly back to Europe in the New Year.

"I'll be traveling a lot in the next couple of months," he said. "Why don't you stay here? My security team will make sure you and the children don't come to any harm."

Jackie decided to give it a try. Caroline and John needed her in New York, and they would be safer with the cushion of Ari's money. He promised to return whenever work permitted.

Before long, Jackie fell into a routine of commuting across the Atlantic the way other people commuted across the Brooklyn Bridge. It was easy when your husband owned an airline. She and Ari were leading separate lives, but in many ways that suited Jackie, just as it had in the early years of her marriage to Jack. She could go horseback riding or shopping, see her New York friends, then jet over to Paris for a few days with her husband, before returning to her children and her own apartment.

Whenever she stepped out her front door, she had a bodyguard hired by Ari to protect her, and she had more personal spending money than she'd ever had in her life. Her allowance was $30,000 a month, and Ari had agreed that on top of that she could send larger bills to the Olympic Airways New York office. To be able to visit designers' collections and pick up six or eight outfits at a time was a novelty that she knew she would never tire of. She bought shoes, handbags, coats, evening gowns, and clothes for the children too. The purchases filled her wardrobes and closets with their enticing smell of newness.

Jackie planned the summer break carefully, inviting groups of guests to stay either on Skorpios or on the *Christina* from June through September, to help celebrate her fortieth birthday. It would be one long sunshiny party, with swimming and watersports, live music, and dancing. That her own sister didn't want to come made her melancholy, but perhaps it was for the best. After the trauma of 1968, this would be her year of recovery.

On August 16, Jackie, Ari, and the children were on board the *Christina* with some American friends when he got a call saying that an Olympic Airways plane had been hijacked. There had been a spate of hijackings that year, with a fresh story hitting the newsstands every couple of weeks. It terrified Jackie that one man armed with a knife or a gun could threaten passengers and force pilots to reroute their planes. Many of them were leftists, who demanded to be taken to Communist Cuba, but for some reason the hijacker on Ari's plane was asking to go to Albania.

Ari spent the afternoon on the phone, talking to police and ground-control staff in Athens. There were twenty-eight passengers on board, and one of them was a pregnant woman who was said to be feeling unwell. Just before five, he told Jackie he was flying to Athens. "I'll offer to take the place of the pregnant woman and, once I am on board, I can make a deal with the hijacker."

"No!" Jackie screamed. Her heart began thumping so hard she thought it might leap out of her chest, and there was a rushing sound in her ears. She grabbed hold of a railing.

Ari seemed surprised by the force of her reaction. "I won't be gone long. It's the best way to bring the situation to a head." He kissed her forehead.

She heard the chop-chop sound of the helicopter's blades and clutched his shirt. "Please don't go. *Please*," she begged.

"Pull yourself together," he urged. "Go downstairs and rest. Perhaps you've had too much sun today." He motioned to a steward. "Could you help Mrs. Onassis to her room and fetch her some water?"

She felt faint as she staggered down to their bedroom

and lay on the silk coverlet. The blood was still pounding in her ears and she was overwhelmed by terror.

What if Ari died? Who would protect her? Who would look after her children? She felt boiling hot one moment, then started shivering the next. Was she ill? Was Ari right about the sunstroke?

After a while she forced herself to get up, take a cool shower, and change for dinner, but still her heart fluttered like a bird trapped under the skin. Her hand shook as she tried to apply lipstick. The children mustn't see her like this. She rang the bell to order a vodka martini and downed it in three gulps.

"Mr. Onassis is on the telephone," a steward told her, and she leapt to her feet and sprinted to the handset in their private sitting room.

"It's over," Ari said. "The hijacker surrendered. I have to talk to the police but I'll be back by bedtime. Are you okay?"

Jackie breathed deeply. "I'm fine now."

She was bewildered when she looked back on her behavior. What on earth had caused her to lose control like that? She had always thought of herself as a strong person. She *was* a strong person. But she couldn't bear to lose another husband. The thought of Ari being in danger had triggered a panicked reaction. With any luck, it would never happen again.

———

A week after the hijacking, Jackie and Ari went for a walk through the woods on Skorpios at dusk. When they reached a secluded beach, he turned to kiss her, then pulled her down onto the ground.

"I need to get back and help the children change for dinner," she objected, laughing.

"In that case, I'll be quick," he quipped, pulling her white cotton kaftan over her head and pushing her bikini top aside so he could lick her salty nipples.

"Are you sure we can't be seen?" She glanced toward an island on the horizon. The engine of a small boat was sputtering just out of sight.

"I'm sure," he said, yanking off his shorts and spreading her legs with his knee.

She was glad it was brief; she preferred the comfort of their king-sized bed to the scratch of shingle on her back, and she knew that the mosquitos would start biting as soon as the last rays of the sun disappeared over the horizon. But Ari liked sex in different locations—on planes, in the backseat of automobiles, and out in the open air—and she was happy to oblige. She enjoyed sex with him. He was a talented lover.

Two days later, when a boat brought the international newspapers, Jackie picked one up to glance at the headlines and screamed out loud: "Telis, look!"

There, on the front page, was a grainy image of them making love on the beach. She felt her heart hammering and heard the familiar rushing sound in her ears.

"How did they get those shots?" she demanded, her voice high and squeaky, while Ari read the story. "I thought we were safe here. They must have landed on the island and crept up on us." She felt feverish and touched a hand to her forehead. Thoughts of catastrophe filled her head, like angry ghosts.

"Don't overreact," he said, unconcerned. "They were just passing and got lucky. You can't make out any details. Besides, what's the harm in people knowing we make love on our own beach?"

Jackie sat down and hugged her knees to her chest, trying to calm her racing heart. "They could have had a gun rather than a camera," she whispered.

"But they didn't." He looked at her with a frown. "You're shaking. What's wrong? This is not worth upsetting yourself over."

Jackie closed her eyes and breathed in and out, trying to calm herself. Why did she keep panicking in such an extreme way? She had married Ari to feel safe, yet her panic was getting worse. What was going on?

In September, she flew to New York with her children in time for the new school year. One day she and John decided to go for a bike ride in Central Park. They had just stepped out of the apartment building and John had climbed astride his bicycle, ready to pedal off, when a man jumped out from behind some shrubbery. There was a flash and a sound like an explosion. John swerved and almost fell. Jackie screamed and grabbed his arm.

John's Secret Service officer, who was only two steps behind them, apprehended the man within seconds, helped by her bodyguard, but Jackie was consumed by full-blown terror. She dropped her bike on the sidewalk and sprinted back into the building, pulling John by the arm, her heart thumping, brain buzzing, ears ringing—all the familiar symptoms.

"It's okay, Mom," John was saying. "It was just another photographer."

She could hear his words but her brain couldn't process them. She pulled John into the elevator and paced around, trembling, till they reached their floor. Her forehead felt scorching to the touch. Was it some kind of flu?

Inside the apartment, she poured herself a vodka and lit a cigarette, hand shaking.

"Can't we go to the park now, Mom?" John asked, but she waved him away. She had to bring her heart rate down and catch her breath.

The Secret Service officer had followed them up to the

fifteenth floor, and now he sat beside her. "Are you alright, Mrs. Onassis?" he asked, his expression concerned.

She nodded but couldn't speak, couldn't meet his eye.

"He's a freelance photographer by the name of Ron Galella. I took his film, but he argued blue in the face that he has every right to photograph you when you are in a public place." He frowned. "Mrs. Onassis, you're very pale."

She opened her mouth to try to articulate the fierce anxiety that gripped her at moments like this. It seemed to have been getting worse lately.

"Why don't you tell me what you are thinking?" he asked, in a gentle voice.

Tears welled in her eyes and she blinked them away. "It's always about that moment," she whispered. "The moment when there was an explosion and part of Jack's skull flew through the air." She traced the arc with her hand. "It's almost six years now and still I keep feeling as though I am back in that Dallas motorcade. I get hot and I can't breathe and my heart goes so fast . . ."

The officer nodded. "It's acute anxiety. I've seen this in soldiers coming out of war zones. I think you need professional help."

"Can anything be done about it?"

He nodded, his expression serious. "I think it has to. You can't live like this."

Chapter 65

Maria vacationed with friends on the private island of Tragonisi, just off Mykonos. The filming of *Medea* had been hard work, but she was excited to learn the new skills required on a film set and hopeful that it might lead to more acting work. Now she was in need of a rest.

It was her name day, and her friends were planning a small celebration that evening in a beach restaurant renowned for its lobster dishes. She spent the afternoon sitting on the sand, enjoying the tranquility.

Yachts sailed through the channel between her beach and Mykonos, and she kept an eye out in case the *Christina* should go past. She knew that Ari and Mrs. Kennedy (as she still called her) had friends staying with them. He hadn't been able to slip away to see her since

June 26, when they had met in Milan to visit Omero's grave, and she missed him badly.

It was easier for him to spend time with her when they were both in Paris, in the fall and winter. Avenue Georges Mandel was not far from Avenue Foch. On the evenings when he was expected, she extinguished the light at the front door so no photographer could catch him entering or leaving. It was best if Mrs. Kennedy didn't find out about their rekindled affair; she might try to stop them.

If Maria dwelled on all she had lost in the past year, she would never have stopped crying. Instead she tried to cherish the time she had with Ari. The three and a half months when they had not spoken had been excruciating. She would rather be his mistress than not have him in her life at all.

She lay beneath her beach umbrella in a state of deep relaxation. Sounds appeared a long way off: the chirping of crickets, the lapping of waves, some distant voices carried on the breeze. She heard a helicopter approaching from afar, but instead of flying past, it grew louder as if toward a crescendo. Maria opened her eyes, shading them against the glare of the sun, and saw that it was coming in to land in a field behind the beach. She sat up to watch as it touched down, and minutes later a familiar silhouette climbed out. It wasn't—was it? She couldn't stop grinning as Ari walked down the sand toward her, wearing a smart gray suit, a white shirt, and a gray tie. He must be on his way to a meeting.

"Congratulations on your name day!" he called. He leaned underneath the beach umbrella and gave her a long kiss.

"Thank you for remembering," she said, touched.

He felt in his pocket and pulled out a jewelry box. "A small token of my love."

Maria opened the box to see some art deco diamond–and–white gold earrings. "They're beautiful," she breathed. "Thank you. But the best present of all is to see you. Can you stay awhile?"

"I have an hour. But I am not dressed for the beach. Shall we . . . ?"

He held out his hand to pull Maria to her feet, and they walked side by side to her villa. They showered together in cool water, then made love on her bed beneath the noisy ceiling fan.

"I miss this so much," he said afterward as he lay on his side, running a hand over her naked body. "Making love with Jackie is like fucking a corpse. She doesn't really like sex, not the way you do."

"I don't want to hear this," Maria said, putting her hands over her ears, but in fact she relished the odd detail he let slip. She knew Mrs. Kennedy refused to try some of the more adventurous activities she and Ari enjoyed; according to him, all she did was lie back and open her legs.

It had upset her when she saw a photograph in the newspaper of them making love on the beach on Skorpios—and then she looked at the angle of the shot. The photographer must have been standing *behind* the beach cottage. A suspicion entered her mind that Ari had commissioned him to take the shot and leak it to the press. It wasn't enough to marry the former First Lady; he wanted the world to see him fucking her.

"I miss your glorious thighs," he said, grabbing a handful. "Jackie's all skin and bone. She eats like a bird and exercises constantly."

"That's healthy," Maria said, then pinched a handful of flesh at his waist. "Perhaps you should follow her lead."

"Healthy—but not sexy," he replied, then slithered down the bed to bury his face between her legs.

They had slipped back into their old routine of speaking every evening at six o'clock, and they always chatted in Greek. If Jackie asked who was on the line, Ari lied that it was Costa Gratsos. Maria knew "the Widow" was close by if he started calling her Costa in the middle of a call.

During their telephone conversations, Ari poured out whatever was on his mind. His son Alexander was still wildly in love with the model Fiona Thyssen, and their devotion showed no sign of lessening.

"Alexander told me she won't accept presents if they are bought with my money. She only likes gifts he has paid for with his own earnings." Ari seemed astounded by this.

"I like the sound of her," Maria replied. "I know it's not ideal, but the one thing I wish for both Alexander and Christina is that they find partners who love them for themselves and not for your money."

Ari grunted. "She's happy to visit the villa in Athens I bought him."

"That is a matter of practicality. I'm living in an apartment you bought me, but I think you know by now that I am not after your millions."

"I do know that." His tone was warm, but it switched suddenly. "You wouldn't believe how much Jacqueline spends on clothes. I get clothing bills that are equivalent to the gross wealth of a small African nation, yet all she ever wears are jeans and shirts. Where does it go?"

Maria refrained from commenting, but she took note. Every black mark against her rival was a point in her favor. "Any news on Project Omega?" she asked.

"It's going in the right direction. I've become a majority shareholder in a British-American oil company, I'm virtually running a Russian one, and the Saudis are all ears." He seemed pleased with himself.

"Are you aiming for a world monopoly on oil?" she asked. "Because I think they probably have laws against that."

"They would have to find out first."

Maria knew his empire was a vast network of shell companies based in different countries and registered under different names. That's what had kept him out of jail when the Americans arrested him back in 1954.

"What about the Niarchos scheme? Has he dropped out of the running?"

"Not yet, but if all goes to plan I will destroy him before this is over."

She chuckled. "What does Mrs. Kennedy think of your crazy rivalry with Niarchos?"

"She doesn't know. I never discuss business with her."

Maria was surprised but pleased to hear it. Another point for her.

She heard a door opening in the background; then Ari said, "Anyway, thanks for the figures, Costa. I'll get back to you tomorrow."

"Good night, my love," she said sadly, before he hung up and went to join his wife.

Chapter 66

New York City
February 1970

J ackie quickly realized that Ari was speaking to Maria
Callas on the phone—often. She'd always had a facility for languages, and her Greek was progressing fast,
but she didn't really need to understand the words to
guess when Maria was on the line. Ari had a particular
tone he adopted with her: soft, tender, confiding.

Jackie could make out enough to know that he discussed his business interests with Maria, and that irked
her; it was as if her opinion counted for nothing. It annoyed her that he thought he was fooling her by pretending he was talking to Costa Gratsos—but she did
not confront him. She had her own male friends, so
at first she was resigned to let him have a female one.
Maria had been a big part of his life, after all.

But soon it became clear that they were doing more

than just talking. She first began to suspect this when she called from New York late at night, Paris time, to be told he was not home. It should have been the perfect time for them to talk: six in the evening for her and bedtime for him.

"I went to a nightclub with friends," he explained. Another time he claimed to have been at a restaurant; yet another, at a dinner party. Always a friend's name rolled off his tongue with plausible ease. Yes, it made sense on the surface, but Jackie knew. She had been married to Jack Kennedy for ten years and had an instinct for detecting infidelity. As with Jack, she decided not to challenge him. What would it achieve? She didn't want a divorce, and Ari was not the kind of man who would change his ways because she demanded it. As long as their affair was discreet, she would close her eyes to it. As she had done so many times before.

Jackie's life in New York continued to be marred by photographers, and Ron Galella in particular. She never knew when he might leap from behind a tree, or lurk in a doorway and then pounce when she passed by. Sometimes he disguised himself with a fake beard or a hat pulled low, so that he could surprise her and get a shot or two before she had a chance to shield her face with her handbag. Every time, her heart would hammer fit to burst and she would gasp for breath; every time, she feared she was about to be shot and killed. It made her reluctant to leave the apartment if she could avoid it. She would rather that friends visit her there than brave the sidewalks outside.

Ari was furious at Gallela's persistence and hired lawyers to force the police to press charges against him. It took months to get to court, and the resulting press was almost unanimously in Gallela's favor when he argued that he had the right to earn his living by taking photographs in public places. It came as no surprise when he got off scot-free.

"What kind of judge will let a man terrorize you like that?" Ari snapped. "I'll have my security team scare him off."

"No, please don't!" Jackie begged. "It would end up in the papers. I need to learn to deal with it and not let him get to me." She hesitated, before continuing. "One of the children's protection officers told me I should see a psychiatrist."

"What nonsense!" Ari scoffed. "Does he want you to lie on a couch and confess that you had erotic dreams about your daddy? Isn't that what modern psychiatry is all about?"

She had guessed he wouldn't be in favor of shrinks. "Not quite. It's because a flashbulb going off in my face brings back memories of the moment Jack was shot. The officer is ex-military and he said that soldiers suffer similar symptoms after battle."

"It's hardly the same, is it? You need to stop dwelling in the past. Do you realize how often your conversation is about Jack and life in the White House and what happened in Dallas? I wish you would start living in the present. If a photographer is bothering you in New York, the answer is simple: spend more time in Europe."

"But the children . . ." Her voice trailed off. This argument kept rearing its head as high school beckoned. She had made up her mind she wanted Caroline and John to continue their education in New York and was steeling herself to tell him, but this wasn't the moment.

"Forget the shrink," he reiterated. "I don't want a docile wife popping happy pills and incapable of stringing a sentence together. We'll find another way of dealing with Mr. Gallela."

Jackie was alarmed when a gossip column reported that some letters she had written to Ros Gilpatric, the very suave attorney who had pursued her before she married Ari, were to be auctioned. She hadn't seen him since March 1968, but she had heard that his latest marriage was on the skids. Jackie wracked her brain to try to remember what she had written him, praying that there was nothing incriminating.

When the letters were published in the press, it was a note written in late October 1968, in which she told Ros of her Skorpios wedding, that made Ari explode. "I hope you know all you are and ever will be to me," she had written at the end. It had seemed an innocent-enough phrase at the time.

"On our fucking honeymoon!" he screamed at her over the phone. "You've made me look a fool! I will not tolerate you carrying on with other men behind my back."

"I'm not carrying on with anyone," she protested. "Anything with Ros ended before our marriage. I haven't seen him since."

"You spend my money, so you can start acting like my wife!" he yelled. "From now on, you must live within your allowance. I don't want to see any more bills for clothes turning up in the Olympic Airways accounts."

"What exactly am I being punished for, Telis? I've done nothing wrong."

She couldn't get him to listen. He ranted for ten minutes without pause, then hung up. She stared in disbelief. He had never raised his voice to her before they were married. She hadn't realized he had a temper, and it came as an unwelcome surprise.

She had always been allergic to conflict. It reminded her of listening to her parents arguing when she was a child and feeling scared that the security of her young life might crumble. She and Jack had disagreed sometimes, like any couple, but they never yelled at each other. She hated being yelled at. It had the effect of making her retreat and pull up the drawbridge.

She decided she wouldn't be the first to call after he'd behaved like that. Ari should call her and, if he were a gentleman, he should call with an apology.

Meanwhile, she decided to go behind his back and make inquiries about the type of professional she should talk to about her feelings of panic. Perhaps the Secret Service agent could point her in the right direction.

Chapter 67

Paris
Spring 1970

"I'm going to divorce her," Ari told Maria, over dinner at Maxim's.

She'd been surprised when he suggested they eat out in his favorite restaurant, and even more astonished when he asked for the corner table by a front window, where they could be spotted by any passing paparazzo, as if he didn't care who saw them together now.

"All I am to her is a bank that never shuts," he continued. "She lives in New York with her children, spends my money like water, and refuses to visit me in the winter months. In summer, she invites her friends for no-expense-spared holidays, but if the weather is too cold for the beach, I might as well not be married. I never thought any woman would make such a fool out of me."

Maria decided not to comment. All she had ever wanted was to be Ari's wife, to look after him, to cherish him. She would have done anything for him—but he had married a woman who did not want to be a traditional wife.

As if reading her mind, Ari said, "I just need to find a way to stop her taking too much of my money. And then, at last, I can marry the woman I should always have been with. The one I should have married as soon as I met her." He lifted Maria's hand to his lips.

"Is that a proposal?" she asked, arching one eyebrow, trying to still the fluttering sensation his words provoked. "You'll forgive me if I don't believe it until you come to me waving a decree nisi in one hand and an engagement ring in the other."

"I will prove it to you. I have learned my lesson. One should only marry for love."

She sighed. "Goodness, Ari, you *are* a slow learner."

"I know. But I get there in the end. You wait and see."

The following evening, Ari wanted to dine at Maxim's again, and asked for the same corner table.

"You're becoming a creature of habit, like a lion returning to its favorite watering hole," she teased.

"Yes, and dragging my lioness along so I can mount her when the urge takes me," he rejoined.

"Not over the steak tartare, please."

Several photographers took their picture that night, and Maria wondered if Mrs. Kennedy would see it in the press.

Ari shrugged. "She might."

"Won't she mind?"

"I don't care," he said. "I briefed my New York lawyers today and they are searching for a solution that will free me from the marriage without diluting Alexander's inheritance."

Maria felt a stirring of hope. Ari seemed resolute. Could it be that she might yet be his wife one day?

That afternoon, he'd had his chauffeur drop off some clothes at her house, along with his hair oil and toothbrush. Seeing his possessions in the bathroom alongside her own gave her a warm glow. Simple pleasures, such as eating breakfast in bed with him, filled her with joy.

Over lunch, Maggie van Zuylen urged caution: "You and I know that the most sensitive part of Ari's anatomy is his wallet. He may retreat when he finds out how much a divorce will cost. I can't imagine the Black Widow accepting any diminution in her lifestyle after the marriage comes to an end."

Maria knew she was right, but once she had allowed herself to hope it was hard to scale back. "I could even accept a situation in which he remains married, so long as we are together. I love him, and I want everyone to know we are a couple again."

"Your friends know that," Maggie said. "Who cares what anyone else thinks?"

But Maria had been publicly humiliated by him and she yearned to be publicly vindicated, so she was delighted when photographs of them dining at Maxim's appeared in the international press, along with cynical comments about the state of his long-distance marriage only a year and a half after the wedding.

"Did Mrs. Kennedy mention the pictures?" Maria asked him over dinner that night.

He gave her a wicked grin. "I don't know. I haven't spoken to her today."

"You're punishing her for something, aren't you?" She scrutinized his gold-flecked eyes, and a suspicion popped into her head. "I hope you are not using me to make her jealous. I'm not a plaything to be dangled, then dropped."

"My God, you think I could do that? You don't know me at all." He put his arms around her. "Oh, Maria, why is life so fucking complicated?"

"Life is pretty simple; it's people who are complicated," she told him.

The next day they went shopping together on the Rue Saint-Honoré, and she helped him choose some new clothes. "For all the money my wife spends on fashion, she rarely buys anything for me," he complained. "I'm down to my last decent suit."

Maria picked a slate-gray flannel for him and sat waiting while the tailor took his measurements, humming to herself. They were dining at home that evening and she'd asked the cook to make lamb *kleftiko*. It was a Greek dish cooked for hours in a low oven; the fragrance of oregano and meat juices would already have filled her apartment.

After they finished shopping, Ari's chauffeur dropped her at Avenues Georges Mandel. Ari wanted to go home to pick up some papers, but said he'd return for a cocktail at seven-thirty.

Maria changed into a fitted black dress with a scoop back and fixed her hair and eye makeup, spraying on some scent. Ari did not arrive at seven-thirty, so she asked Bruna to pour her a glass of champagne while she waited. When he had not arrived by eight-thirty, she began to worry. She called Avenue Foch, where Eleni seemed strangely reluctant to put her through.

"Tell him it's Maria," she insisted.

Ari's voice came on the line, soft and low. "Costa, I'm sorry but I won't be able to make it for dinner tonight."

Maria felt a plunging sensation, as if she were in an elevator. "Is Mrs. Kennedy there?"

"I'm afraid so."

"How long is she staying?"

"That hasn't been discussed yet. I'll get back to you."

"*When* will you get back to me?"

"Just as soon as I can. Have a good evening, Costa," he said, then hung up.

Maria felt a sharp pain in her chest, as if a splinter of glass had lodged there. She poured another glass of champagne and sat, trying to imagine the conversation between them. Would this be the night that he asked for a divorce? How would Mrs. Kennedy react?

All the following day, Maria stayed home, nerves frayed, waiting to hear from Ari. If another friend phoned, she shooed them off the line so she didn't miss his call. She pictured him and Jackie arguing, negotiating. With any luck, she would accept that their marriage hadn't worked. Maybe she wanted out as well.

She picked up a newspaper to distract herself and was shocked to see a picture of Ari and Mrs. Kennedy, taken the previous evening. They were at exactly the same corner table at Maxim's that he had occupied with her, and they were talking. Not kissing, not touching, just talking. Still, it was a shock.

Suddenly she was unable to bear the suspense any longer. She called his apartment and asked Eleni to tell him that Costa Gratsos was on the line.

"It's me," she breathed when she heard his voice. "What's happening?"

"I was about to call you. Jacqueline and I are flying to New York this evening so I won't be able to meet you as planned." From his formal tone, she knew he could be overheard.

"Why are you going to New York? Did you tell her you want a divorce?"

"That will have to be done step-by-step," he said carefully.

Maria swallowed hard. "Why did you dine at our table in Maxim's last night? Was that Mrs. Kennedy's idea?"

"Yes, it was."

Maria had guessed as much. She was staking her territory, sending a message. Ari hadn't told her that he wanted a divorce. They wouldn't be flying to New York together if he had.

"You are playing with my feelings, like a cat with a half-dead mouse," she said. "I didn't think you could be so cruel."

There was a long pause, during which she could hear him breathing on the line. He couldn't think of an answer that would not make his wife suspicious.

Tears started rolling down her cheeks. "That's it,

isn't it? You've made your choice and I am to be abandoned yet again."

"I'm sorry," he said, with feeling. "I'm so very sorry." And then he hung up.

Maria rushed to her bathroom and swallowed a couple of Mandrax, a sedative she had recently been prescribed. She turned on the bath taps, and while the water was running she ran to the kitchen to grab a bottle of champagne and a glass. Back in her sanctuary, she locked the door, then opened the champagne and drank some, before undressing and lowering herself into the steaming water.

Only then did she start to cry properly, with great shuddering sobs. What a fool she had been! She was back in the exact position as before, when Ari had made every excuse under the sun not to marry her. He had her right where he had wanted her all along: as his mistress. He would never divorce Jackie, because it would prove too expensive. She'd fallen neatly into a trap.

Maria couldn't stop crying now. The pain was hideous. She took two more Mandrax and washed them down with champagne. How many more would it take to achieve oblivion? Could anything ever do that again?

Chapter 68

New York City
Spring 1970

When Jackie and Ari arrived at her Fifth Avenue apartment, he rang the Pierre Hotel to see if there were any messages for him. The receptionist told him Maggie van Zuylen had left one, insisting that he call her in Paris straightaway. He dialed her number and Jackie stood nearby to listen. She could hear that Maggie's voice was raised; she was upset about something.

"How is she?" Ari asked; then, "Can I speak to her?" He leaned forward, head in his hand, eyes closed, and Jackie guessed immediately that something had happened to Maria.

After hanging up, he turned to her, ashen. "Maria took an overdose last night. Her maid found her and rushed her to the hospital, but one of the nurses leaked

the story and it's going to be all over the papers tomorrow."

Jackie was horrified. "Why would she do that?"

"They won't let me speak to her," Ari said, ignoring
the question. "And Maggie says that if I return to Paris
her friends won't let me anywhere near her."

"Why not? Do they hold you responsible?" Her chest
felt tight and she tried to slow her breathing, as her new
psychiatrist had advised, to stop the panic from taking
hold.

Ari turned on her. "Why did you make me take you
to Maxim's? This is all your fault. You wanted to score
points against a vulnerable woman."

"That's not fair!" she objected. "I was humiliated
when the papers said our marriage was in trouble. Any
wife would have done the same."

He carried on as if he hadn't heard her: "Then you
dragged me back to New York because you were jealous
and insecure. Yet you have given me far more reason
to feel jealous than I have ever given you." His volume
was increasing. "I'm not the one who wrote fucking
love letters on my honeymoon!"

"Please stop shouting," she said quietly. "You're not
being rational."

"Why on earth did I marry you?" He had worked
himself into a rage now. "It's clear what you got out of

the deal: Gucci, Dior, Chanel, Cassini . . ." He swept an Indian elephant sculpture to the floor, causing the trunk to snap off. "But I haven't had much return on my investment. You're not a wife—you're a professional shopper."

Jackie had never seen him lose his temper so badly. She shrank into an armchair, tucking her feet beneath her, wrapping her arms around her shoulders. His fists were clenched and she was scared he might hit her. He seemed out of control. Should she call her bodyguard?

It was natural he was upset about Maria taking an overdose. He clearly had a guilty conscience. And it was true her shopping habit was getting out of hand. She had a roomful of purchases that hadn't even been taken out of their packaging. But there was no point in saying anything. She would let him have his rant and hope the outburst would soon blow over.

Her silence seemed to infuriate him more. She flinched as he stood over her, shouting in her face. "Maria never took a cent from me! She loved me for myself—but I don't expect you to understand that. She was the best wife I ever had, even though we never married."

It was on the tip of Jackie's tongue to retort that he should go back to her, in that case, but she knew whatever she said would inflame the situation, so she sat quietly, avoiding eye contact.

"Maria knows how to argue!" he yelled. "She fights

back, tells me when I am in the wrong, and after the explosion passes we make up—*passionately.*" He emphasized the word. "All you do is sulk. Silence and sulks: that's what I married."

He stepped back to look out the window toward Central Park, and Jackie took the opportunity to rise from her chair and hurry to the door.

He turned. "I'm not finished yet. Where do you think you are going?"

"I have a headache. I'm going to lie down."

She closed the door behind her, and heard the sound of something else smashing in the living room. Thank heaven the children were at school. She was embarrassed for her staff to hear the ruckus; God only knew what the bodyguards must be thinking.

Lying on her bed, with a cool cloth draped over her brow, Jackie began to tremble. What if Ari divorced her? What would she do then? She would be alone in the world. Who would protect her? The children had a Secret Service man assigned to them until they turned sixteen, but she had lost her right to one when she remarried.

And then she thought of poor Maria, so distressed that she had taken an overdose. Had Ari given her hope and then dashed it? If so, that was despicable. Was that what he had done with Lee? Poor Lee.

She curled into the fetal position, hugging her knees, trying to make her feelings of panic subside. *Don't think about anything else for now; just breathe.*

Ari stayed in his suite at the Pierre Hotel that night, but he returned the following morning, while Jackie was reading in the sitting room. She put her book aside and looked up, feeling wary. Was he going to apologize? Or did he want to continue the fight?

"There's some paperwork I need you to sign," he said, pulling a few typed sheets from his briefcase and flicking through them. He produced a fountain pen.

Jackie took them and looked at the first page. The type was small, but she noticed the word *waiver* and her name and Fifth Avenue address near the top.

"What's it for?" she asked. She had always signed any papers that he asked her to without question, but she felt suspicious all of a sudden.

"It's a standard requirement under Greek law. I'm a bit late submitting it, so I'll drop it off at my lawyer's this morning." He sounded brisk, and definitely unrepentant.

"Should I get my own lawyer to look through it first?" she asked.

"There's no time. I'll have a copy sent for his file, but it's strictly routine. Nothing to worry about."

Still she hesitated, reading the document, trying to make sense of the legal wording. "Is it something to do with your inheritance?"

"That's right; it's making sure the businesses go to Alexander after my death, as we discussed." He glanced at his watch, obviously impatient.

Jackie did not have the strength for another argument. She felt drained by the emotion of the previous evening, and sick at the thought of poor Maria, lying in a hospital bed. She took the pen, signed where he indicated, and handed it back.

"Thank you," he said, putting the papers in his case and preparing to leave.

"Will you be here for dinner tonight?" she asked.

"Of course," he said. "Why not?"

But his eyes were cold, and he left without kissing her.

Chapter 69

Paris
Summer 1970

Maria's apartment was like a botanic garden, full of lavish bouquets and exotic plants. Every surface had a vase perched on it, and the air was filled with fragrance.

Her friends rallied around her so that in the weeks following her release from the hospital she was never alone. They alternately comforted and chivvied her, urging her to get back to singing, to make more movies, to fill her life with fresh challenges, and to never, *ever*, see Ari again. He sent flowers and cards, but her entourage wouldn't let her take his calls. She didn't fight them; she knew she couldn't have coped with hearing his voice.

In the newspapers, she read that he and Mrs. Kennedy had spent the summer on Skorpios, and that Lee had joined them. Didn't Jackie mind that her sister had slept with Ari first? Wasn't that awkward? Lee had been trying to launch herself as an actress, but the drama critics who attended her theatrical debut in Chicago were scathing. Maria smiled when she read the dire reviews: "A star is *not* born," one said.

One afternoon in late September the telephone rang. She picked it up without thinking and was startled to hear Ari's voice.

"How are you?" he asked, his tone gentle.

"I'm well." She felt unsteady on her feet and sat down on the chair in the hall. "Very busy. I'm giving a series of master classes next year for students at the Juilliard School in New York." She was proud to have been invited. It would be fun to work with a new generation of opera singers, and she told Ari about her preparations, chattering to hide her nervousness.

"They are very lucky students!" he said. "And are you performing any concerts?"

"I don't know. There seems to be enthusiasm for the idea of me singing onstage again. I guess people want to come along and be reminded of how great I used to be."

"You're selling yourself short," he said.

She chuckled before she replied. "Even your metaphors involve money."

He paused. "That's the Maria I miss; the one who is straight with me, who tells it like it is."

She didn't answer, scared of where this conversation was heading. She was still too fragile to deal with him, like a smashed porcelain vase that had been hastily glued back together.

"Can I see you, Maria? Please?"

She shook her head firmly. "No."

"What, never?"

"I can't be your lover anymore. It harms me too much. And I don't think I could see you without wanting to be your lover."

She heard him sniff. Was he upset? She listened hard.

"Not even if I come to you waving the decree nisi and an engagement ring?" His voice was emotional.

"I can't wait for that to happen. I need to protect myself, Ari." There was no artifice now; only the truth.

"I understand," he said at last. "But can I telephone sometimes? I can't bear not being a part of your life. There's no one else I trust the way I trust you. We have so much shared history. We can't throw it all away."

Maria considered. Her friends' voices rang in her ears like a Greek chorus: "Have nothing to do with him." "He's arrogant and thinks only of himself." "He manipulates you and poisons any chance of happiness."

And then she thought about the closeness they had

once shared. Could they be friends who spoke on the telephone? Or would it be a slippery slope that would lead to becoming lovers again?

"We can try," she said. "But if you upset me, I will stop taking your calls. And I never want to hear you mention Mrs. Kennedy. Is that clear?"

"Of course. As you wish." He paused, then spoke so tenderly it brought tears to her eyes: "I can't tell you how much this means to me."

It wasn't long before Maria and Ari fell back into their old habit of chatting on the phone most days. She looked forward to their conversations, enjoyed being part of his life again. He called for advice when his daughter, Christina, married a real-estate agent twenty-seven years her senior, who had four children from a previous marriage. He called with mounting alarm as Project Omega began to slip inexorably from his grasp. He called in fury and disbelief when Tina, his first wife, married his archrival Niarchos. To him it was the ultimate stab in the back, and Maria had to work hard to dissuade him when he threatened to send a hit man to murder Niarchos. But she would not, could not, see him.

"Why has my luck run out?" he asked in exasperation. "It's as if the gods have turned against me."

Maria thought to herself that the gods had turned against him when he entered into matrimony for vanity rather than love, but out loud she said, "Since when have you believed in luck? You and I make our own luck. It's one of the things we have in common."

She had begun touring with a tenor named Giuseppe di Stefano, singing medleys of arias and duets to sellout crowds across Europe. That was gratifying, even if she knew her audiences were not hearing the vocals that La Callas had once been capable of. "Watch out for di Stefano," Ari warned her gruffly. "I hear he has a reputation as a ladies' man."

"He's married!" Maria exclaimed, well aware of the irony. In fact, she had begun to sleep with her costar occasionally while on tour. It satisfied her physical needs, but her heart was not in it, and she was anxious that word did not reach the press and, in particular, Ari.

When asked in interviews about her relationship with him now, she told the truth: "He is my best friend. He is, was, and always will be."

Chapter 70

Skorpios
Summer 1970

Jackie was delighted when Lee agreed to bring her children for a three-week vacation on Skorpios. She hoped it would give them a chance to clear the air and become close again, and that Lee and Ari would settle into a comfortable new relationship as brother- and sister-in-law. Whatever the truth about their affair—and each had different versions—it was time to relegate it to the past.

Jackie had assumed that Stas would be coming too and allocated them the largest guest cottage, which she filled with fresh flowers. But when the jeep drove up from the jetty at six in the evening, only Lee and her children stepped out.

Jackie rushed to kiss her in greeting. "Where's Stas?" she asked.

"I couldn't bear to bring him. He's so boring, he would have spoiled our fun."

Jackie glanced at the children, who were shuffling their feet in embarrassment. "Maybe he can join us later. Leave your bags for the staff and come have a drink. You're just in time for cocktail hour."

Caroline and John took Anthony and Tina to explore the island. They were close in age and more like siblings than cousins. Ari joined the sisters on the terrace, kissing Lee's hand with a chivalrous bow.

"Princess!" he said. "Welcome to Skorpios."

Watching them, Jackie couldn't detect any sign of their former intimacy. They seemed for all the world like old friends.

Lee ordered a vodka on the rocks, and when it arrived she gulped it down. "The journey made me thirsty. Can I have another?"

"Of course!" Ari signaled to a waiter.

"I've brought the plans for the villa I'm going to build," Lee told him. "You'll love them."

"What villa?" Jackie asked, wondering where Stas had gotten the money. He did well as a property developer, but he usually needed the profits from his last build to invest in the next.

"Just outside Athens," Lee told her. "Ari gave me a

plot of land—a very generous one. Didn't he mention it to you?"

Jackie glanced at Ari, but his face was impassive. "When was that?"

"At your wedding," Lee said, looking smug. "It was my wedding present from him."

"How kind!" Jackie mumbled, thinking it was odd that neither of them had mentioned it. She wondered what other secrets they might have been keeping from her.

Lee drank red wine all the way through dinner, then returned to vodka, and by the time they retired to the terrace for a nightcap, she was thoroughly blitzed. The alcohol made her conversation dull and monotonous, although she clearly thought she was being hilarious as she described parties she had been to and celebrities she'd met.

"Did I tell you Andy Warhol took me backstage after the Rolling Stones concert in Madison Square Garden? They are such a *scream!*"

She launched into a lengthy anecdote about how one of the Stones wanted her to go to his hotel room, but he kept calling her Princess Radish and she told him she couldn't possibly consider sleeping with anyone who couldn't get her name right.

Jackie glanced around to see if the children were listening, but fortunately they were out of earshot.

Ari excused himself, saying he had a business call to make, and Jackie sat back and watched Lee, rambling on about the artists and musicians who hung out at Andy Warhol's studio, and about her new plan to become an interior designer to the rich and famous.

Jackie wondered if her sister had drunk too much because she found the situation difficult. Maybe seeing Jackie with Ari was painful and she was using alcohol as an anesthetic. Jackie knew all about that. It was a habit she'd fallen into after Jack died.

The next morning, Lee asked for a vodka and lime as soon as they hit the beach, and a waiter fetched her one from the little taverna that Jackie had remodeled there.

"You shouldn't drink if you're planning to swim later," Jackie cautioned.

"When did you get to be so *boring*?" Lee snapped, then lay back on her sunbed with a straw hat over her face.

Ari had taken the children out sailing, and Jackie settled down to read a novel, but she kept an eye on Lee's glass and noticed the level steadily descending. After she got back from a long swim, there was a fresh drink by Lee's side. She drank wine with lunch, then returned to vodka and lime for the afternoon. That evening, she was unsteady on her feet long before they sat down for dinner, and virtually incoherent afterward.

"Do you think I should have a word with Lee about her drinking?" she asked Ari when they were alone later.

"Give me notice before you do and I'll have riot police on standby," he quipped.

"So you don't think I should?"

He shook his head. "I think you are the last person she will take it from, and frankly I don't want our vacation to turn into a battle zone."

"Why did you give her that land when we got married? It's not customary in America to give a dowry to the bride's sister. Perhaps you didn't realize." She tried to speak with a light tone.

"You wanted her to come to the wedding. The only way I could get her to come was bribery. It worked, didn't it?"

Jackie turned away. It was clear now that he had lied to her about the extent of his relationship with Lee. It must have been serious for her to feel quite so upset and betrayed. Had he let Lee believe he would marry her? Or had he used Lee to get close to her? She had a feeling it was better not to know the truth.

———

Lee's drinking continued to be out of control through the rest of the vacation, but Jackie shrank from attempting to restrain her. All she could do was stop her from swimming in the sea when drunk, or behaving inappropriately in front of the children. Confrontation didn't run in the Bouvier family. Difficult issues were swept under the rug. That was the way they'd been raised.

When did Lee start drinking so hard? Was it a trait they had inherited from their daddy?

Jackie had begun to monitor her own drinking after her psychiatrist had pointed out that her anxiety levels were always higher the day after she'd overindulged. There was a direct correlation. She decided to discuss Lee's problem with the psychiatrist upon her return to New York. For now, she didn't have the courage to rock the boat. All her efforts were focused on trying to heal the rift and become her sister's friend again.

ACT V

Chapter 71

Paris
January 23, 1973

Maria was at home in Paris when the telephone rang just before midnight. On the other end of the line there was a howl, like an animal caught in a steel trap.

"Help! Oh, God, help me!" It was Ari. She had never heard him in such anguish.

"What's happened?" she asked, but for several minutes he just roared, unable to speak.

"It's Alexander," he managed at last. "He's dead." He started sobbing: big, ragged sobs that tore themselves from his throat.

At first, Maria couldn't believe it. "No! How is that possible?"

"His plane crashed. Oh, Maria . . ."

She cradled the phone, so shocked she couldn't take it in. "Calm down. Tell me what happened."

"It was a conspiracy. The plane must have been sabotaged. It has to be Niarchos. Why else would a plane fail straight after takeoff? Witnesses say it hurtled from the sky like a stone, but planes don't do that." He was rambling, staccato, not making sense.

"I'm sure there will be an investigation. Don't think about the cause for now," she soothed.

"How can I think of anything else? I just had to ask doctors to switch off the machines keeping my son alive. His brain was destroyed. His poor brain!"

Maria listened as the words poured out, powerless to help.

"I flew in the world's top neurosurgeon and offered him my entire fortune if he could save my son. Last night I kept vigil by his bed: I talked to him, kissed him, sang to him. I even prayed—can you believe it? Me praying? But there was no change. So today I gave them permission to switch off and he died two hours ago." He burst into a fresh fit of sobbing that was dissonant, almost too painful to listen to.

"Oh, Ari, I wish I could have been with you, to support you." Alexander had been twenty-four years old, with his whole life ahead of him. In a flash, she knew this was going to destroy Ari. How would he ever re-cover?

"Why didn't Omero live?" he asked suddenly. "Then I would still have a son. Then I would have a reason to carry on living."

"You have a daughter," she reminded him. "Christina can take over the family business one day." But she knew it wasn't the same. Alexander had been trained for the role from birth. Ari was too old-fashioned to appoint a female CEO.

"What am I going to do?" he whispered. "I don't know what to do."

That was something Maria could help with. She had been in the depths of despair and had lifted herself up again, and she knew it could only be done step by tiny step. "First of all, you will give Alexander a beautiful funeral."

"I don't know if I can cope with a funeral!" he cried.

"You'll do it privately, without cameras, with only close family present," she said. "You must look after Christina, because she will take this loss at least as hard as you. Then you will make sure that Fiona Thyssen is well taken care of, because you know that's what Alexander would have wanted."

He gave a heavy sigh, and she sensed him struggling

for control. "All I want to do is go to the mortuary and lie beside him."

"You need sleep, Ari. Go to bed."

"I'm lying on my bed, but I can't bear to be alone. Please don't leave me, Maria."

She wondered where Mrs. Kennedy was, but didn't want to ask. "Let me transfer this call to my bedroom telephone; then I will stay on the line as you fall asleep."

She picked up her bedside receiver, kicked off her shoes, and lay full-length on the bed. She kept her voice low and melodic as she spoke, trying to lull him to sleep. "You will get through this, Ari, because you are the strongest man I've ever met. One day you will meet Alexander again, of that I have no doubt."

"In heaven?" He wasn't convinced.

"Yes, in heaven, and I think he will watch over you on earth too. A bond like yours does not simply disappear."

"I wish you were here," he murmured. "I need you."

"I *am* here, my love." She lay still now, listening to his slow breathing, and imagining the twitch of his muscles as he slid through the transition into sleep. If only she could take away the pain that would overwhelm him afresh when he awoke in the morning.

She had never loved him as much as she did at that moment. And she had never feared for him as much.

Chapter 72

Athens
Summer 1973

Jackie was astonished by the physical changes in Ari in the months after Alexander's death. He'd always had a muscular physique with a slight paunch, like a prizefighter who had eaten a few too many good dinners. Now he was scrawny, his muscles wasted, and his posture stooped like an old man's, although he was only sixty-seven.

"Stand straight," she urged, pressing the middle of his back. "Head up, shoulders down!"

He raised himself upright, only to slouch again minutes later, as if the effort was too much to maintain. His face had taken on the ruddy look of a drinker, and his eyes drooped as if the flesh were stretched and misshapen by all the tears he had shed.

Their five-year marriage had been through many

trials: Jackie's decision to spend the better part of the year in New York with her children; his explosions of temper about her spending; his affair with Maria Callas; his lies over his affair with Lee. Yet somehow they were still together, and with each passing year she'd grown fonder of him. Life hadn't given him an easy ride, but he drove himself relentlessly in his desire to be "the best," and she respected that.

She felt stronger after her secret sessions with her psychiatrist. As well as helping her control irrational panic, the therapist had also guided her to explore the reasons for her feelings of helplessness. When Jackie was a teenager, her mother had repeatedly emphasized the importance of finding a husband who earned enough to keep her in the style to which she had become accustomed: "Money and power, girls. That's what you need to marry." She'd cultivated in them an appetite for beautiful surroundings: antiques, designer clothes, fine porcelain, French perfume. Owning such things was the measure of a successful life, according to Janet Auchincloss. But because women of Jackie's class did not work after marriage, that left her entirely reliant on her husband. She needed a man to look after her—then Jack was taken from her in a single shocking act of violence. It was no wonder her recovery was taking longer than might be expected for a normal bereavement.

Jackie had never told Ari about her sessions on the psychiatrist's couch. He would have seen them as a sign of weakness. No one knew apart from her, the shrink, and the Secret Service officer who had recommended therapy. It was a place where she could talk about anything that was on her mind, without worrying about it ending up in the press. Quiet, private, just for her.

When Ari fell apart after Alexander died, it came as a surprise; he'd been such a lion of a man before. She couldn't help but compare him to Rose Kennedy, who had stayed so strong after everything that had happened to her. Why couldn't he do the same? Still, she felt huge compassion for him; perhaps it could even be called love.

After Alexander's burial on Skorpios, Jackie arranged a trip to the Caribbean aboard the *Christina* to distract her husband from his grief, but the voyage was marred by his heavy drinking and outbursts of uncontrollable rage. He refused to talk about his loss, refused to be comforted.

They flew to Skorpios for the long summer vacation, taking Jackie's and Lee's children—Lee was too busy to join them, she claimed—but none of his usual pursuits interested him. He had bought a Jet Ski and the children took turns on it, but Ari, who usually loved new toys, sat watching from a deck chair on the beach, his expression inscrutable behind dark glasses.

Previously he used to spend hours in his office, making deals over international telephone calls, but now the only thing that motivated him was hiring private investigators to prove that Alexander's plane had been sabotaged. The first inquiry ruled that the cause of the crash had been mechanical failure, but Ari refused to accept it, offering a reward of $20 million to anyone who could prove that his son had been murdered. It became an obsession. He paced around the villa, muttering to himself about it.

Every night after dinner he took a bottle of ouzo and two glasses to Alexander's tomb, by the chapel in which he and Jackie had been married, and sat, drinking himself into a stupor. He poured a glass for himself and a glass for Alex, and sat in the dark, talking to his son as if he were there. A stray dog that he had adopted always lay on the grass nearby. Jackie crept up to watch sometimes but did not intervene, for fear of sparking his temper.

She often overheard him on the telephone to Maria. He was invariably in a calmer mood after the calls, so she never interrupted. She could look after his physical needs and, if Maria was the person he chose to confide in, she was glad that at least he had someone.

By late summer, Jackie was beginning to wonder if

the drooping around Ari's eyes was caused by something other than weeping. She persuaded him to consult a private doctor in Athens, and he was sent for a
battery of tests, after which he was diagnosed with a
rare condition called myasthenia gravis.

"It's a neurological disorder that causes weakening
of the muscles," his doctor told him. "It can usually be
arrested by taking steroids, but you'll need to come for
regular checkups so we can adjust the dose and watch
for side effects."

"What caused it?" Ari asked.

"No one knows for sure," the doctor said, "but grief
can weaken the immune system so that it malfunctions.
That's one theory."

Jackie reached over to grip Ari's hand.

She considered staying in Europe that winter to look
after him, but he insisted that she fly home to New
York with Caroline and John. Life there had become
easier since a three-year legal battle with Ron Gallela
had finally led to an order that he stay twenty-five feet
away from her and thirty feet away from her children.
Ari was furious at the astronomical lawyers' bills that
arrived in Olympic Airways' New York office. He had
maintained all along that Jackie should either learn to
ignore the man or stay away from New York.

"Congratulations!" he mocked. "You've made Mr. Gallela a household name. He'll get much better rates for his photos now."

"I had no choice," she argued. "You weren't there. It wasn't just me; the kids were petrified too."

Her spending remained a flashpoint, so she tried to be careful. She couldn't seem to curtail her shopping habit, but a store on the Upper West Side bought designer outfits that had been worn only once or twice, sometimes not at all, and paid cash for them. It gave her an extra income stream that Ari knew nothing about.

She knew he was having business worries. The price of oil had gone through the roof because of war in the Middle East, making it more expensive to run his ships; the deal he had been trying to make with the Greek colonels was never mentioned now; and she knew he was negotiating to hand over control of Olympic Airways to the government. Since his son's death, he couldn't bear to have anything to do with it.

October 1973 brought another crashing blow, when his first wife, Tina, died under suspicious circumstances at the home of her new husband, Stavros Niarchos. The autopsy ruled that she had suffered acute edema of the lung, but Ari didn't believe it.

"He wooed her, then murdered her to get at me," he

raged. "I want that man locked up. Or dead. Preferably dead."

The loss of Tina so soon after that of their son devastated him so completely that Jackie began to fear for his sanity. She discussed him with her psychiatrist, who suggested that Ari would benefit from some professional help of his own, but there was no chance of him agreeing to that. His indomitable pride stopped him from admitting weakness. In many ways, he was his own worst enemy.

Chapter 73

Paris
December 1974

Maria still couldn't believe she was meeting Ari, after her final vow back in 1970 that she would never see him again. He had begged her, and this time she had given in. Yes, it was for lunch, not dinner, but after her return from a world concert tour that had taken her across the States and over to Japan, they met in a quiet bistro in the 16th arrondissement.

Huddled together at a corner table, knees touching, they ordered sole meunière with creamy lyonnaise potatoes, accompanied by an ice-cold white Burgundy, but a side effect of the myasthenia gravis was that he had trouble chewing and swallowing solids, and he gave up on the food before long.

"You once said to me that I had behaved with hubris

in marrying Jacqueline, and that the gods would punish me," Ari said.

"That was rather cruel." She gave him a sideways smile. "I suspect I was cross with you at the time."

He looked terrible. The illness had withered the muscles of his face, and his eyelids were clumsily taped open with adhesive that splayed out from behind his black-rimmed spectacles. His hair was thin and straggly, and his hands were covered in an old man's liver spots.

Oh, Ari, she thought, *what has happened to you?*

"I believe you were right," he continued. "All my misfortunes date back to the day I married that woman. Perhaps it's hubris, perhaps it's the curse of the Kennedys, but I need to overcome it. Can you remember your ancient mythology? Was there a way to undo the effects of hubris?"

Maria cast her mind back to the stories she had learned in her youth. "I'm afraid not. Icarus's wings melted; Arachne was turned into a spider; Salmoneus was struck down by a thunderbolt." She laughed. "But I know you don't believe this."

He gave a thin smile. "Perhaps not, but I'm convinced my fortunes will change for the better when I divorce my wife."

"Not that old line. I've heard it so many times." She mock-sighed and picked up her wineglass.

"My lawyers are almost ready to make a move. I've been collecting evidence of her reckless spending. The judge will be astounded to learn what my wife spends each month on shoes alone! And I got her to sign a waiver some time ago that curtails the amount she can be awarded in the event of my death. Then in June last year I persuaded the colonels to pass a law on foreign nationals that means she will only get what I have left her in my new revised will."

"Don't talk about death!" Maria scolded. "You're not going to die anytime soon. I forbid it." He seemed crumpled, she thought: his face was sagging into folds.

"There are some things I need to say to you about my death," he said. "Please let me."

She swallowed hard. She didn't want to hear this, but she knew he was declining fast. Perhaps it was only fair to listen. "You have two minutes; that's all."

He drank some wine before he began. "First of all, you might hear from your mother after I am gone."

"What do you mean?" Suddenly Maria remembered her mother claiming that some men had threatened her. "Have you been warning her off all this time?"

"She doesn't scare easy, does she?" He gave a half smile. "No, since her suicide attempt I've been paying her a monthly stipend on condition she doesn't get in touch with you. I saw how much it upset you when she wrote . . ."

"Ari!" Maria was touched and indignant at the same time. "You might have discussed it with me. I'm embarrassed you were paying her. She's *my* problem, not yours."

"It wasn't much. Just enough to keep her off your back."

Maria wondered what she would do if Evangelia did get in touch again. She had no desire to see her.

"The other thing I wanted to explain is that I haven't left you anything in my will. It would cause too many complications. But if you have any problems after I am gone—whether financial, legal, or if anyone is bothering you—you should call Costa Gratsos. He will help, no matter what it is."

"I'm sure I won't need him, and I didn't expect an inheritance, but thank you. Now, can we get back to enjoying our lunch without all this morbid talk?"

"Just one more thing: I am hoping to be divorced from Jacqueline before I die. She still has no idea. She plans vacations for us and invites friends for cruises on the *Christina* as if we were any normal married couple. Yet we hardly see each other from one month to the next."

Maria swallowed the rest of her wine, and with the slightest movement of a finger Ari motioned to the waiter to bring them another bottle.

"Divorce her or don't divorce her," she said. "It's going to be expensive either way. But I think you should do it with dignity rather than vitriol. The eyes of the world will be upon you and history will judge you."

"Don't you *want* me to divorce her? I promised you we would be married one day and I would like to keep my word while I still can."

Her heart gave a little leap, but she spoke pragmatically. She had heard these words so many times before. "I don't want you to get divorced for my sake. I've got no desire to become the third Mrs. Onassis. We've already got the best of each other."

She wasn't sure if she believed that. They had a close and easy friendship, but sometimes it was hard not to pine for the passion of their earlier years. And then she remembered the heartache that went with it and changed her mind. She couldn't go back to waiting and hoping for him to marry her. Not again.

"Think about it," he said. "I will ask you properly when I am able to wave the decree nisi in one hand and an engagement ring in the other, just as you requested."

The fresh bottle of wine came, and Ari sniffed the cork and tasted it before the waiter poured her a glass.

"Well, I also have news," she announced. "I made my own decision. I sang my last-ever concert in Japan. On the eleventh of November in Sapporo. That's it. *Finito*."

"No!" he protested. "I don't believe you. If the right offer comes along, you'll cave in. You'll miss it too much."

"I won't," she said, very sure of herself. "I'm fifty years old and it's time to retire. I can't be bothered with all the practicing, the diet, the exercises, the discipline. I'm going to enjoy some Brie at the end of this meal, and I will drink wine whenever I feel like it without worrying about my coloratura."

"What will you do with your time?"

She smiled. "Things that make me happy. I'll visit friends, I'll travel, I'll entertain. Singing used to bring me the most profound joy, but I don't feel that anymore. The magic has gone." She was too anxious about reaching the notes to feel that divine sensation of the music filling her from top to toe, and she couldn't bear to listen to her recent recordings, with all their flaws.

"Congratulations on your retirement, in that case." He picked up his wineglass and clinked it against hers. "But I hope you will still sing for me."

"Of course I will. That is one of the privileges of our long and beautiful friendship." When she stroked his thigh beneath the tablecloth, she could feel that he was skin and bone. This horrible disease was taking its toll. Someone should ensure he was eating properly. He needed a wife more than ever. But he had married the wrong woman, and as a result he spent most of his days alone.

Chapter 74

New York City
February 1975

When Artemis phoned Jackie in New York to say that Ari had collapsed and was in an Athens hospital suffering from pneumonia with heart complications, she flew straight over, accompanied by a leading cardiac surgeon. Having money meant she could make one call and these things happened.

The surgeon advised that Ari be flown to New York for heart surgery, but a French doctor Christina had summoned wanted him to go to Paris for an operation to remove some gallstones that were causing him acute discomfort.

Ari was weak but he knew his own mind. "I will *not* die in America," he croaked, thumping his fist on a red cashmere blanket that was covering his legs. "Take me to Paris."

The women around his bed—his sister, his daughter, and his wife—looked at one another in consternation, but no one dared to overrule him. He kept rubbing the red blanket between his thumb and forefinger, as if for comfort. Jackie could see a Hermès label.

"Where did that blanket come from?" she asked Artemis in a whisper.

"Maria gave it to him for his birthday last month."

Jackie felt a pang of guilt. She hadn't flown over for his birthday because she had been busy with the children. When Lee and Stas finally decided to get divorced, Anthony and Tina had begun spending increasing amounts of time at their auntie Jackie's apartment, until she had more or less taken over their care completely. The official line was that it was because Lee was away from home so often in her new career as an interior designer, but in truth Jackie had made the offer to protect them from their mother's drunkenness. She loved them and was happy to look after them, but it meant she was pulled in a lot of different directions at once.

When they arrived in Paris, flown in by private jet, Ari refused to go straight to the hospital but insisted on being taken to his Avenue Foch apartment. A few reporters were waiting outside, and nothing would do but that he walk from the car unaided, giving them a brief wave. Jackie heard him mutter "Vultures!" under his breath.

Once inside, he went to his office and closed the door; then, seconds later, she heard the sound of his voice and knew he was on the phone with Maria. He only ever used that tone for her. Jackie went to the kitchen to speak to Eleni about making something light and nutritious for dinner.

"Eleni!" Ari called down the hall. "Bring me a whiskey!"

Eleni looked at Jackie.

"Are you sure that's a good idea, Mr. O?" she called back.

"Best I've had all day," he replied. "If you don't quit nagging I'll light a cigar to go with it." Just the thought triggered a bout of coughing.

Later, when they were alone, Jackie tried to ask him about his state of mind. How was he feeling about the operation? Where would he like to recuperate? Did he want her to stay in Paris with him?

"Suit yourself," he said, without warmth.

He was cooking up a scheme—she could sense it—but he wouldn't tell her what it was. Over the next couple of days, he sat in his office, the red blanket over his knees, and made a string of phone calls, one after another. Jackie heard him switching languages and knew he was talking to his offices, his ship's captains, and his lawyers around the world. She guessed he was setting his affairs in order so he could go into the hospital without any worries.

At the appointed time, she and Christina took him to the American Hospital at Neuilly for the gallbladder operation and waited while he was prepped by nurses. Just as they wheeled his bed to the door, Jackie leaned over and kissed him on the lips, then whispered in his ear, "I love you."

He closed his eyes tight and didn't reply.

The operation was deemed a success, but when he came to, Ari seemed weaker than ever. Christina tried to feed him Eleni's homemade soups, but he had no appetite and waved her away after a few spoonfuls. The one thing he did still manage was to make telephone calls. He told the nurse to position the phone by his bedside and asked any other visitors to leave the room before he dialed. Jackie assumed he was calling Maria, and maybe Costa Gratsos, but he was too frail to talk business.

A few days after the operation, his doctors reported that the pneumonia was responding to treatment but that his kidneys were not functioning properly and his heart was still very weak.

Jackie spoke to the chief physician in private, asking if he was in immediate danger. Was it safe for her to fly back to New York to check on her kids?

"I am not optimistic about a cure," the doctor told her, "but he's tough and could linger for some time if we keep treating his symptoms."

Jackie told Christina that she was flying home, adding, "I can get here in less than a day if you need me."

When she gave her a hug, Christina briefly rested her head on her shoulder. Poor girl: she'd lost her mother and brother within the past two years. No wonder she seemed so distraught at the thought of her father dying. "Will you be alright?" Jackie asked, rubbing her back. "I'll stay if you want me to."

Christina stepped away. "I'll be fine. My aunt Artemis and I will make sure he's not left on his own."

Was there an accusation in her tone? Jackie wasn't sure. She felt guilty for leaving, guilty for staying, torn between the needs of her husband and her children, as she had been throughout this marriage.

Over the next three weeks, Jackie returned to Paris twice more. She always flew first class, and booked the seat alongside her own to ensure privacy, but she could never fall asleep on planes for fear of someone snapping a photograph. It was a time when she caught up on reading and correspondence. The sleep deprivation and jet lag meant she was permanently frazzled.

On March 7, she left Ari's hospital bed at six-thirty in order to meet Lee for dinner. Her sister had fallen crazily in love with a wildly handsome but utterly penniless artist, and they were in town for an exhibition of his work. Jackie was trying hard not to play the disapproving big sister, but some truths needed to be laid on the line. She was rehearsing her words as she walked along the hospital corridor.

A statuesque woman in a black headscarf came around a corner just as she reached it, and they collided.

"*Je suis désolé*," the woman said.

Jackie looked at the dark eyes rimmed with kohl, with a Cleopatra-style flip at the corners, and recognized her straightaway. "Hello, Miss Callas," she said.

"Mrs. Kennedy." Maria gave a slight nod.

Neither spoke for a moment, then Jackie said, "He's alone. Christina's gone for dinner."

Maria nodded her thanks.

"I wasn't sure if someone was updating you about

his progress," Jackie said. "I'd be happy to arrange that if you like. You should be kept in the loop."

"Ari himself is telling me of his progress," Maria said with dignity; then her voice cracked. "But perhaps you would be so good as to have someone call me when . . . if . . ." She couldn't say the words.

"Of course. Do you want to give me your telephone number?"

Maria wrote it down for her and whispered "Thank you" as she handed it over.

She had aged in the decade since they'd talked backstage at the Met, Jackie noted: there was a fan of wrinkles around each eye, but she was still a beautiful woman, with a real presence about her. How awful it must feel to be an outsider when the man she loved was dying. She too felt like an outsider, with the Onassis clan speaking Greek to one another around his bedside and excluding her from medical decisions, but at least she didn't have to sneak in to visit him.

For a moment she considered embracing Maria and took a step forward, but she got the impression from a slight twitch under the other woman's eye that it wouldn't be welcomed. Instead, Jackie slipped the telephone number into her handbag, gave a polite smile, and went off to join her sister.

Chapter 75

Paris
March 15, 1975

The weather in Paris was gray and somber, with low clouds overhead and torrential rain lashing the streets. Maria stood at her window, watching black treetops swaying, and thought the weather matched her mood.

She could sense Ari slowing down a little more each day, like an old clock. She kept trying to jolt him back to life, the way you jump-started a car with a dead battery, but she couldn't find a way.

During one of her visits, she had tried to provoke him: "Are you really going to let Niarchos outlive you?" she challenged. "You'll give him free rein to dismantle your empire. Christina won't be able to outwit him, but *you* still could."

"I thought you said I had enough money," he replied, his voice husky.

"And you said it's not about money; it's about the game. Are you giving up the game?"

He closed his eyes.

He usually got a nurse to bring him a telephone around six in the evening—their traditional time—pushing aside the plastic oxygen tent that had been erected around him, and speaking in short, breathless sentences. So when the phone rang at 6:15 on March 15, Maria rushed to pick it up.

"Ari?"

"It's Jacqueline," the familiar voice said. "He's gone. I'm so sorry."

Maria sat down hard and covered her mouth with her hand. She had been expecting this for some time but realized she was not ready for it at all. Once she had composed herself enough to speak, she asked, "Were you with him?"

"No, I'm calling from New York. Christina was with him and she assures me it was peaceful. He didn't wake all day. His breathing grew fainter until it finally stopped less than an hour ago."

Tears slid from Maria's eyes and trickled down her cheeks. "It's all over," she said. "Nothing will be the same."

It felt cataclysmic. How could it be that she would never hear Ari's voice again? Never hold him in her arms?

618 · GILL PAUL

"Would you like to come to the funeral?" Jackie asked. "It will be on Skorpios. I'll let you know when."

"Thank you, but no. My grieving will be private. I don't want to give the press any fodder. We had already said our goodbyes."

When she hung up, she sat still, staring at the telephone. There was a vast silence around her. The air itself felt different, because Ari was no longer breathing it.

She wondered where his body was. Would they prepare him for burial in the hospital mortuary? If only she could slip in to kiss him one last time. But she had no rights. She wasn't family, wasn't his wife.

Suddenly she couldn't bear to stay in Paris, to be so close and yet so far away.

"Bruna?" she called. "We're going to Palm Beach. I'll call the travel agent; you pack our suitcases."

Maria read the newspaper accounts of Ari's death, and the many obituaries, while on a plane to Florida. Most journalists focused on his great wealth, estimating figures in the hundreds of millions, some claiming he was worth as much as a billion. They wrote about his love life: his affair with her, his marriage to Mrs. Kennedy; and his children. They employed an entire lexicon of superlatives—*biggest, richest, most famous*—but none of them came close to capturing the devilish *charm* of the man.

Several papers printed a photograph of Mrs. Kennedy arriving at Charles de Gaulle Airport the day after his death, with a peculiar frozen smile on her face, which they interpreted as uncaring. Maria knew how easy it was to be caught mid-expression by paparazzi and did not judge. Mrs. Kennedy gave a statement to the press, saying that Aristotle had rescued her "at a moment when my life was engulfed with shadows." She claimed that she would be "eternally grateful" to him but did not mention love. At least she wasn't hypocritical.

Soon the stories turned to the wrangling over Ari's will. Someone leaked that he had been planning to divorce Jackie and had tricked her into signing a waiver that robbed her of the widow's right to the quarter of his wealth that she would have been due under Greek law. The Kennedys hired lawyers to help her contest it, while the Onassis family, led by Christina, was adamant that Ari's wishes must be respected.

Maria was glad not to be part of the fray. Some jewelry that Ari had given her was still locked in a safe on the *Christina,* but she didn't plan to claim it. Nor would she give any more interviews about her life with Ari. She was no longer a public figure. It was no one's business but hers.

She thought her life would get easier after the initial hammer blow of the bereavement, but in fact it got harder as the months passed. The focus of her life for the past sixteen years had been Ari, and now there was nothing. She cried uncontrollably on the twenty-sixth of June when she visited Omero's grave without him. Some days she didn't get out of bed at all.

There seemed to be no point in worrying about her weight anymore, so she indulged in the foods she had always loved: pasta with heaps of Parmesan cheese, ice cream, Toblerone bars, and the divine cream cornets made by a patisserie just around the corner from Avenue Georges Mandel.

She drank a bottle of champagne most evenings and took pills to calm her nerves, and pills to sleep, because she couldn't bear to be awake in the still hours when she was haunted by bitterness and loss. When her doctor refused to prescribe any more pills, she wrote to Jacinthy in Athens and asked her to buy some. They were available over the counter in Greek pharmacies.

Jacinthy sent several boxes and a letter, in which she said that Maria's mother would very much like to see her. She lived in Athens now and, according to Jacinthy, was a reformed character.

Maria crumpled the letter and threw it into the fire.

Chapter 76

New York City
Summer 1975

Jackie was stunned and hurt when her legal team told her quite how far Ari had gotten in his scheme to divorce her. He had first briefed a divorce lawyer back in 1970, after less than two years of marriage, and it appeared he had been working to get rid of her since then. How could he still make love to her if that were the case? What about all the good times?

Further surprises were to come. It seemed she had been appointed the CEO of a company based in the States that was illegally shipping oil to Cuba via Haiti, and her lawyer warned that she could face arrest and a lengthy investigation.

"Did you sign everything he put in front of you?" the lawyer asked, incredulous.

"Pretty much," she admitted. "He was my husband. I trusted him."

"We'll do our best to keep it out of the press," the lawyer said, "but be ready to talk to prosecutors."

When she told her mother and stepfather about it, Hughdie confessed that Onassis had caused him great embarrassment by buying a large holding in Standard Oil days before the announcement of a merger with British Petroleum, thus making an outrageous profit. That was also in Jackie's name, but he had transferred it to one of his shell companies shortly afterward.

"It's my own fault," Hughdie said. "I shouldn't have told him about the merger, but I assumed he was a gentleman and wouldn't take advantage."

They were cut from quite different cloth, Jackie realized. Hughdie was a gentleman through and through. Ari had the surface polish, but deep down he was a crook. Bobby had been right all along.

She began to wonder if she had ever really known her husband. It was disconcerting to think of all the parties they'd attended and vacations they'd taken together while he was secretly stabbing her in the back. Yet they'd had fun as well. And he had rescued her at the lowest point of her life. She had to hang on to that. Now, no matter what happened, she would never be poor.

The first time Jackie had been widowed, she was thirty-four; the second time, she was forty-five. She wouldn't marry again—on that she was clear. The psychiatrist, whom she still visited regularly, suggested that she find a way to forge her own identity.

"You've been a daughter, a wife, a sister, and a mother, but I'm not sure you know who *you* are," the shrink told her. "The compulsive shopping habit you describe is a symptom I've often seen in those who lack self-esteem. Buying things you don't need is an attempt to exert control over your surroundings and make you feel better about yourself. I want you to think about what you could do over the next few decades that will bring you a genuine sense of fulfillment. What do you *like* doing?"

Jackie was stumped. She'd enjoyed her brief stint as a journalist in her early twenties, but couldn't envision returning to that, given her treatment by the press over the years. She couldn't think of what skills she had to bring to a workplace—until a friend suggested she might become an editor in a publishing house. Books had been her constant companion through life; it felt so obvious she couldn't believe she hadn't thought of it herself. In September 1976, with great trepidation, she began work as an editor at Viking Press, reading manuscripts and making suggestions on how they could be improved. Straightaway she loved it.

The psychiatrist suggested that Lee's drinking could also come from a lack of self-esteem rooted in childhood, and made some suggestions about ways in which Jackie could confront her.

The first few times she tried, Lee reacted with fury. "You think I'm the one who's an alcoholic? Look at yourself, all high and mighty. Don't forget I've seen you lying in your own vomit on the bathroom floor."

It was true; that had been during the year after Jack died. Jackie explained that she had controlled her drinking since then but Lee wouldn't listen. She was cross that she hadn't been invited to Ari's funeral, furious that she hadn't been mentioned in his will, and resentful that Jackie was raising her children, even though she loved the freedom it gave her to come and go with her bohemian friends and her artist lover.

By the end of the year, though, Lee was running out of money and had no choice but to come to her sister for a handout.

"I'll gladly pay off your debts," Jackie said, "but I want you to think again about how much you're drinking. It can't be fun; not really."

Once again, she was rebuffed. It was only the following year, when she caught Lee at a particularly low point, that her sister admitted she had a problem with alcohol.

"I know I need help," she said, "but I'm scared. What would I do without a drink?"

That fall Jackie accompanied her to her first AA meeting, and sat in the car outside so she could drive her home afterward. They still weren't close, the way they had been as children, but it was a start.

The legal disputes over Ari's estate rumbled on, with an astonishing number of people coming forward to claim a share. Some said that he had owed them money or that they were part owners of one of his companies, and there were at least a dozen who claimed to be his illegitimate children by different partners. Jackie was briefed about them in a meeting with her New York lawyer. Some were easily disproved: a cocktail waitress at a bar in Monte Carlo claimed that she had sex with Ari on a date in 1964 when he was demonstrably in New York with Maria Callas; another claimant had "mislaid" the vital documents that would prove his entitlement.

One day in the spring of 1976, her mail included a letter with her name and address written in block capitals on the envelope. Jackie had long received letters from people across the country who felt as if they knew her and wanted to offer their advice. They wrote to her about Jack, about Ari, about the way she was raising her children, and always about her hair—some hating it and others wanting to know how she styled it. The letters had tailed off somewhat since she'd stepped out of the limelight, but occasionally some still filtered through. She tore this one open and saw that it was in Italian. She began to read it in the elevator.

"Dear Mrs. Kennedy Onassis," it began. "I wish to introduce myself. My name is Omero, and I'm the son of Maria Callas and your late husband Mr. Aristotle Onassis . . ."

Chapter 77

Paris
Spring 1976

Maria was astonished when Mrs. Kennedy called to ask if they could meet, saying there was something she needed to discuss face-to-face.

"I'll be in Paris next week on business," Jackie said. "Perhaps we could go for lunch."

Maria rarely left the apartment these days. She didn't want to be photographed at her current weight. Besides, her health was poor. She suffered from dizzy spells and didn't want to risk passing out in a public place.

"Would you like to come to my apartment?" she asked, not without misgivings. She'd seen Mrs. Kennedy as "the enemy" for too long to feel entirely comfortable inviting her into her home—but at the same time she was intrigued about what she wanted to discuss.

Jackie agreed and a time was set.

Maria couldn't decide what to wear; she wanted to look her best when meeting her rival. Eventually she selected a regal green-and-gold embroidered kaftan, accessorized with gold jewelry, and she put her hair up, taking special care with her makeup. It was time to pull herself together and be La Callas once more.

When Jackie arrived, Bruna showed her into the salon, and Maria rose to greet her with a handshake.

"What a beautiful room," Jackie said, looking around. "I love the way you've decorated it. It's so dramatic."

Her voice had a nervous tremor; that was odd. Bruna offered her a drink, and she asked for vodka and tonic, so Maria had a glass of champagne.

"Congratulations on your publishing job," Maria said, once they were seated. "Are you enjoying it?" She studied her rival and noted that she dyed her hair now; there were gray roots visible at the hairline. She was dressed casually in slim black trousers and a black turtleneck with a long, multicolored silk scarf.

"I love it," Jackie said with an instinctive grin. "I've never earned my own living before, and it's a great feeling."

"We are in opposite camps: I've had to earn my keep since childhood and now I'm enjoying my leisure." She sipped her drink, rolling it around her mouth, savoring it.

"I hope you will sing again," Jackie said, but Maria was shaking her head before she finished the sentence.

"Those days are gone. I can't bear the sound of my own voice anymore."

Jackie's regret seemed genuine. "That's a huge loss for the world. Does it not feel like a loss to you?"

"It does sometimes—but I had a longer career than most first sopranos, and for that I am very grateful. I know not to flog a dead donkey."

Jackie mentioned an opera she had recently heard at the Met; then the talk turned to current theatrical productions on Broadway.

"How is your sister?" Maria asked. "I read about her acting debut."

Jackie pursed her lips, with a mischievous glint in her eyes. "She's turned her attention to interior décor now. I hope that will be more successful. Lee is rather a butterfly, flitting from one adventure to the next."

Bruna called them for lunch in the dining room: a cheese soufflé with a green salad and fresh-baked bread. After they ate, Jackie got around to the purpose of her visit.

"I'm sure you will not be surprised to hear that many people have come forward trying to claim part of the Onassis fortune," she began. "Among them, several dozen have claimed to be his illegitimate children." She locked eyes with Maria. "My lawyers have so far not found any of the claims to be credible, but I received a letter that concerns you." She screwed up her mouth. "I'm so sorry if this is awkward, but I have to ask: Did you and Ari ever have a child?"

Maria's hand knocked against her fork, and it clattered to the floor. "Why do you ask?"

"I got a letter from an Italian boy saying that he is the son of you and Ari. I've brought it with me." She reached for her handbag and pulled out the envelope, handing it to Maria. "It may be rather distressing for you."

She read the first line and gasped. "We had a son called Omero, but he died at birth. This can't be true . . . yet how else could this boy have known the name?"

Jackie stayed silent as Maria read the rest of the letter. The author claimed that Mr. Onassis had not wanted another child and had bribed someone to swap Maria's newborn baby with one that had died in the hospital that morning. Hers went to a childless couple, and Mr. Onassis sent them a money order every month to pay for his care. That income had stopped with his death, and they were now seeking their rightful share of his estate.

"This is absurd," Maria said, struggling to comprehend. "Ari was devastated by our son's death. We visited Omero's grave every year on his birthday."

"It's a cruel deception. I'm sorry I had to tell you about it."

And then Maria noticed the signature at the end of the letter: Gallo. "I know that name!" she cried. "Of course! He's the hospital porter. Ari told me about him." There was an address in Milan, and a telephone number.

Eyes blazing, she strode to the telephone on the other side of the room. Jackie started to get up, as if worried that this might be too personal, but Maria motioned for her to remain in her seat as she dialed the number.

"Are you Signore Gallo?" she asked in Italian. "Junior or Senior?"

"Senior," the man said. "Did you want my son?"

"No, you will do. This is Maria Callas."

"I'm honored to hear from you, Signora Callas," the man said, sounding flustered. He clearly hadn't been expecting this call.

"I've read the letter your boy wrote to Mrs. Kennedy. He claims he is my son. Is that correct?"

"Yes, it's true. I'm sorry, Signora." He launched into a complicated explanation, but she silenced him.

"There's one way to settle this definitively. Tell me, what is your boy's blood group?"

There was silence on the line. Mr. Gallo was whispering to someone else in the room. She had flummoxed him. "I'm sorry," he came back. "We don't know."

"You don't know?" Her voice rose an octave. "I suggest you find out. I will call you this time next week and if you tell me the correct blood group, we can talk further. If not, I will ask the police to stop you harassing me. Is that clear?"

She hung up the phone and turned back to Jackie, who was watching, wide-eyed.

"That man blackmailed Ari years ago," she explained.

"I've always been a little bit scared of you," Jackie said. "And now I know I was right to be."

The women returned to the salon, and Bruna brought a tray with coffee and petits fours.

"I'm sorry you lost a child," Jackie said. "I lost three, but I am blessed with the two who lived."

"Omero was born in 1960, the same year as your son. When I see photographs of John in the press, it helps me to imagine what my boy would have looked like now. He would have been sixteen, almost seventeen."

"That must be hard."

"We've both suffered," Maria replied. "And let's face it—Ari was not the easiest of partners." She chuckled.

"He never wanted us to meet, so he would hate it if he could see us now."

Jackie looked down at her lap, and her next words were quiet. "I'm sorry for taking him from you. It was clearly you he should have married, not me."

Maria got goose bumps all over. She had never dreamed that Mrs. Kennedy would admit that.

"You were the bigger prize, and Ari always had to have the best. I didn't blame you," she added, not entirely truthfully. "I only ever blamed him. He could be such a . . ." She sought the right word. "Such a nincompoop."

They both laughed at the inappropriateness, but at the same time the peculiar rightness, of her choice.

Chapter 78

Lefkada, Greece
June 1977

Lefkada Town had become more touristy since Maria had last been there almost a decade earlier. She and Ari used to dine at a favorite restaurant in the town square, and once she had given a concert there for local people. Now the marina was lined with tables where tourists sat by the waterfront, and waiters had to rush across a busy main road carrying their food from the restaurant kitchens.

She got her driver to continue along the coast to the fishing village of Nydri, checking her watch anxiously. Still half an hour to go. The moon was almost full, so there was plenty of light.

When she had called Costa and told him she needed his help, he'd said, "Name it and it's yours." That was kind. She'd always gotten along with Costa.

She stood on the jetty at Nydri and gazed across to the dark shadowy outline of Skorpios on the horizon. It would be strange to set foot on it again: strange but comforting at the same time. She hoped she would feel close to Ari once more. She had dressed smartly in a black dress, with a black shawl over her hair, and circling her throat were some emeralds she'd been wearing the night they met.

She heard the sound of the motorboat before she saw it. It curved around a headland at high speed, before Costa cut the engine and drifted the last few feet toward her. When he was close enough, he held out his arm to help her step on board. She knew how to get in and out of boats after all the time she'd spent on the water with Ari, and she settled herself in the prow, looking out toward Skorpios.

"What did Mr. Gallo say?" Costa asked once they were out on the water.

Maria imitated him: "'B negative. No, I think it might be A positive. They weren't entirely sure but it could be O positive.' He tried every combination." She laughed. "To be honest, I don't have a clue what Omero's blood group was. I was bluffing and he fell straight into the trap."

"Was there a part of you that was disappointed?"

She shook her head. "God, no! If it had been true, it would have meant that Ari had deceived me about our son. That would have been appalling. He was a scoundrel, but I knew he would never sink to that depth."

"He shouldn't have paid off Gallo all those years ago. He was just trying to protect you but the man clearly got a taste for extortion."

"I bet you advised him against it. You were always the sensible, cautious one of the pair of you."

"Really?" Costa said. "What I'm doing tonight is not very cautious . . ."

"I'm so grateful," Maria said quickly. "But you already know that."

When they pulled in at the jetty on Skorpios, a long-haired Greek boy was waiting for them.

"This is my nephew, Konstantinos," Costa told her. "My sister's boy. He's going to help."

"Good evening, madame," he said to Maria. "The coast is clear. Christina is in Athens, so you can take your time. I've brought the jeep to drive us up the hill."

Costa passed him the cargo that had been in the stern, then tied the boat to a cleat. Maria took a deep breath, smelling the scent of eucalyptus mingled with salt. It was silent on Skorpios apart from the murmur of waves.

They climbed into the jeep and drove up to the white-painted chapel, with bougainvillea and jasmine climbing the walls and sea lavender lining the paths.

Lanterns were burning by the tombs of Ari and Alexander, and the air was sweet with incense. Maria examined a little shrine by the tombs. Someone had set out bottles of whiskey, brandy, and ouzo, along with two glasses. There was a dish of Ari's favorite olives, all the way from Smyrna, a jar of caviar, and an old photograph of him with Christina and Alexander as children, playing on the decks of the *Christina*.

Konstantinos was holding a crowbar. "Are you ready, ma'am?" he asked her.

She stood back to let the men do the work of prizing open Ari's marble tomb. Inside she saw a white-painted coffin with silver handles. The flowers that had decorated the top had long since decayed into brown streaks.

"Hello, Ari," she whispered. "It's me. You knew I would come, didn't you?"

She stopped, unsure if she had been speaking out loud or inside her own head.

"Would you like us to say a prayer?" Costa asked.

"No. I will have a priest bless them another time. I'm sure the gods will forgive us for now."

Costa walked forward, holding the cargo.

"Is there enough room?" she asked.

"Plenty of room," he said.

For the first time, she let herself look at the tiny box he held, and the memory came back to her with full force, of holding Omero in her arms all those years ago. The tufts of soft dark hair, the frog legs, the plump cheeks, the tiny fingers. All that potential. All the hopes and dreams she had invested in him.

Everything would have been different had he lived.

"Put him in," she said, and Costa lowered the box down gently beside Ari's casket.

"There you are," she said, and a wave of happiness washed over her, like sunlight emerging from behind thick clouds. "My boy is a proper Onassis at last."

"I'm sure Ari would be delighted we've done this," Costa said, putting an arm around her.

"It doesn't matter whether he would or he wouldn't," Maria replied with a smile. "For once in our lives, I am going to have the final word."

Acknowledgments

Barbara Douka, to whom this book is dedicated, is a social media friend who lives in Athens, and at the time of writing we still haven't met in real life (although I hope to remedy that soon). Back in September 2017, she messaged me suggesting I write about Maria Callas, Jackie Kennedy, and Onassis, and straightaway my brain lit up like a pinball machine. Their story has all the elements I look for in a novel subject, and I knew I wanted to write it. My incomparable U.S. editor, Lucia Macro, jumped on board without hesitation, and Helen Huthwaite in the UK was close behind. All I had to do was get the words down. . . .

As it turned out, the writing of *Jackie and Maria* took longer than any of my other novels so far. I went through many, many drafts, trying to balance the women's stories and decide which bits to include, which to leave out. Karen Sullivan, Lor Bingham, my agent Vivien Green, and author Tracy Rees and her mum Jane were early readers, and I was grateful for their honest reactions. Barbara Douka advised me on all matters Greek, while opera singer Heather Keens helped with singing techniques, and Lor Bingham was my go-to expert on pregnancies. As always with my novels, any mistakes that have crept in are my responsibility alone.

Karel Bata came to the Ionian Islands with me for a recce and drove a motorboat repeatedly around Skorpios while I took photographs and imagined my characters swimming in its coves and lying on its beaches. It's a private island, closely protected by security guards—who asked us to move off more than once—but I managed to swim ashore and feel the sand between my toes, just as Jackie and Maria felt. Thanks for your assistance, Karel, aka James Bond.

My grateful thanks to all those who helped in the making of the book, including copyeditor Jane Hardick, who corrected several matters relating to U.S. politics and terminology to spare my blushes. I also want to thank the entire team at Morrow for their energy, enthusiasm, and professionalism: Lucia Macro, Asanté Simons, Jennifer Hart, Amelia Wood, Danielle Bartlett,

Jean Marie Kelly, and Jessica Rozler are the ultimate publishing dream team!

I'm incredibly grateful to all the imaginative bloggers and Instagrammers who have supported my recent novels, in the U.S., Canada, the UK, Australia, New Zealand, and around Europe. It makes my day when someone photographs my book with a beautiful backdrop, writes a considered review, or lets me post on their website, and I wish I had space here to thank you all individually.

Thanks also to the author friends who keep me (comparatively) sane in this crazy business, to Hope Bingham for making me laugh, to my sister Fiona for letting me share her children, and to all the pals who buy my books and even read them. I love you all!

HARPER
LARGE PRINT

We hope you enjoyed reading
our new, comfortable print size and found it
an experience you would like to repeat.

Well – you're in luck!

Harper Large Print offers the finest in
fiction and nonfiction books in this same larger
print size and paperback format. Light and easy to read,
Harper Large Print paperbacks are for the book lovers
who want to see what they are reading without strain.

For a full listing of titles and
new releases to come, please visit our website:
www.hc.com

HARPER LARGE PRINT

SEEING IS BELIEVING!

DISCARD